PRAISE FOR THE NOVELS
OF SHELLEY SHEPARD GRAY

"Packed with an enticing mix of heartening emotional engagement and inspirational sweetness, the light, joyous plot has . . . ample food for thought."
—*Publishers Weekly* (starred review)

"[A] feel-good winner."   —*Library Journal* (starred review)

"Shelley Shepard Gray is beloved for her swoon-worthy Amish love stories, and her latest exudes charm and joy."
—*Woman's World*

"[A] heartfelt love story . . . This is sure to please."
—*Publishers Weekly*

"The camaraderie between all is open and honest, as the characters are well described and credible, each with their own fears, sorrows, joys, and heartaches. . . . A feel-good book."   —New York Journal of Books

"A sweet, straightforward story about how love can be tested by family, faith, and personal insecurity. Enjoyable and heartwarming."   —*USA Today*

"This gentle, uplifting story admirably models values of genuine respect and open communication."
—*Publishers Weekly*

Coming Home

SHELLEY
SHEPARD GRAY

BERKLEY ROMANCE
New York

BERKLEY ROMANCE
Published by Berkley
An imprint of Penguin Random House LLC
penguinrandomhouse.com

BERKLEY is a registered trademark and Berkley Romance with B colophon
is a trademark of Penguin Random House LLC.

ISBN: 9780593438084

First Edition: November 2022

Printed in the United States of America
1   3   5   7   9   10   8   6   4   2

Book design by George Towne

For my mother-in-law, Pat Sabga

Courage is fear holding on a minute longer.

—GENERAL GEORGE S. PATTON

Chapter 1

MARCH

"Ma'am? Can you hear me, ma'am?" Anderson was standing off to the side as his coworkers worked to secure the vehicle with rescue struts—the adjustable tools used to steady wrecks.

"Her eyes were open a second ago, Anderson," one of them muttered as he pulled out the combi-tool. The hydraulic power tool was a work of art. It could both cut and spread an opening with relative ease.

It was going to be a lifesaver for the middle-aged woman trapped inside. Her Honda Accord had slid onto an embankment off Ute Pass in the storm that had just passed. The vehicle was now gently rocking like it was trying to decide whether to linger on the road or give in to temptation and careen off the cliff.

Boy, he hoped those struts would hold.

"We're getting there, Doc. Two minutes," Mark called out.

"Hope so," he murmured before raising his voice again. "Almost there, ma'am. Hold on, okay?"

The woman inside was sluggish to respond. The airbag had deployed but it hadn't completely prevented her from hitting her head on something. She had a pretty good abrasion on her forehead. All head wounds bled a lot but this blood flow—from what he could see of it—showed no sign of lessening as it slid down her face and into the neck of her sweater.

"How's it going, Greg?" he asked.

Greg, once his captain in the army and now his co-worker in the Woodland Park Fire Department, grunted as he worked with two other men to cut open the door. "Hold on, Doc."

Another time, Anderson would've rolled his eyes at the nickname, which he'd received after delivering a baby while transporting the mother from a fire.

Now, though, all he cared about was the fact that the woman in the car was now motionless. "I need her out."

"If we mess up it won't matter because the car's going to be down the mountain," Mark snapped. Mark had been his unit's sergeant and had all the necessary attributes to run a small country. He was a natural-born leader and had an innate sense of what to do and when to do it.

Though Anderson was the paramedic on staff, he elected not to prod them again. Everyone there knew what was at stake. Two more minutes passed. Then three. Sparks flew from the hydraulic cutter as Mark continued to patiently cut through the steel.

Then, just as the car began to creak and groan again, Greg stepped back. "It's stable, but hurry," he murmured as he pulled a two-foot section of metal out of the way.

Anderson stepped closer and leaned in. His hands were covered in two sets of gloves and his jacket sleeves were pulled up. "Ma'am, my name is Anderson Kelly. I'm with the Woodland Park Fire Department. I'm going to get you out."

Behind him, he could hear Mark mutter something under his breath. Anderson knew that it likely had to do with his innate need to follow protocols. However, he could care less what they were saying behind him. All that mattered was getting the victim out of the vehicle without either doing further injury or killing them both.

Even though she hadn't moved a muscle, he kept talking. He'd learned from experience that even your tone of voice could cause someone in distress to relax. "Ma'am, I'm going to wrap my hands around your chest and pull you up. It's better if you don't help."

"Cut the straps and come on, Doc," Mark said.

"I'll cut," Greg said. "You got her?"

The woman opened one eye, seemed to tense, then gave up fighting as Anderson adjusted his grip. As Greg worked around him, Anderson thanked the Lord that the woman was relatively small. The hole they'd made wasn't big and it would've been harder if she'd been bigger. "Got her," he replied at last.

Curving his body to one side, he was able to create just enough room for Greg's right hand to slide in and clip the seat belt.

As soon as it was clipped, her body sagged, and he moved to retain his grip, half catching Greg's hand against the jagged metal. He was barely aware of Greg's sharp exclamation before pulling back on his heels and yanking the woman toward the hole.

When her head was safely out, Greg helped guide her shoulders through the hole while Mark and two other firefighters helped support Anderson's weight as he continued to use brute strength to pull her to freedom.

The moment she was out, a backboard appeared. Though he would've preferred to immediately carry her to the waiting ambulance, Anderson knew better than to transport her without more information.

While one firefighter searched the inside of the vehicle for the woman's purse in order to get her identification, Mark checked her vitals. Anderson listened for the numbers while methodically locating the source of the bleeding. After ascertaining that she wasn't in cardiac distress, he quickly applied pressure.

He was vaguely aware of another team arriving, along with a pair of men from the sheriff's department. Voices sounded over radios, lights flashed, and sirens continued to blare. However, it might as well have been a mile away, he was so focused on the victim in front of him.

"You ready, Doc?" Greg called out. "She's stable enough to travel."

His buddy's deep voice, so familiar, floated over him like a balm. It brought back memories of being with his team in the desert, the sand coating everything within seconds, as he worked to help a medic save a different life. It was why he became an EMT.

"Anderson?" Mark called out in his former officer's voice. "We got to go now. We're about to lose the vehicle."

"Roger that," he responded. "Count of three."

Greg counted and then, just as they'd done so many times on foreign soil, they stood in unison and carried the woman on the backboard to the ambulance.

Anderson nodded to Dave, their newest hire, and Chip, the usual driver, before leading the way inside. Four minutes later, the ambulance was zipping down Ute Pass. In the back, Anderson began her IV and spoke to the emergency room, relaying the woman's injuries and vital signs. Dave continued to monitor her vitals and check her bleeding.

Ten minutes later, she'd been whisked into emergency and he was standing outside the ambulance, feeling that same curious combination of adrenaline and exhaustion that he always did. They'd done it. They'd freed Mrs. Kemp from the vehicle, got her stabilized, and brought her to the hospital.

"Ready, Anderson?" Chip asked.

"Yeah." He climbed into the back and closed the door as Chip slowly drove back to the station house. Dave was sitting up front with Chip, leaving Anderson to spend a few blessed minutes alone to regain his bearings. He loved his job and enjoyed both the comradery and the way they made a difference. But every so often he was hit with a memory so vivid he had to remind himself that he was no longer in Afghanistan.

When Chip parked in their designated bay at the station, Anderson began the long process of disinfecting, organizing, and restocking the supplies. It was their team's responsibility to make sure everything was in order for the next call, whether they were still on shift or the next team was. Chip and Dave helped, each performing tasks they'd done dozens of times over the last year. When Dave turned on the hose to wash the exterior of the ambulance, Anderson removed his coat and boots, and then at last trotted up the stairs to the showers.

Greg and Mark were exiting as he was entering the locker room.

"She make it?" Greg asked.

"Yeah. Mrs. Kemp is in surgery now, but I think she's going to be okay."

"You did a good job up there," Mark added.

"We all did. For a minute I thought those struts weren't gonna hold and we were all going to get a close-up view of that ravine."

"One day, maybe," Greg said with his trademark humor. "But today?"

"Today ain't that day," he and Mark finished. They'd taken to saying that during all the skirmishes and close calls they'd faced back in the army. As cheesy as it sometimes sounded, they were now superstitious enough to never risk *not* saying those words.

"We're headed to Granger's Last Stand when we get off shift. Want to join us?" Greg asked.

It was not only rare for the three of them to all be working the same day, but also for them to get off the same shift at the same time. But for some reason, going to the same place with the same group of guys didn't hold as much appeal as it used to. "Yeah, maybe. I'll let you know."

Greg looked like he was about to argue, but simply nodded before walking away.

Only later, when Anderson took the time to glance at his reflection in the mirror after showering, did he admit what was holding him back: the multiple scars on his face that always invited a second and third look . . . and the fact that there was always a chance that Chelsea Davis would be at Granger's.

Though he was pretty much used to the scars—and the second and third looks he received—every time he caught sight of Chelsea, the pain felt fresh and new. They'd broken up years ago, but every time Anderson caught sight of her face, still so perfectly beautiful, the pain of her betrayal returned. On his worst days he feared it would never heal.

Chapter 2

Chelsea's back was to the main entrance of Granger's but it didn't stop the fresh burst of cold air from sinking into her skin. She was starting to wish she'd chosen a thicker sweater for her night out with Mallory and Kaylee.

Granger's Last Stand wasn't the only option in Woodland Park for burgers, wings, and beer, but it was hands down everyone's favorite spot. Located on the main drag through town, the restaurant had been expanded multiple times over the last twenty years. Now it boasted indoor, patio, and rooftop dining. Local bands played all summer and from time to time in the winter high school and college kids played acoustic guitar near the fireplace.

Tonight, since there was still a chill in the air, most everyone was inside. A couple of people were keeping the old jukebox playing and the buzz from the crowd provided the rest of the noise.

After eight hours of working at the Woodland Park Senior Center, Chelsea was ready to relax and catch up with her two best friends. "Mal, you never finished telling us about the couple who came into the boutique today," she said.

The petite brunette shrugged. "It wasn't all that notable . . . beyond the fact that the husband sat on the pink velvet chair by the door while his wife spent *almost a thousand dollars* on end-of-season fleece!"

"To be fair, that stuff adds up," Kaylee said. "Last time I bought a Patagonia jacket, I paid three hundred."

"Are you still wearing it, Kay?"

Kaylee picked up the sleeve of her jacket that was draped over her chair. "Obviously."

"Well, there you go."

Chelsea hid her smile by taking another sip of wine. The conversation was nothing new. Kaylee liked to carp about the prices at Mallory's store but always managed to stop by to drool over every new shipment of high-end ski, aprés-ski, and mountain gear. Since Chelsea couldn't afford any of it, she enjoyed simply listening and being supportive. "Well, that's great. I'm glad they stopped in."

"Me, too," Mallory said with a smile. "They were on their way to Cripple Creek to gamble. I hope they come in again before they head back to Kansas City."

"I'm really happy for you. Congrats." Chelsea knew that sales like that kept Mallory's spirits up, especially in the spring. A lot of folks were still paying off Christmas bills in March, so the shop suffered a lot of slow days until the weather warmed up and she began selling biking and hiking gear.

"Thanks." Mallory smiled again, but she kept glancing past Chelsea's shoulder.

"What's going on behind me? Am I boring you?" she teased.

"I think she's having a hard time concentrating because the hotties from the fire station just blew in," Kaylee said. "Who can blame her though? It's hardly fair that five guys can look so good."

Chelsea's stomach sank. Of course the firefighters had to show up. It was the first night in ages that she'd gone out instead of hurrying home to Jack.

Not even pretending to look anywhere else, Mallory murmured, "That Mark Oldum is dreamy."

"So is Chip," Kaylee said. "I met him at the gas station a couple of weeks ago."

Oh brother. "How do you know those guys' names?" Chelsea asked her friends. "I didn't know you hung out with firefighters."

"I don't, which is the problem," Kaylee joked. "And, just for the record, I don't know all of their names. Just one or two. And I know because I asked Wendy up at the bar." Flipping her hair over her shoulder, she asked, "Why all the questions? I didn't think you were interested in dating. Or have you finally changed your mind?"

"It would be great if you did start going out," Mallory said. "All you do is work and go home."

"No, that's not all I do. I have Jack, remember? He keeps me plenty busy."

"I get that, but I think it's time you started doing more for yourself. Jack's almost nine, you know," Mallory added.

"Ha-ha, I know."

"Then you also know that he's going to want to start doing more things with his friends instead of just his mom, right?"

"I know that, too." But she also hated to think about it. When had he gotten so big, anyway?

Kaylee sighed. "If you know all that . . . isn't it time you started dating?"

"I've dated," she protested. Though, to be fair, she hadn't dated very much. She'd promised herself years ago to always put her little boy's needs ahead of her own. And, though he probably wouldn't mind if she dated occasionally, she never wanted to risk hurting him.

Or maybe she was simply afraid to risk hurting her heart again.

Anxious to push the attention elsewhere, she smiled at Mallory. "Who are you looking at now?"

"I'm trying to find where Mark went. I lost him in the crowd. I tell you what, half the station must be here."

Chelsea tried not to tense but it was next to impossible. Whenever she was someplace there was a chance of seeing Anderson Kelly, she couldn't help it. "What do the other guys look like?"

Mallory raised an eyebrow. "Uh, like hot firefighters?"

Great. Now she was going to have to peek around and make sure Anderson wasn't there. So far, she'd been doing pretty well at avoiding him, but chances were that it was just a matter of time before their paths crossed. She just hoped that wouldn't be for a while. Or when she had Jack with her.

Jack was her pride and joy, but she feared that her son would be nothing but a reminder to Anderson of their breakup. There was no way she ever wanted Jack to feel like he was a *mistake*, no matter how her parents used to describe the way he'd been made.

She took another sip of her soda. Being a single mom meant it was a very rare evening when she could let down her guard enough to have a beer or a cocktail.

After another thirty minutes, she decided to head on home. Her neighbor Camille had offered to watch Jack, and since she usually came with cookies and an activity, Jack hadn't complained at all. It was a godsend that Chelsea lived across the street from the nicest lady in the world.

Putting a ten on the table, she pulled on her coat. "I'm out of here."

Her friends frowned. "Chelsea, are you sure?" Kaylee asked. "It's barely six o'clock."

"I'm sure. It was a long day at the senior center and I'm tired. Plus, I promised Jack I'd make sloppy joes for dinner. He's probably starving."

Whether her girlfriends were simply kind, or just used to her bailing out early, they let her leave without further protest.

"Maybe I'll see you at church," Kaylee said.

"I'll look for you at the ten o'clock service." Chelsea smiled, grabbed her purse, and started making her way through the crowd to the door. Realizing that she hadn't checked her phone in almost twenty minutes, she reached down into her purse—and promptly ran smack into another patron.

"Whoa," he said, holding one of her shoulders so she could regain her balance.

"Sorry!" She looked up with a smile, about to thank him for saving her from a fall—then froze, because there was the very man she'd been hoping to avoid. Before she realized what she was doing, she scanned Anderson's face, taking in for the first time the scars around one of his eyes and near his mouth, which were more pronounced than she'd thought. They had to have hurt badly, she thought, wincing at the idea of his pain.

Another second passed but it might as well have been an hour. All she was aware of was Anderson. After so many years of avoiding even the mention of him, there they were, standing in the middle of the restaurant, his hand protectively curved around her shoulder.

And just like that, a fresh wave of sadness flowed through her. He still towered over her. Still gazed at her with an intensity that took her breath away. Still made her wish for . . . things that were close to impossible.

"Chelsea?"

His voice sounded rough, like her name was the first word he'd spoken in hours. And, just like it had years ago, hearing her name on his tongue brought chill bumps to her arms. She hated that it could still affect her after all this time. She tried to summon some manners. "Hey, Andy," she said before she could catch herself. She might not know him anymore, but she knew he'd dropped that nickname when he joined the army. "I'm sorry, I mean Anderson." She shook her head. "I mean, sorry, I should've watched where I was going."

He dropped his hand. "No worries." He swallowed. "Are you heading out?"

She nodded. "I've got to get home to Jack."

A line formed between his brows. "Jack?"

That bit of confusion was all she needed to get her head screwed on straight again. "My son," she murmured before turning back to the door and weaving through the crowd again. When she got outside, she took a deep breath, enjoying the way the cold air seemed to drop her body temperature and clear her head at the same time.

She needed to put all thoughts of Anderson Kelly out of her mind. It didn't matter if he was still gorgeous in spite of his scars. What mattered was the way he was underneath. She reckoned he was still the same judgmental guy. People didn't change. Not really.

Chapter 3

*N*ot every firefighter in the station house enjoyed off-site visits, but Anderson did. He saw the benefits of getting to know community members when he wasn't in his turnout uniform. He served the community and that meant that he was there to address concerns, answer questions, and generally represent the department.

First, he and Samantha were headed to Meadowbrook, one of several over-sixty-two living communities in Teller County. There, they would meet with the residence managers and do smoke alarm checks. After that, it was over to the Woodland Park Senior Center, which was located in the center of town. They were scheduled to give a short presentation about fire safety as well as check the smoke detectors in the building.

Sam was the newest firefighter in their house and had quickly become everyone's favorite. She had come to them with extensive experience as a volunteer and high marks from the academy. She was not only a first-rate firefighter but could cook a mean pot roast, and she was always ready to lend a hand, whether it was cleaning the trucks, helping to give tours to visitors, or doing community outreach like this.

Her only flaw, as far as Anderson could tell, was her driving. She drove her tricked-out Jeep like a ninety-year-old woman. Slow as molasses and twice as carefully.

That was why they were in his Jeep Cherokee. It was comfortable, broken in, and kept her firmly in the passenger seat.

"Your truck's a mess, Kelly," she said as they headed toward Memorial Park, the large community space in the center of town recently remodeled with basketball courts, picnic areas, walking trails, and paths to the elementary school, library, city offices, and the senior center. Picking up an empty to-go cup, she wrinkled her nose. "They have trash cans for this, you know."

"Yeah, whatever. Toss it in the back if you don't want to look at it."

"I would if there wasn't an inch of sludge on the bottom." She shifted in her seat. "We should have taken my Jeep. It's spotless."

"If you were driving, we wouldn't get downtown until this afternoon."

"Ha-ha."

"I wasn't joking."

If Sam saw his lips twitch, she didn't let on. "For your information, there's nothing wrong with being careful."

"Or driving the speed limit," he countered as he pulled into a visitor space. Turning off the engine, he said, "Seriously, thanks for coming with me."

She was already unbuckled and reaching for her backpack from the backseat. "No problem. You know I like community visits. Plus, these guys have the best chocolate chip cookies."

"And you know this how?"

"My grandma used to come here to paint and play

bridge. Sometimes she'd take me along when I was at her house visiting."

Grabbing a box of smoke detectors and a packet of fire safety brochures, Anderson grinned at her. "Snag me a cookie if you find one."

"Don't worry. I've got your back." After smoothing back her hair and adjusting her fleece WPFD jacket, she grabbed her backpack and started walking to the front entrance.

Anderson followed, intentionally taking his time to postpone the inevitable. Chelsea was the activities assistant here and he'd gotten a text from the director that Chelsea would be their escort today. After over a year of essentially avoiding each other, he was going to have to work by her side. He was dreading it.

Their run-in at Granger's last Friday had done something to him. For the first time in months he'd been forced to remember the things he'd said when he found out about her pregnancy. He was embarrassed that he'd been so thoughtless and cruel. It didn't make things any better to realize that even after all this time he still hadn't apologized. He owed her that.

When he walked inside, Sam was already chatting with a couple of vets wearing ball caps emblazoned with their former units and squadrons. He wondered if they'd been friends with her grandma or if Sam had simply struck up a conversation with them because that was her way.

"Hey, Anderson," she called out. "I was just telling the guys about you."

He walked over and shook their hands. "Don't believe anything she says," he joked.

Samantha put one hand on a hip. "Not even that you did three tours in Afghanistan?"

Anderson shrugged. "She might be right about that, but obviously I'm not the only vet in the room."

"Looks like you brought yourself home a couple of badges of honor, son," one of the men said.

The guy was talking about his scars, of course. That's what everyone saw first. What Chelsea had stared at the other night. "It's been my experience that we all brought back some kind of badges from wherever we served. Mine just happen to be in plain sight." As much as he didn't care to be stared at in bars or clubs, around these vets, he felt safe. "Where did you all serve?"

As they shared stories about Korea and Vietnam, Sam turned and greeted a new arrival. And, by the faint scent of honeysuckle, he knew exactly who was there.

"Anderson, have you met Chelsea Davis?" asked Sam.

He braced himself and turned around. "I'd say so," he said with what he hoped was more ease than he felt. "We went to high school together. Thanks for having us, Chelsea."

In a look he used to know well, Chelsea scanned his face before replying. "Of course. Helping visitors is my job. Plus, everyone's been pretty excited to see you today. Seeing real firefighters never gets old." She winked. "We've got a good crowd in the activities room already waiting for you."

"I figured you would," Sam said. "My gram used to love to hear the speakers . . . and enjoy the coffee and cookies."

Chelsea grinned at her as she led the way down the hall. "Oh, I know, our cook bakes the best chocolate chip cookies. My boy is always after me to bring him home a couple."

"You have a son? How old?"

"Eight, almost nine."

"Oh! You don't seem old enough to have a nine-year-old."

"Believe me, I am."

Anderson knew there was no reason he should feel like a part of their conversation, but he still felt its pinch. Was it from guilt . . . or a longing that things could have been different?

"Are you married? What does your husband do?"

"I never married. It's just Jack and me."

Samantha visibly winced. "I'm sorry. I didn't mean to pry."

Chelsea waved a hand. "Please, you didn't pry. I'm happy raising Jack on my own. What about you? Are you married yet?"

Samantha snorted. "No way."

"Not even when you're surrounded by all those cute fire-fighters?"

"I can't think of those cute firefighters as anything but a bunch of brothers—mostly annoying ones at that—and most of the men I meet outside of work don't seem to be able to handle dating a woman who can bench-press as much as they can . . . or runs into burning buildings."

"I guess that could be tough for a guy to handle."

"Maybe it is . . . or maybe I just haven't met the right guy yet, I don't know. I *do* know that dating around twelve-hour shifts and a semipermanent state of exhaustion is pretty darned hard." She turned around to meet Anderson's gaze. "Right, Doc?"

"Don't look at me, sis."

Chelsea led them into the activities room. "I set a table and two chairs up front for you. Would you care for coffee or a cookie?"

"Coffee will do fine for me right now," Anderson said.

"Do you still take it with cream and sugar?"

Ignoring Sam's look of interest, he shook his head. "I gave all that up in the army. Black's good for me. Sam?"

"A little milk, if you could, please, Chelsea."

"Of course. I'll be right back."

When they were alone, Sam whispered, "*Still* with cream and sugar? How well do you know Chelsea?"

"Don't go there, Sam. Don't even go near there."

Her eyes widened but she nodded. "Understood. Do you still want to start?"

"Yeah. I'll be happy to." Sam was now studying him like his past was a new puzzle to figure out, but Anderson did his best to ignore it . . . and the visceral way he was still drawn to Chelsea, despite the years—and the hurt—that separated them. He stood in front of the table and smiled. "Good morning, everyone. I'm Anderson Kelly and this is Samantha Carter. We're here to talk about fire safety."

*C*helsea had been dreading this day from the moment her boss, Jill, had told her that a firefighter named Anderson Kelly was going to present the lecture on fire safety. It didn't make sense but, no matter how many years passed, where he was concerned her emotions were still raw.

Luckily, he'd come with his colleague Samantha, who was well-known to about half the assembled group. She'd provided a great buffer between Chelsea and Anderson, and her outgoing personality engaged everyone, allowing Chelsea to linger in the back, serving coffee and getting a good long look at her former boyfriend with his dark-blond hair, brown eyes, and broad shoulders.

Well, her and every other woman in the room.

He was beyond handsome. Standing several inches over six feet, he towered over Samantha and commanded everyone's attention. Somehow the scars on his face only emphasized his gorgeous features instead of detracting from them.

Not that she was still attracted to him.

It was just that the calm way he spoke, always so patient and kind to the older folks, warmed her heart. Even his modesty and the way he graciously deflected all the questions about his service were attractive.

Yep, she could see how he could be a lot of women's dream guy. If, say, they were never on the receiving end of his lacerating words questioning her morals.

"Miss Davis?" Sam called out. "Is that all right with you?"

Suddenly noticing the whole room's attention on her, Chelsea felt her cheeks start to burn. "Um, I didn't catch that, sorry."

"I was just asking if it was okay for me and Anderson to split up, in the interest of time? You could take him around to check the smoke detectors while I stay here and answer some more questions."

"Yes. Yes, of course, that would be great." Forcing herself to meet his gaze, she said, "I'll wait for you out in the hall."

Before he could respond, she walked right out of the room.

Be professional, she cautioned herself. *Be polite. The past is the past.* But half of her wanted to yell at him for making a really scary time in her life even worse . . . and half still ached to hold him close and let him know how glad she was that he'd survived whatever had happened to him during his deployment.

Chapter 4

The time had come. Time to address the hurt between them. Anderson had been thinking about it nonstop ever since he'd returned home. Imagining what he would say, how he would repair the terrible rift. He knew it wouldn't be easy, but he had to try. There were a dozen things he could tell Chelsea, but only one that really mattered: *I'm sorry.* His lips tried to form the words. Failed. Maybe he was being a coward, but it didn't feel like the right time.

Instead, all he managed was, "I guess it's no surprise that I was pretty apprehensive about coming over here today." *Smooth, Anderson. Very natural.*

"I actually am surprised," she responded. "I would've thought you did these talks all the time."

"You know that's not what I'm talking about." Lowering his voice, he added, "After our run-in at Granger's, I knew things between us would be rough."

Her expression flared but she tamped it down. "Here's the first room. The smoke detector is to the right of the door."

After giving her a look, he went inside, checked the batteries and the condition of the detector, then walked back to where Chelsea was waiting by the door. "It's good."

She checked off the room on the list he'd just noticed she was holding. "Okay, the next room is just to the left."

Dutifully, he went in, examined the detector, and met her back at the door. "We're good here, too."

After placing a check mark on her sheet, she walked him to the next room. He was going to lose his mind if the only thing they said to each other was about the smoke detectors. "Chelsea, Woodland Park is a small town. It's too small for us to keep dodging each other."

"I haven't been dodging you, Andy."

She'd averted her eyes. The movement was so familiar, it almost made him smile. Chelsea never could lie well. But instead of pressing her on that fib, he pressed on. "Can we just talk? At least get to a détente?"

"We have a détente. I really don't think there's anything more we need to talk about."

Since she was still avoiding his eyes, Anderson knew she was giving him lip service. "Sorry, but it feels like the opposite. I think there's a lot we need to talk about—starting with the fact that we're barely even talking."

"This isn't the time or the place."

"Name it, then." When her eyes widened, he added, "Come on, Chelsea. You know we need to have an actual conversation. I don't want us to keep avoiding each other. Woodland Park isn't that big, you know."

"We're not exactly avoiding each other. We've seen each other twice in the last week. I saw you at Granger's and now we're both here."

He was disappointed that she was pretending not to understand what he was talking about. The Chelsea he knew had been a lot more open.

Well, maybe she'd gotten less open when he broke up with her, when he enlisted in the army. And when he completely lost his cool when she told him she was pregnant.

Firmly pushing that bit of recrimination away, he murmured, "You know what I'm talking about. Chels, can't we
figure out how to put the past behind us?"

Her expression went ice-cold before she regained her
composure. "Here's the next room, Anderson. The smoke
detector is—"

"I think I can find a smoke detector." Irritated with the
way the conversation was going—even though he knew it
wouldn't be easy—he marched in, checked the batteries,
then dutifully returned. "This one's good."

"Great. The next two rooms are right across the way."

And so it continued. Chelsea pointed out rooms, he
checked smoke detectors and reported back. Unbidden, he
recalled walking her to class. How she used to look up at
him with her soft smile, tempting him so much that he'd
kiss her in the middle of the hallway. Everyone had teased
them, of course, but he never cared. He got to wrap his
arms around her or hold her hands that were always a little
cool, and kiss those sweet lips . . .

Fifteen minutes later, they were done and walked back
to the community room. At the door, they both reached for
the handle, and she turned to gaze up into his eyes again.

And, there it was. That electric awareness that had always been between them was alive and well. Unfortunately,
it was now flavored with a giant dose of regret and hurt.

Flustered and unsatisfied, Anderson made one more attempt to start a conversation. "For what it's worth, I'm sure
Jack is a great kid since you're his mother. I hope I get to
meet him one day."

She seemed to make a visible effort to compose herself before saying, "Anderson, look. I realize that we once
had a thing."

A *thing*? How could she say that? They'd been in love.
"What we had was more than a *thing*." As much as he wanted
to be understanding, he was losing his patience. "Chelsea, I

might have really messed up with you, but I was never shy about my feelings. You know you were special to me."

Chelsea kept talking as if he'd never said a word. "I'm also proud of your service and grateful for the sacrifices that you made." She glanced down—away from his scars—before meeting his eyes. "I'm sorry that you were hurt so badly—"

His mouth went dry. "I'm fine."

"—but I'd also rather not hear your opinion of my parenting or what you think Jack is like. He is none of your business."

"Noted." Her coldness stung, but he supposed he really couldn't fault her.

"Good." She went into the community room and Anderson followed, thinking that they had a long way to go before they were going to be anywhere close to being friends.

He wanted to remind her that she wasn't the only person who'd been having a difficult time over the last few years. He'd been injured, badly. After his discharge he had to learn a new occupation, which wasn't easy. He'd also had to live with the knowledge that he had hurt the woman he loved in so many ways that they might never even be friends again.

But I'm not giving up.

"Anderson!" Sam called out with a bright smile. "You're just in time to help me demonstrate how to stop, drop, and roll."

"Are you serious?"

Sam grinned at the crowd, many of whom were chuckling. "They might have put me up to that—but we should still do a demonstration."

"Sure," he bit out. He was surrounded by women who were having a great time putting him in his place. Moments like this made him wonder whether the army was easier.

Looking like she was enjoying the moment too much, Samantha said, "I'm sure most of you learned to stop, drop, and roll back in elementary school. But how many of you have actually practiced it since you were six or seven years old?" When no one raised their hand, she nodded like she'd just uncovered a dark secret. "That's what I thought. Now, shall we get our able model here to demonstrate what to do in case you've forgotten?"

Anderson dutifully dropped to his knees and rolled while Samantha called out warnings about hot doors, smoke, and the importance of calling 911.

As he got to his feet, Samantha smiled brightly. "Everyone, let's give Firefighter Kelly a round of applause for that helpful demonstration." She lowered her voice. "Ladies, it doesn't hurt that he's easy on the eyes, right?"

When a few of the women in the audience old enough to be his grandmother whistled and clapped, he finally gave up fighting the response and bowed.

Laughter rose as he straightened—and looked toward the back of the room.

Chelsea was . . . smiling?

It hit him like a punch in the chest. Even if he'd wanted to, he couldn't look away. She'd always had the most beautiful smile. Not just her straight perfect teeth or the faint suggestion of dimples. She smiled with her whole heart. That smile was infectious—and it had never failed to mesmerize him.

Everyone commented on it. Even his own mother used to say that Chelsea could have made the cheerleading squad on her smile alone. All he'd known was that whenever Chelsea had treated him to one, it told him he'd done something right.

Boy, he hadn't thought about that in years.

There was no telling if Chelsea was smiling for Sam's benefit or because she was getting a kick out of the teasing directed at him. Maybe it didn't even matter.

For the first time in years, she was looking at him in the way that had always made his heart melt.

It was such a relief, he smiled back.

Chapter 5

It felt as though Samantha and Anderson had taken half the oxygen out of the senior center when they departed. The staff seemed a little melancholy, the seniors who usually chatted while they played bridge were almost silent.

And, as she walked down the hall toward her office, Chelsea couldn't help but think that even the colors on the usually bright bulletin board didn't seem as vibrant.

Or maybe that was how she felt—emotionally drained and half-consumed by guilt and regret. If that was the case, well, it wouldn't be the first time.

She sat behind her computer and opened the calendar. It was a sorry attempt to look busy but she hoped it would give her a couple of moments of peace before the craft class she was scheduled to lead.

When her cell phone rang, she rolled her eyes. Of course her mother would decide to call right at that very moment. She had the uncanny ability to seek her out at her lowest points. It was a gift, really.

But, as she'd learned, ignoring her mother didn't do Chelsea any favors in the long run.

"Hey, Mom. What's up?"

"A lot, as a matter of fact."

Chelsea put down the pencil she'd just picked up. "Oh?"

"I heard you spent time with Anderson today."

Wow, her mom sure wasn't messing around. "Why do you say that?"

"You aren't the only person at the senior center who knows how to text, Chelsea."

Oh brother. "Who texted you?"

"That's my secret."

Her mother had a mole at the senior center who was keeping her up to date on Chelsea's life? On another day, that would have made her chuckle. Today though? Not amusing. Deciding to pretend she wasn't rattled, she asked, "Any special reason you called?"

"Obviously I'm wondering how it went." When Chelsea didn't say anything right away, her mom fired off more questions. "Chelsea, what happened? How was he? Are those scars of his giving him trouble? Did you two finally talk and clear the air?" Hope tinged her voice. "Are you going to see him again?"

In her parents' world, Chelsea's life was divided into two parts: before and after she lost the handsome, heroic Anderson Kelly.

No matter how much her parents loved Jack—and they adored him—they'd never shied away from expressing their disappointment at how he came into the world. Well, Chelsea was just as disappointed by their inability to accept her past and move on.

Though it was tempting to simply get off the phone as quickly as possible, Chelsea forced herself to reply. "We both live in Woodland Park. I'm sure we will see each other again. And, as far as his scars go, I don't think they're hurting him." She really hoped that was the case.

"I'm glad. That poor boy was so handsome."

"He still is, Mom."

"Well, you know what I mean." She took a deep breath. "Anyway, I heard you two spent quite a bit of time alone together. Did he ask you out?" Her voice was filled with hope.

"He was here for work, Mom. It wasn't a reunion."

"But I bet there were sparks, right? You two used to be so close."

What? Of course not! But once upon a time there absolutely had been sparks between them. Sparks and attraction, oh yes. Chelsea's throat grew tight as she remembered how she'd watch his every move when he wasn't looking . . . and get all warm and languid whenever he met her eyes across the room.

She'd loved him so much.

But that was almost ten years ago, and she was no longer the dreamy girl who was sure she was going to live a fairy-tale life. A lot happened in a decade. A whole lot.

"We're not going to start dating, Mom." She tried to ignore the feeling of regret that formed in her belly.

"Why? Is he dating someone else?"

"I have no idea."

"Really? Did you tell him you were still single? You're still pretty, you know. And you two have so much history. I bet if you gave him a little bit of encouragement—"

"*No.*" Patience gone, she got to her feet. "Mom, I am at work. I really need to go. I have a lot to do."

"Oh. Of course, honey. I'm sorry to have bothered you."

Chelsea closed her eyes and tempered her tone. "Jack is looking forward to seeing you and Dad on Sunday afternoon. Is that still okay?"

"Of course. You know we enjoy spending time with him."

"See you then. Love you, Mom."

"I love you, too, dear." Sounding deflated, she hung up the phone.

Of course Chelsea felt a rush of guilt rise up. She'd never aspired to be perfect, but sometimes it hurt that her parents seemed to focus on her flaws.

Shaking off her gloomy thoughts, she grabbed the plastic tote that held her crafting materials for the class on scrapbooking and hoped it would take her mind off things.

And it probably would have, if Eunice had greeted her with anything other than, "We think you and that Sergeant Kelly make a real cute couple. How can we make that happen?"

Aarrgghh! She was living in a nightmare.

*O*ver the years, Chelsea and her neighbor Camille had come up with a pretty good system. About ten or fifteen minutes after Chelsea pulled her Subaru into her driveway and texted Camille that she was home, her neighbor would open the door and watch Jack cross the quiet residential street from her house to Chelsea's.

Chelsea was always grateful for those few, precious moments of solitude. It gave her time to go to the bathroom, look over the mail, or even change her clothes.

Or, on days like today, to unpack the groceries, then sit down, take a deep breath, and recharge. It was amazing how even ten minutes could help a single mom get through the second half of her day.

They'd adopted this routine when Jack was in kindergarten. Before, Chelsea would pick Jack up the moment she got home. She was always delighted to see her little boy, but never taking even a few minutes for herself was exhausting.

*F*ifteen minutes after she texted, Jack opened the front door and called, "Hey, Mom."

Realizing that she'd fallen half-asleep, Chelsea jumped to her feet and tried to sound alert. "Hey! I'm in the kitchen. How are you?"

"Good." He came into the room, looking serious.

"And school? What's going on?"

"Mrs. Thomas is going to have a baby."

"That's exciting." But he looked pretty grumpy about it. "You're not happy for her?"

"She's going to go on maternity leave."

"Not for a while, right?"

"In three months."

"Hmm, let's see. Three months will put you at the end of the school year."

"Not all the way. Mrs. Thomas said we'll probably have a substitute for the last three weeks."

"Oh my goodness, I think you'll survive for three weeks, don't you? Besides, that's a long ways away, right?"

"It doesn't feel like that, Mom."

"I guess not." She pulled out a knife and started cutting up the rotisserie chicken she'd bought. "Have you finished your homework?"

"Yep." Eyeing the chicken, he said, "What are we having for dinner?"

"Pasta with chicken and broccoli."

"We haven't had that in a long time."

"I guess we haven't." She shrugged. "It sounds pretty good though, right?"

"Yeah." He snatched the drumstick and sat down on the small banquette seat Chelsea had put in when he was five. "Hey, Mom?"

"Yes?"

"Did you take a maternity leave after you had me?"

Why she hadn't expected the question was beyond her. Carefully, she set down the knife and fork. "You know my circumstances were different than Mrs. Thomas's, Jack."

"Because you weren't married."

"True, but I mean because I was in college, remember?" They'd discussed this before. Several times, even. So why did Chelsea suddenly feel like she was wearing a scarlet letter?

"I remember." He wasn't frowning, but it was obvious that something was bothering him.

Inwardly, she sighed. It wasn't that she wanted to keep her past a secret, it was that this conversation, on top of seeing Anderson today, felt like one too many trips down memory lane. But years ago, she promised herself to be as open as possible with Jack. "Do you have any questions for me?"

He bit his lip. "Kind of."

"All right. Ask away whenever you're ready." Inwardly, she held her breath as she reached for the broccoli and started chopping. *Please don't ask about making babies. Please don't ask about making babies.*

"Mrs. Thomas said Mr. Thomas is going to help her a bunch with her baby."

"Yes, I imagine he would." She smiled. "I'm sure they're very excited to be parents."

"He's even taking time off from his job, too."

Chelsea wondered where Jack was going with this, but she continued to chop broccoli. "That's wonderful. New babies are so special, but also a lot of work."

"How come my dad never wanted to help with me?"

Though it hurt to be honest, she'd realized that lying about the way things were wouldn't help either of them. She put down the knife and walked to his side. "He wasn't ready to be a father."

Jack's expression turned stoic. "I guess he's still not ready, huh?"

Oh, this was so hard. She didn't want to hurt his feelings, but she didn't want to give him false hope, either. "Jack, I don't know how he feels. Back when I was pregnant, I think he was young and scared."

A line formed between his brows. "Weren't you young and scared, too?"

"I was, but I was also excited to meet you." She paused, then added, "Maybe one day he'll change his mind, but I don't know."

Of course, that wasn't exactly the truth. From the moment she'd told Ryan that she was pregnant and he'd said that it meant nothing to him, that *she* meant nothing to him, Chelsea had written Ryan out of her life. He'd never reached out to her, either.

Because of all that, she hadn't even told Jack his name. There was no point.

But, she was realizing, some decisions that sounded okay in one's mind . . . were still hard to live with.

Pulling herself together, Chelsea looked at her son, this person she loved more than anything else in the world. "Honey, every once in a while, God gives us a gift. He turns what might seem like a mistake into the best surprise ever. That's what you were to me. That's what you are to me."

"Do you think one day my dad is going to want to meet me?"

As much as she wanted to make him feel good, Chelsea knew the danger of false hope. "I honestly don't know."

A muscle in his cheek tensed. "I don't know if I want to meet him, either."

"That's okay. That's always going to be your choice."

"Yeah."

"Jack, you and I are a family. It might not look like everyone else's, but so far I think we've been a pretty good one. Don't you?" When he nodded, she said softly, "I'm sure that sometimes you wish things were different and that you did have your dad around. But what do we always say? It is what it is, right?"

"Right."

"Even if everything isn't perfect, I'd never change a thing. You're good as gold, Jack. I've always loved being your mom."

His shoulders relaxed slightly. "Always?"

She rolled her eyes as she reached out to ruffle the hair hanging over his brow. "Well, maybe not when you make a big mess and forget to clean it up," she teased. "But other than that, you've made me really happy."

He looked up at her. "Me, too."

Before she could say another word, he walked down the hall to his room. That was probably for the best, since she now had a lump in her throat.

Thinking back over their conversation, she felt a degree of peace. They'd likely have another couple dozen similar conversations, and maybe they'd always feel just as hard; but at least they talked to each other openly. Whatever she'd done so far as a mom had been enough for him to feel comfortable asking tough questions.

And given her the strength to answer him as honestly as possible.

Chapter 6

*A*nderson didn't like grocery shopping. After spending so many years in the military—much of that time deployed overseas—he was no longer comfortable with the crazy number of choices in the store. For several months after his last tour, even the bright colors and the number of other shoppers had bothered him. So had the shocked expressions of old classmates or family friends seeing his injuries for the first time.

Inevitably, those shocked expressions would turn into awkward conversations about what had happened to him. No matter how many times he pretended their intrusive sympathy didn't bother him, it had. He'd started to simply avoid supermarkets.

Now that he'd been back for a year and his scars were no longer bright red and angry-looking, he no longer received as much unwanted attention and he was relatively content to wander around the local Safeway.

Unfortunately, now it was his dismal cooking skills that plagued him. Even though other guys seemed to have no problem following recipes, Anderson couldn't summon up any interest in them. He wasn't sure how it was possible, but he found it easier to treat a gunshot wound than to make a decent stack of pancakes.

All of which explained why his cart usually looked like he was a teenage boy on a keto diet. Meat and junk food, plus a couple of protein bars.

However, today he was determined to change that. Seeing Chelsea again had been a good reminder that life moved on. If Chelsea could raise a kid on her own, he ought to be able to make dinner.

Maybe even lasagna. Armed with his cousin Aubrie's recipe, he stood in the pasta aisle searching for something called no-boil noodles, whatever that was.

Why were there so many different kinds of lasagna? And what the heck were gluten-free noodles?

When he noticed a cart approaching to his left, he attempted to pull his cart to the other side. "Sorry, ma'am," he muttered as he continued studying the two boxes in his hands.

"That's all right."

Shocked to hear the familiar voice, he turned to face Chelsea. Today her golden hair was in a high ponytail and she had on jeans, a faded red long-sleeved T-shirt, and a navy Patagonia vest. She looked so young and pretty, almost exactly the same as when he used to watch her at cheerleading practice.

He felt sheepish for calling her ma'am instead of recognizing her immediately. "Sorry. I—I was reading the boxes."

"So I see."

He held up the two packages of lasagna noodles like they would mean something to her. "I'm trying to figure out the difference between these two brands. Do you know why one is almost double the price of the other?"

Instead of helping him out, a line formed between her eyebrows. "Why are you here?"

"Um, I'm shopping?"

"I shop here all the time and I've never seen you before. It seems strange that we've never run into each other before now."

Is she accusing me of stalking her? "Coming here is kind of a new thing." Realizing that that sounded pretty vague, he added, "I mean, when I first got back, I tried to shop late at night, when there weren't lots of people around. But I kept blowing it off and going home to an empty fridge. So I decided to give shopping in the light of day a try."

"I see." Her words were still terse, but her expression had softened slightly.

It was pretty obvious that she didn't entirely get what he was talking about, but it didn't matter. He couldn't blame her for being wary of him and he certainly couldn't change her mind in the middle of a grocery aisle.

Instead, he reverted to what he'd learned in the army: focus on what you can control. In this case, dinner. "Do you know anything about no-boil lasagna noodles?"

At last, she smiled at him, albeit in a puzzled way. "Some. What's your question?"

Feeling like a putz, he held up Aubrie's recipe. "I'm going to make a lasagna."

Instead of laughing at him, she scanned the paper. "See, with some recipes you boil the noodles first, then layer them in the baking dish. But with this, you use the oven-ready noodles straight from the box, to save time."

"Oh, that sounds good to me. Did you know there's like ten different brands of lasagna noodles?"

"I didn't, but—"

"Mom?"

When she turned to face the kid with the dark hair trotting up the aisle, Anderson felt his stomach drop. This was Jack.

Chelsea's complete focus was now on her little boy. Her

whole vibe seemed to change as she bent down slightly. It was like his very appearance made her happier. "What do you have there?"

"Cinnamon Toast Crunch. Can we get it?"

She took the box from him as she straightened. "Oh, Jack. Really?"

"What's wrong with it? A lot of kids eat Cinnamon Toast Crunch, Mom."

The kid's voice was so serious, so sincere, Anderson couldn't help but be charmed.

Now seemingly oblivious to him standing there, Chelsea remained focused on her son. "I'm sure they do." She gently shook the box. "And there's a lot of it, too."

Jack grinned. "That's 'cause it's family size. It's more economical," he enunciated carefully. "So, can we?"

"Go big or go home, huh?" Anderson said before he could stop himself.

As if he'd just noticed Anderson standing there, the boy looked up at him. "Hi."

"Hi, Jack."

Confusion wrinkled the boy's brow. "Do we know each other?"

"No, we've never met. I've known your mother for a long time, though." He held out his hand. "My name is Anderson Kelly."

Jack shook his hand but his expression said he clearly didn't know what to make of him.

"Jack, this is Sergeant Kelly," Chelsea interjected. "Anderson, this is my son, Jack."

"It's good to meet you."

"Are you in the army?"

"I used to be. Now I'm a firefighter." He noticed the boy staring at his scars but he didn't mind. These days, he would rather be stared at by a child than someone pretending his face looked like it used to. After giving Jack another couple of seconds to look his fill, he said, "I kind of like how you got the biggest size box to show your mom. I used to do that, too."

"Yeah, but my mom doesn't ever let me get cereal like this." He frowned. "She says it's not a good choice for breakfast, on account of there's sugar in it."

"Ah."

"What do you think?"

Feeling both of their gazes on him, he hesitated. Who knew having an opinion about cereal was the equivalent of maneuvering around a land mine? "It doesn't matter what I think." Pointing to the boxes of lasagna noodles, he added, "I stink at picking out stuff. I've been trying to figure out what kind of noodles to get for about five minutes."

But instead of letting him off the hook, Jack stared at him intently. "Do *you* like this cereal?"

Man, but this kid was cute. Intent but cheerful, respectful but aching to be independent. No doubt about it, Jack was a winner. The kind of son any man would be blessed to have. And with one phone call, he'd thrown it all away.

Even though Chelsea might resent him stepping into the cereal war, he couldn't just ignore Jack's question. Anderson decided to err on the side of honesty. "I haven't had Cinnamon Toast Crunch in years, but I reckon it still tastes pretty good," he said at last.

Triumph shone in the kid's eyes when he turned to Chelsea again. "See?"

"Oh, Jack." Glancing Anderson's way, she raised an eyebrow. "Any other opinions you care to share?"

Chelsea still had her backbone and he loved that about her. But because smiling was no doubt a sure way to get even further from her good graces, he simply shook his head. "No, ma'am."

When she raised her other eyebrow, he added, "Sorry, but I figured I better tell the truth instead of lying."

Jack grinned. "See, Mom? Anderson likes it and he's telling the truth."

She sighed. "How much is this box of *pretty good* cereal?"

"It's on special. See?" He pointed to the endcap, across the aisle. Sure enough, there were a slew of brightly colored boxes on sale for two-fifty a box.

"Fine. Put it in the cart."

Jack tossed the box in the cart, grinning as though he'd just accomplished an amazing feat. "Thanks, Mom."

"You can have it as an after-school snack. Not for breakfast."

"Fine." He smiled up at Anderson. "You should get some, too."

"I might, but I've got to tackle lasagna noodles, first."

Finally scanning the shelves of pasta, Chelsea murmured, "This is the brand you want." She tried to reach a box on the top shelf, but it had slid toward the back.

Anderson took hold of it easily. "This one?"

"Yes. It's not the most expensive and doesn't taste like cardboard."

He tossed the box in his cart, saying, "Who helps you get the stuff off the top shelf when I'm not around?"

Unfortunately, she didn't take the bait and didn't crack a smile. "That doesn't happen often."

"Sometimes I help," Jack piped up. "Remember, Mom?"

"I do." She smiled at him. "I held you up and you got a can of soup for me."

Anderson chuckled. "Remember how you used to swear you were going to get taller one day?"

A pretty pink hue tinged her cheeks. "I can't believe you brought that up."

"It was hard to forget." Like pretty much everything about their relationship. Amazing how the challenges he'd faced since then made all those hours spent in Chelsea's company even more memorable.

"When did you meet each other?" Jack blurted.

He felt a flash of hurt that she'd never mentioned him. *Well, of course she hadn't, genius. He said terrible things to her, and pretty much broke her heart.* "We were friends in high school," he said at last. How could he explain how it really was?

As soon as he saw her flinch, though, he knew he should've thought of something better—or at least continued to tell the truth.

Chelsea's cautiously warm expression had turned carefully blank. "Sorry, but we've got to go."

"Oh, sure. Hey, thanks for the help with the noodles."

"I hope your dinner turns out." She pressed a hand to the back of Jack's neck. "Ready, buddy? We still have a ton to do today."

"I'm ready. Bye," he said to Anderson.

"Bye, Jack. It was good to meet you."

The little boy looked at him curiously before moving away.

Chelsea met his eyes for a long moment before turning to walk away.

Anderson couldn't help but think about how she used to cling to him when they kissed good night at the end of their dates. They'd hold each other tight and he'd inhale the fragrance of her shampoo—mint and vanilla, he could still recall—feeling like the luckiest guy in the whole state of Colorado.

And then, always with just two or three minutes to spare before curfew, she would disappear inside her house.

It was torture—and not just because he knew her daddy was somewhere watching. No, it was literally painful to know he wasn't going to see her for at least another twelve hours.

But all that was in the past. Chelsea Davis wasn't any of his business. For all he knew, she had a boyfriend—and didn't want him knowing it, either.

But either way, he stood no chance with her.

He'd made sure of that, all those years ago.

Chapter 7

The rest of Chelsea's grocery run went smoothly. Jack stayed by her side, seemed pleased when she said she was going to bake a blueberry pie, and acted like he could care less about having pork chops for dinner.

Normally, Chelsea wouldn't have thought twice about any of that, but their recent talk about his dad—or lack of one—combined with the way he'd stared at Anderson, made her think Jack was acting a little out of the ordinary.

To be fair, she was probably acting a little out of the ordinary, too. It seemed every little thing that happened during the rest of their grocery visit felt amplified.

Which was all Anderson's fault.

It was only later, after they dropped off the groceries, picked up his cleats, and headed off to baseball practice, that Jack mentioned Anderson.

"Hey, Mom?"

"Yes?"

"Do you think Sergeant Kelly got all those scars on his face in the army or from fighting fires?"

"I'm pretty sure he got his wounds in the army."

Jack seemed to think on that for a moment. "I bet they hurt a lot."

"Yes, they may have," she replied calmly. Feeling like Anderson's sacrifice deserved something more than her mess of confused feelings, she added, "I think Sergeant Kelly was very brave. We should be grateful for his service."

"Do you really mean that?"

She looked at him in surprise. "Jack, of course I do. You know how I feel about all the veterans in town. Why would you ask such a thing?"

He looked down at his tennis shoes. "Because you didn't seem very happy to see him," he mumbled.

She hated that her discomfort had been so obvious. "I was happy enough."

Raising his chin, he rolled his eyes. "Mom."

"Okay, fine. The truth is that Anderson Kelly and I have some history that I'm afraid didn't end on a very good note. He made me pretty mad." Forcing herself to continue, she said, "That doesn't mean I don't think Anderson is a good person. He is." When Jack continued to look skeptical, she added, "I do respect him and I am thankful for his service. Plus, he's a firefighter now, which is another important job."

"He seemed pretty cool."

She couldn't deny that. "He is, I'm sure." She exhaled, pleased to have finished the awkward conversation.

"Mom, what do you mean by having history?"

Feeling her cheeks flush, she stammered, "I—I mean that Anderson was my boyfriend in high school."

Jack's eyes went big. "Really?"

"Really." Was he surprised she'd dated Anderson—or that she'd had a boyfriend in the first place?

"But then you broke up."

He looked so world-weary, she had to chuckle. "Yes, we did. Like I said, it was a long time ago."

"I guess that happens."

She chuckled. "You know what? You sound awfully mature for an eight-year-old."

"I'm almost nine," he said indignantly. "I already know a lot about relationships."

On another day, she probably would've teased him. Now, though, she was thinking that Jack understood a lot more of the world than she realized. She needed to respect that.

Or at least deal with it.

Struggling to keep her voice light, she said, "I guess you do."

"How come you two broke up?"

At least there was a simple answer she could give him for that. "Because Anderson went into the army and I went to college."

"And that was that?"

She rumpled his hair. "No, but that is all *you* need to know about it."

He pursed his lips. "He seems nice, though."

"He is nice. He's a good man, Jack." With a sigh of relief, she pulled into the practice parking lot. Luckily, the coach and several members of Jack's team were there, but not all of them. She wasn't late. Forcing a smile, she said, "Okay, grab your gear and your water bottle. I'll be right here the whole time."

He put his hand on the door. "Hey, Mom?"

"Yes?"

"Sorry, but I think it seems pretty mean to stay mad at Anderson for so long."

"Jack . . ."

"You're the one who always tells me that it's better to look forward than backward. Right?"

"Right." Ooh, that trite little phrase was coming back to bite her.

He went right on. "High school was a really long time ago, Mom," he said like he was talking about ancient Greece. "I mean, that's a really long time to stay mad at someone."

"You'd better get going. Practice is about to start."

She was still trying to come to terms with this little counseling session when he jumped out of the car and ran toward his coach.

Chelsea leaned back and thought about what Jack had said.

Darn it, her kid was probably right. She *was* holding a grudge against Anderson and had been for a long time. She realized now that she'd been thinking about their relationship in extremes. Either they were together or they were nothing. But that was ridiculous.

If Mallory or Kaylee had said something like that, well, she would roll her eyes and tell them that they weren't being realistic *or* healthy. The fact was, she and Anderson lived in a small town and they had friends in common. Surely she could learn to be friends? They didn't have to start anything.

And, honestly, he was still so handsome, he probably had a girlfriend. Apparently not a girlfriend who could make lasagna . . . but probably a beautiful girlfriend who appreciated the fact that he put his life on the line every day as a firefighter, and he'd done the same thing while in the army.

She nodded. Yes. That was the way to start looking at things. Anderson Kelly was her past, not her future, and in the present they could peacefully coexist.

Just as she pulled out her phone to check for messages, two fire engines and an ambulance sped by, their lights and sirens causing almost everyone in the area to stop, turn, and watch. She caught sight of the woman in the next car bow her head to pray.

Chelsea wasn't shocked. Fires were a huge concern in Woodland Park and in the state as a whole. At least once a year, a fire burned out of control and razed whole communities before it finished raging.

Usually, she would be praying, too—praying that the fire wasn't near her own home. After all, everything she and Jack had was in their little rental house.

But now she was more focused on the men and women in turnout gear inside the vehicles. Anderson and Sam—even the men that her girlfriends had kept tabs on during last Friday's happy hour at Granger's Last Stand.

Taking a moment, she closed her eyes and prayed for their safety as well.

Oh, who was she kidding? She could fool her heart but she couldn't fool God. It was obvious whom she was really praying for.

Everything she'd been telling herself and Jack had been essentially lies. No matter how much she might have wished otherwise, things weren't over between her and Anderson.

Not by a long shot.

Chapter 8

$\mathcal{F}$orty-seven hours into their forty-eight-hour shift, Anderson, Mark, and the rest of the crew were basically just waiting to go home. Too restless to hang out in the kitchen or on the couch, Anderson had gone to the garage bays to double-check that everything was in order for the next shift.

Of course it was. They'd already thoroughly cleaned and inventoried everything twice.

Anderson had just decided to make some notes about projects he wanted to tackle during his next shift when Mark joined him.

"Kelly, I would say that I can't believe you're back in here, but you've been looking stressed for two days straight," he said as he walked to his side.

"I know."

"What's going on?" Without waiting for a reply, Mark continued in his usual serious, confident tone. "It can't be anything going on around here. Everything's been running like clockwork. At least I thought so."

"You aren't wrong. Things are good here, especially

since we've gotten so much rain and snow this spring." Everyone in the fire department allowed themselves to take a bit of a breather in the spring. Usually the cap let them, too, knowing that July, August, and September were just around the corner.

Those three months were the stuff of nightmares for every firefighter in Colorado. They were traditionally the driest months in the state as well as prime camping time. And every day some numbskull decided to do something stupid, whether it was leaving trash out and attracting bears, getting hurt on a trail, or ignoring multiple CAMPFIRE PROHIBITED signs. Of course, the last was the most dangerous. One simple spark could start a wildfire that raged through hundreds of acres before a team could even get to the vicinity and put it out.

But that wasn't what had kept him from sleeping the last couple of nights.

Mark raised an eyebrow. "So, if you're not worried about work, what's been going on with you?"

Anderson shifted his shoulders. "Nothing. Don't worry about it."

"Come on, buddy. I know you like to keep everything to yourself, but it's obvious that whatever you're dealing with isn't going away on its own." He stepped closer. "Sorry, but we've been in too much bad to ignore each other's rough patches. Tell me, *what is going on?*"

Mark had brought out his sergeant's bark, the one that gave many a new recruit nightmares. While Anderson certainly wasn't intimidated by Mark's tone, he couldn't simply ignore his questions anymore. "I've got it handled. Give it a break, Mark."

His buddy took a step back. "Okay."

Anderson knew Mark was confused and maybe even a little hurt, since it seemed to be his goal in life to fix things. Frustrated with himself—especially since he actually *had* been acting short-tempered lately, Anderson softened his tone. "I mean, you're right. I have been off, but it's just a feeling."

Another guy might relax at that news, but not his former sergeant. He and Mark—along with Greg—had been through far too much overseas to ignore each other's problems—or a hunch that something bad was about to happen.

Mark's expression tightened and he gave Anderson a hard look. "How bad a feeling?"

He shook his head. "Don't worry about it. Not *that* kind of feeling." When Mark's expression said he wasn't buying his excuse for a second, Anderson blurted, "If I seem stressed, it has more to do with me and Chelsea than anything work-related."

Mark's expression eased. "So you've got female problems."

"Not 'female' problems. *Chelsea* problems." He hadn't thought about another woman since he'd run into Chelsea at Granger's.

Mark leaned against the tanker truck. "I'm sure she's a nice gal, but she's in your past. You ought to keep it that way. Do you actually not remember how you felt when she told you what she'd been up to at college? You telling me you're still not over her?"

Now he would never blame Chelsea for making a couple of bad decisions when she was eighteen years old. He'd sure done some stupid stuff.

But back then, when he read her letter confessing she was pregnant? He'd been devastated. It hadn't mattered that he'd broken up with her, saying he didn't want to be tied down during his first year in the service. All that he could think about was that she'd forgotten him so easily. Or that's the way it seemed.

He'd been such a wreck, multiple guys from his unit had had to talk him off the ledge. "I know I should get over Chels. And I will, too."

Maybe.

Somehow.

"Listen, I met a cutie hiking near Divide last weekend. She and I didn't really click but I think she would with you. I got her number." Smiling like it was a great idea, he added, "I could set you up."

"Yeah, no thanks."

"Sure about that?"

"Positive." He couldn't imagine thinking about another woman, let alone trying to form a relationship with her. All he could think about was Chelsea Davis.

Mark shifted, obviously ready to launch another idea, when the bells rang out.

As the dispatcher called out "House fire" and the address, they ran to their lockers and grabbed their lids and gloves, then headed to the trucks and stepped into their turn-out gear. Thirty seconds later, Samantha and Greg joined them; they'd be in the fire truck while Anderson and Mark were taking the SUV, which was easier to drive in some of the mountain regions than the ambulance.

Within another sixty seconds, both vehicles were speeding toward Midland Avenue.

"What do you think about the two of us going up to Breckenridge soon? They've been getting a ton of powder. We could ski all day, then head over to Ollie's for a while. It will be great," Mark said, just as if they weren't racing toward a house fire.

"Thanks, but I already said no."

Ollie's was the most popular bar in that ski town. In the summer, it was a popular pickup spot for the locals.

"I'm not saying you should meet someone. Only that going out might do you some good," Mark continued.

"Maybe. I don't know." Going to Ollie's didn't have much appeal, but spending the day at Breck didn't sound bad. It had been a couple of weeks since he'd been skiing.

"Just think about it, okay? You've got to do something to get your mind off that girl."

Hearing the faint bark of laughter, he said, "What I

think is that I really don't want you discussing my love life while we're all on radio."

"Come on, Doc," Samantha coaxed from the ladder truck. "I want to hear all about the girl you can't stop thinking about."

Making eye contact with Mark as he slowed to make a right turn, Anderson mouthed, *You'll pay for this.*

"Just trying to help."

"I've got more information," Greg radioed. "Cops are on-site. They say the home's owner is out safely."

Anderson felt his body relax a notch. "Does the owner need medical assistance?"

"Roger that, Doc. He's rattled and receiving oxygen but stable."

Checking his oxygen tank and face mask, Mark said, "Anyone else inside?"

"Checking, though one of the neighbors said there might be a cat."

"Lord, don't make me go in after that cat," Mark murmured.

"I'll second that." It wasn't that Anderson didn't like cats, it was that fear made most of them hide and go silent. Trying to rescue a cat who didn't want to be rescued—through a veil of smoke, no less—was a thankless task.

"The cat is out and owner assures us no one else was inside. Building only," Greg said over the radio as the engine pulled to a stop in front of a small bungalow that was engulfed by flames.

Mark and Anderson pulled over to one side and exited the vehicle. Immediately Mark joined Greg and Sam and went to work attaching the hose to a nearby hydrant.

Seeing that the captain had arrived, Anderson jogged over to him. "Where do you want me, Cap?" he asked. Usually, he would have gone right to fighting the flames, but he wanted confirmation that there weren't any victims who needed medical attention.

Captain McGinn pointed to a fire truck that had just pulled up from another station.

Anderson hustled over and helped the guys unwrap the hose and hook it up. Just as he braced himself for the burst of water pressure, the wind changed direction and sparks flew to a shed nearby. It ignited like it was filled with TNT.

A few of the men cursed as the captain started barking out orders.

Anderson heard his name and his mind hastened to process the words, but his muscles had already clenched and he was moving in sync with the other firefighters toward the shed to extinguish the new fire.

As he approached, he could feel the heat surround his turnout gear, the sweat trickling down his neck and back. His body's reaction was almost comforting in its predictability. This, he could deal with.

The confusion surrounding all things Chelsea? Well, that was another story.

"I was afraid of that," said Pete, the driver from the other truck.

"What?" he asked, and Pete pointed to a cat running from the shed toward the burning house. The poor thing was obviously scared and confused. It froze, caught sight of the crew and trucks, then darted off again.

He swore under his breath. "Someone's got to get that cat."

Pete grinned. "Thanks for volunteering, Kelly."

Anderson rolled his eyes but trotted toward the cat, which was once again frozen in fright.

"Hey, kitty," he said, though his voice couldn't possibly be heard over the noise of the fires and the water hoses.

Anderson knelt down and held out his arms. "Come on, cat. Don't be a fool. Come to me." *Like this is gonna work,* he thought.

It hissed and arched its back. *I've seen this movie. You're gonna make me chase you all over kingdom come, aren't you?* But when he didn't move, the cat actually took two tentative steps toward him. "That's it," he murmured. "I'm your best option right now. The alternatives aren't all that good, right? Now, come on." He forced himself to remain motionless even as a batch of boards fell to the ground less than ten feet away.

The cat yowled and skittered in fright—then slowly, delicately, trotted right to him. Anderson picked it up and held it tight against his chest. Glad to get off his knees, he stood up and carried the cat to safety.

"Here you are, sir," he said to the homeowner.

The elderly man, who was perched on the back of the ambulance, had a blanket wrapped around him and was sipping a cup of hot coffee. He didn't answer; truthfully, he looked a little shell-shocked. Well, it wasn't easy to watch your house go up in flames.

"Sir, I have something for you."

Hope filled the man's eyes. "Did you save the pictures in my kitchen?"

The guy's house was toast. Anderson could tell nothing was salvageable. "Ah, I don't know about the photos," he hedged. "But I do have your cat." He thrust the cat forward even though it looked completely determined to stay rooted in his arms.

"What does Tab have to do with me?" The man scowled.

"Tab?" When the guy continued to look at the cat with distaste, Anderson stepped closer. "She's pretty scared. Don't you want to take her?"

"No. She's just a stray. I only call her that because she's a tabby cat."

Obviously content that the man hadn't touched her, Tab the cat rested her head against Anderson's coat.

He tried once more. "She seemed pretty upset. I found her next to your shed."

"I bet. The sneaky little thing likes to sleep in there when she can. I let her, though, since she usually gets herself a mouse to eat."

Anderson was starting to realize that the cat was on the skinny side—and she didn't seem any more of a fan of the old guy than he was of her.

But what was he supposed to do? He was reluctant to just let her loose again. "Are you saying you don't want her, sir?"

Another scowl. "Why the heck would I want a stray cat when I've just lost all my belongings? Of course I don't want it." He thrust out his foam cup. "Now, can someone get me another cup of coffee?"

Anderson looked around and motioned to a tech. "Would you please get him another cup, Denny?"

"Sure, Anderson. No problem." Turning to the man, Denny's voice lowered. "How do you take your coffee, sir?"

"With a little cream and not too much sugar. Hear me?"

What a . . . Taking a breath, Anderson reminded himself that all that mattered was the man was safe and the fire was out. But now what? He walked over to Mark, who was wiping his face with a blue bandanna. "Any idea what to do with this cat?"

"It's not the homeowner's?"

"Nope, it's a stray." Anderson looked around at the mess of ashes, wet ground, and bits of firefighting foam. "I don't feel too good about leaving it here."

"Why don't you keep it?"

"As what, a firehouse cat? Is that a thing?"

"I was thinking more along the lines of your new pet. He looks pretty fond of you."

"It's a she."

Mark grinned. "See, you two have already bonded."

The little thing *was* snuggled up to him in kind of a nice way. "I don't know . . ."

Two other guys came over and grinned. "Looks like you've got yourself a cat, Doc."

"Maybe the firehouse—"

"Not on your life, Doc," said Captain McGinn. "Take it

on back, though. If you don't want it, we'll give it to the shelter."

"Fine. Anyone want to hold her while I help with the hoses?"

"Nah, keep her with you. We've got this," Mark said. "Just about done now anyway."

So, Miss Tab, you think there's a future for you and me? Anderson climbed into the engine and settled Tab on his lap. He was half expecting her to jump off and bolt toward the door, but instead she closed her eyes and purred.

He'd never admit it, but he kind of melted right then and there. The poor thing was obviously so desperate for some kindness that she was willing to get it from anywhere.

Pulling off one of his gloves, he ran a hand over her soft coat. "You and me both, Tab. You and me both."

Chapter 9

*W*hat do you think, Chelsea?" said Camille, holding up a pot holder she'd just made out of stretchy bands intertwined on a plastic grid. "Do you think anyone is going to want to pay money for this?"

Honesty kept Chelsea from answering immediately. Though the ladies at the senior center were making pot holders to raise money for a local food bank, even the most charitable-minded would hesitate to hand over a five-dollar bill for the misshapen pot holder in an unfortunate combination of orange and brown.

"Er, what made you choose those colors, Camille?"

"Because I'm from Cleveland, dear."

That didn't make a lick of sense to her. "I'm sorry?"

The woman sighed like Chelsea was trying her patience. "I'm referring to the Browns, dear." When Chelsea continued to look blank, Camille cleared her throat. "The Browns are Cleveland's pro football team."

Chelsea propped a hand on her hip. "I know about the Browns. I just didn't put two and two together."

"Or orange and brown, perhaps?"

That Camille. She was so put together, so witty and, well, busy, Chelsea was sometimes surprised that she hung out so much at the senior center. Camille looked like the type of woman who would be working part-time in a fancy boutique or maybe lunching with her friends.

But that was obviously a stereotype, since she not only was at the senior center a lot but she also watched Jack after school one or two afternoons a week.

"So?" Camille prodded. "Do you think this is a money-maker or not?" She raised her eyebrows.

"Well . . ."

"Come now, don't be shy."

"Fine. I have to say that it might be a stretch. I don't know if there are a lot of Browns fans around here." And no one but a die-hard Browns fan could possibly want that pot holder in their kitchen, especially since it was rather stretched out and misshapen.

Camille frowned at the pot holder. "I was thinking the same thing. Besides, it looks plumb awful."

"I wouldn't say that. But you could always give another one a try?"

"That's the problem, dear. I don't want to."

At the other end of the long craft table, Susan and Bar-bara giggled.

"What's so funny, girls?" Camille raised an eyebrow.

"You know what," Susan said. "You're teasing her like nobody's business."

Chelsea turned to Susan. "Camille has been teasing me?"

Looking a little embarrassed, Susan nodded. "Camille doesn't like crafts."

Chelsea let out a gasp of frustration.

"You know I was an accountant," said Camille. "I worked on a computer and crunched numbers all day. I don't know why I'm suddenly supposed to get crafty in my old age."

"I totally understand, but if you don't like crafts, why did you sign up for this session?"

"The girls are good company." Eyes sparkling, Camille added, "Plus, there's some rumors going around about you and that cute firefighter and I wanted to know if they were true."

"Hold on." Chelsea looked at the ten or so women looking back at her. "There are *rumors* about me going around the senior center?"

"Surely you can't deny that there were sparks flying between you and that young man."

"Hmm."

Barbara held up her perfect pot holder. After accepting compliments, she said, "So, are they true, Chelsea?"

"Is what true? What do you think you know?"

Everyone spoke at once.

"That you and the fireman used to date."

"That you were an item. Were you?"

"That he was always into you."

"You used to be hot and heavy."

Chelsea bit her bottom lip while she debated different ways to respond. If she denied it, she was sure they would be able to tell she was lying. If she refused to answer, they would be offended at her reluctance to share. And if she was honest . . . well, she'd finally have to be honest with herself.

"Anderson and I did date for a while." *For a whole year.* "A long time ago." *A lifetime ago.*

"What happened?"

"We grew up. You ladies know how high school relationships are. They rarely go anywhere."

"I don't know about that," Susan said. "I married my high school sweetheart."

"Maybe you're the exception that proves the rule."

Susan smiled but looked like she was busy scheming. "You're single now, right?"

"Well . . . yes."

"That's what I thought. Now, I've been asking around about that cute Anderson Kelly."

"Please, no." But Chelsea couldn't deny she was interested in hearing the answer!

Susan continued. "Guess what? He isn't dating anyone, either! Isn't that lucky?"

"I don't know . . ."

"Isn't that a shame? He's such a catch!" said Camille. "Do you think women are avoiding him because of his"—she lowered her voice—"scars?"

Chelsea had never imagined such a thing . . . until just this minute. "I certainly hope not!"

Blue eyes fastened on her. "Do they bother *you*?"

"*No*. Of course not."

"See, I told you, Camille!" Susan said. "Chelsea finds Mr. Kelly very attractive."

And, it was official. Her private life was fodder for anyone walking by to hear. "Can we *please* not do this right now?"

Susan folded her arms across her chest. "Oh, Chelsea. You can't think that we'd all rather make pot holders than help you? Now, don't you think it's time you gave Anderson another shot?"

Barbara nodded. "There's no time like the present to get back into the swing of things."

Barbara was acting like poor Anderson was a horse on the merry-go-round. Before she knew it, Chelsea had gone from trying to shut down the conversation to being engaged again. "It's not that easy to date someone you have history with."

"It's not that hard," Camille said.

"Besides, I'm busy with Jack."

Camille's expression warmed. "I know, dear. And Jack is a nice boy. He's a terrific boy."

"Yes, he is."

"But he's in school all day, and he's getting to an age when he wants to spend more time with his friends than with his mother. And dear, you're not *just* Jack's mother."

"I'm not sure what you're getting at."

"You're a young lady, not an old goat like us, dear," Susan said. "That means you shouldn't be sitting around by yourself every night."

The ladies' comments were starting to get a little too close to the bone. "Can we just move the conversation back to pot holders?"

"Of course, dear." Barbara handed Chelsea her pot holder, a perfectly square, tightly woven piece in an appealing combination of red and white. "I hope someone will enjoy using this and that it will bring a couple of dollars to the food bank."

"Yes, I hope so, too. Thank you so much."

Moments later, Chelsea was holding ten pot holders and a cardboard box with the extra craft supplies. The women had thanked her for her time and gone on their way without another word about her and Anderson.

Maybe they'd listened to her after all.

Even though she'd apparently won the battle, Chelsea felt curiously deflated. She feared the ladies had a point. Like Mallory and Kaylee had been trying to tell her, there was more to her than just being Jack's mom—maybe there was a lot more. However, she was never going to discover what that was unless she made some changes in her life. It was probably time to think about dating.

Just *not* Anderson Kelly—no, she couldn't imagine being in a relationship with him again. He'd let her down too badly.

Yes, she used to love him. Yes, she'd almost hated him for a while, too.

But the Andy Kelly she used to know was firmly in her past. He was nothing to her anymore. Just another guy in Woodland Park.

Chapter 10

Standing in the coatroom of the senior center, Camille kept a smile on her face as her girlfriends said good-bye and headed out to their cars. She chuckled when Barbara joked that they should become Chelsea's matchmaking service. Then she made a good show of flipping through some of the flyers and coupons neighborhood retailers had dropped off for them.

Only when she was alone did she dare allow her true feelings to show. She sighed as she sat down on the long wooden bench, slipped off her cute flats with tasteful rhinestones on the toes, and pulled on her heavy leather and navy canvas L.L.Bean boots that were almost as old as she was.

All right, that might be an exaggeration, but they certainly were several decades old. The darn things were as good as the catalog said. They lasted practically a lifetime and had certainly seen her through many winters.

It was just a shame that they looked old and worn-out—kind of how she felt some days.

Not that she was all that old. Only sixty-six. She had

many, many more years before she completely slowed down. After all, Barbara was in her seventies and kept very busy.

Unfortunately, her children seemed to think that she was on death's doorstep, or at least the retirement home's.

She absolutely wasn't. She intended to live in her cozy little house until the Lord decided he needed her up in heaven. She'd moved to Woodland Park with her husband and intended to be buried next to him one day. Until that moment came, she was just fine.

All she had to do was convince Janie, Clayton, Briana, and Bo.

After organizing her tote, Camille grabbed her things and shook off her doldrums. She was healthy as a horse and just fine.

Actually, she was better than fine. The only thing she couldn't do anymore was drive. Her darn eyes had failed her. Now she had to walk to where she wanted to go or rely on her children or the senior services van or an Uber. It was humbling but not a crisis.

At least she kept in good shape.

Her mind firmly on the positives in her life, she stepped out of the coatroom—and ran right into Frank Robards.

Next thing she knew, two strong hands were gripping her shoulders in an effort to prevent her from losing her balance. "You better watch where you're going, young lady," he said.

No, he *boomed*.

Frank had a really loud voice. It was actually too loud, in her opinion. And she would tell him that—if he ever asked her.

She decided to settle for correcting his statement. "I don't believe our near collision was my fault. After all, you came barreling around the corner like you were late for supper."

His gray eyebrows rose over a pair of pale eyes surrounded by fans of wrinkles. Then he smiled like he'd found her amusing.

"Was that a jab at my waistline?"

"It was not. I've never even noticed your waistline." Not much, anyway.

He placed a hand on his heart. "Whew. You're tough on a man's ego."

"Not at all. I'm simply honest. Now, if you'll excuse me, I need to head on out."

He stepped back. "Of course. Excuse me."

To her consternation, he walked back out of the coatroom with her, just as they crossed paths with Ernie, the longtime custodian of the building and an all-around good guy.

She smiled at him. "Hello, Ernie."

He bobbed his head. "Afternoon, Camille, General."

"Good to see you, Ernie," Frank boomed.

After Ernie disappeared down the hall, she looked up at Frank. "Why do you continue to let people call you that?"

A line formed between his brows. "Call me what?"

"General. You're retired, aren't you?"

"Of course."

"Then?" she asked impatiently. Really, conversing with him was about as much fun as walking in the rain.

"Not that it's any of your business, but old habits die hard."

"Hmm."

His eyebrows snapped together. "What is that supposed to mean?"

"Nothing. Now, if you will excuse me, I really need to go. It's supposed to rain this afternoon. I'd like to be home before that happens."

"Of course. Let me get the door so you can find your way out."

He might have been an old general with a bit of a paunch, a booming voice, and eyes that were—well, lovely, actually— but he kept her on her toes. She did like that. "Thank you, Frank. Good afternoon."

"Good afternoon to you, ma'am," he replied. "Be careful heading home, now."

Even though the polite thing to do would be to thank him for his concern, she kept walking. Frank got under her skin. She didn't know why. But she did know she needed to keep her distance from him.

*F*rank couldn't help himself. From behind the partially covered front windows, he watched Camille Hudgens walk daintily down the sidewalk. It was uncanny; that woman looked as attractive walking in a pair of snow boots as others did in high heels. Curious as to what she drove, he craned his neck to see the parking lot. The lady surprised him, however. She bypassed the parking lot and kept walking straight down the street.

Even though it was none of his business, he wondered where she lived.

Jill looked up from the mail that had just been left on the welcome table. "Everything okay, General?"

"Hmm? Ah, yes." After debating a moment, he decided to dig for a little bit of information. "I was just noticing that Camille Hudgens didn't climb into a vehicle in the parking lot. Does she live nearby?"

"She does." Jill shrugged. "She always tells me that walking is good exercise."

"Ah yes, of course." She certainly did look fit and trim.

"Are you here for the card games?"

He nodded. "We're playing euchre this month."

Jill smiled. "The card room is bound to get busy, then. I'll make sure we put some coffee and water out for you."

"Thank you, Jill."

Tucking the mail under her arm, she said, "Have a good time. See you later, General."

Camille's comment rose in his mind. "No reason to call me that anymore, you know. It's just Frank now."

"Did I offend? I'm sorry. I guess after hearing so many other people call you that, it stuck in my brain. It suits you."

Frank smiled as he walked down to the card room, but inside his mind was churning. He was sixty-eight years old. He'd been retired for almost a decade. Why *had* he allowed everyone to call him by his former rank?

At first, it was because he was used to hearing it more than his first name. But now? He didn't know what his excuse was. Was it pride in his achievement? Or was it something worse? Like if he lost that label, he'd also lose his self-worth?

What else did he have? A serviceable house full of new furniture and old memories. His wife had died years ago and his children lived far away.

No point in thinking of any of that, he decided as he lifted his head and strode down the hall.

And when the other guys grinned and called out, "Hey, General," all he did was smile back.

Chapter 11

When Chelsea picked Jack up from school a little after three, she agreed to take him to Memorial Park for a little while before they tackled homework, dinner, and a load of laundry.

But now, as the clock headed toward five, Chelsea's patience was ending. For the last fifteen minutes, she'd been waiting for Jack to finish his conversation with two boys from his class so they could get home.

Unfortunately, even though Jack occasionally glanced in her direction, he didn't seem to see her.

"It turned into a great day, didn't it?" a man asked.

"Hmm? Oh yes, it is."

To her dismay, he moved to stand next to her. "I'm glad last weekend's rain didn't stay around here long."

"Me, too."

"My name is Drew. Do you come here often?"

Her stomach knotted as she realized she was getting picked up at the park. She smiled tightly. "Only with my son."

As she'd expected, Drew's interest waned. "Oh. Well, have a good afternoon."

"You, too."

Now that Drew had gone on his way, her patience was really thin. As much as she yearned to march over and tell Jack that it was time to leave, she sat down on a nearby bench and glanced at her phone. Jack would hate it if the boys made fun of him for having a hovering mother.

Maybe Camille really had been right. Jack wasn't her little sidekick anymore. Maybe he hadn't wanted to be that for a while now and she hadn't realized it.

"Uh-oh," said a deep voice behind her. "Is it happening already?"

Startled, she turned, then wished she hadn't. Here she was again. Standing face-to-face with Anderson Kelly. Her mouth went dry as their eyes met. "Hey," she said.

"Hi." He stopped a few feet away. Far enough to give her some space, close enough for her to notice his muscles beneath the long-sleeved navy WPFD T-shirt and how those faded jeans he had on seemed to fit him almost too well.

"So, is it happening?" He looked entertained.

By what, though? And why was she still far too aware of every little thing about him? "I'm not following you."

"No worries. I was making a joke that obviously fell flat. I was only talking about your son growing up. You had the kind of look my mom used to wear whenever I acted embarrassed to walk with her in the mall."

She chuckled softly. "I probably did look like that. I was just thinking that Jack is growing up on me. In spite of my best efforts to keep him little, too."

He looked at her sympathetically. "I heard that happens to everyone sooner or later."

"I've heard that, too." Hearing the wistfulness in her own voice, she chuckled. "And, just for the record, my younger self is currently rolling her eyes. All I did was tell my mother that I needed more space."

"Me, too."

There it was again. That reminder that as much as she'd

tried to forget the memories, it wasn't possible. Especially since so much of what came to mind was so sweet.

Hesitantly, she said, "Things are so different now. Everyone texts."

"Twenty-four/seven."

Opening up a bit more, she added, "I guess kids don't need those lectures about talking on the phone too much anymore."

"My mom always used to say anything I had to tell you could wait eight more hours until we were at school."

Chelsea chuckled. "I heard the same thing at least once a week."

Anderson folded his arms, the movement pulling the cotton a little more tightly across his chest. "Our moms probably have tons of stories about those days. Trying to keep a handle on teenagers can't be easy."

"I guess it comes with the territory." Without stopping to wonder why she was talking so freely to Anderson, she added, "When Jack was a toddler I used to fervently wish for just ten minutes to myself. Now, though? I wish he wouldn't grow up quite so fast."

"I'm not a father, but I have a feeling a lot of parents do that, too."

"I guess. But still . . ."

Anderson looked like he was about to add something but then he redirected his attention. "Hi, Jack."

Chelsea turned around to see Jack approaching with a curious look on his face.

"Hi," he said. "How come you're here at the park?"

"I got off my forty-eight-hour shift about an hour ago and I'm meeting some buddies for a game of HORSE."

"Horse?" Chelsea asked.

"It's a basketball game, Mom," Jack said, just this side of snarky. "Where are you going to play, Mr. Kelly?"

Anderson pointed to the courts. "Over there. And you can call me Anderson."

"Can I watch?"

"You can if you'd like, but I'm guessing that your mom might have something to say about that."

Jack pivoted on his heel. "Mom, can I? Please?"

Chelsea didn't know what to say. She had wanted to hurry him home. But how could an on-time supper or homework at the kitchen table compete with a basketball court full of guys?

Still, did she *want* Jack around her old boyfriend? Of course, she'd just acknowledged that he was growing up, even if she wasn't ready for him to—and seeking out new people was part of that. Plus, hadn't she decided to try to be friends with Anderson?

"Please, Mom?"

How could she refuse when he asked so sweetly? And well, to her surprise there was a part of her that wouldn't mind being around Anderson for a little bit longer. "What do you think?" she asked him. "Do you mind if we stay and watch for a while?"

His gaze was warm, like he knew what a hard time she was having. "Not at all."

"*You* want to watch them play basketball, too, Mom?"

"I don't mind hanging out here for a while. Besides, it's not like you can drive yourself home, bud," she teased.

"I can bring him home, if you'd like."

Watching him play basketball was one thing. Driving Jack around was something else entirely. She wasn't ready for Anderson to get that close to Jack. "No, thank you. We come as a pair." She ignored her son's obvious discomfort.

Anderson waved a hand, saying, "I get it."

"All right then. I'm going to take Jack to get a hot dog and then we'll be over to watch you guys play Horses."

His eyes crinkled a bit. "Sounds good."

After he walked away, Jack looked up at her impatiently. "We don't have to get hot dogs, Mom. I'm fine."

"You haven't eaten a snack and neither have I. And,

since we're staying here at the park, dinner is probably just going to be some soup and cheese and crackers." When he sighed, she hardened her voice. "Pick your battles, buddy."

"Okay. Fine."

Resting her hand on his shoulder, she walked him to the food cart parked at the edge of the green. Three people were already in line and other folks were sitting nearby eating hot dogs, hot pretzels, and it looked like chili and sodas were also on the menu.

Her stomach grumbled in appreciation. Hot dogs might not be the healthiest choice, but they sure were good.

At least she was giving Jack a little bit of space and taking care of most of her dinner worries at the same time.

Perhaps she should be picking her battles as well?

Chapter 12

*H*e was a grown man. He fought fires for a living. He'd been deployed on foreign soil and had more than once come pretty close to giving his life for Uncle Sam. He had the scars to prove it, too.

So, why was every nerve ending on alert just knowing that Chelsea and Jack were watching him play a game?

Probably because every time he glanced their way, both mother and son were watching him avidly, and Jack was cheering for him like he was the best ballplayer around, which was nowhere near the truth.

Chelsea didn't look quite as impressed, but still she watched closely enough for him to be distracted by her attention. And maybe by the way her golden hair flowed around her shoulders.

Having his own cheering section was a bit of an ego boost, he couldn't deny it.

Luckily, the other guys didn't seem to mind that they had a small audience.

"*R*," Mark called out.

Anderson dribbled a couple of times and launched his

shot, which bounced off the backboard. Greg reached for it, dribbled it twice, then took his shot.

He missed, too.

Anderson almost gave him grief before he remembered that he had two pairs of eyes watching his every move. So instead of teasing Greg, he glanced Jack's way and grinned.

Jack grinned back. "Come on, Anderson!"

That little show of support was as cute as all get-out. So much so, he didn't even care that the other guys were going to tease him for weeks to come.

"*S*," Finn yelled as he dunked the ball.

Anderson reached for the ball but stepped out of bounds.

"Kelly, get your head in the game," Greg said.

"I hear you."

"Hope so."

All too soon, Mark called out "*E*" and the game was done.

"Give me five minutes, guys," Anderson said.

Greg leaned in. "Take seven, Doc. You've got a little guy over there chomping at the bit to see you." He winked. "His mom, too."

"Thanks." He drained half his water bottle before walking over to talk to Jack.

The boy was up on his feet, smiling broadly.

Reminding himself that Chelsea probably had no desire to stand near a sweaty guy, he focused on Jack. "So, what do you think? Do you like HORSE?"

"Yeah, but it looks kind of hard."

"Nah, it's easy." He grinned. "Besides, it's just for fun."

Jack seemed to think about that for a moment before speaking. "Are you mad that you lost the game?"

Chelsea, still sitting on that bench, looked embarrassed. "It's rude to ask things like that, son."

Jack looked down at his feet. "Sorry."

"Nah, don't be. It's a legitimate question. And the answer is nah, things like that don't upset me."

"Really?" The boy was looking at him so intently that Anderson felt like his next words actually meant something.

"Really." Anderson knew that boys Jack's age tended to look up to anyone older. Nonetheless, it made him feel about ten feet tall.

All at once, everything inside him felt lighter than it had in weeks, maybe even months. So much so that he found himself opening up a bit more. "First of all, I just got off a very long shift, remember, so, it's not like I'm at my best. Secondly, someone's got to lose, right? That's kind of what sports are about."

"But still, losing doesn't feel good," Jack said.

"True, but my dad used to tell me that if I couldn't be a good loser, then I shouldn't be playing any game at all." He drew a breath. "Back when I was playing football, I didn't really agree with him, but I've come to find out he had a point."

"Yeah, maybe you're right."

"Nothing wrong with losing every now and then, especially if it's just a game for fun."

Chelsea looked pleased with how Anderson had handled the conversation. Thoughtful, too. "He's right, Jack," she put in. "Games should be fun. Neither of us gets mad when we lose at Uno, right? Sports don't have to be any different."

"Doc," Greg called out, "you gonna play or are you done?"

"I'm playing! One sec." Turning back to the boy, he said, "Sorry, but I've got to go."

Chelsea stood up. "That's okay. We need to go on home anyway."

Jack frowned. "Mom, really?"

"Really. And you'll appreciate it at eight o'clock when you aren't still doing your homework." With a shy smile, she turned to Anderson. "Thanks for letting us hang out for a while. It was fun."

"Anytime."

Holding out her hand, Chelsea turned to her son. "Ready, Jack?"

He glared at her hand like it was a stick of dynamite. "I'm way too old to hold hands, Mom."

Looking contrite, she pulled her hand back immediately. "You're right. I'm sorry."

Even though the guys were waiting on him, Anderson called out, "Hey, Chelsea?"

"Yes?"

"If I call or text you, would that be okay?" He couldn't believe it, but his palms were sweating.

"Oh, I don't know, Andy."

Lowering his voice so Jack would hopefully not hear every word, he murmured, "I love that you still call me Andy, but that guy really isn't me anymore. I promise, I'm better."

"You don't need to be better for me."

That was crushing, but he wasn't going to give up. Not now that they'd come this far. "I do, Chels. I really do. Will you try to trust me just this little bit? If you try, I won't let you down."

After a pause, she nodded. She opened her mouth and then closed it again. Felt the pockets of her slim-fitting slacks—an action he tried hard not to notice. "Sorry, I don't have a pen handy," she said.

"I don't need it written down. What is it?"

"I can tell it to you," Jack blurted. He rattled off the seven numbers.

"Thanks, buddy. Chels, I'll call you later."

The boy's mouth gaped. "You can remember that many numbers?"

"Yep." Turning to Chelsea, he softened his voice. "Thanks for that. Drive home safe, yeah?"

"Always."

"Doc, now!" Mark called out.

After bumping fists with Jack, he ran back to the game. "Sorry."

"Whatever," Finn said.

Spinning the ball on his fingertip, Greg said, "You three looked pretty tight."

"I wouldn't say that. We're all just getting to know each other."

All the guys laughed.

"What?"

"Anderson, you might have been getting to know the kid, but there were still enough sparks between you and that woman to light up the sky."

Only Greg could say something like that and sound earnest. "Maybe. I don't know. We still have a lot to work through."

"That may be, but it's obvious that she's willing to give you a chance."

"I wouldn't go that far."

"I would," Mark said. "Chelsea gave you her number in front of her kid, dude. That's huge."

Maybe . . . unless it was only Jack who wanted him to call. Maybe Chelsea intended to tell him in private to leave her alone. Just as Anderson was about to ask the guys what they thought about those chances, Greg tossed the ball at him. "Okay, Romeo, let's play."

Anderson made his shot and called, "*H*."

The game began again. But he had his mind on other things.

Chapter 13

Jack was quiet during their short drive home. Chelsea was glad; she'd needed a few moments to reflect on Anderson's rapport with Jack and how it felt watching him play basketball. For the first time since Jack was born, she'd felt like it wasn't just the two of them. Instead, just for a little while, it had almost seemed like she and Jack were watching the third person in their group.

Oh, she might as well admit it to herself . . . she'd gotten a glimpse of how it would feel to have a husband and a father for Jack.

Not that she thought it was going to be Anderson. No, it was just the idea of not being so alone.

Unbidden, a memory returned, of a day when cheerleading practice ran long and she had no way to get home. Riley was supposed to take her home . . . but had forgotten and left without her. So Chelsea was feeling panicky, knowing how angry her mother would be if she had to drop everything and come get her.

She was standing outside the gym, worrying what to do, when Andy walked by with five or six guys, all sweaty and with a cut on his cheek from football practice. When he caught sight of her, he walked right over and asked what was wrong.

"I'm just trying to get up the nerve to call my mom to pick me up. My ride home fell through."

"I'll drive you."

She jutted her chin at the guys who were waiting for him. "You don't have plans?"

He smiled. "Not anymore. Come on, Chels."

It was such a little thing. But all these years later, she still remembered feeling special. Cared about.

Not alone.

Of course, that was a long time ago. She and Andy were no longer a couple.

They weren't anything. In fact, until just a few weeks ago she'd been going out of her way to avoid the man! Actually, any man.

That said, she couldn't deny that she still felt something for him. A pull that had a little to do with his good looks and a lot to do with his kindness and the memory of how happy they'd been together.

She continued to stew on her mixed-up feelings as she parked the car, shuttled Jack inside, looked over the mail, and cleaned out Jack's backpack and lunchbox.

But as soon as she sat down at the kitchen table where Jack was doing homework, he pounced. "Do you think Anderson is going to call you?"

"I think so, but I'm not sure."

"If he did, maybe you could go on a date."

"Well, um, I don't think we're quite ready for that."

"But one day, right?"

She knew Jack was smitten with Anderson and she didn't want his feelings to be hurt. But she also didn't want to allow him to think that there really could be a future with Anderson. "Sometimes people say they'll call but don't." It wasn't easy to be so frank, but it would be a lot harder if she allowed

Jack to have a lot of expectations that were never met. Anderson seemed to have grown up, but she couldn't forget how badly *Andy* had let her down.

Jack tilted his head to one side. "Why not? Do you think he couldn't remember all those numbers?"

She actually thought there was zero chance he'd forget her number. He'd always been smart, plus she had a feeling that he'd learned to memorize all sorts of important data during his military training. "Honey, sometimes people do and say things in the moment but then change their minds. Anderson might decide he really doesn't want to call." As in, Andy might change his mind about *her*.

Chelsea heard herself sigh and was surprised at the feeling of disappointment that crept into her stomach. She was determined to be fine either way. Anderson Kelly would *not* disappoint her again.

She didn't want to think about the topic anymore, but Jack was unrelenting.

"I hope he doesn't change his mind."

Hurt flared in his eyes, which made her feel terrible. Maybe she was pushing realistic expectations just a little bit too far.

No, maybe she should admit to herself that all these "realistic" expectations weren't in place to protect Jack as much as to protect herself. Honestly, when was she going to learn that not everything was about her?

"If he does call, I'll let you know. Okay?"

"Promise?"

"Promise."

As she saw Jack draw in a breath, obviously ready to relay further thoughts, she held up a hand. "Son, I love you, but I don't necessarily want to hear your opinions about me and Anderson. We're grown-ups, and things between grown-ups sometimes don't make any sense to kids and that's just how it is."

"Fine."

He was now wearing a mutinous expression—one he'd perfected when he was four and really, really liked getting his way.

It was past time to change the subject. Seeing that it was nearing seven o'clock, she said, "Let's get your things organized for tomorrow. What's your report going to be about?"

"Sea lions."

"Do you want to get started on it now?"

"No. I got a library book and we're gonna work on our reports in class tomorrow."

He stood up and walked to the refrigerator, running his finger over the lunch schedule, which was attached to the door with a magnet. "I want to buy tomorrow."

"What is it?"

"Tacos."

She grinned. "Do you want a snack for school, too?"

"Nah, I'm good. And I still have money on my lunch card."

"Okay, now that that's covered, let's get to work on that homework. It's getting late."

"I'm going to do it in my room."

This was new. "I don't know, Jack."

"That's what I want to do, Mom."

She was about to argue but decided to take some of her own advice and allow him some space. "All right. Take a shower when you're done. Do you want some ice cream when you get out?"

"Uh-huh."

"Sounds good, then."

Jack trotted up the stairs with more energy than she'd had at nine that morning. Realizing that she finally had some time for herself, she poured herself a glass of wine from the bottle of chardonnay that she'd bought last week. She wasn't much of a drinker, but every once in a while, a glass was delicious.

Grabbing a couple of Wheat Thins from an open box,

she wandered back into the living room and sat down next to the fireplace. Now that she was alone, she could admit that she'd been kidding herself. If Anderson didn't call, she would definitely feel disappointed.

Andy Kelly had turned into a pretty great guy. Even with his scars, he was still gorgeous. Well, at least to her, he was. But more important, she was beginning to realize that even if nothing ever happened between them in the future, there were parts of him that were still the same. Inside, he might very well be the same guy who would leave all his friends to give her a ride home so she wouldn't be standing around by herself.

"Now what?" she said to the empty room.

Now it was time to glance at her phone to see if he had maybe, possibly, already texted her. Not that there was a chance.

It had been about an hour since they'd left the park. Maybe he'd decided to try out her number. Just to see if he remembered the digits, right?

Or because he'd been thinking about her?

She took a sip of wine for fortification. Took a deep breath. Then picked up that darn phone and glanced at the screen.

She had four notifications from various apps, including the very important fact that there was a sale going on at Macy's. Two texts, one from Kaylee and one from an old friend who'd moved to Iowa.

Nothing else.

She put her phone back down, picked up a magazine, and told herself to grow up.

An hour or so later, Jack trotted back downstairs, had a bowl of ice cream, then kissed her good night with a promise that he would brush his teeth and go to sleep soon.

She made her lunch, prepped the coffeepot for the next morning, and took a shower.

Then glanced at the time.

Made a cup of tea to calm her nerves.

Checked the time again.

It was almost nine. Anderson had said that he'd just come off a forty-eight-hour shift. He was probably asleep. Or out at Granger's having a beer with his buddies before going home.

Or watching ESPN. Whatever guys did at night.

Just as she was taking a sip of tea, her phone both vibrated and rang.

Which promptly caused her to spill tea on the front of her sleep shirt. Boy, was it hot!

Her phone rang again. She picked it up, and was hit with a smattering of nerves when she saw who it was. "Hello?"

"Hey, Chels," Anderson said.

"Hey." She smiled, remembered he couldn't see her face, and tried to think of something to say that was easy and low-key.

When nothing came to mind, a couple of seconds passed and his voice turned a little less confident. "Is now a good time to talk or are you tied up?"

"Yes. I mean, yes, it's a perfect time. We've already had showers and ice cream and Jack's in bed." And . . . she'd just told him way more than he wanted to hear.

"I thought that was what you'd be doing."

"Sorry?"

"No, I'm sorry. I sound like an idiot, don't I? I promise, I didn't mean that in a creepy, I'm-imagining-what-you're-doing way. I was . . . well, I didn't want to risk calling when you were in the middle of his homework or getting him to bed or something."

"You don't sound creepy at all," she said with a smile. "I'm impressed that you even thought about an eight-year-old's nighttime routine."

"He's a great kid, Chels."

The last time he'd said something similar she bristled. Now the compliment warmed her heart. "I think so. We've almost made it to his ninth birthday, as he reminds me about a dozen times a day."

"I haven't thought about things like that in years, but it's so true—birthdays and getting older used to mean so much."

"No, it used to mean *everything*. It was the difference between going to movies with your parents and without them."

"Or moving up to the next league in sports."

"Or getting a learner's permit," she added.

"Or driving."

"Or dating."

"Chels, I swear I waited forever until you could date."

And just like that, she was fifteen, trying to convince her parents to let her go on a real date. But her parents had stood firm. Andy Kelly could come over and sit on the couch with her in the living room. Or, they could meet with a group of kids to go to the movies or basketball games. But Chelsea couldn't go on a real date until her sixteenth birthday.

Even though the memory felt bittersweet now, she murmured, "I could barely sleep the night before I turned sixteen."

"I still can't believe your parents let me drive you to school that morning."

"I wore them down." After making sure that Jack hadn't sneaked down the stairs, she said, "You were pretty much all I ever talked about." The moment the words were out, she wished she could yank them back. It wasn't like he didn't know how she'd felt back then . . . but did she really need to remind him?

"I was the same way," he admitted. "But I was cooler about it, I'm sure."

She giggled. "Uh-huh."

"Yeah, probably not that cool at all. The guys gave me so much crap." He chuckled. "So did Carter and Kim— they were too young to think dating was cool. I think even my parents were pretty amused."

"What? I didn't know that."

"I wasn't going to tell you." His voice was both rough and teasing. "I had a reputation to uphold, you know."

"Well, you *were* the quarterback."

He laughed. "I thought that was something, too. Lord, I was so full of myself."

"Not so much." Oh, maybe he had been full of himself, but he'd also been the best guy she'd ever met. "Anyway, I'm sure I was pretty full of myself, too."

"You were the prettiest cheerleader on the squad. And the smartest."

Boy, their life back then had felt positively charmed, and she'd naively thought it would be like that forever.

By May of senior year, he'd committed to the army. By June, he'd broken up with her. By July? He was long gone.

He cleared his throat. "Chelsea, I . . . listen, I didn't call to relive our high school days."

Swallowing the lump that had formed in her throat, she nodded. Then realized he was still waiting for a response. "Okay."

"What I mean is, I'd really, really like to be friends again, and I hope to earn your trust so we can do that. But first I know we need to talk about how I behaved when you wrote me you were pregnant."

Back came all the pain that she'd tried so hard to get rid of. "I don't think we need to talk about that."

"I'm sorry, but I think we do." Before she could protest again, he said, "At least, I do."

Oh Lord, she wasn't ready for this. When *would* she be ready to unpack that hurt and live it all over again?

"I don't want to talk about it over the phone," she managed to say. It wasn't only that she needed time to prepare herself, she didn't want to take a chance that Jack might overhear.

"I understand. Would you like to go out to breakfast or

lunch one day soon?" With a surprisingly boyish laugh he added, "I'd say dinner, but I'm afraid you won't think I'm worth a babysitter."

The way he was talking was so sweet, she wanted to pretend that their rocky past didn't exist. "Anderson, are you *sure* we have to do this?"

"I'm sure." After a slight pause, he continued, "I need to apologize."

She had no need to make him grovel, though. "Andy—"

"You know a simple sorry isn't enough. I want to attempt to explain myself." Before she could say a word, he added, "I very much want to know the woman you are now, Chelsea. I want to be a friend to you and to Jack. I'd like to be able to talk to you at the park or bring a pizza by your house without it being awkward. I'd like that a lot. So, will you, Chels? Will you at least have breakfast with me?"

"Andy . . ." She hesitated, then replayed his words in her head. No longer having to avoid him would be a relief. Maybe even one day being his friend would be okay, too. "Fine. I'll have breakfast with you. I drop Jack off at school at seven thirty and I can go into work at ten."

"How about Friday morning?"

That was in two days! What had she done? Forcing herself to sound like her schedule was busy, she said, "I can make Friday work."

"Great. Where would you like to meet? Want to go to Jo's Kolache Hut?"

She loved that place, but so did half of Woodland Park. "Would you mind if we went somewhere quieter? Like Bridget's?"

"Uh, sure. So, eight A.M.?"

"I'll be there. Now I guess I better go make sure Jack's asleep and not sitting in bed playing a game."

"Good night then. See you Friday, Chels."

"See you then."

Hanging up, Chelsea got to her feet. But instead of hurrying to Jack's room, she forced herself to take a deep breath and calm her nerves. In just two days, she was going to be alone with Anderson for the first time in ten years and they were finally going to rehash everything that had pushed them so far apart. Their breakup had taken a piece of her heart, and that loss had left a gap neither time nor any other man had been able to fill.

Was it possible their talk would succeed in doing what nothing else had been able to do—to mend her heart at last?

Chapter 14

$\mathcal{E}$very other Thursday, the senior center hosted a bingo game. Much to Frank's amusement, it was kind of a big deal. Bingo started at one o'clock on the dot and was extremely popular. So popular that if you didn't get in the line outside the door by half past twelve, you probably wouldn't get a spot.

Frank knew this because the first time he wandered in at five minutes to one, every chair in the community room was filled and not a person seemed to care that there wasn't a seat for a former general.

He'd felt a little stung, both by the way everyone had looked at him like he should've known better . . . and by his own feeling of regret. After spending a good portion of his life surrounded by dignitaries and government bigwigs, he never would've imagined he'd be so disappointed to miss a bingo game.

Which meant he was now usually the first guy in line.

Today, the crowd was raucous. Jill had acquired a slew of gift cards from restaurants and stores around town to use as prizes, and today's grand prize was a twenty-dollar gift card for Granger's Last Stand.

Frank had gotten in line right at twelve thirty, but somehow he'd gotten sidetracked talking politics with two cronies, and now he was forced to take the next to last seat in the back corner of the room. It wasn't ideal. It was too far back to see well and if Jill strayed far from the microphone, it was difficult to hear, too. Not that he'd ever admit it.

"You okay back there, General?" Alan teased from the front row, Frank's usual spot of choice.

"A-okay."

Jill rang a bell. "All right, everyone, it's one o'clock and since it looks like we've got a full room yet again, it's time to close the doors."

"Oh, are you sure the chairs are all gone?" Camille said as she raced inside. "I got stuck at the crosswalk."

Jill looked around the room. "Please raise your hand if there's an empty chair near you."

"I promise, I don't take up a lot of room," Camille joked.

She was petite, for sure, and also as cute as a bug, thought Frank. Feeling like his day had just gotten a lot better, he held up a hand. "I do!" he said.

Jill smiled and pointed. "You're in luck, Camille. There's one last chair available in the back corner."

Obviously trying to locate that empty chair, Camille scanned the room.

Frank could tell the second she saw him because a slight look of discomfort appeared. After thanking Jill and accepting a bingo card, she weaved her way through the room and then slowly sidestepped down his row. Two men stood up so she could get by more easily.

Frank stood up as well, though it wasn't necessary. Camille was taking the seat before his. But it seemed like the gentlemanly thing to do and he was half hoping his good manners would be noticed.

After murmuring "thanks" and "sorry" to several people as she passed, she sat down next to him without a word.

So much for his attempt at chivalry.

Just as he was taking his chair again, Camille attempted to wiggle out of her coat. Since they were in such close quarters, he automatically reached out to help her.

But instead of smiling up at him, she froze. "I can do it, General."

She said *General* like *war criminal*. "Don't turn my help into something it's not, ma'am."

Her eyes narrowed and she looked like she was about to give him what for before appearing to realize that they had an audience. She pinned a bright smile on her face. "I'm all settled at last, Jill," she chirped. "Everyone, thank you so much for your patience."

Jill smiled as more than a few people reassured Camille that they didn't mind waiting in the least.

Frank couldn't think of another person in the room who would get such a nice response.

Ringing the bell again, Jill stepped in front of the microphone. "Okay, gang. Let's get started. Our first round will be four corners. Is everyone familiar with that?" She pointed to a whiteboard showing a drawing of a bingo board with the four corners darkened. After the briefest of pauses, she pushed a button, a fancy electronic machine started, and then a ball popped out. "B5!"

Frank glanced down at his card, located B5, and clicked the tab on his card. Next to him, Camille glanced down at hers and then continued to get settled.

He barely knew the woman, but even he could tell that she was flustered. Her cheeks were flushed and she sighed more than once.

The game continued. Jill called out numbers at a lightning speed, slowing down only to make the tried-and-true bingo jokes (How many times had he heard about B12, the vitamin of bingo?) while old Emmitt grumbled every time his numbers weren't called. Frank played, but he also continued to keep an eye on Camille.

When she missed O71, he pointed out that she had it on her card.

She clicked her board and neatly covered the number. "Thank you," she said.

"No problem."

Moments later a gal in the third row won. Jill checked her card, and then handed her a ten-dollar grocery store gift card. There was good-natured groaning from all the losers, then Jill stepped back to the microphone. "Clear your cards, everyone, we're heading back in time with classic bingo. For this next game, all you have to do is get your numbers in a straight line—horizontal, vertical, or diagonal."

As expected, someone made a crack about being a whiz at all things horizontal, which made their little director blush. To her credit, Jill didn't respond to the joke. She just started calling out numbers.

Frank was amused. They might be a bunch of old coots, but they'd all led full lives.

However, as the round continued, Camille seemed to grow even more distracted. It was becoming evident that she wasn't simply uncomfortable sitting next to him. No, there was something bothering her that she was having trouble shaking off.

When she pushed up her sleeves, he noticed an ugly dark bruise on her forearm.

Now he was worried. She was such a little thing and that was a good-sized bruise. When she noticed him gazing at her arm, she hastily pulled her sleeve back down and looked straight ahead.

And now he'd gone and embarrassed her.

He turned and looked straight ahead, too. And after a few minutes he realized that Jill might as well have been calling out the numbers in Greek, because all thoughts of bingo had disappeared. It was starting to seem like he'd gotten in line at twelve thirty for nothing. All he could think about was the woman next to him . . . and that hadn't happened since his darling Donna passed away.

*C*amille knew she should never have come. The day had been a disaster from the beginning.

First Clayton and Briana texted that they wanted to Face-Time. That was puzzling; her two eldest children were rarely in the same room together, much less looking to FaceTime in the middle of the week.

She'd clicked on apprehensively, and found them looking her over like she was under a microscope.

Then things got worse.

Briana immediately began hinting that Camille wasn't as spry as she used to be, and that she probably shouldn't be alone so much.

Every time Camille had opened her mouth to protest that she had a very full life and wasn't alone all day, Clay had jumped in with his two cents. Finally, frustrated by the lecture, she'd asked them to cut to the chase and tell her the real reason for the call.

Clay took a deep breath and dropped the bomb.

"Mom, we think it's time you moved."

She hated the fact that they could see her face! She did her best to keep her expression serene and not scowl. "Why is that?"

"You're getting older, and already you can't drive," said Briana. "Walking everywhere has to be difficult for you."

"I haven't driven in almost a year but I'm still okay, dear. I get around just fine."

"You walk a lot of places on your own. All by yourself."

Oh, for heaven's sake. "Yes, I do. The doctor said it's good for me and I agree. I'm getting fitter every day."

"I don't know about that, Mom. Walking in all kinds of

weather? It can be dangerous for a woman your age," Clay said.

"At the risk of sounding like a broken record, I think I should point out that I'm sixty-six, not eighty-six. By most people's standards I'm middle-aged."

"I think that's not quite true," Briana replied. "Don't forget, you've been retired for years now."

"I haven't forgotten, dear."

"Plus, think about what Dad would have wanted for you."

Scott. The love of her life. Her husband of thirty-seven years, whom she had lost far too young. As hard as she tried to hide the dismay on her face, she knew she wasn't successful. The kids softened their tones but it didn't disguise the fact that they were going in for the kill.

"Mom, that's why we're bringing this up. We all expected Dad to be around a really long time. You never know what the future holds. We don't want anything to happen to you."

"I realize that."

"Then at least think about it. We've been researching communities in Florida and we found some really nice retirement places. You'll have your own town house but all the upkeep is taken care of."

"I don't want to live in Florida."

"You can be near me, Mom."

"Briana, dear, I love you. But I do not want to move into a town house in Sarasota."

Clayton cleared his throat. "We all thought it would be better for you to be in a warm climate."

"We all?" What was going on?

"All four of us," Clay supplied. "We had a family meeting."

A family meeting without her? Because it was *about* her. "I see." And what she was "seeing" wasn't good. Actually, she was downright irritated.

Briana, her pretty, headstrong, successful Realtor daughter, spoke in her sweetest voice. "Mom, please, just think about it.

I asked for some brochures and when they arrive I'll send them to Woodland Park."

"Thank you, dear."

Briana's eyes lit up. "So you'll think about it?"

"I don't think I have much choice." She smiled to take the edge off her voice. It was enough to fool the kids. They both appeared visibly relieved.

She was glad she'd put their minds at ease . . . because inside, she was seething. "I'm so sorry but I need to get off the phone. I've got quite a few things to do before I head to the senior center for bingo."

Both Clayton and Briana gave her a look that spoke volumes. Obviously her eagerness to play bingo was another sign that she was decrepit.

"Okay, Mom. Have fun and thanks for not freaking out."

Enough was enough. Giving Clayton a cool look, she said, "I do a lot of things but I do not freak out."

His smile evaporated. "No, ma'am. Of course not."

They hung up, leaving her fighting the insane urge to throw something.

She'd settled for turning around too fast, tripping on a throw rug that was wrinkled, and knocking her arm against the side of a counter.

And that, of course, had started a round of tears which she'd barely finished before it was time to put her face back on and get ready for the senior center.

For whatever good it had done. She couldn't concentrate on the game at all.

"Camille?"

She glanced at the general. "Yes?"

"I hate to pry, but . . . are you all right?"

She was tired of lying. Looking directly at him, she shook her head. "No. Frank, I hate to say it, but I'm really not all right at all."

Chapter 15

$\mathcal{T}$ime was a funny thing. Ever since Chelsea had agreed to meet him at Bridget's on Friday morning, Anderson had been both waiting impatiently . . . and hoping that the moment would never arrive.

He wasn't used to this flip-flop of emotions. He'd never been the type of man to procrastinate or shirk from what had to be done. Not when he played football in high school, and for sure not in the army.

But this was different. If he messed up his apology, there was a good chance Chelsea wouldn't give him another minute of her time—and he was starting to believe that losing her all over again would be devastating.

So that morning he'd attempted a dry run of his speech, but it sounded so stilted, he decided just to wing it. But now, as he entered Bridget's Bistro, another case of nerves settled in and his mouth went dry. He wondered if Chelsea had picked this spot just to make sure she had the advantage.

Bridget's Bistro was small, with about six tables covered in gingham and polka-dot tablecloths in sherbet colors. The menu was heavy on things like scones, quiche, and organic granola, with fancy-sounding lattes and fresh-squeezed orange juice.

Bridget's was a favorite of his mother's. Of a lot of people, no doubt.

Until five minutes ago, he'd never stepped foot inside. The feminine aura kind of reminded him of being in a little girl's playhouse. He didn't have a problem with that, but it wasn't really his kind of place. Even beyond the decor, he tried to stay away from baked goods and he'd choose a cup of black coffee over a cherry almond latte any day.

But he would have gone anywhere and eaten five cinnamon rolls if it meant Chelsea agreeing to meet with him.

"You order at the counter, sir," a woman called out from the table she was clearing.

"Thanks."

A couple of minutes later, he was sitting in a tiny wicker-backed chair, sipping a latte and eyeing the food selections written on the chalkboard with what he hoped was an open expression.

Obviously he wasn't too successful, since the moment Chelsea walked in the door and spied him, she broke into a laugh.

He stood up as she approached his table. "What's so funny?"

"You, looking like you're trying to fit in."

"I guess I'm doing a pretty poor job of it?"

"You are, but I won't hold it against you. It is a rather froofy place, I realize. I promise it's good though."

He held up his drink. "The coffee is."

She pulled off her coat and slipped it over the back of her chair. "I'm so sorry I was late. There was a backup in the drop-off lane."

"You aren't late, I got here early." He gestured to the chalkboard. "Ready to order?"

"I am. I'm starving."

He motioned for her to precede him, remembering just in time not to place his hand on the small of her back as they navigated their way through the tables.

A woman who looked to be in her midforties greeted them with a smile. "Chelsea, hi! I haven't seen you in a while."

"I know. I miss coming in, but I don't always have the time anymore."

"Do you know what you'd like? We've got some terrific berry scones and this morning's latte is coconut java."

"I'll have a berry scone and a plain latte," she replied as she reached inside her purse for her wallet.

Even though he'd cautioned himself not to touch her, old habits died hard. Covering her hand with his own, he said, "I'm taking care of both of ours."

"Are you sure? There's no need to pay for mine."

"There's every need," he murmured. Raising his voice, he said, "I'll take another plain latte, some of that granola and yogurt, and a berry scone, too."

After paying and taking everything to their table, Anderson took a healthy bite of his granola and yogurt. It *was* really good, he thought, dipping his spoon in again.

Chelsea was watching him with a half smile on her face. "So, what do you think?"

"I think I need to stop worrying about pink tablecloths and come here more often."

She laughed. "I promise, I didn't ask you to meet me here for any other reason than that it's usually pretty quiet and the food is delicious."

"You made a good choice." He realized that he'd already made a huge dent in his food while she was still slowly sipping her drink. "Sorry, I'm used to eating fast."

"I bet. You never know when you're going to get called out for a fire."

"The alarms do seem to always ring at the worst times, like when I'm in the shower. Once, I didn't even get all the soap out of my hair."

"At least you were clean before getting surrounded by smoke."

"At least." Watching her take another nervous nibble of her scone, Anderson knew he couldn't put it off any longer. "Thanks for agreeing to meet me, Chelsea. I—I've been wanting to talk to you about how I acted all those years ago."

"Like I said on the phone, I don't know if that's necessary."

"I'm sorry but I think it is." His words felt like a jumbled mess inside his head, but he continued. Even if he messed this up, at least she would know he tried. "Listen, Chelsea, it's like this. You know how much I liked you back in high school."

"You told me you *loved* me, Andy. We were in love." She swallowed. "I mean, I thought we were."

He was already messing this up. "You're right. I did love you. I—sometimes I'd even think about the future. I used to think it was possible—I mean I hoped—well, that we would end up together." Revealing so much left his heart pounding. Could Chelsea hear it? Could she hear how much he still cared for her?

"That isn't what you said before you went off to basic."

"My parents were worried about me getting through basic. They didn't want me pining for my girl back home and messing up. Most of my friends thought the same thing. I figured they were right."

When she continued to stare at him, he added, "I . . . I guess I was also worried about fitting in. A couple of guys I knew who'd enlisted said that everyone went out a lot. That's how they bonded. I didn't want to be the guy who was left behind." His palms dampened as embarrassment set in. It was hard to admit just how much of a small-town kid he'd been back then. "Even though it sounds stupid now, that's why I said I wanted to break up for a while."

"No, you said you wanted to break up, Andy. You didn't say *for a while*!"

"I know, I'm sorry. I was young and confused. I wanted

to ask if we could just take a break, but it sounded lame, so I said all the wrong stuff. I know it's no excuse, but I've always regretted breaking up with you that night."

She shook her head, like she didn't believe a word he was saying. "That may be true, but you didn't tell me any of that. All you did was end things." Looking him directly in the eye, she said slowly and deliberately, "You broke my heart."

"I know." She'd cried right there in front of him. It had been hell not to pull her into his arms and take back everything he'd said.

He ran his hand through his hair and forced himself to continue. "I know it doesn't matter now, but I was also worried about the kind of future I could offer you. I kept hearing that once you're in the service, your life is no longer your own. I didn't know where I'd be at after basic. How could I force you to wait for me? It wouldn't be fair."

"You never told me any of that."

She was right, but instead of apologizing again, he tried to further explain his thinking. "Chels, you were going to college. You deserved to focus on that. You were sweet as all get-out and gorgeous, too. As much as I wanted you to wait for me, deep down I was afraid you'd be better off without me. There'd be a ton of college guys for you to date."

Brushing her hair away from her face, Chelsea swallowed hard. "I didn't want to date other guys. I loved you."

"And I loved you. I told you, I regretted breaking up almost as soon as I did it. I was planning to call you after I got through AIT—"

"Through what?"

"Sorry. Advanced Individual Training. You go through one or two AITs before being assigned your specific MOS."

She raised an eyebrow. "Which is?"

"Sorry, your Military Occupational Specialty. Your job, in other words." He remembered that heavy feeling of having so much to learn, all the time worrying that every one of his sergeants and commanding officers was going to think he was an idiot.

"Anyway, I was going to call you when I finally got settled and ask if we could see each other during my first real leave." Feeling his cheeks heat, he added, "I had it all planned out. I was going to admit how much I missed you and wanted you back . . . and then ask you to come see me."

"And then you got my letter."

Barely able to swallow the lump in his throat, Anderson nodded. "And then I got your letter."

Looking miserable, Chelsea leaned back in her chair. "I wanted to tell you the news in person or at least on the phone, but your parents said there was no way we could talk." She looked up at the ceiling. Was she trying to hold back tears?

"I didn't know you talked to my parents, Chelsea."

"I didn't tell them I was pregnant, just that I really needed to speak with you." She shook her head. "Your mom was super sweet but she told me that recruits couldn't have phone calls in basic training."

He shook his head in dismay. "I only told her that! She'd been calling every other day, then would get upset when I didn't call her back for a week . . ." Again, that pinch of regret. If only he hadn't told his mother that, he would have actually spoken to Chelsea. Maybe things would've worked out differently if he'd heard her voice. *Maybe.*

Chelsea released a ragged breath. "As you know, she did give me your mailing address. Writing that letter was the hardest thing I ever did. But I was afraid *not* to write you in case you somehow heard about everything from someone else."

"I don't know if hearing it in person or even on the phone would have made things any easier." Remembering the visceral shock of reading her letter, combined with how lonely he'd been during basic, Anderson figured he'd have started either crying or shouting at her.

"Looking back," Chelsea said, "I think I could've handled you being hurt and disappointed in me." She drew a circle on the table with one of her fingers. "What I couldn't get over was that you never wanted to hear my side. It was like you didn't care about me. Only your pride."

Oh God, every word she was saying was true. "You're right. I should've listened to you."

"Will you listen now?"

Gazing into her blue eyes, Anderson felt some of the fear he'd been feeling slip away. They were finally, finally going to get everything out in the open. It wasn't too late. "That's why I'm here."

"All right." She drew a breath. "I was heartbroken that you ended things. I thought you just wanted to date other people, Anderson. Like I wasn't good enough for you."

Even though he knew he should stay silent and let her speak, he couldn't help himself. "You *were*. You always were."

"I pictured you in your uniform flirting with all these girls." She shook her head as if to clear it. "Anyway, I rushed and got into a great sorority house. I tried to fit in, which meant I drank too much at the very first party. The next thing I knew, it was morning and I was in a guy's bed." Turning her head away, she said, "Of course I threw on my clothes and had to do the walk of shame back to my dorm. I can't tell you how awful that felt. But all the girls from my sorority laughed about it, like it was no big deal."

Anderson clenched his fists. He hated everything about that story, but especially that no one had looked out for her. "The older girls should've watched over you. They knew what the parties were like and that you were just an innocent freshman."

"Maybe they should've, but it wasn't anyone's fault but my own. I should've looked out for myself. It was my fault. Sleeping with that guy was *my* mistake."

Her bottom lip trembled before she bit on it, obviously

trying to retain her composure. "All I could think about were all the times we talked about waiting. How patient you'd been, saying that you'd waited until I was sixteen to take me out, and you could wait as long as I wanted until we had sex." She lowered her voice. "And what did I do? I gave it away to some random guy. I hated myself for that."

Her honesty floored him—and forced him to be honest with himself as well.

The truth was, Anderson *had* felt betrayed. Upset that all his patience and understanding had been for nothing. Wasn't that why he'd written such nasty things back to Chelsea? His face reddened at the memory of what a jerk he'd been.

"I couldn't believe it when I found out I was pregnant," Chelsea said. "All those girls I was hanging out with acted shocked when I told them, even though they were pretty wild." She wrapped her arms around herself and took a shuddering breath. "Next thing I knew, everyone was treating me like I was a slut, my parents were furious, and I was completely alone."

He swallowed, pushing his own feelings away. "And then you had to deal with me and my anger."

Chelsea straightened up. "You know, listening to ourselves now, with the wisdom of closing in on thirty, I realize that we were just kids then. We were scared kids trying to navigate new situations. We made mistakes, but I think we learned from them." Her voice grew husky. "While I regret the circumstances, I can honestly say that I've never regretted Jack. He's been everything to me."

"I get that. You should be proud of yourself." When she rolled her eyes, he reached for her hand. "No, listen. *You should be proud.* You told everyone the truth and you kept on keeping on. It's not easy being a single mom, but to do it at such a young age? I have *so* much respect for you, Chels. And you're right, Jack is amazing."

She looked down at their hands. "Where do we go from here?"

"I want us to be friends." Remembering the promise he'd made to himself, he shook his head. "No, that's not the complete truth. I want more than that."

"More?"

"Chelsea, I want to date you," he blurted. "To date you and Jack."

"I don't know . . ."

"At least think about it, okay?"

"Being involved with a single mother is a commitment," she warned. "I can't be casual where Jack is concerned."

"I'm not afraid of commitment. I don't know if I ever was. I *do* know I'm not afraid of committing to you—even if you only want to be friends right now."

Her eyebrows raised. "You'd do that, even if we became nothing more?"

"Friendship counts for a lot, Chelsea. If we only became friends, I'd count that as a win." It was the truth. Maybe even more so now, since she'd shared so much and been so honest.

She gazed at him for what felt like five minutes but was probably just five seconds. Then, to his delight, she curved her hand and linked her fingers through his. "Okay."

He exhaled a breath he hadn't even realized he'd been holding. "Okay," he said back.

As their eyes met again, Anderson could have sworn that they'd just promised each other a whole lot more.

Chapter 16

$\mathcal{T}$hey finished breakfast and went to their cars. As they said their good-byes, Chelsea did her best to smile and look relaxed.

But inside? Inside, she was as rattled as she could ever remember being.

Since their cars were parked next to each other, Chelsea pulled out her phone and made a big show of reading her messages, though there were only two inconsequential work emails and a notice about a sale on candles at one of her favorite stores.

Anderson waved as he pulled out in his SUV. She smiled and waved back, just like having breakfast with him was a normal thing.

Like she wasn't completely flustered because she'd been holding hands with Anderson not twenty minutes ago. And liking it.

Honestly, for a few sweet moments, it felt like being back in high school, when she was in love with Andy Kelly. With her hand encased in his, she'd felt protected and cared for.

Where had *that* come from?

Then there was their conversation! He'd shared so much, and so honestly, which had encouraged her to share way more than she'd intended to.

And instead of all that bare honesty tearing them apart, it seemed to bring them closer together. Why, she'd practically melted at his words and wanted to immediately forgive him for all the heartache he'd put her through.

How could she do that? Where was her backbone?

She needed a minute. No, she needed more than a minute.

She called Jill at work.

"Hey!" Jill said the moment she picked up. "I was just about to text you and see if you could take over the chair exercise class at one o'clock. Can you do that?"

Chelsea hated to refuse, but there was no way she could run that class today. Swallowing hard, she said, "I'm sorry, but I can't come in today."

"Are you sure?" Jill sounded panicked.

"I am. Uh, I'm feeling under the weather and I'd hate to get anyone sick. I'm sure you understand," she added quickly. Jill was a good woman and a good boss. But she also had a tendency to overcommit herself and then hope that Chelsea could pick up the slack. Usually Chelsea could . . . but not today.

"Well, yes, I guess I do," Jill murmured.

Hearing her take in a deep breath, Chelsea was determined to get off the phone before Jill could say anything else. "Thank you for being so understanding. I'll see you tomorrow. Bye." She clicked off without even waiting for her boss to reply, which was pretty rude.

But this was a special circumstance—she was having a mini meltdown in the front seat of her Subaru. She needed some space and some time to pull herself back together.

Where could she go in order to do some thinking? If she went home, all she would do was clean, do laundry, and feel guilty about ditching work.

No, she needed someplace outside, someplace where she could do some soul-searching. Her mind hit on the hiking trail just to the east of town.

The Deer Park Trail was one of the easiest around and rarely frequented by serious hikers. Usually only families walked on it, which meant it was very popular on Saturdays and Sundays but usually pretty empty on Friday mornings. It was a perfect spot for wandering and heavy thinking.

Feeling better, she drove out to the trailhead, parked next to the three other cars, pulled a jacket from the trunk, and after making sure she had her cell phone, headed down the path of packed dirt.

Within minutes, she was surrounded by glorious-smelling pine trees and huge, jagged red rocks that sprang from the earth. The sound of traffic from the interstate gradually faded away, while the dirt under her feet was soon replaced by bark and pine needles. Only a few birds and the occasional rabbit kept her company.

It was a pure Colorado moment—a reminder of why she had never considered living in another state . . . or even in a bigger city than little Woodland Park. This was her happy place. At last, a sense of peace slowly filled her.

Energized, Chelsea picked up her pace, enjoying the rare opportunity to take a beautiful solo walk in the middle of the day. She couldn't remember the last time that had happened. She usually didn't long for solitude; she was a people person and she adored being with Jack. But there was something almost spiritually healing about being so alone on the woodland trail.

Suddenly, a memory appeared, of a spring Saturday when Anderson asked her to take a walk around the track at the football stadium, which they liked because it was the best place for them to be alone. They both had parents who kept a tight leash on their whereabouts, so they spent most of their time together at each other's houses.

Boy, was that frustrating.

The two of them had joked about their parents' annoying rules many times. After all, if they'd really wanted to do something inappropriate they could've simply lied about going to the movies.

But that wasn't who they were. They didn't lie, didn't behave irresponsibly. Anderson wasn't just the varsity quarterback, he was on student council. She was not only a cheerleader but did choir and student council and the yearbook committee, even candy striping at the hospital. Everyone said they were such good kids. Good role models. And that they were the perfect couple.

She had thought so, too.

But that afternoon walk around the track had shaken her up. Instead of pulling her in for a few kisses, Andy revealed that he'd enlisted in the army and that he was leaving for basic training just weeks after graduation.

She was so shocked, she didn't even cry. No, not until she got home, and sobbed to her parents. Hours later, armed with their admonition to support Andy's decision and not be so selfish, she'd gone over to his house and said she was proud of him.

He'd looked so relieved and grateful, she continued to bottle up her pain and dismay. She pretended that she wasn't at all worried about being apart for years. Soon, as they neared graduation, she'd almost come to believe they were going to be okay.

Until he announced that he wanted to break up—for her sake. *Her* sake.

His little speech had been so full of himself. So practiced. He'd managed to look both sad and stalwart while neatly breaking her heart.

Only now did Chelsea realize that she'd cared for him so deeply that she'd suppressed all of her negative feelings. Yep, every time she'd gotten mad or admitted to herself that she wasn't okay with his decisions, she'd pushed it down deep.

Maybe that's why she'd clung to her new friends in college. She'd felt so alone and so hurt that she'd been willing to do anything in order to fit in.

And then Jack came along.

And a new sense of peace came over her. Her parents' wishes didn't matter anymore because *she* was a parent. The girls' comments didn't matter because they weren't who she was anymore. And Anderson's disappointment and anger didn't matter anymore because he was the one who had set everything in motion.

Besides, she had Jack. She had Jack, and never looked back. Except that wasn't really true. She'd held on to all that secret disappointment and anger and nursed them in private. And now, here she was at almost thirty and she was finally giving them up.

She didn't know what was going to happen with Anderson now. Sure, she'd agreed to try to be friends, but was that even possible, when she still found him to be one of the most attractive men she'd ever met?

And there was the quiet, steady way he acted now. That appealed to her—both as a woman and as the mother of an impressionable boy.

And he was so strong. She pictured being held in his arms . . . winding her arms around his neck . . . and kissing him.

She groaned. She mustn't think about kissing Anderson Kelly. Never again.

"Ma'am, are you okay?"

With a start, Chelsea looked over at a pair of young men with short military buzz cuts, the kind new recruits got when they entered the service. "Yes. Why?"

They exchanged looks. "No reason, ma'am," the taller of the two murmured. "Sorry to disturb you."

Chelsea realized then that she'd been standing like a statue in the middle of the trail. "No, I'm sorry. I, um, I guess I was daydreaming. Sorry I was in your way."

"No worries." They smiled at her and moved on.

It was time she moved on, too. At long last.

Chapter 17

Six hours later, Chelsea was feeling a whole lot less rattled and more like her usual self. Kaylee had promised to come over after work with dinner. Then, Jack had come home with news that he was invited to go bowling with a friend's family.

Now she and Kaylee were sitting on the living room couch sharing a bottle of red wine and a spinach pizza with a cauliflower crust. Kaylee had also brought some of her latest designs for her bridal gown business and a whole lot of stories about her clients, including one who sounded like she was auditioning for a bridezilla reality show.

Kaylee's stories made the cauliflower pizza a little more edible, especially since Chelsea could hardly eat a bite without dissolving into laughter.

"I can't believe she blamed you for the dress not fitting," Chelsea exclaimed after Kaylee finished her latest tale of woe.

"It would have been really terrible except that she'd brought her mother and her two best friends and I saw them trying not to laugh when she was chewing on me about how tight her dress was." She shook her head. "When she went to take it off her friends told me that she'd been stress-eating whole pints of ice cream at a time."

Chelsea giggled again. "What did you do?"

"Not much."

"What? That doesn't sound like you!"

Kaylee pointed to the intricate design. "Look at all that beadwork. I sewed every one of those stinking seed pearls in that bodice. There wasn't any way I could let out the dress."

"So, what did you say?"

"I told her what her friends should have told her—that she was going to have to lose the weight she'd gained if she wanted to fit into the dress."

"Ouch."

"Don't look at me like that. There was nothing I could do. She insisted on a mermaid gown with a thousand seed pearls. At this point it's all about the dress."

"So . . . what happened?" Chelsea said around another bite of pizza.

"She left in a huff after refusing to pay me the next installment."

"No, she did not. Kaylee!"

"I was really upset until her mother paid me and told me she would talk to the bride."

"Do you think that will help?"

"I hope so, because she's getting married in six weeks. She's not going to find another dress. Especially not one as pretty as the one I made for her."

Chelsea was both amused and impressed by her friend's way of looking at the situation. "At least you haven't lost your confidence."

"Oh, don't get me wrong. I felt bad getting cussed out in front of her mother and her friends. She wasn't nice, Chels."

Chelsea raised her glass of wine and toasted Kaylee. "Congratulations, then. I have a feeling that bride is going to lose the weight and post a dozen pictures on Instagram.

Everyone is going to see the photos and give you a call. You're going to get tons of orders."

"I hope so." Kaylee sighed. "Boy, wouldn't that be so great?"

"It's going to be amazing! Though, I have to say that hearing your stories makes me happy that I never had a big wedding."

"Oh, Chels, I'm sorry."

"What? I promise, I didn't mean it in a 'please, feel sorry for me' kind of way."

Kaylee's distinctive dark-green eyes turned troubled. "Do you ever wish that Jack's dad had married you?"

Chelsea had a hard time stopping herself from glancing over her shoulder, just to make sure Jack hadn't suddenly appeared in the house and overheard. "Of course not," she said with a shake of her head.

"Really? Things might have turned out differently. Maybe y'all could've been happy."

"After dealing with awful brides, how are you still a romantic at heart?" she teased.

"I'm just saying that if he would've done the right thing—"

"If he and I had done the 'right thing' we would never have gotten drunk and had sex in the first place. I promise, no matter how hard some of my days as a single mom have been, I've never thought entering into a loveless marriage would have made things better."

"Well, one day I'm sure I'll be making you a gorgeous wedding dress to go on your gorgeous figure."

She had a far-from-gorgeous figure but there was no way she was going to debate that with Kaylee. "If I ever do fall in love and decide to get married, I'll be begging you to design my gown."

"You won't have to beg. I'll be honored to make that dress."

"I know it will be gorgeous, too. You are so talented."

"All right. I hear you." After another sip of wine, Kaylee shifted to face her more completely. "So, moving on . . . how's work?"

"Good."

"Are you ever going to start looking around for another job?"

"Not at all. I love working at the senior center."

"But doesn't Jill plan to stay there forever?"

It was obvious that Kaylee wasn't a fan of Jill, but she'd never shared exactly why that was. "She does, but that's okay. I have no desire for her job."

"Are you sure? I bet you'd do a better job."

"She's fine and yes, I'm sure. I don't want all the responsibility she has. I love my job but I also don't want to work any more hours than I already do. I like being around for Jack."

"But you need to think of your future." Kaylee took a deep breath, obviously gearing up to deliver a lecture.

Chelsea held up a staying hand. "I love that you have big dreams and work hard to accomplish them. But that isn't me."

"I'm sorry. I sound pretty self-absorbed, don't I?"

"No, you sound like a woman who is going to be a huge success one day. It's okay that we're different."

"Different is good."

Thinking they both needed a break from heavy conversation, Chelsea handed the remote control to Kaylee. "Turn on Netflix. Let's binge."

"On it." Kaylee put her portfolio away and started clicking like she'd navigated her way around Chelsea's ancient television for years. Which she had.

After settling on a new series based on a popular set of historical romance novels, Kaylee tucked her feet under her and settled in. Chelsea tried to concentrate, but her mind kept drifting.

As the characters on the screen chatted and joked while enjoying really good hair, Chelsea, almost against her will, let her mind wander. For just a minute, she allowed herself to imagine what it would be like to wear one of Kaylee's beautiful creations, hold a bouquet of pink roses, and walk down the aisle on little Jack's arm toward the most handsome man in the room.

Sitting on all the pews in the church would be their families and friends from every part of their lives. Everyone would be watching them with so much happiness that the church would practically radiate with warmth.

But she would have eyes for only Anderson.

He would be standing in his uniform, looking like everything he was: proud, serious, and a hero multiple times over.

When he saw her, his eyes would light up and he'd smile.

It would be perfect.

"Oh, Chelsea, don't you just love this series? This guy is so dreamy."

She blinked and belatedly looked at the screen. The couple was standing close together—it was obvious they were trying really hard not to kiss in the middle of the ball.

"Chels?"

"Sorry. I guess I was too caught up. Yeah. He's great." She sipped her wine and tried to focus on the show, *not* on how she couldn't seem to stop thinking about Anderson. Or how, yet again, she wasn't thinking about him with bitterness but with something a whole lot different. Something that felt a little bit like longing.

*A*nderson had joined a couple of guys for dinner but passed on going to Granger's afterward. He'd told Greg he was still beat from going on a five-mile run that afternoon. Greg hadn't looked like he believed him, but hadn't tried to change his mind.

Instead, he'd settled on the couch in front of the TV. Tab, looking pleased to have company for once, curled up by his side. He found some reality show about hunting for gold in

Alaska but was barely aware of what any of the guys were saying.

All he seemed able to do was think about Chelsea's face when she shared how hurt she'd been. Even after all this time, she looked visibly wounded, which was a punch in the gut. Why had he listened to everyone's advice when he should have simply trusted his gut and tried to make things work long distance? Even if they had eventually drifted apart at least they could have *tried*.

When at last he couldn't castigate himself anymore, he'd ended up doing the next best thing, which was stare at the most recent addition to his phone's contact list: Chelsea Davis.

Feeling more nervous than a high school freshman with his first crush, he let his fingers hover over the screen. He knew he needed to text her something—otherwise she was liable to think he'd changed his mind about renewing their friendship, and that was the last thing he wanted.

Hey, he texted, then erased it immediately. *Think this through*, he told himself. *Sound like a grown-up.*

After another five minutes of internal debate, he texted **How was your night?**

There. It was pretty lame but at least it showed he was thinking about her. He pressed send before he erased it and wrote something stupider.

Of course, the minute he clicked send, he found himself staring at the screen again, waiting impatiently for Chelsea's response.

Like she had nothing else to do on a Friday night but stare at her phone and write him back.

But then, just as he was about to actually try to care about panning for gold in Alaska, the telltale dots appeared on his screen. He couldn't help but grin.

Less than a minute later, Chelsea's reply popped up.

My friend Kaylee came over. She brought cauliflower pizza.

Let me guess——you're not a fan.

I'm not. But it wasn't too bad. She also brought wine.

What did Jack think of it?

He wasn't here. He went bowling with a friend. What about you?

Anderson couldn't believe how easy it was to text with her. It was comfortable, like they did it all the time. **Nothing much. Went out with a couple of guys for Italian. Now I'm home hanging out.**

Where?

The couch

Haha

La Bella

It's been forever since I went there. What did you get?

It was such a Chelsea thing to ask, it made him grin.

IDK, some kind of pasta

That's it?

I had a salad and garlic bread too

Feel me rolling my eyes. I need to eat out vicariously through you. Seriously, going out for me usually involves food wrapped in paper.

Noted. I'll take you and Jack next time.

When she didn't reply immediately he started worrying again. Had that been too much? Was he not supposed to mention Jack?

He put down his phone and grabbed a glass of water, trying not to spiral. Ten silent minutes later, he came to the conclusion that he'd really messed up.

Chelsea still didn't trust him and naturally she was protective of her son. He should have waited for *her* to bring Jack into the conversation.

Irritated with himself, he got up and started pacing, then finally decided to call it a night.

But just as he was pulling off his T-shirt and climbing into bed, he heard his cell phone ding. Picking it off his nightstand, he read.

That sounds fun. I'm headed to bed. Night.

He was so relieved, he fired off one last text and sent it before he started overthinking everything again.

Night, Chels. Sleep well.

As he lay on his back and watched his ceiling fan spin, he couldn't help but smile. Maybe he hadn't completely messed everything up with Chelsea after all.

Chapter 18

*B*riana's packet of brochures had arrived yesterday. Though Camille wanted to do nothing more than throw it out, she'd placed it on the counter. Later that evening, after fortifying herself with a steaming cup of peppermint tea, she opened up the envelope and glanced at the brochures. Then, because she loved her children, she dutifully read all about three retirement communities in the Sarasota area.

Every photo showed gray-haired, fit, smiling people engaged in tennis, golf, biking, even gathering for cocktails in various clubhouses. When they weren't actively doing all those things, they were taking "enrichment" classes and being waited on hand and foot.

Camille was sure they were models, and directed to pose like they were very happy living in the Sunshine State. However, even if they were actual residents, they were strangers to her. Strangers with whom she didn't want to sip wine, join a book club, take cooking classes, or play tennis. She already had friends, a community clubhouse, and a nice place to live. It was already paid for, too. Then there were all of her things.

She understood the wisdom of divesting, but there was only so much she was currently willing to part with.

To make matters worse, Briana had gone so far as to star her favorite floor plans. Each one looked about the size of a shoebox and the kitchens were minuscule, in no way big enough for Camille to make a pasta dinner for her friends or roast a chicken with all the fixings. Who even knew where she was supposed to store all her pots, pans, and kitchen appliances?

But perhaps that was the point. She wouldn't need to make big meals like that because she wouldn't be near anyone she knew.

Just thinking about that made her sad.

This morning, she approached the stack of flyers once more. Resisting the urge to walk them straight into the garbage can, she picked up the trio of brochures, skimmed through them yet again, then finally set them on the corner of her kitchen table. Though the brightly colored covers seemed to glare at her like obnoxious beacons, she forced herself to keep them in sight.

Now, like a surly child, she was ignoring the table, refusing to even look at it. What was she going to do?

A fast-moving storm had come in overnight and dumped six inches of snow. Though her fourteen-year-old neighbor had already shoveled her driveway, Camille decided to stay inside. She had plenty of food and hot tea and three new books from the library.

Determined to immerse herself in characters' problems instead of her own, she'd just settled in front of the fireplace with a book when her phone rang. It was tempting to ignore it, but of course she couldn't. If it was any of her four children, they'd be nervous wrecks if she didn't answer.

When she saw it was Janie, she sighed. No doubt the great plan to move Mom had reached her ears and she was ready to weigh in.

"Hi, Janie."

"Hey, Mom. Are you home?"

"I am. I'm staying in today."

"Good. I'm almost there."

Janie lived on the northeast side of Colorado Springs. It could take her anywhere from an hour to ninety minutes to get to her in good weather, let alone snow. "What for, dear? And why are you braving the pass in this weather?"

Janie ignored her questions. "I'll be there in fifteen minutes, and I'm bringing lunch. Bye."

Unsure whether to feel amused or irritated, Camille put down the phone. Well, at least everything was picked up. She walked to her bathroom mirror to make sure she looked put together. Yes, her hair was clean and styled, her makeup was on, and her casual velour outfit wasn't stained or worn. Her bed was even made.

Satisfied that Janie wouldn't take one look at her and see an old lady who needed a caregiver, Camille looked out the windows by the front door just in time to see her youngest child's Chevy Blazer pull into the driveway.

Parents weren't supposed to have favorites. She and Scott had loved all their children with all their hearts. But there was just something special about their second daughter. From the time they brought her home from the hospital, she'd been a bright light in their lives. Janie was easygoing, full of smiles, and a magnet for friends. By high school, she was rarely home without two or three of her friends there, too.

Camille had sometimes joked to Scott that their youngest was responsible for their huge grocery bills. He'd agreed, saying that the whole town came over for supper or snacks at least once a week. Ironically, the smaller food bills didn't make things easier when Janie went away to college. Instead, the half-filled grocery carts just made Camille sad.

"Hi, Mom."

Camille hugged her tight. "Hi, honey. Talk about a big surprise."

"I know. I'm glad you were free." She hefted the shopping bag in her hand. "I've got Chinese from Wok On By."

Her favorite place in Monument. "Well, I was glad to see you, but now I'm thrilled."

Janie grinned as she ignored Camille's attempt to take the bag from her. "I've got it, Mom."

Camille led the way toward the kitchen. "Now, to what do I owe this pleasure?"

"Oh, no reason in particular." Janie smiled at the fleece blanket that was folded over the back of the couch. "I always did like this blanket of yours. When did you get it, Mom? When I was in high school?"

"Before that, I'm afraid." In no hurry to discuss the blanket, or to hear any more lies, since Janie never could lie worth beans, Camille folded her arms across her chest. "Janie, why did you drive out to see me today? And I'd like the real reason this time, if you please."

"How about we eat first? I'm starving."

Tamping down her impatience, Camille went through to the kitchen and pulled out two plates. "You take the food out. I'll get the forks and the serving spoons."

"Yes, ma'am."

As her daughter set the bag on the table and pulled out carton after carton of food, Camille took a moment to look her over. Today she had on a black wool jumper over a black turtleneck and bright-pink tights with some really fabulous black ankle boots liberally embroidered with fuchsia, green, red, yellow, and purple flowers. Her dark hair was in a ponytail and her usual Buddy Holly glasses were perched on her nose. Janie looked adorable and Camille thought there wasn't another thirty-eight-year-old in the world who could pull off the outfit so well.

Janie noticed her gaze. "What do you think? Too much?"

"Nope. I was just thinking you look as cute as a bug."

"Travis told me he thought my shoes were kind of loud."

"Travis wasn't wrong. They're as loud as a rock concert in July . . . but I still like them."

Janie's expression softened. "Thanks, Mom. I like them, too." Putting both hands on her hips, she said, "This is it."

Looking at the spread, Camille shook her head in mock dismay. "Orange chicken, beef and broccoli, pork fried rice, and spring rolls?"

"And a side of pot stickers for good measure!"

Her daughter had spent a small fortune on Chinese food. Suddenly, she had a bit of foreboding. "No one else is joining us, are they?"

"Who, like Bo and Clay?" Janie wrinkled her nose. "No. It's just us."

Starting to feel a little worried about what was going on, Camille picked up her plate and started serving herself a portion of each dish. Janie followed suit.

Camille smiled. "Boy, here I was just planning to spend the day in front of the fireplace with a book and now I've got you and orange chicken. I feel blessed."

"I'm glad I made you happy."

Camille dug in. After swallowing her first bite she smiled. "This is so good."

"It is. It's great."

Though a dozen questions were burning her tongue, Camille kept her mouth busy with their food instead of conversation. But after ten minutes, she noticed that while she had practically cleaned her plate, Janie had taken only a few nibbles. How strange. That girl had always loved Wok On By.

Unable to hold back any longer, she carefully set her fork down. "Janie, I appreciate the meal, I really do. But we both know that you didn't bring Chinese food to Woodland Park just to make your mother happy. What is on your mind?"

"Why, isn't Wok On By a good enough reason?" Setting

her fork down, she added, "We don't get together for lunch often enough."

"That's true, and I do appreciate it. The food is as scrumptious as always. But I think something else is on your mind."

"There isn't."

But her daughter still looked guilty. It looked like she was going to have to continue guessing. "So, there's nothing wrong with Travis or you?"

"What? No. We're fine."

"Then . . . what is it?"

Looking even more uncomfortable, Janie pushed her plate to one side. "Mom, you have to know that Bri and Clay reached out to Bo and me about retirement communities in Florida."

And . . . time for some fancy tightrope walking. "I figured they had. The four of you are nothing if not a cohesive bunch."

"Honestly, Mom, I wasn't all that excited about Briana's idea. And just so you know, Bo isn't real keen on it, either."

"Oh?" Camille was afraid to sound too pleased in case Janie said something to the others, but inside she was delighted.

Janie gaped. "That's all you're going to say?"

"There's not too much to say. I promised Briana and Clayton that I'd look over the brochures and I've done that."

"Did you like any place in particular?" Janie reached for the brochures and flipped through the top one.

"Not especially."

Janie looked back up at her. "You didn't like any of them?"

"I'm not in any hurry to move across the country, dear. I like my life here."

"Really?"

"Really." There. Even though she'd essentially already made up her mind, it felt good to actually say it out loud. "I might be older but I'm in good shape."

Janie flipped through another leaflet. "Bri is worried about you spending so much time alone. She's worried you're gonna fall on one of your walks in the snow."

"I don't spend all that much time alone and I rarely go walking in the snow, dear. Which I've already told all of you."

"You know Clay; he's already looking four steps into the future. He thinks if you move now, you'll be a lot happier when you're seventy-five."

"So a decade from now?"

Janie shrugged. "You know Clay."

"Well, that's three of you I've heard from. Might as well tell me what Bo had to say."

"Bo said if you needed help he would move closer."

Her eyes widened. Bo was a sheriff for the county and spent most of his time in other parts of the area. "That was nice of him."

"He said Woodland Park has a real good police department and that he wouldn't count it a hardship to be in a small town. I think he's really considering it, Mom. That is, if you don't decide to move."

"Dear, it sounds like you've decided that maybe Briana is right after all."

"I'm not sure *what* I think. I just hate the idea of you living alone for much longer. It might not be what's best for you."

"I'm fine here, and I am not that old."

"But maybe it's time to make a fresh start. At first I didn't think moving you to Florida was the best option, but I have to say, you have seemed kind of blue lately." She held up a hand. "I know, you miss Dad, but something else might be going on." Lowering her voice, she said, "Maybe you need some medication or something."

Heavens to Betsy! She'd tried to be patient. She'd even tried to be diplomatic. But this . . . this was too much.

Looking Janie directly in the eye, she said, "I do not need depression medication. I do not need a change of scene. I *do* need my four children to stop worrying so much. You each have one parent fussing over you, while I've got four bossy children. It's enough to drive a girl to drink." She pressed a palm flat on the table. "Do you understand?"

Janie looked chastened. "Yes, ma'am."

"Good. Now, may we please just enjoy our food and talk about something other than my old age and infirmity?"

"Yes, ma'am," Janie said again. "Let me just get some more and heat it all up in the microwave."

And, for now, the crisis had been averted. "Of course, dear. Take your time."

A moment later, Janie started chatting about work and Travis and her apartment and some of her girlfriends from high school and what they were up to.

She was talking a mile a minute, hardly stopping to get a fresh breath.

Camille smiled lovingly at her daughter and said the appropriate things . . . but in the back of her mind she wondered if maybe her interfering children might have made one good point. She had been something of a sourpuss lately. She needed to shake things up.

And with that thought came an image of Frank. In spite of her intention to keep him far from her mind, Camille remembered how it had felt to walk beside him the other night after bingo as he escorted her home. She hadn't hated it.

She hadn't hated it one bit.

Chapter 19

"Mom, aren't you ready yet?" Jack called out impatiently. "How come you're taking so long?"

Upstairs in the bathroom, Chelsea inwardly groaned. Jack had been dogging her all morning, asking what time they would leave, where they were going to eat, and if they could go early.

At first, she'd tried to patiently answer her little boy's questions as best as she could. But now that they had begun to sound a bit bossy, the cuteness of his enthusiasm was starting to wear off.

Still, she was glad he was excited about visiting Anderson and the firehouse, especially since she was pretty excited about their little field trip, too. Ever since Friday night, she and Anderson had been exchanging texts several times a day. They kept it light and easy, but she was starting to know the man Anderson was today, all grown up. It was enough to erase most of the lingering doubts she'd had about him. She was starting to look forward to being his friend.

"Mom!"

Give me a break. All she wanted was five minutes to look in the mirror to see if the new jeans she'd bought online really did make her look a size smaller.

"Mom?" He knocked on the bathroom door. "Mom, are you ready yet?"

"No, Jack, I am not ready. That means you need to sit tight and stop asking me if I'm ready."

"But you said we'd be leaving now."

Opening up the door, she glared at him. "I also said you need to give me some peace and quiet, but that never happened." Before he could argue, she walked down the hall to her bedroom door and said, "I need to get a few things out of my room, but I'm warning you now, the more questions you ask the longer it's going to be."

He searched her face, obviously looking for clues to gauge her level of seriousness. Whatever he saw there made him turn and go back downstairs.

When she heard the refrigerator door open, she hurried back to the full-length mirror and examined her reflection once again. She had on her new jeans, a flowy, V-neck top in emerald green, her favorite designer knockoff flats, and gold hoops that Kaylee and Mallory had gone in on together to get her for her birthday. Her hair was hanging loose down her back. She'd put on eyeliner and lipstick.

All in all, she looked pretty good. Probably too dressed up for a firehouse visit, but there was no way she was going to be around Anderson and all his buddies in her regular Saturday clothes: faded jeans and an old flannel.

After returning to her bedroom for a spritz of perfume, she grabbed her purse and hurried downstairs. "I'm ready."

Jack popped up to his feet. "Mom, you sure took a long time to get ready today."

That might be true but she wasn't going to admit it! "I took the same amount of time that I usually do. I think you've just been really excited to see the fire station."

"Oh."

"I don't blame you for being excited, though. This is going to be really neat."

"Nobody says 'neat,' Mom."

"I do."

"Well, I think it's going to be cool." He lifted his chin.

"Whatever," she teased, and off they went to Anderson's firehouse.

*J*t was a large redbrick building, with four garage door bays on one side. After parking in the small lot off to the side, Chelsea grabbed her purse and got out of the car.

Jack was standing by her side within seconds. "I don't know anyone who's gotten a private tour of a fire station!"

"This is pretty special. Remember to thank Anderson for arranging this visit."

"He must really like you a lot."

"I told you, we went to high school together."

"And he was your boyfriend."

Oh, why had she ever told him that? "Yes, he was. Anderson and I are old friends, but I'm certain he is taking us on the tour because of you. He likes you."

A small flash of happiness lit his eyes before he carefully tamped it back down. She could see that along with his excitement was a degree of jittery nervousness. "We're going to have a good time together, okay? Please don't worry."

"I'm not."

"Okay. I'm glad. Let's go then." Jack didn't waste another second before hurrying toward the entrance. Anderson stepped out onto the walkway and she thrilled to the sound of his deep voice.

"Hey, Jack. You made it."

"Uh-huh. Are we late? Mom took forever to get ready. I didn't think she was ever going to get out of the bathroom."

Chelsea was sure her whole body turned bright red. "Jackson Henry Davis, you need to watch your mouth."

Her boy just grinned. "Sorry, Mom, but I still don't know why you had to get all dressed up just to come here."

"I do," Anderson said.

Chelsea saw pure appreciation in his gaze.

"Pretty ladies like your mom like to fuss from time to time, Jack. When you get older, you're gonna learn not to complain about it."

She couldn't help but smile at him. "Thanks for sticking up for me."

"Anytime." He stepped forward and gave her a quick embrace. "You look gorgeous," he said softly. "Smell good, too."

He did, as well. She felt goose bumps appear on her skin but tried to act unaffected. "You look good in your uniform." He did, too. He was wearing faded jeans, thick-soled boots, and a snug-fitting blue T-shirt with the letters WPFD over his heart.

"Mom, that's not his uniform."

"It actually is," Anderson said. "The majority of the time I wear this uniform. Firefighters have a whole lot of other things to do besides fight fires and rescue people in accidents."

"Like what?" Jack asked.

He crouched down to look Jack in the eye. "Like inspect houses and businesses for fire hazards and maintain our vehicles and equipment." Straightening, he smiled at them both. "Are you two ready to come inside?"

Jack nodded. "Yep!"

Anderson led them to the garage bays. While they were talking, someone had opened two of the garage doors, and now two large red fire engines were visible. Inside, Chelsea spied several men, and Samantha, wearing the same uniform of jeans and T-shirt as Anderson.

"Everyone, this is my friend Chelsea and her son, Jack," said Anderson with a broad smile. "I'm giving them a tour today. This is Mark, Dave, Chip, Greg, and Samantha."

"Welcome to Fire Station 1," Samantha said. "Chelsea, it's good to see you again."

"Thanks. Thank you, everyone, for letting us disrupt your day, too."

"Our pleasure," Mark said. "We live to be disrupted."

When they all chuckled, Chip said, "Be sure to ask lots of questions, Jack. Especially long, involved, detailed ones. Anderson loves those."

"Really?" said Jack innocently.

"Really," Anderson replied, "though they're all teasing me because they know I'm pretty bad at telling stories."

"Doc can make the most exciting day sound more boring than watching paint dry," Greg added.

After shooting Greg a pointed look, Anderson turned back to Jack. "Ignore those guys, buddy. They just like giving me a hard time."

"How come that man called you Doc?"

"Because in addition to being a firefighter, I'm a paramedic. If someone is hurt in a fire or accident, I help them until we can get them to the hospital." He tapped the side panel of one of the trucks. "We'll come back and I'll let you climb into one of these, but let's do that last. Let's go inside first, okay?"

"'Kay."

Eyes wide, Jack glued himself to Anderson's side, trotting to keep up with the man's large strides. Chelsea stayed a few steps behind, content to let Jack have this time with Anderson and ask all the questions he wanted.

To her surprise, the first place he took them was the kitchen and what looked like a rec room.

"This is where we hang out when we're done with our chores."

"You have to do chores?" Jack asked.

"Oh yeah. Some are really big, like help wash the trucks or inventory our supplies. Others, though, probably don't seem that much different than yours." Leading them to the kitchenette, he pointed to the sink. "Sometimes we have to cook, and someone's got to wash the dirty dishes."

Jack frowned. "I didn't think firefighters did dishes."

Anderson chuckled. "No one minds doing dishes too much. I mean, we all like to eat, right? So we have to clean up afterward."

Jack nodded.

Chelsea squeezed his shoulder. "See? Even strong firefighters have to do dishes."

"I guess so." He walked over to the large cast-iron pot on the stove. "Is that your supper?"

"Yep. Greg's making soup." Walking over to the seating area, he added, "Sometimes we play video games over here, when chores are done or we're on a night shift and we aren't tired."

"Where do you sleep?" Chelsea asked.

Anderson walked them down the hall where there were a dozen or so large cabinets labeled with everyone's last name. "In our firehouse, everyone gets assigned a cabinet like this to store our personal items like shampoo or contact lens solution or stuff. All of us have a couple of extra sets of clothes, too. That way, since we're on forty-eight-hour shifts, we can shower or nap for a few hours in one of the sleeping rooms."

"Do you all go to sleep at the same time?" Jack asked.

"Nope. We usually have at least two firefighters on duty at all times." He looked thoughtful. "There's a lot of shifts when hardly anyone gets more than a safety nap."

"What's that?" Chelsea asked. "Is it like a power nap?"

"Affirmative," Anderson replied.

He opened one of the doors and showed Chelsea and Jack a small room with a bed, a bedside table, and a lamp. The bed was neatly made. "This is another one of our chores: every time you use a room, you have to strip the bed and make it up with fresh sheets for the next person."

Leading them down the hall, Anderson said, "This is my favorite part." Opening a big cabinet, he showed them a metal attachment inside. "This here's the laundry chute. We can put the dirty sheets and towels in here and they'll pop out into a big laundry basket next to the washer and dryer."

"That's cool!" Jack said.

"Right?" Anderson chuckled. "It's really cool . . . until it's your turn to do laundry. Then you feel like telling everyone to stop showering or taking naps."

Chelsea loved the way Anderson explained everything to Jack. He wasn't just clear and thorough, he was showing Jack that doing his chores helped the whole team and that it was an important part of the job. Even though it was just the two of them at home, she hoped Anderson's words would sink in. "It's just like a family here, isn't it?" Chelsea murmured.

"Yeah," agreed Anderson. "It really is. We not only have to work together, we have to live together. Just like in a real family, if someone doesn't do a chore, we all notice. Plus, it makes extra work for everyone else."

"Which isn't fair," Jack said.

"You're right about that. Remember, when we're out on the line, we have to trust each other. If I can't trust someone to do their chores in the house, it's kind of hard to trust them to have my back at a fire." Anderson stuffed his hands in his pockets. "Now that we've got most of the living quarters covered, how about we go look at the trucks?"

"Show me the one *you* ride in," Jack said, taking Anderson's hand and pulling him along.

Anderson bent down to listen to something Jack was saying and a lump formed in Chelsea's throat as she watched Jack have a moment with his new hero.

The moment of privacy allowed her to collect herself. Seeing her son connect with the man she'd once thought she'd marry—who would have guessed it would affect her as much as it did? The more she and Anderson talked, the more she realized that there was too much between them to ignore. All their history, yes, but also something simmering in the background like a pot of water just waiting to reach the boiling point.

Okay, maybe that wasn't the best analogy. She and Anderson weren't about to boil over with lust . . . but there *was* something simmering between them that was genuine. As much as she might want to pretend that attraction didn't exist, it was impossible.

"Mom, you coming?"

She popped up her head and saw Anderson and Jack watching her with twin expressions of confusion.

"Everything okay, Chels?" Oh, that voice . . . it did something to her.

"Uh, I'm good. Sorry, I was just looking at . . ." She scanned the area. "This, uh, fire pole."

But instead of nodding, Anderson smiled. "That's not a fire pole."

"Really? I was kind of hoping you still used them."

"We do," interjected Sam, who was there to witness her embarrassment! "But that is just a plain old load-bearing column."

"Oh."

"There's no hole in the ceiling, Mom," Jack piled on.

She felt herself flushing. "Sorry, I don't know what I was thinking."

Anderson studied her for a moment before gesturing to the biggest fire truck in the bays. "This is the tanker engine. It holds lots of water in case we get to a fire where there isn't a hydrant or water source nearby."

Jack's wide eyes got even wider. "It's huge."

"It is. But that's not why it's everyone's favorite. There's kind of a cool reason," he said, leading the way to the front of the tanker truck. "Look at this."

Anderson was pointing to the hood ornament. It was a silver-and-black dog wearing a yellow fireman's uniform. On its helmet was a red seal with WOODLAND PARK across the top and FIRE DEPARTMENT on the bottom. "That's adorable!" Chelsea exclaimed.

Anderson nodded. "It really is. Everybody loves this little guy."

After he lifted Jack to get a good look at it, Anderson guided him over to a slightly smaller fire truck, saying, "Let's go on the engine. Your mom can catch up when she's ready."

"I think you might be mom of the year today," Samantha said with a wide smile. "Your cute son has stars in his eyes."

Chelsea was pleased about how happy her son was, but being so close to Anderson—and hearing him say that she looked gorgeous? Well, it was a lot to take in.

Not that she was going to share that.

"I'm grateful that Jack was able to have such a special visit," she said instead. "It's so nice of you all to do this for the community."

"We enjoy giving tours. The community supports us and has blessed us with an amazing facility. Of course we want to show it off." She stuffed her hands in her back pockets. "I could be wrong, but I'm kind of thinking that as great as the firehouse is, there's something else that's gotten Jack's attention."

Samantha meant Anderson of course. Attempting to play it cool, Chelsea said, "It would be hard for any boy not to admire Anderson. He's pretty impressive."

"He truly is, Chelsea. Anderson always gives a hundred and ten percent. A lot of people around here look up to him."

Hearing Anderson spoken of like that filled her with pride. The boy she'd once loved had turned into an exceptional man.

Feeling even more confused about her feelings for him, she cleared her throat. "I better go make sure Jack's okay."

"He is," Samantha said. "I promise, he really is."

Chelsea nodded her understanding, but she knew Samantha's words would be resonating with her for the next few hours, if not days. Maybe it was true. Maybe Anderson really was okay for both her and Jack.

Maybe he was even more—if she was willing to take that chance.

Chapter 20

$\mathcal{A}$nderson didn't need to see his coworkers' knowing looks to grasp that inviting Chelsea and Jack to tour the station house would be a topic of conversation. He knew guys who did it all the time. One had even said that he loved showing off the station to impress the women he was dating, almost as if it was proof that he was heroic. Of course, everyone gave him a lot of grief for that remark—especially Samantha!

For his part, Anderson had never questioned anyone's motive for taking folks on private tours. Actually, he'd taken it in stride. Visitors were usually very respectful of their jobs and the fact that the tour might be interrupted at any time. Besides, any type of community awareness was good for everyone.

He'd never been the kind of guy to mix work and dating. He usually liked to keep different parts of his life compartmentalized. But then again, Chelsea hadn't been in the picture until now.

Now she was on his mind all day long. He looked forward to telling her good morning and seeing her texts about work and Jack. Thinking about the night before, he grinned. Chelsea had texted a round-by-round account of her and Jack's marathon game of Uno played while eating ice cream sundaes—a reward for something the kid had done at school. Her texts were so funny and adorable, they left him longing to one day be invited, too.

At least he was with them now.

From the time they'd arrived, he'd felt so proud. She'd become such a beautiful woman inside and out. It was all he could do not to constantly touch her, just so everyone in the firehouse would know that she was his.

Whatever. All that mattered was that Chelsea was no longer treating him like someone to be avoided and Jack was gazing at him like he was Superman and Batman combined.

It had been such a long time since he was on good terms with Chelsea. Anderson held the knowledge close like a good jacket on a cold day.

"You two came on a great day," Anderson said as they sat down at a picnic table next to the station. Just as he was about to bid them farewell, the lieutenant's wife had brought in homemade chili, Fritos, cheese, and onions.

After everyone assured Chelsea and Jack that there was more than enough to go around, the three of them had spooned chili and cheese into the individual chip bags and taken their meal outside to eat. "It's always a treat when someone takes pity on us and brings us food."

"This is real good," Jack said. "I've never had a walking taco before."

"I think we've called them Frito pies, Jack," Chelsea said, looking at her corn chip bag filled with chili, cheese, and onions. "It's the same thing. We just eat them in a bowl."

"This way is better. You can do things while you hold them, Mom."

"That's true." She shared a smile with Anderson before scooping another bite of chili with her plastic fork.

"I'd never heard of these until I met Greg," Anderson

admitted. "We shared quarters when we were deployed and one night he spent a good hour telling us all about his favorite dinner, including walking tacos."

"It's nice of everyone to share their meal with us," Chelsea said.

"There was plenty."

"I'm already done!" Jack announced with a grin.

"Hey, Jack," Greg called out from another picnic table. "I'm heading up to get more. Want to come get some, too?"

"Sure." He jumped to his feet before looking at his mother. "Is that okay, Mom?"

"Of course, honey. Go on."

He tore off to Greg's side and practically skipped all the way into the station house.

When the door closed behind them, Chelsea grinned. "Now I know he's officially on cloud nine. At any other time, he'd be scowling at me for calling him honey in public."

Anderson chuckled. "He's a great kid, Chels. You've done a good job with him."

"Thanks, but I can't take much credit. He seemed to be born with an easygoing way about him. I'm grateful for that."

"I don't think he was born being so polite. You might have to take at least a *little* bit of credit."

Chelsea shrugged. "If we get through the teenage years unscathed, then I might feel like I was a decent mom."

Anderson started to smile but then he realized that she was being completely serious. "Chelsea, don't say *if*. You're going to get through those teenage years just fine. We did, right?"

"I guess we did." For a second, her bottom lip trembled, but then she regained her composure. "Sorry about that. Seeing him here, seeing the way he looked up at you, it reminded me that I'm just a mom and that his dad's out of the picture."

Anderson had a sudden urge to go track down the idiot who'd never wanted to be a part of his own son's life and whack him upside the head. He knew more than one guy who didn't marry the girl he got pregnant but moved mountains in order to do the right thing—even from Afghanistan! For this guy to just walk away without ever looking back? Well, it was a crime.

"Does he pay child support?"

Her brow furrowed. After glancing toward the door, she shook her head. "No. But that's okay."

"Chelsea—"

"I didn't want him in my life, Anderson. Look, I didn't bring it up to talk about child support. Only to say I'm glad Jack is getting to spend some time with guys like you."

Her words made sense, but he couldn't deny that it was getting hard to simply play the part of a casual friend. Chelsea meant so much to him. Every time he thought of her being hurt, it twisted his insides. He didn't want her to feel alone. Or Jack, for that matter.

"I meant what I said, that I'd like to be his friend."

Her expression brightened. "I know."

"And your friend," he added. Of course, he was realizing more and more that his desire went beyond friendship. He wasn't going to push, though.

"I haven't forgotten that, either," she said with a soft smile.

"Do you think it's possible?"

"I do. I . . . well, I'm starting to realize that I can't have too many friends."

"Good."

Bells rang out, ending their quiet moment. Immediately he got to his feet. "Sorry, Chelsea, but we're getting called out."

She sprang to her feet as well. "What should I do about Jack? I don't want him in the way."

"Come on. I'm sure Greg's ushering him to the door right now." He grabbed his bag and hers, tossed them in the receptacle by the door, and strode inside, Chelsea on his heels.

"Code 3," a voice called out over the public address system. Immediately, a new sense of urgency filled the area.

"Chelsea, hey!" Greg called out. "Sorry, but duty calls."

"Of course," she said as Jack hurried to her side. "Be careful!"

"Always," Anderson said, with a warm smile before heading toward the bays. "Go on out to your car and wait for the trucks to pull out, okay?"

She nodded, but he had already disappeared.

The whole station was practically reverberating with every firefighter in motion, speaking on earpieces and jumping into the fire engines, which roared to life.

"Come on, Jack, let's get out of the way." She ushered him around the side of the building toward the parking lot.

Jack followed along at a far slower pace, looking back over his shoulder every couple of steps. By the time they got to her car, one truck had left, lights flashing and sirens blaring. On the heels of the first truck went a smaller red SUV, which they now knew was what Anderson usually took to the scene instead of an ambulance.

"There he goes," Jack said.

Unable to help herself, she watched the SUV speed down the road and fade into the distance. An unfamiliar mixture of fear and pride welled up inside of her—fear for Anderson's safety and pride that he was the type of man to do whatever it took to help others.

"Mom?" said Jack as they buckled themselves in.

"Yes?"

"Are you worried about Anderson?"

"A little bit," she admitted. "I guess I can't help but be worried about all of the men and women on those trucks. They're putting themselves in harm's way." She ran a hand over his hair. "What about you? Are you worried?"

"Uh-huh, but he'll be okay."

Struck by the confidence in his voice, she turned back to look at him. "You sound very sure."

"He's tough, Mom. I mean, think about how much pain he was in when he got all those scars. If he can handle that, he can handle anything, right?"

"Right." She smiled at her boy before pulling out onto the street. "Want to go get you some new sweats? Yours are getting too small."

"Yeah, sure."

Usually she would have joked a little and teased him for being so unenthused about something he'd be cheering for on any other day.

But she just couldn't think about that at the moment. Instead, she said a silent little prayer for Anderson and the rest of the firefighters they'd met today.

Chapter 21

*T*here were three of them in the SUV that was custom-
ized to function as the station's ambulance. Of course,
they often called for ambulances as well, but it had been
proven time and again that the SUV could get to emergencies faster and far more easily than an ambulance.

Now they sped along the back roads of Woodland Park
with Chip in the driver's seat, Dave in the backseat, and
Anderson up front in the passenger seat.

Because he was the paramedic, he was in charge of their
group, though on-site he would defer to both his captain
and the fire chief.

They were wearing abbreviated turnout gear. Though
their primary job was to assess and treat the victims, not
actively fight the fire, they knew from experience that anything could happen and often did! They could do any job
that was needed.

Chip wore the headset and was in communication with
Mark, who would inform him of any changes in location as
well as available information about injuries on the scene.

Usually Anderson would use this time in transit either

to check his equipment or to prep Dave, who was a fairly recent hire. But since Anderson knew everything was already in good order and Dave was acting calm and level-headed, he allowed himself the luxury of thinking about Chelsea for a few more minutes.

Man, she was still sweet.

Thinking back to the first time he'd noticed her, he almost laughed. He'd been standing with a couple of guys, laughing at Rick Wallace's story about his camping trip. When Rick threw back his arm to illustrate trying to fly-fish, his hand had flown right into Chelsea's armful of books. Two seconds later, all her books were on the floor, Rick was mortified, and Anderson was gazing at the prettiest girl he'd ever seen.

He'd knelt down to help her, gotten a whiff of some kind of honeysuckle scent that she was wearing, and practically forgot his name.

"Thanks," she'd said.

"No prob. I mean, it's the least I can do to make up for Rick. Are you okay?"

She nodded as she stood up. "I'm fine. Just embarrassed."

He couldn't believe it. Most of the girls he'd been hanging out with would've acted like getting knocked into was a tragedy. At the very least they would've yelled at Rick. Instead, she'd acted like somehow she had been at fault.

A tenderness he hadn't known was possible filled him. "You've got nothing to be embarrassed about . . . What's your name?"

"Chelsea."

"I'm Andy."

Just as she smiled at him, Rick had broken the moment. "Sorry about that, Chels. I was trying to show the guys how bad I was at fly-fishing."

"It's okay. I'm fine."

"You get all your books?"

"Yeah. I mean, Andy got them."

"Oh. Cool."

Anderson had shared a smile with her. That was Rick, all right. Goofy but essentially harmless.

"Need help getting to class?" he'd asked.

"What? Oh no. I'm in here." She pointed to the class two doors down. Right then the bell rang. "I better go. Um, see ya."

He'd nodded, all cool. But inside, he was thinking she was *definitely* going to be seeing him again.

As much as possible.

He blinked. Of course, things were different now. She wasn't as shy around him and he wasn't as cool. But he was also starting to realize that she wasn't completely different from the girl he'd once escorted to every class back in high school.

She was still oh-so-sweet. But she was also confident, successful in her job, and a great mom.

The person she was now surpassed everything he'd imagined over the years. He'd been torn between wanting to simply watch her and bombard her with compliments.

Yeah, he admired the woman she'd become.

But there was also that one moment when Jack had been looking at the trucks that kept playing on repeat in his head. Chelsea had glanced his way and then stilled as their eyes met, and suddenly he'd been certain that he wasn't the only one of them remembering what their kisses had been like. Or how it had felt to be in each other's arms.

*B*rush fire's jumped," Chip announced, shattering all thoughts of Chelsea.

"Casualties?"

"No reports of any, but the chief just called in another crew from Divide to check houses and vehicles."

"Oh man!"

Dave's exclamation summed it up. If the fire had jumped and crews were actively checking houses, that meant evacuation, and chances were good that things were about to get bad, fast.

There was always someone who refused to leave their house. Then there was his least favorite scenario: someone who used their vehicle as their safe house, thinking they could stay nearby but speed away if the fire got too strong.

Of course, they always forgot that fires aren't predictable foes. They change course on a dime, melt tires, and turn vehicles into portable ovens.

Pushing all thoughts of Chelsea away, Anderson turned to look at Dave. "Check your equipment."

"It's checked, Doc."

"Check it again, then get on your radio. Keep it on. Understand, probie?"

"Affirmative."

"ETA, Chip?"

"Two minutes. Cap wants us parked just to the south of the new control line."

Anderson frowned. He would've preferred to be closer to the action but knew the captain had a reason for the directive. "Roger that."

Ahead of them, he could see a burst of bright-orange flame in the distance, and the echo of more sirens rushing to the scene.

They were going to be there for a while.

He grabbed Dave by the shoulder. "You keep your head, you hear me? Follow my orders or the captain's."

Dave nodded. "I will."

"Good. Let's go."

The moment Dave opened the door Anderson could feel a burst of heat through his thick protective gear. Yeah, they were going to be there awhile.

He headed straight for Captain McGinn and reported, "Anderson, Dave, and Chip here."

McGinn, who rarely got rattled, looked grave. "Crew from Divide just radioed. They rescued a pair of fifty-year-old men. Both have sustained second-degree burns. One has a broken tibia. They're transporting them over."

"Got it." Anderson turned to go, but the captain spoke again.

"Hold up, Doc. I'm not done. Another crew has a thirty-year-old woman and two kids. All are suffering from smoke inhalation. The mom has some minor burns and possible concussion."

"Roger that."

"Thanks. No, wait." Cap held up a finger as he received another radio message. "A crew member just got a good cut on his arm. Someone needs to sew him up before he goes back."

Anderson was starting to feel like he should be taking notes. "Anything else?"

Captain McGinn gave him a sad smile. "Not yet, but it'll happen. Chief's already asked for assistance out of the Springs."

Anderson barely had time to nod before their first patients appeared with a team of firefighters. "Triage, Chip," he called. Looking to his right, he saw a grumpy-looking gray-haired guy holding his hand in the air. "Stitch him up, Dave."

"Yes, sir!"

Anderson took a deep breath, pleased that his team had their game faces on and were all business. They were good men and they'd trained hard.

He spied Greg approaching with a woman in his arms, and Anderson emptied his mind of everything but what had to get done.

Chapter 22

$\mathcal{A}$lmost twenty-four hours had passed since the ringing bells had disrupted their lunch at the firehouse
and they'd watched the line of fire engines rush down the
road. Though Chelsea had hoped and prayed that the fire
would be put out quickly and all the firefighters would return to the station without a scratch, that wasn't the case.

According to the news bulletins, the situation worsened
by the hour. The smoke looming in the distance, along with
the faint scent, served as a constant reminder of the danger
just to the east of Woodland Park. When there were reports
that a firefighter had been life-flighted to Memorial Hospital in Colorado Springs, it seemed no one in the community
could talk about anything else. Radio announcers even began to offer advice on what citizens should pack in their
vehicles in case of a sudden need to evacuate.

Chelsea hoped everyone was safe, but she couldn't help
but focus on Anderson and the danger he was in. Every time
she thought about him knowingly being in harm's way, her
stomach clenched. This was a man who'd served in the army

for almost a decade. A man who had been deployed multiple times and even had the scars to show for it.

Yet Anderson was once again putting himself between danger and the rest of the population. She was scared to death that he was going to get injured again, joining the other firefighter in the hospital, or worse.

His bravery was humbling . . . perhaps a little guilt-inducing, too. She'd been so focused on her own hurt feelings after telling him about her pregnancy, she'd pushed aside all consideration of his feelings. She wished she had given more thought over the years to the sacrifices he made.

As she watched a helicopter fly toward the dark cloud of smoke, Chelsea's worries intensified. Everyone she'd met at the station house had been fighting the fire for a full day. She couldn't get them out of her thoughts.

And neither, it seemed, could Jack.

Yesterday, after assuring Jack that the crew would probably be back at the station house before long, she'd taken him shopping for new sweats followed by a quick trip to the grocery store. Back at home, she changed from her cute outfit into old black leggings and an even older sweatshirt. Jack played a couple of games on his Xbox but then walked out to the front yard to stare at the sky. He'd been really worried about the firefighters and it was obvious that he still was.

"Could you look online again about the fire, Mom?"

"I could, but I don't think there's anything new. It's only been thirty minutes since last time we checked."

"You don't know that for sure, though. Couldn't you check again?"

His concern broke her heart. Though she didn't want to discourage his empathy, she also didn't want to encourage him to worry. "Jack, I'll check in another hour."

"That's forever from now."

She held up her cell phone. "If something major happened, I'll get a notification on my phone. I promise I'll keep you posted."

He sighed. "What if Anderson is really hurt bad, though? I hate having to wait."

"I know, but we shouldn't expect to get too many reports. The firefighters are busy and it's not like they're going to let reporters near the fire or give them interviews. We need to keep our faith and try to be patient."

"But couldn't you text Anderson or something?"

"No, honey. We need to leave him alone so he can do his job." She smiled slightly, realizing that she was speaking as much to herself as to him. She had been tempted more than once to text Anderson, just to let him know that she hoped he was okay.

Jack frowned but nodded. "All right."

"I know it's nerve-racking. The best thing we can do is pray that the fire will get contained soon and that everyone involved will be okay."

Staring up at the distant smoke again, he said, "I hate sitting around."

"I know, I do, too."

"Can't *we* do something to help?"

Chelsea hated to see how stressed Jack was. And even though worries were a part of life, she almost felt like she'd put this burden on his shoulders. If she hadn't taken him to the firehouse, he wouldn't be so upset now.

Just as quickly, she pushed away that thought. Jack wasn't a baby and there was nothing wrong with being concerned about others or even being upset that someone was in a dangerous situation.

"I have an idea. Since the firefighters like when friends and family help with the cooking, we can make a meal." Mentally reviewing what was in her freezer, she added, "How about some pulled pork sandwiches? The support staff can let them know that there's a meal waiting for them back at the firehouse whenever they are able to take a break."

"I guess that would be okay."

She should've known that Jack would think making pulled pork wasn't very important. He was probably right.

Impulsively, she said, "How about this? I'll call Anderson's parents and ask them to call or text me if they hear any news."

At last, he started to look hopeful. "You can do that?"

"I can." She smiled, even though she felt slightly sick inside. Though she had seen Anderson's parents around town from time to time, she'd done a good job of avoiding them. Her parents had been glad about that, of course. They'd taken Anderson's harsh words to her very personally.

Jack stood looking at her expectantly, obviously waiting for her to pick up the phone, but Chelsea couldn't do it with an audience. "Hon, why don't you go make a sign or something? We could put it out by the sandwiches when we bring them."

"All right." Jack wandered back to his room.

Chelsea didn't know if he'd make a sign or not, only that he'd be upset if she didn't follow through on her promise to reach out to Anderson's parents.

She sat down, wondering whether they still even had a landline. Remembering the number was easy; it was still lodged in her brain, thanks to the hundreds of times she'd called Andy when they were dating.

When they'd first started going out she worried about being too needy—all the girls said guys hated that. She even asked him about it once. "You sure you don't mind if I call?" she'd whispered one night after he walked her to her door.

"Of course not."

"I don't want to be too clingy or anything."

"Cling all you want, babe," he said right before he claimed her lips.

She still felt chills every time she remembered it.

After that, though, she did call him whenever she felt like it—and he almost always answered, too, like he was waiting for her call, even if six of his buddies were hanging out at his house. All he had to do was murmur, "Hey Chels," and she'd feel warm all over. "Hey," she would reply. "Are you busy?"

"Not too busy for you."

Oh, to her those words were swoon-worthy. Her girlfriends always teased her about being obsessed with Andy Kelly. But *obsessed* wasn't the right word. She was in love. So very in love.

Chelsea cleared her head. Reminded herself that there were more important things to think about than memories of first love. Such as giving Jack another bit of hope. Before she could chicken out, she dialed the Kellys' number.

"Hello?"

"Hi, Mrs. Kelly?"

"Yes? Who's speaking, please?"

"It's Chelsea Davis, ma'am."

"Chelsea? Well, my goodness. Now this is a surprise."

Did she mean it was a good surprise or a bad one? Chelsea couldn't tell. Gripping the phone a little tighter, she continued. "I'm sorry to bother you, Mrs. Kelly—"

"It's Missy, dear."

"Yes, ma'am. I mean, Missy." Oh, but she was making a mess of this. Taking a deep breath, Chelsea attempted to explain. "I'm calling because my son, Jack, and I were at Anderson's firehouse when they were called out to a fire yesterday morning. We're both pretty worried about Anderson and the rest of the firefighters, since the news says that it still hasn't been contained. Have you heard from him, by chance?"

"From Anderson? No, honey. I'm sorry, but I haven't."

Missy definitely sounded worried. Feeling like she had made things worse by calling, she said, "Oh. All right. I'm sorry to bother—"

"No, wait. I did hear something. We receive automated messages in situations like this. Not a lot of information, but it helps keep the families from staying up all night," she explained.

"Yes?"

"So far, Anderson and the rest of the firefighters from his house are okay. They've got support from the Springs and the winds have died down."

Chelsea breathed a sigh of relief. "That's good news. Thank you for sharing that."

"You are so welcome. Not knowing anything is the worst part. I'm glad you called." Missy paused. "Chelsea, it's good to hear from you, dear. I didn't realize that you and Anderson had begun seeing each other again."

Chelsea couldn't tell if Missy was pleased about that or not. "Actually, I wouldn't say that we're seeing each other as much as becoming friends again. And Jack has been enjoying his company."

"Ah yes. How is your little boy?"

In spite of the uncomfortable circumstances, she smiled. "Not so little now. Jack's almost nine."

"My goodness! That's hard to believe, isn't it?"

"Yes, ma'am. It is."

"Chelsea, why don't you give me your phone number and if I hear anything more I'll give you a call?"

"Thanks. I mean, I don't want to be any trouble."

"It's no trouble at all. I'm glad you're thinking about him. Porter and I worry about him, too. It never gets easier, even though we had plenty of practice when he was in the army."

"I suppose you did." After passing on her phone number, Chelsea felt awkward. She never thought she'd feel like apologizing to his parents for their breakup, but now it felt like the thing to do.

Or was it?

"Well, thanks again for your help," was all she could manage.

"No, Chelsea, thank *you* for caring." Missy cleared her throat. "Maybe I shouldn't say this, but well, you're going to find with Jack, as I did with Anderson, that sometimes it's very hard to be the parent when it comes to your kids' relationships. When you went off to college and Anderson joined the military, Porter and I missed seeing you."

"I missed you both, too."

Missy continued, sounding tentative, "And then, when, um, everything happened . . . well, I guess I didn't want to say the wrong thing, so I didn't say anything about your boy. Unfortunately, that silence was probably hurtful in its own way. I'm sorry if that silence made things harder for you."

Tears pricked Chelsea's eyes. Missy would never know just how much those words meant. "Thank you, but it's all in the past. Anderson and I were young. I don't think I would've known what to say if you had called me, anyway."

"Isn't that the truth of how things go? We worry so much about finding the 'right' words that we forget that it's the thought behind the words that matters."

"It is the thought that counts, you're right."

Sounding more like her usual self, Missy said, "I am looking forward to meeting your son one day. I'm sure you're very proud of him."

"I am."

"We'll have you all over one night when Anderson joins us for supper. I mean, if you'd like to."

"I would." Well, she would if it was all right with Anderson. "Thank you, Mrs. Kelly."

"It's Missy from now on."

"I'll try to remember, but it might take me a minute to get the hang of it," she joked.

"We've got lots of time to get to know each other again. Now, please try not to worry. Andy is smart, a good paramedic, and has been through tougher situations than brush fires. He'll be all right."

"Yes. I'll try to remember that."

After they hung up, Chelsea considered what Missy Kelly had said. Doing the right thing really was more important than finding the right words. She and Anderson were slowly showing each other that they were stronger than they used to be. That they'd both learned how to be better versions of themselves.

As if he'd been listening at the door, Jack burst into the kitchen and disrupted her thoughts. "What did Anderson's mom say?"

She motioned him over. "Mrs. Kelly said she heard that Anderson is still on-site but that he's okay, they've gotten help from the fire department in Colorado Springs."

"Really?"

"Really." She reached out and wrapped her hands around both of his shoulders. "Mrs. Kelly wouldn't lie about that. So, we need to keep thinking positive thoughts. There's every chance that he's going to be okay."

"That's great."

"I think so, too."

"Are you still going to make pulled pork sandwiches?"

"I sure am. After I get the Crock-Pot going, you and I can run to the store and get hamburger buns and foil to wrap them in."

Jack smiled. "Thanks, Mom."

"For what?"

"You know." He shrugged. "Just because."

She gave him a brief hug and grabbed a pen to make a shopping list, but instead found herself thinking about having dinner with Anderson and his parents.

She wasn't sure if she was ready to be involved with his family again—but maybe she'd never really stopped. Missy had responded warmly to her, and she felt the same way in return. After all, you can't just turn off relationships like a light switch.

Or, it seemed, fall out of love.

Chapter 23

ey, Doc!" Mark called out from the firehouse kitchen. "Come over here. You've got to see this."

Anderson had just finished restocking the SUV along with Dave and Chip, then put fresh sheets on the bed he'd slept in two days ago. He'd heard that no one had had time to do anything more than short power naps during the past couple of days. The skeleton crew that had been left at the station still had to see to the needs of the town and surrounding areas.

Even the small task of changing sheets had felt monumental. He was so tired and sore, even walking down the hall to the kitchen seemed like too much trouble. In truth, he was still reeling from helping load a firefighter from Cripple Creek into the life-flight helicopter. The guy's injuries, combined with the whirring of the blades, had done a number on him. For a few seconds, he'd been back in Afghanistan, the blood from his wounds running into his eyes while two medics loaded him into the bird.

"Doc, I'm serious. Come see this!"

Mark was sitting on one of the barstools, relaxing like

he hadn't a care in the world. Anderson was just about to tell him exactly what he thought about being ordered around when he spied what was arranged in front of the guy. A whole spread of sandwiches wrapped in foil, baked beans, chips, coleslaw, and brownies. It looked amazing and smelled even better.

"What is all this?" he asked.

Mark held up the unwrapped sandwich in his hand. "It's really good pulled pork in barbecue sauce. There's pickles and more sauce, too."

"Where did it come from? The town council?" Sometimes they used discretionary funds to furnish a meal for the crews.

"Nope." Mark smiled. "Look at the note."

Only then did he catch sight of the construction paper sign. "It's from Jack and Chelsea?"

"Yep."

Samantha appeared in sweats, her hair damp. The bruise she'd sustained was vivid on her cheek, though it didn't dim the bright smile on her face. Grabbing a sandwich and a paper plate, she said, "Monica in dispatch texted that there was a great meal waiting for us."

She placed a frosted brownie on her plate. "This meal was the only reason I didn't go straight home to shower. Why settle for a can of soup and some stale crackers when I could have this? I'm starving."

Anderson was still trying to wrap his head around the fact that Chelsea had gone to so much trouble for the crew. "This does look pretty good."

"It's better than that," Captain McGinn said as he came in. "I'm not gonna lie—I grabbed a sandwich first thing."

"I'll have to give Chelsea a call and thank her for thinking of us."

Mark smirked. "Yeah, you could sure do that . . . or you could finally ask her out on a real date."

Feeling everyone's gaze on him, Anderson shifted uncomfortably. "I don't know if we're ready for that. We're going to be just friends for a while. We might do something with Jack from time to time, but it's too soon to get serious."

Samantha raised her eyebrows but didn't say a word, for which he was grateful.

Mark wasn't nearly as shy about voicing his opinion. "You know as well as I do that life is what happens while you're making other plans. Anything can happen, man. You ought to stop being so wary and dive in."

Actually, he'd been thinking something along those same lines. He had a dangerous job; a job that occasionally cost a man his life. "I hear what you're saying."

"And?" Mark raised an eyebrow.

"And I'll think about it. But, ah, first, I'm gonna go get cleaned up."

"Want me to save you a sandwich, Doc?" Captain asked. "At this rate, they're not going to be around long."

"Thanks, Cap. That would be great."

Half-convinced the three of them were watching his retreat, Anderson forced his sore legs to step a little faster and went back upstairs to his locker and the showers. After emptying his pockets, he grabbed a pair of navy sweats and a T-shirt and headed to the showers.

As he walked into the large tiled bathroom, two members of his unit walked out. He guessed the remaining firefighters on his shift had already gone home to shower and rest.

Anderson knew from experience that the new shift was already down in the meeting room by the bays getting updated, not only on the brush fire but also any other calls that had occurred in the last forty-eight hours. He, Chip, and Dave had done a quick inventory and cleaned the ambulance so it was ready in case of an emergency, but the new crew on duty would clean and stock it more thoroughly as time allowed over the next forty-eight hours.

Heading to one of the enclosed showers, he stripped and then turned on the water as hot as he could bear it. Immediately, the faint scent of smoke wafted from his hair.

Soaping up, he closed his eyes and let the hot shower attack the knots in his shoulders and loosen the muscles in his neck. Once again he had to push back the image of Cal's nearly lifeless body strapped to the board as they carried him to the helicopter.

As his brain finally began to detach from the stress, he allowed himself to think about Chelsea, wondering what to do about his feelings for her. Was he really ready to try to win her love again?

Was he willing to risk hurting her—and her son—if things didn't work out between them? That was a terrifying prospect. Jack already had to live with the hurt of a deadbeat dad. Anderson just couldn't stomach setting him up for another failed relationship.

But what if things could be good again? What if he and Chelsea got back together and then he was seriously hurt in the next big fire? She had already lost so much . . . what would she do if he left her again?

Anderson realized he was too tired to think about anything rationally. He needed to go home and sleep for at least six hours. Then, maybe, he could contemplate his future.

Feeling more like himself and satisfied with the decision to postpone any decisions, he quickly dressed, threw his soiled uniform in a tote, and headed downstairs. A couple of firefighters from the new shift were standing around eating brownies.

What had looked like enough food for a platoon had dwindled to almost nothing. Oh well, you snooze, you lose . . . then Anderson saw a foil-wrapped sandwich set off to the side, his name written on it in Sharpie.

He grabbed it, said good-bye to the guys, and headed out. Before he was halfway home, the wrapper was balled up on the floor of his passenger side and he was regretting that he hadn't grabbed another sandwich and some cole-slaw, too. He might not know what to do about Chelsea but he couldn't deny that she had a way with barbecue.

Tab gave him a resentful greeting. Apparently having the neighbors look in on her didn't excuse his absence. He had to laugh inwardly at how attached Tab was to him. Weren't cats supposed to look down on humans? This one was glued to his side! She followed him to the bedroom and lay down beside him.

Exhausted, he closed his eyes expecting to drop off immediately . . . and saw the hospital tent where doctors pulled shrapnel from his face while nurses injected him full of drugs.

Anderson pushed them away. Forced his mind to drift to other things. Better things.

Back to senior prom. Chelsea's pink dress, almost prim-looking in the front, was practically backless. It was the sexiest thing he'd ever seen, and it was all he could do to keep his hands off her.

Well, after he survived pinning on her corsage . . . right in front of her father. He'd thought Mr. Davis was going to shoot him before it was done.

But the awkwardness was completely worth it when Chelsea gazed up at him like he meant everything to her.

And in that moment, he'd imagined that he actually could be everything she needed.

Then, like an idiot, he'd ruined everything just a couple of weeks later. If he hadn't been so worried about basic and doing what other people thought he should, things might have been a whole lot different.

Maybe he'd be sleeping next to Chelsea instead of real-izing that he'd forgotten to call to thank her for the food. Maybe he'd be holding her in his arms—or she would be the one holding him, reminding him over and over that he was okay.

Chapter 24

$\mathcal{A}$lmost a week had passed since the brush fire. Less than that since she and Jack had made sandwiches and brought them to the firehouse. So, not too long at all. It was really too bad that it felt like it had been a month.

Anderson Kelly had been MIA.

Even though Chelsea told herself not to do it, she brushed her thumb over her phone's screen and clicked on Anderson's text.

THANKS

That was it. There was nothing else. Nothing about how good the food was or whether the rest of the team had appreciated it. No response to the voice mail she'd left in a moment of weakness, in which she'd confided how worried she was about him. And certainly nothing about how his mom had invited her and Jack over for supper one day soon.

Missy Kelly wasn't the type to say something without meaning it.

So that meant she'd probably talked it over with Anderson and he had put the brakes on it.

All of which made Chelsea feel awkward. Really awkward. Should she just forget how right it had felt when she'd toured the firehouse by his side? She'd been so sure they had moved forward at last.

But now, after all those days of texting each other . . . he'd gone silent.

Could he actually be waiting for her to reply to him? What could she even say to his six-letter text? That it was no trouble to go to the supermarket, cook all that food, then carefully box it all up and bring it to the station, all of which hadn't taken more than, oh . . . four or five hours?

She didn't expect a medal or anything, but Chelsea would be lying if she said she didn't think she deserved more than a one-word text.

She was feeling a little miffed that her efforts seemed to be taken for granted. And that didn't come close to how she felt about Anderson's ignoring Jack's feelings, too. He had to know how worried Jack would have been about him.

"Mom, you never answered me about going to Dillon's house for dinner. Can I?"

"Hmm? Oh sure."

"Okay, then I've got to use my phone to text him."

Still stewing, she nodded. "Okay . . . that's fine."

"Mom! You know you locked it up."

"Sorry." She shot him an apologetic look as she got up, unlocked the phone from the desk in the kitchen, and turned it on. "I was thinking about something." When his little disposable phone clicked on, she quickly scanned his incoming texts to make sure there was nothing inappropriate, then handed it to him. "Here you go."

"Can I have it for a couple of hours? Dillon said all the guys would have a text string going after school. I don't want to be the only one not on."

"Sure, honey." She had to smile at his look of delight before he walked away. She hadn't felt good about getting a kid his age a phone but it turned out that most of his friends already had one—and anyway, he needed to be able to get ahold of her if she was at work, so she'd given in and bought a cheap phone with a generous texting plan. They had a deal that if he didn't do anything stupid she'd get him a real phone when he turned ten, which was getting to be just around the corner!

A few minutes later, Jack came running back.

"Hey, Mom, Dillon said I could come over in an hour and his dad would bring me home around nine. Okay?"

"Nine?" She blinked and finally pulled herself together. "It's a school night, Jack."

"It's Thursday night. Everyone does stuff on Thursday night now. And I'm not asleep at nine anyway."

"Well . . ."

"Please?" Jack held up his cell phone. "He's waiting."

She leaned her head back with a sigh. Her son might be *almost nine* but at the moment he was acting like he was *almost a teenager.* "Fine, but if you're grumpy tomorrow morning—"

"I know, I know. You won't let me go again."

She smiled. "Glad we're on the same page."

As Jack trotted back up the stairs, Chelsea realized that she was about to have a whole evening to herself—a Thursday night, no less. She texted Mallory and Kaylee.

Any chance one of you can go out to dinner? Jack has plans.

Kaylee texted first. **I'm heading to Giovanni's with my neighbor Shannon. Want to join?**

I'm out, Mallory said. **But it sounds like fun.**

It did sound like a good time. Better than sitting at home and wondering about Anderson. She sent off another text. **Are you sure you don't mind? I feel like I'm crashing your plans.**

Not at all. It's pasta night, with half-priced bottles of wine. You can eat carbs and share a bottle of red with us.

Carbs, a glass of wine, and being around friends. It sounded like the perfect antidote for her Anderson blues. **Tell me the time and I'm there.**

Twenty minutes later, she was brushing her hair out, putting on a new pair of jeans, a pair of really cute loafers, and a black turtleneck sweater.

"I'm ready when you are!" she called out.

Still holding the cell phone in his hand, Jack appeared in a pair of his Nike sweats, his new tennis shoes, and a clean long-sleeved T-shirt. She supposed in Third Grade World, this was pretty dressed up. "You look nice."

"Thanks." He stood a little straighter. "So do you, Mom."

She smiled at him. "Ready? Do you remember where Dillon's house is? I don't."

"I'll ask him his address," he said as they got in the car and she pulled out.

"I'm pretty sure he lives over by the school. Does that sound right?"

"Yeah. Oh, here it is. He's on Juniper."

"Got it."

As she drove down their street and waited for the light to turn left, Jack played with the radio. "Pick a station, son."

When he at last settled on some awful pop station, he glanced at her again. "You're awfully dressed up just to drop me off." His eyes widened. "Wait, you're not going in, are you?"

"No, I am not. I happen to have some plans of my own. I'm going out for Italian food with some girlfriends."

"Really?"

"Well, it is Thursday night," she teased.

He grinned—then his expression turned hopeful. "Do you think you're gonna see Anderson there? Because it's okay if you are."

"No, I'm only going to see some girlfriends."

"Oh. Maybe you should text him to see if he wants to join you." Fiddling with his sleeve, he said, "That's okay, right?"

"Not really. Girlfriends don't really appreciate it when you have plans and you invite a boy there, too." Besides, there was no way she was going to ask Anderson to do anything—at least until he called.

Jack seemed to think about it for a few seconds. "I guess that makes sense."

"Glad you approve," she joked.

"Do you think you'll do something with Anderson soon? I mean, he wants to see us again, right?"

Oh, but this was crushing her. The last thing she had wanted was for Jack to get attached to Anderson, but she'd let down her guard when he asked to be friends. Now all her fears seemed to be coming to fruition. He was ghosting her, Jack was disappointed, and all her good feelings about Anderson returning to her life were evaporating.

Realizing that her boy was waiting for a response, she said, "I'm sure he's just busy. It's only been a few days since the fire, right?"

"Yeah. I guess."

"We're on Juniper. What's the address?"

"Three something. It's the house at the end of the street with the Jeep in the front."

She pulled up. "Have a good time. Take your phone and don't forget it there, either."

"Okay."

Pulling on her best "Mom face," she said, "And don't forget, nine is the latest you get to stay out. If his dad can't bring you home then, text me and I'll come get you."

"Fine." He opened the door. "Okay if I go now?"

"Nope, one more thing."

"What?"

"I love you."

He smiled back at her. "Love you, too. Bye."

She waited until he got inside then headed over to Giovanni's. She loved the adorable, old-school Italian decor there, and the Tony Bennett standard she could hear in the background.

Kaylee and her friend Shannon waved her over.

Except, to her surprise, they weren't alone. Two guys were sitting with them. She was horrified. Had she just crashed their date night? Awkward.

She decided to be up-front. "Uh, did I somehow manage to insert myself into your double date?"

"No way," Kaylee said with a laugh. "Shannon knows Rob from work and when we all started talking, the hostess asked if we would mind sharing the big table. I didn't think you would mind."

"And by the way, I'm Shannon," said the other woman. "I think we might have met at a Christmas party a few months ago?"

"Yes, I'm sorry. Hi. And hi, Rob."

The other man, all six foot four inches of him, stood up and smiled at her. "I'm Will, I guess you're Chelsea?"

"Guilty." She held out her hand and shook Will's. He had the perfect handshake, too. Solid but not crushing her hand or holding it like a limp fish.

When she sat down, Chelsea found herself glancing at him a little more closely. Close enough to notice that he wasn't wearing a wedding ring.

"So, Chelsea, Kaylee says that this is a rare night out for you?" Shannon asked.

"It is. My Thursday nights usually involve frozen pizza and scrambling to make sure Jack gets all his homework done."

Shannon smiled. "He's your son, right?"

"Yep, he's a third grader at Woodland Park Elementary."

"Hold on. *You* have a nine-year-old kid?" Rob asked.

Comments like that used to bother her, but now she felt nothing but pride. "He's eight, actually. And the best thing that ever happened to me."

"Where is he tonight? With his dad?"

Chelsea was beginning to feel a little awkward. She

never minded talking about Jack, but this guy made her feel a bit defensive. She shared a look with Kaylee before replying. "No. His father isn't in the picture."

Rob looked like he was about to ask yet another question, but Will stood up and said, "Our server is good, but she's swamped. How about I go get you a drink? What would you like?"

"A glass of red wine, please? Pinot noir, if they have it. Thanks." As she reached for her purse, he held up a hand to stop her.

"My treat. Hey, Rob, why don't you come help me bring back a couple of beers, too?"

Rob looked like he was about to refuse but then he must have seen something in Will's eyes because he stood up and joined him at the small bar near the entrance.

Only when they were gone did she remember that they were going to share a bottle of half-priced wine. "Sorry—I'll still help pay for the bottle."

Kaylee shrugged off her apology. "No worries. At this point, I've half a mind to ask Rob to buy it. He was so rude!"

"I don't know why he's being like that," Shannon added. "He's usually not nearly so nosy. I'm really sorry, Chelsea."

"It's not your fault. I don't mind talking about Jack . . . I just didn't love being bombarded by questions the moment I sat down."

"Right?" said Shannon. "Don't worry. If he starts interrogating you again, I'll put a stop to it."

"I don't think you're going to have to do a thing," Kaylee said with a small smile. "I've been watching them and it was pretty obvious that Will was telling him to back off."

It was tough to not turn around to see. "If he did, I'd be grateful."

"He did. And he bought you a glass of wine, too." Kaylee smiled. "Hmm."

"Oh, stop."

Kaylee shook her head. "I'm not going to stop. You're

not a sixty-year-old woman with one eye on retirement, okay? You've got a lot of living to do!"

Where was this lecture coming from? Feeling her cheeks heat from her girlfriend's interested regard, Chelsea lowered her voice. "Kaylee, thanks for the reminder. But, stop, okay?"

Obviously seeing the guys return, Kaylee smiled. "Fine, but months from now, don't say I didn't warn you."

Will placed a wineglass in front of Chelsea. "Sounds like you've been talking about something serious."

"Not so much. We were debating the pros and cons of heading down to the Springs for Memorial weekend," Chelsea said, thinking quickly. "I never want to do anything and Kaylee was reminding me that I'm going to regret staying home."

"She's got a homebody problem," Kaylee said. "It takes a lot to get Chelsea out of the house."

Luckily the server appeared. "So sorry, gang. We're one short tonight. It looks like you boys took care of the girls' drinks?"

"We did," Rob said.

"How about ordering, if you don't mind? I hate to rush you, but things in the kitchen are going to take a bit longer than usual."

"That's fine," said Kaylee. "I get the same thing every time I'm here. I'll have the pasta carbonara."

"Get me last, will you?" Chelsea asked as she scanned the menu.

Around the table they went, Rob and Shannon ordering lasagna and Will getting stuffed shells. When it was her turn, she ordered the fettucine. After the server promised to return with bread and salad, Chelsea glanced at her phone, just to make sure Jack hadn't texted or called.

"How are things at work?" Kaylee asked Shannon and Rob.

Telling herself that her son was fine, Chelsea slipped her phone onto her lap. "Now, what is it you two do again?"

"We work for a mortgage company," Shannon said. "It's constantly busy with people either moving to town or refinancing."

"That sounds stressful," Kaylee said.

"It is."

"But there's always something going on," Rob added as the server brought their salads and a big bowl of bread.

As Rob continued, Chelsea speared some lettuce and relaxed, happy to let someone else talk for a while.

Will leaned over. "I'm sorry about earlier. I feel like we crashed your girls' night."

"Nothing to apologize for. Like I said, any night out is fun for me." Not eager to start talking about herself and motherhood again, she said, "What do you do, Will?"

"I'm in the air force."

"At Peterson?"

"Yes, and at Cheyenne Mountain at times. I'm kind of a jack-of-all-trades."

Thinking about Anderson's scars, she said, "Thank you for your service."

"You're welcome, but it's my honor."

There was something about the way he'd said those words that got her attention. It sounded less like a line and more like he actually meant it. Curious about what he did, she asked, "How long have you been in?"

"Ten years." He grinned. "I'm a lifer."

"Military life really suits you, then."

"It always has. My dad was in the army, so military life runs in the family."

"Our Major Will oversees a bunch of top secret units," Rob interjected. "He's modest, but there's a lot that he'll never share."

Shannon laughed. "Rob, I think you're the only guy who can get away with calling William Eustace Hamilton III 'Major Will.'"

* * *

*B*efore she knew it, it was eight and time for her to be on her way. She was ready, though. The evening had been fun, but it had also left her feeling flat. The sad truth was that even when she was irritated with Anderson, she found him to be better company than Rob or even Will.

And that was the problem, she guessed. No matter what happened or how much time passed, Anderson would always be her first love. For a little while, he'd shown her what it felt like to be treasured. That's what she yearned to have again.

She just wasn't sure if it was possible.

Chelsea handed a few bills to Kaylee. "Would you mind paying my share when the check comes, Kay?"

"Stay, Chels. I thought Jack wasn't coming home until nine."

"His buddy's father was going to bring him home by nine. I need to be there in case he gets dropped off early."

"Boy, you sure take this parenting thing seriously," Rob joked.

"Always," Chelsea said with a tight smile. "Good night, everyone."

To her surprise, Will stood up as well. "I'll walk you out, Chelsea."

"Thank you, but that's not necessary."

"It's a dark parking lot. Of course it is."

"Well, uh, good night, everyone."

As they walked out side by side, Chelsea noticed more than one woman's appreciative gaze. When a teenager almost ran into her, Will pressed a hand on the small of her back and guided her to the side. It had been so long since anyone had done that for her, it caught her off guard.

She relaxed when she realized Will was only making sure no one else knocked into her.

"Sorry about that," Will said when they stepped outside. "I didn't expect that kid to pass by so close to you."

"It's okay."

"Where's your car?"

"It's over to the right. It's the dark-gray Subaru."

Will didn't say anything as he walked her to the driver's side door. When they stopped so she could get her keys, he spoke at last. "Chelsea, I've been trying to figure out how to apologize again for tonight, but I can't think of the right words."

"I'm not sure why you'd be apologizing for anything. It was a great evening."

"Rob is a good guy, but he's . . . well, he's kind of a jerk, too." He winced. "Maybe more than that at times."

Seeing that Will really was embarrassed, she pressed a hand on his arm. "Rob's a grown man, and not your responsibility. And, to tell you the truth, the things he was saying weren't anything I haven't heard before. A lot of people our age have a hard time relating to a woman who got pregnant at eighteen and now worries more about her son conquering long division than buying a new purse or planning a vacation. I don't blame him."

"I hate that you come across a lot of people who think that way."

"Like I said, I've long made peace with my choices. As much as only having to worry about myself or my career sometimes sounds refreshing, I'd have a huge hole in my life without Jack. He means the world to me. As far as I'm concerned, everything has happened for a reason and I'm blessed." She felt her cheeks flush. Usually she didn't open up so much—and never to strangers. Will was probably counting the seconds until he could say good-bye.

"Can I take you out?" he blurted.

"What? I mean, pardon me?"

He ran a hand over his dark-brown eyes. "Sorry, that came out of nowhere, didn't it? Listen, I know you don't know me at all, but I want to change that. I mean, what I'm trying to say is that I want to get to know you better." Looking frustrated, he closed his eyes then tried again. "May I take you out to dinner?"

"Dinner? Well, um . . ." Chelsea had no idea how to respond. Did she even want to get to know Will?

"Do you ever date? You know, like get a babysitter and go out?"

"To be honest, I haven't dated in a while."

"So, is that a no?"

He was giving her a way out. All she had to do was nod, thank him for the invitation, and say that she just wasn't comfortable leaving Jack.

But what if she regretted not taking a chance? What if nothing was ever going to happen with Anderson? Did she really want to stay home and watch movies instead of living?

"You know, Will, I think I'd like that. Thank you."

His serious expression lightened into a gorgeous smile—revealing one crooked tooth that was endearing. "Thank God."

She giggled. "Were you that nervous about asking me?"

"Close to petrified. While we were walking out, I was rehearsing a half dozen ways to ask you, but all of them sounded either sappy or pathetic."

She was charmed in spite of herself. "Pathetic?"

"I'm pretty good at ordering people around on the field, but not so much when it comes to asking gorgeous, accomplished women to have dinner with me."

"Well, no worries from me. I think you did a good job of it." Aware of the clock ticking, she added, "I really do have to go, though."

He pulled out his phone. "What's your number?" He punched it in as she recited it. "Thanks, Chelsea. I'll be in touch."

"Thank you. I . . . well, I'm glad we met, Major Hamilton." Smiling softly, she added, "Don't worry. I'm not going to start calling you Major Will."

Even in the faint glow from the parking lot lights, she could see a glint of humor shine in his eyes. "It's always just Will to you, okay?"

"Okay." She got in her car and liked how he stood by until it started up and she pulled out of the parking lot.

He was the type of guy to look after her. The type of man to depend on. The type of man whom Jack would love being around.

Maybe, just maybe, he was even the type to stick around, too.

Chapter 25

$\mathscr{F}$riday was one of those long, tedious days at work that seemed to go on forever. Every time she checked her phone, only twenty or thirty minutes had passed instead of two or three hours. To make matters worse, Chelsea wasn't in the mood to be there.

That was frustrating, too, since she usually loved her job.

And today she had a full day of activities, there were no crises that drained all her energy, and everything was fine at home.

The problem rested within herself.

She couldn't stop thinking of a man. Two men, actually. There was Will Hamilton, who didn't send mixed messages. Not only had he walked her out to the parking lot and politely asked for her number, but he had texted her last night to make sure she'd gotten home okay.

Which was why she shouldn't be thinking about Anderson instead.

They'd agreed to try to be friends, just friends. So why was she so upset that he hadn't been burning up her phone with texts or calls? He was presumably just taking her at her word when she said she wanted to take things slow. Anderson was the type of man who listened and respected what he heard. Even though he'd broken her heart, ever since talking to him again she found herself remembering the *good* things. The way it felt to see him standing outside her classroom waiting to carry her books and walk her to her next class. Holding hands and snuggling at the movies. Dancing and celebrating at a friend's house after football games. The perfect couple, everyone said and she'd believed. Of course she was just a kid then, but now that she was all grown up . . .

Chelsea knew she hadn't been wrong. Things between them *had* been good.

"Hey, Chelsea. Do you have a minute?"

Anderson's appearance in the middle of her office just about gave her a heart attack. Okay, maybe not that, but she was startled enough to almost drop the pile of papers she'd been sorting. "What are you doing here?"

"I wanted to see you." He stepped closer. "I know that you're busy, but do you have a minute for me?"

Her mouth went dry as she caught a whiff of his cologne. He was wearing a pair of jeans so faded and worn, they were almost white, a long-sleeved T-shirt, and flip-flops. Only a guy born and raised in Colorado would find an outfit like that comfortable at the end of March.

Realizing she was still staring at him, she answered, "I guess." She stood up and walked around to the front of her desk. Leaned against it like she was completely at ease. "Ah, what do you need?"

"I wanted to apologize for being kind of distant this past week."

"It's okay. I mean, it's not like you said you'd call as soon as you got off your shift."

"I kind of did, though, right?" Still looking uneasy, he

stuffed his hands in his pockets. "I guess the fire spooked me enough that I wanted to give us some more time."

She wasn't going to let him off that easy. "Time for what, exactly?"

"I don't know. Maybe for me to get used to the fact that I could one day have you and Jack hoping I come home safe?" He swallowed. "And maybe you getting used to the fact that I might not?"

His words hit her hard. She inhaled sharply and all the irritation she'd been feeling toward him faded. It was obvious he was trying to hold it together. "Do you really think that way?" she asked gently.

He pursed his lips and nodded. "In Afghanistan, the reality was that not everyone makes it home." He paused, seemed to debate something, then pulled up the side of his T-shirt.

At first, all she saw was an expanse of smooth skin—then a large scar toward his back. It looked a lot like the ones on his face, but worse. Imagining the injury when it was fresh nearly took her breath away. "Anderson. I . . . Oh my gosh. I mean, I'm so sorry."

He didn't meet her eyes as he tucked his shirt back in. "I wasn't asking you to feel bad for me, I . . . well, I just wanted to show you something that I see every day. The wounds on my face are ugly but superficial. Usually I just look at them as reminders that I survived." His throat worked. "This one, though? It's been a little harder to get used to. It's more of a reminder that I almost didn't come back home. If the IED had been any closer, I wouldn't have made it." He swallowed. "When one of the guys at the brush fire sustained serious burns and was airlifted to the hospital, a lot of what I went through came back and hit me hard. I guess I'm not as over my time in the desert as I thought." He studied her face for a moment. "And then I started wondering how my mess would affect you."

"Me?"

He waved a hand. "You know. If I'd been the guy injured in the fire. Or if I came home from a blaze and was PTSD-ing for a couple of hours."

"I would have taken care of you after Afghanistan, Andy. If you'd been the one airlifted from the fire, I would have helped you. No matter what our status is, I would want to be there for you."

"Chelsea, I love my job, but I don't want to cause you more pain," he said with a shuddering breath. "Maybe everything is good and I'm just freaking out because that guy getting hurt brought back some memories. I . . . well, I've just been trying to come to grips with it, that's all."

"I understand." She actually thought she did, too.

"If you do, thanks." He sighed, looking tired. "I still want to be friends, Chelsea. What I don't want to do is be another burden for you. I know that we wanted to be careful of your heart and Jack's heart . . . but maybe I'm the one who needs to take things slow, huh?"

"There's nothing wrong with that."

Anderson gazed at her for a moment before replying. "Okay then. I'm going to take off now."

Chelsea wanted to hug him. She wanted to push him into one of the chairs in her office and ask when he'd eaten last. But everything between them felt too tentative. "Thanks for stopping by."

Unable to think about anything besides Anderson's visit, Chelsea decided to take a walk through the center before helping to serve lunch. She needed to get out of her head.

A quick glance affirmed that the new paint-by-numbers class had started in the main community room. Because there was a fee to enroll, unlike most classes, she was curious to see how many people actually showed up.

After glancing inside the two restrooms to make sure everything was spick-and-span, she followed the sound of excited voices and laughter down the hall.

Jill was leaning against the doorway when she approached.

"I was just coming to find you," her boss exclaimed. "Look at this turnout!"

Peeking in, Chelsea whistled low. "There must be at least thirty people."

"Thirty-three, to be exact." Jill's smile widened. "And just look at everyone. Not a single person looks bored or disengaged."

Chelsea had to agree that Jill was exactly right. The twenty women and ten or so men were all on their feet, chatting with one another and smiling. "I wish I had my camera with me. It would be so good to post some photos on our website. This is amazing."

"I already took a couple of snaps. They're going to be terrific on our Facebook page."

Chelsea smiled at her. "They sure are."

"I already touched base with the instructor and asked her to set up another class. Can you nail down the details?"

"Of course. I'll let you know what we decide."

"Sounds good. Congratulations, Chelsea! It was your idea and you got it all organized. If it was up to me, I probably wouldn't have followed through on it."

"Sure you would have."

"No, I wouldn't. The twenty-dollar fee scared me—I was sure we'd get a ton of complaints. But it turns out that everyone thinks the fee was worth it." Jill sighed happily. "And because of the number of attendees, we're going to be able to fill the food bank a bit. We were able to get three dollars from every class member."

"That's really wonderful."

"You're a real asset here. I hope you don't ever forget that." Jill smiled at her again before walking down to her office.

Encouraged, Chelsea stepped inside.

"Come over here, Chelsea," Camille called out. "What do you think of my woodland scene?"

"I think it's amazing." The eleven-by-thirteen canvas of trees, deer, and assorted other animals was half-finished, but it looked surprisingly detailed and it was obvious that the finished project was going to be really pretty.

Looking at the canvases of the three nearby women, she said, "Everyone's painting is going to be gorgeous, and each is going to look a little bit different, too. I'm surprised."

"I was, too! I think that's the best part. Trish had three different scenes for us to paint and each of those had three color palettes to choose from."

"We're artists and we didn't even know it," Mary Anne quipped.

"You really are! Bravo," said Chelsea before moving on to the next group.

Thankfully, every other group was just as enthusiastic. By the time Chelsea got to the art instructor's side she couldn't wait to book another event. "Trish, I can't tell you how impressed I am. Everyone is so into it."

Trish smiled, obviously as pleased as everyone else was. "It's a good group. Lots of enthusiasm and comradery. I'm enjoying myself."

"Can we book another class in two months? I have a feeling that some of these folks will want to paint again and there will be others who are going to hate that they missed out."

"As soon as class is done, I'll check my schedule, but I don't see why not."

With renewed energy, Chelsea walked through the rest of the activities going on that afternoon.

An hour later, just as she was exiting the building, she spied Frank walking to his vehicle. He was moving slowly, as if he was deep in thought.

Taking a chance, she hurried over to him. "Hey, Frank!"

He turned to her with a jerk. "Yes, Chelsea?"

"I'm sorry, I didn't need anything. Well, not anything beyond wanting to ask if you were all right."

"Why wouldn't I be?"

There was a man's answer if she'd ever heard one. "No reason, other than I noticed you seemed a little blue today." When he lowered his thick eyebrows at her, she held up her hands and took a step back. "Or, it could've just been my imagination."

For a moment it looked like he was going to argue, but then his entire posture slumped. "It wasn't your imagination. To be honest, I'm not exactly myself."

"I hope you're not sick."

He chuckled softly. "No, I'm not sick. Just a little sick at heart."

"I'm sorry."

"Me, too." Just as he was about to turn away, he seemed to think better of it and faced her again. "It has to do with that Camille. You know her, right? I mean, I saw you speaking with her during that art class."

"I was." She racked her brain but couldn't recall seeing him. "Were you in there? I somehow missed you."

"Heck no. I don't paint, not even when it's just paint-by-numbers. But I couldn't resist peeking in when I saw Camille standing by the door."

"What's going on with you and Camille? Why does she have you so tied up in knots?"

"She's got me tied up for a lot of reasons, but the main one is because I asked her out."

"Hey, that's great."

Frank frowned. "I don't know if it is or not. At first she was kind of playing hard to get, but then it really seemed like she was warming up to the idea."

"That's good, right?"

Some of the fire in his eyes faded. "No. I must have mis-read things, because now she'll hardly give me the time of day. Worse, she won't even talk about what's bothering her." He folded his arms over his chest. "It's frustrating as all get-out."

"I bet. What are you going to do?"

"I don't know. I'm a reasonably confident guy, but around her I start feeling like a new second lieutenant on a battle-field."

Quickly she tried to interpret the analogy. "Qualified but unsure of what to do next?"

"You got it." He sighed. "What do you think I should do next?"

"I'm not anything close to being an expert on dating, but I think you should give her another chance." When he looked like he was going to argue, she added, "And by that, I mean ask her out again. Or, better yet, just ask her what's go-ing on."

"You really think it's that easy?"

"No. But I do think it will be worth it." Half feeling like she was talking to herself, she added, "Sorry to sound trite, but if relationships were easy, falling in love wouldn't be so hard, right?"

Frank nodded, like she'd just given him the encourage-ment he'd needed. "So, be honest."

"Yes, General."

He looked skeptical. "Does being open and honest work for you?"

Thinking about Anderson, she shrugged. "I want it to, though, to be honest"—she chuckled—"I probably need to take more of that advice. I'm currently trying to figure out some dating problems myself. I've discovered that being vulnerable is harder than it looks."

"What have you decided to do next?"

Thinking of her conversation with Anderson, she said, "Be open about what I want. Not expect a single conversa-tion or even two to smooth out all the problems. But if some-one's worth it, be patient."

"Those are good things to remember," said Frank.

"I hope I do." She smiled. "Until then, I'm going to just try and live my life. Right now that means I need to make my son some tacos like I promised."

His light-blue eyes lit up. "How old is your boy?"

"Eight."

"Tacos never get old, do they?"

"Not for little boys, they don't. Speaking of which, I probably ought to get going. Camille would be babysitting him but she wanted to take this class, so he's at a neighbor's house. He's going to be anxious to get home, though."

He nodded. "No doubt. Good night, young lady. And Chelsea?"

"Yes, General?"

"Thanks for flagging me down. It's appreciated."

"You helped me, too." She smiled at him. "Good night, then."

"Good night."

The whole way to her car, Chelsea replayed the things she told Frank. It was all good advice, she was sure of it. Unfortunately, it was advice that she hadn't followed.

After she retrieved Jack from the Chungs' next door and they walked in the door, Jack tossed his backpack on the floor. "Mom, guess what?"

"What?"

"My friend Jenny knows Anderson."

"Is that right?"

"Uh-huh. Jenny said Anderson's parents live next door to her grandparents. She said hi to him last night."

"Well, um, that's interesting."

"Mom, are you still talking to him?"

"Some." Feeling dazed, she pulled out a package of ground beef from the refrigerator. "Hon, give me a few minutes to start on dinner or it won't be ready until late. 'Kay?"

"Are we still having tacos?"

"We are."

He grinned. "I finished my homework with Mrs. Chung. I'm going to hang out in front of the TV. Okay?"

"Yep."

As soon as the hamburger was browning and she'd shredded the cheese and chopped lettuce, she glanced at her phone. She had three new messages. One was from her mother. She scanned it quickly and replied to her question about Jack's baseball schedule.

The next was from Will, engendering a little zing of disappointment. She read his note.

Hey, it's Will. How does Saturday night sound? Or, is it too soon? I kind of suck at this.

She chuckled to herself before opening the next text.

Chelsea, thanks for speaking with me today. Would you and Jack like to come to my folks' house for dinner one day soon? They've been asking about you and would love to meet Jack. Well, just let me know when you can.

Two invitations. One for Saturday night and one for dinner with Anderson's family. Which to choose?

Or, should she say yes to both? Was that allowed?

She was starting to think she should've gotten the general's phone number. At the very least they could commiserate.

Everyone always acted like dating was fun. She was learning that even when it was good, it was still as bad as it was when she was sixteen.

No, scratch that. Dating was harder now. At sixteen, she was dating dreamy Andy Kelly.

Chapter 26

Camille loved her children, she really did. She was grateful for their concern and how they never acted like doing something for her was too much trouble.

But these days she was tempted to tell them to worry about their own lives. They were acting like she was incapable of doing even the smallest thing for herself.

Or having a mind of her own.

Tapping her foot as she listened to Clayton avoid the real reason for his call, Camille silently counted to ten, then did it again.

After another two minutes passed, she cleared her throat and took charge. "Dear, you know I love hearing about your golf game, but I'm afraid I don't have too much time to talk right now. I've got an appointment."

"What's wrong? Which doctor?"

Oh brother. "An appointment to get a manicure, Clayton."

"Oh. Well, um, Mom, I actually did call for a reason."

She smiled. At last! "And what would that reason be, son?"

"I called to tell you that I tentatively booked us flights to Florida next week."

Every drop of her amusement faded away. "Did you say next week?"

"Yeah. I was able to move a couple of meetings around. So I have three days free to take you to Sarasota."

Oh, but she couldn't believe this! Standing up, she began to pace. "I don't recall telling you I wanted to travel to Florida, and even if I did want to visit—which I do not—I can't possibly go next week. I have plans."

"Mom, it wasn't easy for me to move everything around. You're just going to have to reschedule next week's manicure or hair appointment or whatever you've got going. This is important."

"What is so important, Clayton?"

"We're going to visit some retirement communities."

"No, we are not. Furthermore, I'm sure you know that Janie already spoke to me about this. She came over, plied me with Chinese takeout, then tried to make me see the benefits of living with a bunch of old ladies in ninety percent humidity."

"It's not like that."

Oh, like he even knew. Continuing to pace, she said, "I told your sister that I would let all of you know when I was ready to look into those retirement places. That day has not come yet."

"You only have a negative view because you haven't given it a chance. I'm sure once you live there for a few months, you'll wonder why you didn't want to go. It's sunny there."

She rolled her eyes. He was speaking to her like she was an idiot. "Believe it or not, I'm perfectly aware of how sunny it is in Florida. I'm also aware that there are lovely retirement communities and a great many people my age who love everything about them." She paused, then added firmly, "But son, that is not me."

"Come on, you know what I mean about the sun. In Florida, you won't have to worry about snow."

"Just hurricanes?"

Ignoring her, he plowed on. "Plus, these planned communities give you lots to do. You won't be sitting home alone."

Honestly, it was like he wasn't listening to a single thing she was saying. "I already have a lot to do. I also have lots of friends here. Friends I've had for twenty and thirty years. The only time I sit home alone is when I feel like it, son."

"Still, this will be better."

It was time to stop this verbal tug-of-war. "Clayton, I think it's time we got off the phone. I don't want to argue with you, but I don't know how to be any more direct. I am not going to Florida next week. I do not want to move to a sunny retirement community."

He sighed. "I told Briana you were going to be like this."

She didn't appreciate his irritation or his attitude. "Clayton, I'm sorry to say this, but you are acting like a know-it-all bully, just like you did when you were on the football team and started acting far too big for your britches. Your father and I had to give you a good talking-to and bring you down a peg, and this is feeling very similar."

"I cannot believe you brought that up."

"You were quite unpleasant back then. It's hard for me to forget."

"I was fourteen!"

She sat back down. "So you don't like that I brought up something that has nothing to do with the person you are now? If that's the case, then welcome to my world, because I could say you and your siblings are doing the very same thing to me."

After taking a cleansing breath, she rushed to continue. "Now, I've had as much of this retirement home nonsense as I can stand. You listen to me and listen to me good. I am not going to Florida next week."

"I heard you the first time, Mother."

Oh, if he was calling her *Mother* he must be really annoyed! "I'm glad you heard me. I hope that you actually listened to me as well, because I have no intention of traveling with you anytime soon. I'm also in no hurry to have another of these conversations, so you'd best think twice before you get on the phone with your bossy attitude. Do you hear me?"

"Yes."

She was irritated enough to badger him a bit. "I don't believe I heard you correctly."

He sighed. "Mother, don't you think I'm a little old for this game of yours?"

"If you are suddenly too high and mighty to put a 'ma'am' on the end of your sentences, you've got a whole lot more wrong with you than a difficult mother who doesn't want to get stuck in a Florida retirement home with a bunch of strangers."

"Come on, Mom . . ."

She felt like throwing her phone. "Clay, I love you but I'm hanging up."

"Wait, Mom—"

"Have a good day now," she said, and she clicked off. Then she tossed the phone on her kitchen counter, slipped her feet in her tennis shoes, and walked outside.

Oh, but she felt like screaming. And crying. Maybe both at the same time. She couldn't believe how failing a driver's test had triggered this chain reaction.

Realizing that a few quick deep breaths in her front yard wasn't going to cool her temper, Camille hurried back inside and grabbed her backpack, put on a better pair of sneakers, and, with reluctance, slid her phone into her jacket pocket.

It looked like Briana had called just a minute ago, which meant that Clayton had wasted no time in reaching out to his sister for reinforcement.

Finally satisfied that she had everything she needed, she locked her door and started walking toward Jo's for a cup of coffee and a kolache. She definitely needed some sustenance!

By the time she made it to Jo's, she felt almost like herself. She'd spent some time praying for patience and giving thanks for children who cared about her. Yes, she was still irritated with them, but at least she appreciated them, too.

Ready for a cherry kolache, she stepped inside, waved at Jo, and turned her head toward the tables . . . to spy Frank Robards.

He looked as surprised to see her as she was to see him. Shoving the paper he was reading to one side, he stood up. "Good morning."

Feeling flustered, she rubbed her palms on her jeans. "Good morning to you. I was just coming in for some coffee and a kolache."

"They're terrific today. I've had two of them. You're welcome to join me if you'd like."

Though her first instinct was to refuse, Camille realized that she didn't want to do that. He'd offered her friendship and she needed a friend today. "Thanks, I would like that. I'll be right there."

She could practically feel his surprise at her easy acceptance, and she couldn't blame him. She'd been prickly and standoffish from the moment they'd met. But for some reason, her attitude hadn't seemed to put him off. It occurred to her that his persistence had less to do with her charms than with the type of man he was. After all, there had to be a reason he was a general. He probably never gave up easily.

As soon as she had her kolache and a large coffee, she sat down across from him and smiled. "You, Frank, are an answered prayer."

"Normally I'd be very flattered to hear that, but something tells me you're troubled." Looking at her intently, he added, "What is going on?"

"Nothing."

"Mm-hmm. Want to try again?"

She thought about telling him the whole story, but she didn't feel like dwelling on her children and their bossy ways for one more moment. "Honestly, I could really use a break from it."

He frowned but nodded. "I guess we could. It's your pre-rogative."

She couldn't help but laugh. "Did your wife teach you that, or your daughter?"

A genuine smile lit his face. "Daughter. My youngest. She's stubborn and smart and has never wanted anyone's help until it's halfway to being too late."

"In short, a handful."

"Yes, but in a good way. When Allison was four, her favorite expression was 'Daddy, I got it.'"

She could only imagine the amusement that engendered on the base. "How did you respond?"

"Half the time I'd let her do it but hovered nearby. Other times I'd tell her mother that Allison needed her."

Camille laughed. "I can see it now."

"I guess you have one of those?"

"I have four children. None of them were quite like Al-lison, but my third, Bo, was born scrappy. His older brother and sister found out real quick that it was a mistake to boss him around."

"What does he do now?"

"He's a county sheriff bossing other people around," she said with a grin. "What about Allison?"

"Al's a sergeant major in the army," he said with obvious pride.

"But she didn't want to be an officer like her father?"

"Nope. She wanted to go her own way, and damned if I'm not proud of her for doing that." He chuckled. "I've seen her in action, too. She's a formidable presence. Even I'd think twice about disobeying one of her orders."

Amused, she grinned at him. "Kids do grow up, don't they?"

"They do. And so do we." Gazing at her over his cup, he sipped his coffee. "How are you doing?"

"You know what? I think I'm better. Thanks for reminding me that kids are who they are—even at a young age."

"If I did that, you're welcome, though I feel like I should add that just because they're who they are practically from birth, it doesn't mean that they're a barrel of laughs all the time."

"Mine aren't. But perhaps I'm not, either." Eager to change the topic, she said, "Now, tell me why you didn't go to the painting class the other day."

Frank looked surprised but recovered quickly. "Painting isn't really my thing."

She wasn't going to let him off that easily. "It was paint-by-numbers, Frank. There's no skill involved."

"You're right, it's just not my thing. No offense."

"Sorry, but if you're implying you're too young for paint-by-numbers I am a bit offended. You're not the only spry oldster."

"If you're talking about yourself, then that's an understatement. You're as pretty as any woman ten or fifteen years younger than you."

"Thank you. But even if you hadn't wanted to start a career in paint-by-numbers, I would've still liked it if you had stopped by to say hello."

Again he looked surprised. "The truth is that I didn't know what to say."

"You could have just said hello."

"You make it sound so easy, but we both know you're not actually that approachable. Some days, it's felt like you were going to bite my head off if I stopped to chat."

Everything inside her wanted to protest, to tell Frank he was imagining things, but she knew he might be right. Over the last few weeks she'd found herself repeatedly snapping at one person or another. Why, hadn't she gotten a little too irritated with the butcher last Saturday? Since when had she ever really cared how much her favorite stuffed pork chops were? Two chops easily fed her for three meals.

"As much as I'd like to argue, I'm afraid you're right." She tucked a lock of hair behind her ear. Even though she'd planned to keep it to herself, she found herself saying, "My children's quest to move me out of my house has taken a toll, I'm afraid."

Compassion filled his gaze. "Camille, what's going on now?"

"Clayton, my oldest son, called me a little bit ago. He wants me to go to Florida with him next week."

"Somehow I'm guessing it's not to vacation on the beach?"

"Not even close. It was to visit retirement homes. He had already made several appointments."

Just thinking about that high-handedness made her fume. "Frank, it would take almost a full day to get there and another one back, leaving one day to cart me around to all those places like an unwanted puppy."

He raised his eyebrows. "Perhaps not like that."

"Close, though. Can you imagine what would have happened? Every time I even hinted I was tired he would take it as a sign that I was old and frail."

"Even though you'd have a day of travel and a two-hour time difference to contend with."

"Exactly. Worse, I got the feeling that the other kids were more than fine with his cockamamie idea. I think they were hoping I'd pick a place and put a deposit down on the spot."

"Oh boy."

"I know." She released a ragged sigh. "I love my children and I know they love me, but they aren't listening to me and I'm getting extremely tired of it."

"What are you going to do now?"

A lump formed in her throat. Frank had just said the

very last thing she had expected, and it struck her deeply. A part of her expected him to react to her worries the same way Scott had. He'd been so very good at dispensing advice, even when she hadn't asked for or wanted any.

"I'm not sure," she said at last. "All I do know is that I'm not going to move out of Woodland Park to please my children."

He smiled. "I thought you might say something like that."

To her surprise, Camille found herself chuckling, too. "I might be an old bird, but I'm not a helpless one. At least, not yet."

Frank lifted his cup. "Cheers."

"For what?"

"For growing older with grace."

They toasted with their paper cups, then Camille leaned back in her chair. "I'm beginning to see why I can't seem to stay away from you, Frank Robards. There's something about you that's hard to resist."

"I reckon there are quite a few folks who'd say the same thing about you, Camille. Including me."

If she were a younger, sillier woman, she might have sighed at that.

Instead, she just smiled back at him—and tried to ignore the fact that her insides had just turned to mush.

Chapter 27

*Y*ou don't look too good, son," said Anderson's mother as she hugged him hello on Sunday evening. "That bandage on your arm . . . And you've got a pretty good shiner there, too."

"It's nothing," Anderson said as he leaned down to kiss her cheek. He'd forgotten about the bandage. "It doesn't hurt. And it's just a black eye."

"Is it a burn?"

"No. I got a little tangled with a tree during a training exercise this morning. I'll be fine."

His mother frowned. "It must be a serious abrasion."

"I kind of ran into a branch." Hoping to distract her, he added, "I haven't had a black eye since high school, remember?"

"Oh, that awful child from Castle Rock."

Even after all these years, his mom still insisted he'd been an innocent victim in that wrestling tournament. "That 'child' ended up winning state in his weight class," he said, not for the first time. "He was a tough competitor, but he gave me that black eye by accident, Mom."

"If he was anything like his father, he was also a jerk," Dad said as he joined them. "We had the misfortune of sitting near him for eight hours that day. The man couldn't shut up."

After hugging his dad hello, Anderson pulled off his fleece vest. "Just like back then, this black eye will heal up in a couple of days. I'll be no worse for wear."

His mom cast a long look at him. "I suppose."

"Mom, I'm fine."

"If you're fine, you can come on into the kitchen and talk to us while I finish up supper."

He noticed then that the table had only three place settings. "No one else is coming over?"

"Not tonight. Even though Carter is in town for a while, he's got other plans."

His younger brother had graduated from the Air Force Academy and was now a hotshot pilot. When he wasn't deployed he lived nearby at Schriever . . . but liked to keep parental visits down to once or twice a month. "What about Kim and Sean?"

"Paige was under the weather so they decided to stay home tonight."

Anderson was disappointed to not see his siblings or his niece but also felt a little relieved. When everyone got together, it was a little loud and the conversation almost always centered on him and his lack of a significant other. Even his younger brother had been dating the same woman for years.

"It will be nice to have you both to myself for a change," he joked.

"I told your mother that very same thing," Dad said. "After all those years of you stationed all over creation, I feel like I'm still making up for lost time."

Every time one of his parents said something like that, Anderson was struck again by how little he'd understood their worry. He'd always been glad to get their letters, emails, and care packages, but sometimes waited days or even weeks to write them back. He'd blamed it on exhaustion, but he wished he'd been more considerate of their feelings.

Just like he should've been more understanding when he received Chelsea's letter.

It seemed wrong to dwell on his regrets after his mother had gone to so much trouble to make him dinner, so he shook it off. Instead, he walked to the cabinet, got himself a glass, and filled it with water from the refrigerator.

By the time he'd drunk half the glass, his regrets were firmly pushed aside again. "How was your week, Dad?"

"Good enough. We got a new contract on a building down in the Springs. It will keep us going for a while."

His dad always said that. He was an electrician by trade but now mainly ran his company from his home office instead of working out in the field. Although the company was doing well, he always worried about the guys who worked for him and looked out for their future.

"That's great. I'm glad."

"What about you? I haven't heard about any more brush fires in the area."

"That's because things have been pretty calm these last couple of days."

"Have you been working?"

"Yep. Everything's been fine. Beyond my run-in with that tree."

His father nodded. "Good. That's what I like to hear."

"How are Mark and Greg?" Mom asked as she pulled a meat loaf from the oven.

"They're fine. They're doing pretty much the same things I am. Working and sleeping."

His mother smiled. "We ought to have them over soon."

"They'll love that, Mom. You know how much everyone appreciates your cooking." That wasn't a lie, either. His mother never made anything too fancy, but everything she did make was delicious. She was also the queen of side dishes, so there was always a lot of variety—something three army grunts could appreciate.

"I'll text you on Tuesday or Wednesday so we can make plans."

"Yes, ma'am."

"Supper's ready. Let's eat."

Anderson waited until his mom and dad had served themselves. He'd started doing that during his first leave, after his sergeant joked about getting his hand slapped with a spoon when he'd dared to serve himself before his mama. For some reason that story had stuck with him.

After his father said a brief prayer of thanks, they dug in to heaping plates.

"Mom, you outdid yourself."

"Oh goodness. It's just meat loaf and mashed potatoes, Anderson."

"And green beans and corn and fruit salad and a pie for dessert."

His mother blushed with happiness but only murmured, "I'm glad you're hungry. You know how much I love having you over for supper."

As soon as he'd eaten three bites, his father put his own fork down. "Strangest thing happened the other day. I heard talk about you and Chelsea Davis."

"Is that right?" After glancing at his mother—who was wearing a poker face—Anderson set his fork down, too. "What did you hear?"

"Oh, just something about how the two of you had a nice little breakfast together at Bridget's Bistro." His father speared a strawberry. "Is that true?"

"It is."

"I forgot to tell you, she called me when you were fighting the big fire," his mother added.

"Did she?" How come he was just now hearing about this?

"She was really concerned. Her boy was, too."

"I'm sorry they were so worried."

His mother picked up her water glass. "So . . . what is going on with you two? Are you seeing each other again?"

What could he say? "Kind of."

"What does that mean?"

"It means we're becoming friends but not dating." Not yet, anyway.

His mother sipped her water, then leveled her gaze at him. "Is it because of her little boy that you don't want to date Chelsea?" she asked. "Are you still upset about that?"

"Of course not. Whether we date or don't date doesn't have anything to do with Jack. He's great."

Feeling uncomfortable, Anderson ate another few bites, dwelling all the while on how confused he was where Chelsea was concerned.

Though usually he would rather do just about anything than discuss relationships with his parents, he was starting to think they might actually have some good advice.

Unlike Mark and Greg, they knew Chelsea. They also knew how hurt he'd been after receiving her letter . . . and how guilty he felt about his response.

With that in mind, he cleared his throat and began. "Even if she and I did want to get back together, it's not that easy. We're a lot older now. We've changed. We're gun-shy."

"That sounds about like most folks, Andy," Dad said.

"I know." Anderson leaned back in his chair. "Look, the truth is that I don't know what to do. I don't want Jack to be hurt if things don't work out. And . . . there are times when I wonder if I'm even ready for a relationship."

His mother blinked. "With Chelsea or with anyone?"

He took a moment to think about that. "With anyone, but maybe especially her." Gathering himself together, he added, "Every once in a while, something triggers my PTSD. Last weekend it was loading a coworker onto a bird."

"Maybe you should speak to someone again, Andy," his dad said.

"I was going to, but then after I got some sleep, I was better."

"You sure?" his mother asked.

"I promise. The episode wasn't too bad, nothing like how it used to be. It did put me on edge, though. I don't want to mess things up with Chelsea again."

"Ah," Mom said, and took a small bite of potatoes.

"What does that mean?"

She cast a quick glance at his father, then plunged in. "Only that I understand now."

Dad scowled. "Well, I sure don't."

"Oh, Porter, it's simple. Anderson is not only suffering from PTSD, but from a bit of romantic PTSD, too."

Stung, Anderson held up a hand. "It's not like that, Mom."

"It really does sound like it—"

"And, by the way, PTSD is very serious. Don't go throwing that phrase around for everything."

"I know, but I think your problem is serious, too. I'm sorry to be blunt, but you're not just scarred from that IED. You're emotionally scarred from your relationship with Chelsea."

"Mom, you're talking like my shrink."

"Just hear me out. Andy, we were so proud of you back in high school. It seemed like you were living every boy's dream. You were smart, popular, and talented on that football field. And you had the homecoming queen on your arm." She laughed softly. "It's no wonder you thought you knew everything."

Thinking of the way he'd broken up with Chelsea so he wouldn't be distracted, how he was sure that she'd forgive him as soon as he called her, he winced. "I was so full of myself."

"Yeah, you were. But you were also just eighteen," his father added. "We knew you had a lot of growing up to do."

"I sure did."

His mother continued. "I've always thought that the

army made you realize you had a lot to learn about life and being a real adult. Then, when you discovered that Chelsea had also been struggling—and that you were partly to blame, for breaking up with her—you totally closed down."

He opened his mouth and shut it almost immediately. She had just summed up in a nutshell what had happened.

Unsure of how to react, he turned to his father.

Dad shrugged. "I can't help you there, son. The fact is, I think your mother might be right. She's smart like that, you know."

He was in between a rock and a hard place. And, it seemed, he was sitting across from a woman who was pretty wise about relationships. "Mom, what do you think I should do now?"

"I think you should do some soul-searching, dear. Stop pretending you're only worried about Chelsea and Jack and face the truth."

"Which is?"

"That you're just as worried about getting hurt as you are about hurting Chelsea." Her voice softened. "But there's nothing wrong with being worried about that. Getting hurt isn't fun. The pain you suffered would make anyone cautious."

"Just as long as you're honest with yourself," Dad added.

"I see." Though it was all about as clear as mud.

His mother stood up. "I'm glad. Now, would you like ice cream on your apple pie?"

"Yes, ma'am."

"I'm so glad. Get your father's plate and bring it into the kitchen."

Feeling a little bit like he'd just gotten hit by a gale-force wind, Anderson did as he was told.

Chapter 28

wo days had passed since Anderson's text about dinner with his parents. Chelsea had responded with a
vague, stupid-sounding **Let me check my schedule**.

He was either still waiting or hadn't been too impressed
with her reply, because he hadn't written another thing since
then.

Frustrated with herself, she'd gone ahead and texted Will
back the next morning. He'd been nothing but nice and she
didn't want him to feel ignored like she did.

Unlike Anderson, Will had texted her right back, and
then had called her later in the evening. He didn't play any
games; he told her flat-out that he'd been thinking about her
and wanted them to get to know each other better.

How refreshing! Going on a date didn't have to be stressful. It wasn't a commitment, it was simply a way to get to
know someone better.

With that in mind, she'd agreed to go out to dinner with
him on Thursday night. Thursday seemed safe because they
both had to go to work the next day. They could keep the

evening relatively short. In Chelsea's mind a Thursday night was also a little more low-key than a big Saturday-night event.

Though, who even knew anymore? She was certainly out of dating practice!

Will was agreeable to Thursday night, and insisted on picking her up. She didn't think it was necessary, but he said he wanted to *do this date right* so she agreed to let him pick her up at half past six.

Unfortunately, the only person who wasn't agreeable was Jack. Like, not at all. From the moment she'd told him about it, he'd followed her around the house complaining.

He wasn't much better on Thursday. "I don't understand why you're going out with this guy."

"Um, because he's nice and he asked me?"

He rolled his eyes. "I'm being serious."

"I know you are." She meant that sincerely, too. For most of Jack's life, it had been just the two of them. Now, she had added not only Anderson to the mix, but Will, too. Though it was tempting to admit that she was just as confused about dating as Jack was, Chelsea knew he needed reassurance, not more things to worry about.

"Jack, honey, this is what adults do. They go on dates to see how much they like each other. I'm not sure if Will and I are going to click or not. But if I don't get to know him better, I'll never know!"

"That's it?"

She nodded. "That's it. So, may I now get dressed?"

But instead of walking out of her bedroom, he sat down on the edge of her bed. "What if you really like him? What happens with Anderson?"

"I don't know. I guess I'll figure that out when the time comes."

"That's a pretty bad answer, Mom."

She did feel for him—grown-up relationships were hard to explain to an eight-year-old—but she was starting to lose patience with his attitude. "Jack, if it's a bad answer, it's because you're asking me questions that don't have real answers. You're jumping from A to B to S or T. Like I just said, there's a whole lot of stuff that has to happen in between."

"In between B and S?" A line formed between his brows. "You're not making any sense."

Sitting down next to him, she tried to come up with another way to explain herself. "I promise, one day, six or seven years from now, you're going to be asking girls out and then you'll have a better idea of what I'm going through. You have to take time to get to know all different people before you know who you like best. That's what I'm doing."

Jack seemed to think about that. Then he crossed his arms over his chest. "I'm not going to wait until I'm seventeen to ask a girl out, Mom. It's going to happen a lot sooner than that."

"How soon are we talking about?"

"Kids start going out when they're thirteen or fourteen."

"Well, if you do, I hope you're not going to plan to marry any of them right away." When she saw a hint of a smile, she ruffled his hair. "Are we good now?"

"I guess. Where am I going tonight? To Miss Camille's?"

"You're not going anywhere."

For the first time since she'd told him about the date, Jack looked pleased. "You mean I get to stay home alone?"

"No, Mallory is coming over to stay with you."

"Is she bringing her dog?"

"I hope not. Snowball leaves a trail of white fur over practically everything he touches. But I do know she's bringing over two fried chicken dinners."

"No way!"

"Yep. She's running by Momma's House right now."

"That's awesome!"

"Now, I better get ready or Will's going to take one look at me and change his mind!"

Jack shook his head like her jokes were the worst—which Chelsea thought might not be wrong.

When the doorbell rang thirty minutes later, both Mallory's and Jack's eyes lit up.

Chelsea pressed a hand to her heart as she tried to push back her nerves.

"Want me to get the door? I can tell him that you're still getting ready," Mallory said.

"No, I better answer it myself. Now you," Chelsea said, turning to Jack, "have a choice. Would you like to meet Will or not?"

"I'll meet him."

"I'm proud of you," she said as she led the way to the door.

Feeling both giddy and nervous, Chelsea took a deep breath and opened the door. "Hey, Will," she said with a smile. "Won't you come in? This is my son, Jack."

Will looked directly at Jack and held out his hand. "Will Hamilton. It's nice to meet you."

Jack thawed slightly, and smiled as he shook Will's hand. "Same."

"Is Jack coming out with us?" Will asked Chelsea, without sounding disappointed.

"No! I mean, no. My friend Mallory is here to babysit."

"She's in the kitchen," Jack explained. "Hey, Mallory, come meet Mom's date!" he yelled.

Feeling like her face was now beet red, Chelsea smiled at Will. "Welcome to my world."

He looked even more amused. "Glad to be here."

When Mallory came out of the kitchen, Chelsea could feel herself tense. She looked so pretty, even dressed in faded jeans with holes in the knees and an even older sweatshirt.

Even though Chelsea knew she looked just fine, for a

split second, she felt a burst of jealousy and wondered if Mallory's very existence was going to be enough for Will to be a little less enthusiastic about their date.

But Will only held out his hand. "Nice to meet you. Will Hamilton."

"Mallory Lee." Wrapping a hand around the back of Jack's neck, she said, "Now listen, we're good here, so you two should get on your way."

"You ready?" Will asked.

Chelsea slipped on her jacket and picked up her purse. "I won't be home late," she said to Mallory. "Maybe nine at the latest?"

"We'll be fine," Mallory said. "Right, Jack?"

"Yep. Bye, Mom." His face showed the moment he remembered his manners. "Bye. And um, nice to meet you."

"It was good to meet you, too, Jack," Will replied.

After exchanging another look with Mallory, Chelsea smiled at Will and walked through the front door.

He drove a shiny black Range Rover. She couldn't help but admire it as he helped her into the passenger side. "This is a great SUV."

"Thanks. Some of the guys at the base give me grief about having a, quote, fancy car, but I haven't had a single problem since I bought it five years ago."

Running her hand down the smooth leather, Chelsea mused that she probably wouldn't mind if it was full of mechanical problems. It was that comfortable.

As he backed out of her driveway, Will said, "I made reservations at Champions. Do you like steak and seafood? Or, if you don't, we can go to a Thai place I like."

"I haven't been to Champions in a long time. That sounds wonderful. Thank you."

He grinned. "Don't thank me yet. We haven't eaten."

"That's fair, but I feel like I should be thanking you for everything you've done so far." When he glanced at her in confusion, she rushed to explain. "You know, being patient with me, picking me up. Meeting Jack and my friend Mallory."

"Chelsea, I don't think you get it. I want to get to know you. I'm happy to get to know your son and your friends, too."

Feeling flattered, she smiled. "I'm looking forward to getting to know you, too."

"Jack seems like a good kid."

"He's the best." Realizing how she sounded, she chuckled. "And yes, I know I'm a little prejudiced."

He grinned. "If you weren't, I'd wonder why. I think moms are supposed to feel that way about their kids."

"Everyone told me that my whole world would become all about him from the moment he was born but I didn't really believe it. I was wrong, of course. The moment the nurse put him in my arms, I was in love."

"You said his father wasn't in the picture?"

Ugh, she didn't want to talk about that. "The short answer is that I made a mistake when I was eighteen and didn't want to make two mistakes by marrying a guy I barely knew."

Slowing as he turned into the Champions parking lot, he frowned. "Hey. I wasn't judging you. Sorry if it seemed like that."

"It didn't. I . . ." She took a deep breath as she tried to form her thoughts into something that resembled coherence. "To be honest, if I sound defensive, it's because it's hard for me to come to terms with my actions. I can't believe I used to be so different."

"I think it's more like you used to be younger, right?" he asked as he parked his vehicle. "And, for what it's worth, when I was young I did plenty of stuff that I wish I would've thought harder about. But I've also given myself a break, especially because some of those 'mistakes' have made me into the person I am right now."

"I feel the same way. Jack made my life better."

"I'll come around and help you out, Chelsea."

Maybe another time she would have felt awkward waiting, but she was pleased to have a few seconds to regroup. Will was even nicer than she had imagined. She hadn't expected him to be so easy to talk to.

She smiled up at him when he opened the door and held out a hand to help her up. The heels of her leather boots clicked on the gravel as she stepped toward him.

"Have I told you how pretty you look tonight?" he asked as he closed the door. "I like your outfit."

Will would never know how much she appreciated the compliment. She had exactly one nice outfit, which consisted of a slim-fitting light-brown wool skirt and a few different tops that went with it.

She'd had doubts about whether it was dressy enough for a date but hadn't had any time to shop.

"Thank you. This is my 'professional' outfit. I wear it whenever we have someone from the state or county visit the senior center."

"If I saw you wearing this at work, I wouldn't have a doubt that you're a professional."

She noticed that while his expression looked serious, his eyes were dancing. "And tonight?"

"Now, I just think you look hot. And yes, I realize that I probably shouldn't have said that out loud."

"I'm not offended."

He gestured to the plaid button-down he was wearing untucked over dark jeans and a pair of dark, polished cowboy boots. "I can't say anything about what I have on except that it's clean."

It also just happened to fit him like a glove. "You clean up good," she teased as they walked into the restaurant.

Champions was in a converted bank building and was divided into several small eating areas featuring white-tableclothed tables, mismatched chairs, funky light fixtures, and a really big bar. Almost every barstool was occupied by someone about their age sipping wine, beer, or cocktails, all looking happy to be out.

That's when she realized that she probably looked the same way.

"Hey, you okay?"

"Yes." Looking up at him, she added, "I was just thinking that I was glad I accepted your invitation."

As he held her chair for her, his expression warmed. "Funny, I was just thinking the same thing."

Conversation flowed. Oh, she wouldn't call it magical or anything, but she and Will definitely had a lot to talk about. His kind, half-formal manner of speaking also made her feel comfortable. It was like he was giving himself boundaries. She could tell Will wasn't going to push her to discuss things she wasn't ready for.

Because of that she relaxed. They shared an appetizer and two sides to go with her fish and his steak. She had a second glass of wine because she wasn't driving and he'd already switched to water.

And when the server asked if they'd like dessert, at Will's encouragement she ordered crème brûlée.

He tried a bite, then leaned back while she savored the fancy dessert just a little too much. Realizing that she probably should've left half of it on the plate, she set her spoon down. "Sorry. I guess it's obvious that I haven't gone out for anything beyond fast food for a while."

"You don't have a thing to apologize for. I am surprised that you haven't gone on more dates, though."

She didn't feel the need to share how her experience with Jack's father and Anderson Kelly had messed with her head for way too long, so she simply said, "You have to be picky when you're a single mom."

"I'm glad I passed the test."

She laughed. "Me, too, though I guess I should say that I probably haven't passed a lot of guys' tests."

"Why do you say that?"

"Well, not every man my age wants to suddenly be in a relationship with an eight-year-old."

"I have a sixteen-year-old brother, so an eight-year-old doesn't sound all that young. I played a lot of Legos with Luke whenever I was in town or stationed nearby."

"I guess so," she murmured. What a big age gap, she thought, not that it was any of her business.

He chuckled. "Are you mentally calculating the age difference? My brother is from my mother's second marriage."

"Are you close?"

Will shrugged. "Fairly close enough, considering Luke's in high school and I've been stationed all over the country the last ten years."

"Where does he live?"

"In Monument. Not too far." His eyes lit up. "Luke's a drummer in the Lewis-Palmer High School band. He's great."

Something inside her melted a little bit more. Will was so approachable and his love for his brother made him seem even more attractive.

"You're full of surprises, Will," she said as they walked back to his car.

"Not so many, I promise. I don't have any secrets, so feel free to ask me anything you like. I want you to be able to trust me."

Later that night, after he'd given her a chaste kiss on the cheek and she'd promised to give Mallory all the deets the next day, Chelsea took a hot bath and then crawled into bed.

Feeling snug in her flannel sheets, she decided that the evening was a success. Jack had done okay, dinner was delicious, Will had been a surprise, and she hadn't said anything stupid.

She should be really pleased.

However, all she could seem to think about was the way Anderson had looked when he'd lifted his shirt in her office. He'd been showing her his scar, of course. And while that had been hard to see and had cemented the meaning behind his words . . . that wasn't all she'd noticed. There had been so many muscles, that line of dark hair on his belly, the deep emotion in his voice that was so raw she'd felt a lump form in her throat.

She had never seen a man more handsome.

As she drifted off to sleep, she realized she probably never would.

Chapter 29

*C*amille wasn't sure what to do about her children anymore. Yesterday Briana had called to chat about yet another retirement community that she'd found. She kept speaking over Camille, determined to overrule her every objection.

After repeating herself several times, Camille had hung up the phone in tears.

Never before had she felt so weak and vulnerable. Not even when her dear Scott had died.

For the first time, she was really starting to worry about her future. She was losing control and, she feared, her children's respect. It felt as if every word she said was being analyzed for early dementia. If she acted flustered by a telemarketer, they would scold her for not screening her calls better.

If she left a credit card statement on the counter, one of them would think nothing of inspecting it and then lecture her about her finances.

It wasn't just aggravating, it was offensive. She'd been an accountant for thirty years! It was like they'd all blocked out the memory that she was the one who paid bills, filed the taxes, and handled investments. Not their father.

Camille had started to feel kind of alone, too. Normally, she would joke about her children's bossiness with one of her friends. Now she was so nervous and on edge, she was afraid that any complaints she made would eventually get back to her kids.

That was silly, of course. Her children were far too busy to interrogate her friends—but that's where her mind seemed to go these days. Always to the worst possible scenario.

Since she'd always been a generally happy person, this was yet another cause for concern.

Maybe she was getting paranoid? Or too sensitive? Her children loved her and for most of their lives she'd enjoyed an easy relationship with all four of them.

Frustrated, she put some chicken on to boil for a casserole, lit a favorite candle so the kitchen wouldn't smell like boiled chicken, and went outside to check on the mail.

"Hey, Camille," her sweet neighbor Chelsea called out from across the street. "How are you today?"

"Oh, okay."

Chelsea's cheerful smile dimmed as she walked closer. "That doesn't sound too good. Is something wrong? Do you need anything?"

"Oh no, dear. Nothing for you to worry about." She pasted a chipper smile on her face. "Thank you for asking, though. How's Jack?"

"He's fine. Now that he has baseball twice a week I've been carpooling with some of the other moms or taking him directly from school."

"I'm sure he's glad about that, but I do miss him."

"He misses you, too."

"Tell him that I bought a brand-new box of Cinnamon Toast Crunch."

"You did not!"

"Of course I did. I've got to keep that boy on my side!"

"He's always on your side, Camille."

For some reason, that sweet comment touched her heart. "You tell him I said hey."

"I will." After giving her another long look, Chelsea said, "Well, I better let you go. But listen, if you do need something let me know; Jack and I are around all weekend."

"I'm sure we'll see each other sometime, then. Tell Jack to stop by tomorrow afternoon. I have a feeling I'll be making some peanut butter cookies."

"I will. You know how much he loves your cookies. Thank you."

"Of course, dear. Have a good day now."

"You, too." Chelsea gave her a little wave before heading back home.

As Camille opened up her mailbox, she tried to shake off her blues, but they seemed to linger, grabbing hold of her emotions and refusing to let go. She sorted through the assortment of junk mail and magazines to find four bills and yet another brochure for a senior living facility.

Appalled that she was now on their mailing list, Camille walked to the ornate wooden bench that she'd ordered from a nearby garden center almost a dozen years ago. She'd always loved the curlicues that made up the back of the bench and the bright colorful paint on the legs and seat.

With a sigh, she sat down and took a deep breath. *Everything is going to be okay,* she promised herself. *This is just a little bump in the road and it, too, will pass.*

Unfortunately, her pep talk didn't do much good. Then, out of the corner of her eye, she found a true sign of hope. Several of her crocuses were about to bloom. It was like the Lord had given her a little sign that life continued, no matter how hard a winter might be. At last, she felt a break in the cloud that had overtaken her.

Those crocuses were lovely and they would soon brighten her whole flower bed—if they were freed from the mess of weeds that had seemed to spring up overnight.

A burst of wind blew, knocking over the trash can at her curb. She hurried to pick it up, and carted it back to the garage.

Just as she was placing it in its cubby, she heard a faint, high-pitched beep. Concerned, she opened the back door to see what was going on—and found her small kitchen enveloped in smoke.

Camille froze, trying to put together what she was seeing and hearing and smelling. It was as if her brain had forgotten how to function.

Then she remembered she'd put a pot of chicken in a shallow pan of water to boil. Was that what was wrong? Was the chicken burning? Afraid that the pan would scorch and be ruined, she hurried through the smoke to the range.

Suddenly, she was completely surrounded. She inhaled and started coughing, and her eyes watered. Then, through her foggy, confused daze, she was assaulted by a wave of heat and a burst of light.

Fire.

The kitchen was on fire. Only then did she remember the candle that she'd left burning. She'd set it near a cracked window. Had the breeze knocked the candle to the ground? It must have set fire to the old rag rug in the center of the room.

Feeling as if she was thinking through a thick cloak of fog, she tried to get a grip on herself. If the children found out about the fire, they were going to make her move for sure.

She had to put it out. She *had* to.

It seemed that so far only the rug was on fire. Camille looked around, trying to recall where the fire extinguisher was. The alarm got louder and higher pitched, and her ears started to ring.

Suddenly, there were too many senses being bombarded with pain. She rested a hand on the wall but pulled it back when she felt singed. Were the walls on fire, too? It just didn't make sense.

A wave of dizziness overtook her.

She backed up a step but bumped into the corner of the counter. She tried to catch her breath but it was as if all the oxygen had been pulled out of the room and she was left gasping. She bent over, her hands on her knees.

"Camille?"

She turned, wondering if she'd actually heard her name being called or if it was her imagination.

"Camille!"

"Yes!" she gasped, but even to her own ears her voice was faint and strained. She turned around, searching for the door, every instinct propelling her to flee. To hurry to safety.

"Camille, where are you?"

"I . . ." she began, but could say nothing more. She reached out a hand, even though she knew there was nothing to hold on to.

It didn't matter. She'd already sunk to her knees, braced a hand on the ground, and noticed how warm it was.

And then there was nothing but black. Black smoke, faint pain, and the sense that there was nothing to do but close her eyes and stop fighting.

Anything to stop the burning in her lungs and the heat surrounding her body.

Chapter 30

Chelsea knew her son was a good kid, but he was still a kid. And . . . she was still a mom, which was why she was holding on to her patience when she'd much rather be lying on the couch and watching a Hallmark movie.

Instead of debating homework.

"I don't see why I have to do my homework. It's only Saturday afternoon," Jack complained.

"I already explained the reason. We have church tomorrow and then you are getting together with Brian and his dad, remember? You're going to the batting cages."

He brightened. "I forgot about that."

"Well, I didn't. So you'd best get busy."

"Can't I do it tomorrow before church?"

"No."

"How about after I get home tomorrow night?"

"We don't leave our homework until Sunday night, period. Just go do it, Jack." When he groaned, she propped a hand on her hip. 'What is the problem? I thought you only had your science project to do."

"I do."

"Then?"

"We have to come up with twenty things about our animal."

"I know. I went over the assignment with you, remember? After you list your twenty facts you get to make a model or draw a picture of the animal." Honestly, she couldn't understand what he was complaining about. It sounded like a fun project.

"She won't let us design it on the computer. I don't know why."

Chelsea wasn't sure why, either, but she hoped it was because third graders needed to get off the computer sometimes and do something with their hands. "You're a good artist. I'm sure your sea otter is going to be fantastic." When he only grunted, she hid her smile. After all the work she'd done that week, she would have *loved* spending a few hours thinking about cute sea otters.

When Jack sat down at the table with his two library books, she breathed a sigh of relief. Sitting down on the couch, she clicked on the television and pressed mute. Maybe she could see when the next movie was on.

"Hey, Mom?"

"Hmm?"

"Mom, come look at this."

Vexed, she got to her feet. "Jackson, I don't want to debate this any longer."

"But—"

"Do you remember what I said? What your teacher said at our conference? You're a smart boy but you need to work on focusing and getting tasks done. This is your homework, not mine. I'll help you fix things up when you're finished."

"Mom, this is important. Come here!"

Now she could tell something was wrong. "Jack, what?" She hurried to his side.

"That!" he said, pointing to the window. "Look!"

She gasped. "Oh no! That's Miss Camille's house."

"What should we do?"

She was already running to the kitchen to her cell phone. "I'm dialing 911."

He kept pace with her. "Didn't you see her earlier? Do you think she's over there? Mom, what if Miss Camille is hurt?"

That was exactly what she was afraid of. "Put on your shoes but don't you leave this house," she said in a rush as the phone rang.

"911 operator. What's your emergency?"

"The house across the street from us is on fire."

"Address?"

She rattled off hers. "I'm sorry, that's mine. I forget what her house number is. But it's on fire."

"I understand."

"Will you hurry? Please?"

"I need your name first, ma'am."

"Chelsea Davis," she replied as she ran to the closet by the door and stuffed her feet into the first shoes she could find. "Please, is someone on the way? It looks bad and there's a lady who lives there. Her name is Camille Hudgens."

"Stay on the line, ma'am."

Jack was standing by the door. "Mom, come on! We should go see if we can help."

"Stop! Stay there! The operator will tell us what to do. Oh, I guess we can go stand outside."

Luckily, some of their neighbors were outside as well. Right away, she noticed that several of them also had phones in their hands. She breathed a sigh of relief. "Looks like other people have called, too, Jack."

He looked stricken. "I hope Miss Camille's okay. What if she's not? Do you think we should try to help? Maybe we should go over there," he said all in one breath.

The fire seemed to have gotten even bigger in just the

last two minutes. "There's nothing we can do except wait for the fire department, honey." It hurt to say, but there was no way she was going to risk Jack's life.

He paced back and forth on the porch while she stayed on the line with the operator. "Can I go over and talk to the Chungs?"

"You may, but only if you stay where I can see you."

"'Kay."

"I mean it, Jack," she warned. "Don't make me have to wonder where you are."

She knew just how worried he was when he didn't so much as roll his eyes. She watched as Jan Chung enveloped him in a hug and he hugged her back.

"Chelsea, are you still on the line?" the operator asked.

She'd practically forgotten that she was holding the phone to her ear. "Yeah. I mean, yes, I am."

"The fire department is on the way," the voice said in a soothing, calm tone. "They're less than two minutes out."

As if in response came the faint sound of sirens. "I hear them! Thank you!"

"Thank you, ma'am. Take care now."

After she hung up, she considered walking over to the Chungs but decided to stay put for a moment. She was worried sick about Camille and needed to get herself together or risk making Jack even more upset.

Then, too, she was worried about Anderson and the rest of the crew. There were several fire stations in the area and several shifts for each station, so it was a long shot that he would be called out. But she couldn't help thinking of him.

Her musing was interrupted by two fire trucks and an ambulance rushing onto their street and pulling to a stop in front of Camille's.

Jack ran back to her side. "Is Anderson there?"

"I don't know."

They watched two pairs of firefighters ready the hoses

and start spraying the flames while another pair entered the house.

She caught her breath, unable to do anything but watch helplessly as they disappeared inside.

"I sure hope Miss Camille isn't in there, Mom."

"I hope she isn't, too, but if she is, I pray they find her easily."

Jack nodded and leaned into her slightly. Slipping her cell phone in the back pocket of her jeans, she wrapped an arm around his shoulders and said a silent prayer for everyone's safety.

Soon the smoke and flames were fading, and, judging by the posture of the man who looked to be in charge, she guessed that the worst of the fire was out.

After what was probably only five minutes but felt closer to thirty, the two firefighters came out of the house.

One of them was carrying Camille in his arms. "Oh, dear Lord," she breathed. Camille looked limp, like she wasn't moving at all.

"Mom," Jack said with a hitch in his voice. "She looks really bad."

"I know."

He jerked out from under her arm. "We should go over there. She knows us. We're her friends. Maybe that would make her feel better."

Tears pricked her eyes; she shared every bit of her son's helplessness and fear. "I'd love to go over there, but we need to stay out of the way. She needs medical attention right now." She leaned a little closer to him. "I think you know that, too."

"It's hard just standing here."

"It really is." She watched Jim, another one of their neighbors, speaking with the man in charge. Then he walked over to the Chungs and seemed to be filling them in. Anxious to get an update, she grabbed Jack's hand. "Let's go see what Jim found out."

For once, Jack didn't try to pull away. Instead, he stayed by her side.

Jim smiled as they approached. "Hey, you two. How are you doing?"

"We're pretty worried," Chelsea said. "What's going on? How's Camille? Do you know?"

"I spoke with the captain and he seemed to think she's going to be okay. She breathed in some smoke and has some bruises and burns, but she was conscious when the guys found her, which is a good sign."

"Is she going to the hospital?" Jack asked.

"Yep," Jim said. "They're loading her up now."

"Thank goodness."

Suddenly Jack started bouncing on his feet. "Mom, look! That's Anderson."

Chelsea turned quickly and saw that Jack was exactly right. Anderson had his helmet off and was standing by while two other people loaded Camille into the ambulance.

When she saw him look their way, she raised a hand in greeting.

He raised his own before getting inside the ambulance. Moments later, the vehicle was out of sight.

"He's gone."

"Yep. I guess to the hospital."

"Can we go, too?"

"Of course."

"You know one of the firefighters?" Jan asked.

"Anderson Kelly. We've been friends since high school."

"Well, when you talk to him again, thank him for his service. They got here just minutes after we called."

"We called 911, too," Jack said importantly.

"I hope Camille is all right," Jan said.

"Her house is going to be unlivable. What the smoke didn't damage, the water from the fire hoses did," Jim said. "Does she have family in the area?"

Chelsea tried to remember. "She has four kids, but I'm

not sure where they all are. I think she has a daughter in the Springs and maybe a son in Denver." She thought some more. "There might be another son nearby?"

Jim looked relieved. "I guess she'll stay with one of them, then."

Chelsea wasn't so sure about that. Camille had mentioned more than once that she liked her independence. "Let's wait to see what Camille says," Chelsea said. "Maybe her house isn't as bad as we think."

"I hope it isn't, but I'm not going to hold my breath," Mo Chung said. "That fire was pretty bad."

When Jack gazed up at her in concern, Chelsea rubbed his back. Usually she did her best to reassure him, but there was nothing she could think of to say. At least, not yet.

One of the trucks left, then an official-looking Suburban arrived and a uniformed man got out to talk to the captain. The excitement was at last winding down and the onlookers started to go back into their houses.

Well, she wasn't going home. She was taking Jack to the hospital to see Camille. Hopefully they'd allow her visitors and she could ask Camille how she could help. Chelsea wasn't sure what she could do, but she wasn't about to simply sit by and do nothing.

And she made another decision as well. She was going to stop waiting around and call Anderson herself. Seeing him on the scene had given her a whole new appreciation for his job. She was proud of him and he needed to know that.

She also needed to make sure that he wasn't hurt. And to tell him that no matter what happened—or didn't happen—between them, she still cared about him.

At least she could admit it to herself. She still cared about Anderson Kelly, no matter what their future had in store.

Chapter 31

*E*n route to the scene, Anderson heard that not only was the fire on Chelsea's street, but there was a female victim. His heart jumped, then calmed when Mark said the woman was older. Anderson was torn between giving thanks and feeling guilty that his first thought wasn't compassion for the victim.

Thankfully, by the time he arrived, someone on his team had already carried the woman to safety and started her on oxygen.

The moment Chip pulled to a stop, Anderson rushed to her side. "Ma'am, my name is Anderson. I'm a paramedic and I'm going to help you out. Okay?"

Her eyes, filled with pain, struggled to focus on him, and she didn't attempt to speak or nod her head.

He knew that could be caused by a number of different things, some of them serious. As he began to check her vital signs, Mark spoke in his ear.

"She's rattled, but that goose egg on her head's concerning."

"Affirmative." The wound on her head was bleeding only slightly, but the size of the swelling worried him. She could be bleeding in her brain.

Pulling out a penlight, he gently checked her pupils. "What's your name, ma'am?"

"Camille." She paused for a moment, then added, "Hudgens."

"Camille's a pretty name," he said. "Unusual, too."

"Nowadays," she whispered.

Pleased that she was responding well—and that both of her pupils were equal and reactive, he said, "Camille, we're going to take you to the hospital, okay? That means we're going to transfer you to a stretcher and carry you to the ambulance that's waiting. Do you understand?"

"Can't leave my house," she rasped.

"I'm afraid that's not the best place for you, Camille," Dave said smoothly. "We need to take care of you first."

"That's right," Anderson said. "Plus, if we don't take you with us, it'll look like we came out here for nothing," he joked as he carefully checked for broken bones. "You can't have that, right?"

Looking woozy, Camille murmured, "I suppose."

Meeting Dave's eyes, Anderson counted to three, then, just like they had in countless training exercises and other calls, together they transferred the woman to a stretcher in one fluid motion.

She moaned slightly and closed her eyes.

"Almost there, Camille," he said as he led the way toward the ambulance. With Chip's help, they got their patient safely into the vehicle. Before he climbed in, he found himself glancing across the street to Chelsea's house.

And there she was. Standing beside Jack. Her eyes were trained on him, and he felt her steady gaze as assuredly as if she was in his arms. The awareness was almost unsettling. What was it about Chelsea that made the rest of the world fade away, even in the midst of an emergency?

After waving in her direction, he met Chip's gaze. Though they were so in tune with each other that no words were necessary, he never skipped a step. "Ready. One, two, three."

His muscles flexed as they easily guided Camille into the ambulance, Dave quietly reassuring her until they strapped her in and got her settled.

Seconds later, Chip was speeding down the road and Anderson was starting an intravenous drip while Dave adjusted the oxygen cannula under her nostrils.

Camille drifted between awareness and grogginess, which Anderson was thankful for. The woman's lungs were going to feel sore and the burns she'd sustained were going to sting. In his experience, even a small burn in the wrong place hurt as much as more serious wounds. Checking her vitals again, he exhaled. She was stable.

When she groped for his hand, he shifted so she could see his face. "You're safe and in the ambulance, Camille," he said. "We're almost at the hospital."

"My house? Is it still there?"

"Yes, ma'am."

"Bad shape?"

"I can't speak to that, ma'am. You're gonna be okay, though. That's what matters, right?"

Unfortunately, she didn't nod or look relieved. When Dave gave him a pointed look, Anderson felt his cheeks heat. He knew how to be more diplomatic. He certainly knew how to be more caring.

When she closed her eyes, he checked her vitals again. Still stable. In less than five minutes, they were in the emergency bay, a nurse and two CNAs—certified nurse assistants—hurrying toward their bus. Dave opened the door and hopped out in one fluid movement.

"Here we go, Camille. Just relax, okay? I've got you." When some of the tension in her face eased, he felt some of the tension he didn't realize he'd been holding ease as well.

As they followed the CNAs into the hospital, they were met by Michelle, the admitting nurse. "Whatcha got?"

"Smoke inhalation, minor burns, hematoma, some disorientation," he said. Dave filled Michelle in about Camille's vital signs and other information.

As he knew she would, Michelle immediately began giving directions to several people around them.

"Thanks, Michelle." —

"Anytime." She gave him the once-over. "You okay, Doc? You're looking a little peaked today."

"I'm good. You?"

"I'm good, too. See you," she called as she moved away.

As he always did, Anderson took a moment to process what had just happened and to give thanks that his patient had traveled safely from the burning house to the hospital's triage area.

He and Dave returned to the ambulance. "We good?" he asked Chip. There had been times when no sooner had they dropped off a patient than another call came in.

"Yep. McGinn said the fire is out and no other injuries."

Anderson hopped into the passenger seat and buckled up while Dave climbed into the back and closed the back doors.

Anderson pulled out his phone and smiled when he saw a text had come in from Chelsea.

I'm so glad you were there for Camille! I hope she's okay and that you are, too.

He replied immediately. She's in the hospital now. I can't say for certain but I think she's going to be okay.

Thank goodness. Jack and I are about to head there to check on her.

I'm sure she'll be glad to see you. He had to smile, at both her compassion and her enthusiasm. She really was a woman anyone would want by their side.

He should have remembered that.

Hey, you ought to wait at least two hours, he added. She's

going to need some tests. With that hematoma, he figured, Camille would need a CT scan and at least an overnight stay.

Oh. Okay.

Try not to worry. The docs are good at what they do.

I hope so. Are you still there?

We just left. I've got another five hours on shift, then I'm going to go home and sleep.

Okay. After a slight pause, she added, **Will you call me tomorrow?**

He felt guilty that she'd had to ask. **Absolutely,** he texted.

Okay

He could practically feel her doubt in that one word. He'd really messed up by being so silent. **I promise, I will.**

Okay:)

Seeing they were pulling into the bay, he quickly added, **Sorry gotta go.** Then he slid the phone back into his jacket pocket.

As Chip parked, he elbowed Anderson. "You chatting with that gal again?"

"Yeah. Chelsea lives across the street from the fire. She and Jack were standing outside when we loaded the victim into the ambulance."

"Wow. This world of ours is turning smaller and smaller."

"Sure feels that way."

Two hours later, after they cleaned the ambulance, checked supplies, and showered, Anderson sat down in the rec room while two of the rookies finished setting up a taco bar.

Beside him, Mark was stretched out in a pair of sweats and new WPFD T-shirt. He looked way too relaxed and easy for a guy just finishing up a forty-eight-hour shift.

"What's going on with you?" Anderson teased. "You look like you just had a two-week vacation."

"That's because my brother's in town and I'm heading out to Winter Park for the next four days." He grinned.

"Twenty-four hours from now, I fully plan to be drinking beer on the side of the mountain after skiing all day."

"I'd be smiling, too."

"When are you scheduled for vacation?"

Anderson shrugged. "I haven't booked any."

"Really?"

He shrugged. "I will, I just haven't decided what to do yet."

Mark's expression turned serious. "Hey, I know you haven't asked me for any advice—"

"You're right. I haven't."

"Okay, how about if I put it this way? Someone needs to give you some real talk. It might as well be me."

"About what?" he prodded, even though he was fairly certain he knew what Mark was about to say.

"You need to move on or get some help."

"Get help with what?" he asked warily. Had Mark noticed something off with him lately? Was he concerned that his PTSD was acting up again?

"With everything that goes hand in hand with coming home."

"My transition has gone fine. I'm having no trouble."

"Reintegration can be ugly, man." His former sergeant waved a hand. "And you've got it tougher than a lot of us, since you came back to such a small town where everyone knows you. It's hard to fade into the background."

"Roger that, but I'm handling it."

"Fine. I hear you. Just give yourself some slack, right? Maybe try something new in your downtime. Maybe date someone new . . ."

"My social life is none of your business."

Mark swallowed. "I'm not trying to be nosy, I'm trying to show you I care." He sighed. "You know what, I even read the other day about some plastic surgeons who are donating time over at the VA hospital . . ."

"Are my scars bothering you, Sarge?"

"Of course not, but don't knock the idea of making them

a little less noticeable. Some guys have said getting them fixed can help the reentry."

"Look. I know you were my sergeant and I know you mean well, but I don't care about the scars."

"Hey, listen. Sometimes things from the sandbox stay with you and you're not even aware of it. We both know why Greg hates to be taken by surprise. And I still have a hard time when I get sand or dust in my eyes."

Only years of friendship and a healthy dose of respect for his former sergeant kept Anderson from walking away. Mark was famous for initiating heart-to-heart talks with his men back when they were deployed.

Sometimes the guys would roll their eyes or make fun of his cryptic philosophy on the one hand and well-meaning pep talks on the other.

Anderson took a moment to mentally step back and drew a deep breath before speaking again. "Mark, I get what you're trying to say and I know that you mean well, but there's nothing wrong with me—nothing that a doctor can fix anyway." He forced a laugh.

"Are you sure about that?"

"I'm positive. I'll take vacation when I feel like taking one." When Mark continued to study him intently, Anderson shrugged. "Look, all that's wrong is that I've still got a thing for Chelsea. It has nothing to do with reintegration and everything to do with my heart. Just run-of-the-mill stuff."

Mark raised his eyebrows but didn't say a word.

"Okay, fine. I obviously have some garbage to deal with. It's been noted."

"Good. Listen, I know I kind of suck at these conversations, but I care about you. I'm on your side no matter what."

"I know. You do suck, but it's appreciated."

On his way home Anderson took a chance and stopped by Chelsea's house.

She opened the door with a look of surprise. "I can't believe you're here. Hi."

She was wearing some beat-up white leather tennis shoes, cropped jeans, and a Broncos sweatshirt. "You look cute, Chels."

She stepped back. "Do you want to come in?"

"No. I'm on my way home. I—I just wanted to tell you thanks for reaching out to me. Thanks for caring."

She shifted. "Jack's not here. He's going to be upset he missed you."

"Let's plan something soon."

"Sounds good."

"All right, well, I better go get some sleep. I just wanted . . ." He trailed off, realizing he'd already said why he was there. "Nothing. See you later."

"Hey, Andy, wait."

"Yeah?"

Without a word, she reached up, wrapped her hands around his neck, and hugged him tight.

Closing his eyes, he held her close, inhaling her sweet scent. Unable to help himself, he pressed a kiss to the top of her head.

When she pulled away, she looked a little flustered. "I'll uh, see you later."

"Yeah. See you." He stood there like a fool as she smiled at him, blushed slightly, and then closed the door.

When he finally got back inside his vehicle, he admitted the truth. Having her in his arms again had felt right. Perfect.

And he absolutely couldn't wait until he had her there again.

Chapter 32

Camille's precautionary overnight stay had turned into two full days and now a possible third. The doctors said the goose egg on her head was large enough to require daily CT scans to check for internal bleeding. In addition, although she was breathing better, she was still coughing quite a bit, and the burn on her arm was quite painful.

She'd never been one for lazing around, but there had been times over the last two days she'd been privately grateful not to have to do anything but rest.

Especially since she also happened to be worried sick about the damage to her house. Though she and Scott had done some remodeling, she'd never imagined doing such a big project on her own. Even thinking about exchanging phone calls with insurance agents and contractors was wearying.

So between her pain, the medical tests, and the looming construction project, she had more than enough on her plate. This visit by two of her four children was about to send her over the edge.

"Do you want anything else to drink, Mom?" Janie asked.

"The nurse said you could have cranberry juice if you'd like! Maybe that would perk you up, hmm?"

Her daughter was talking about cranberry juice like it was a shot of vodka, which was starting to sound pretty good. "Thank you, but water suits me fine."

"Maybe a snack?"

"Dear, I'm pretty good at ordering food from the little menu myself." When Janie opened her mouth to speak again, Camille said firmly, "Please sit down. I'm good."

As soon as her daughter finally took a seat, her son stood up. "Bo said he was going to come this afternoon," Clayton said. "Plus, I've been texting Briana. She's looking at flights into the Springs."

Usually seeing all four of her offspring at one time would make her beam with happiness. Unfortunately, the only thing it made her feel now was tired. "Briana certainly does not need to come all that way."

"She wants to, Mom," Janie said. "She doesn't like being so far away from the action."

"I'm hardly action."

"You know what I mean. She's worried about you."

"A phone call would suffice. I don't know why she hasn't called me." When she saw Clayton and Janie exchange glances, Camille felt her blood pressure rise. "Let me guess. You told her not to call?"

"No, not at all," Clayton said. "I only told her you were still in the hospital."

For some reason she was sure there was more to it. "Is Bo on the way to the hospital, too? If so, we're going to need another chair in here." Of course they didn't register her sarcasm.

"Bo's stopping by later," said Janie. "He's over at your house now."

At least one of them was doing something productive. "I hope he's taking lots of pictures to show me the damage.

We're going to need those pictures for my insurance agent, too. I can't wait to get started on renovations." Okay, that wasn't quite true, but she did feel that her house needed to get fixed up and become livable as soon as possible. Like yesterday.

Clayton frowned. "Mom, I've been by your house. Your kitchen is ruined."

"I knew that. How is the rest of it, though? It's driving me crazy that I can't see the damage for myself."

"There's damage to most everything. What wasn't directly affected by the fire was either soaked by the fire hoses or smells like smoke."

"I figured as much." Refusing to let that news get her down, she grinned. "I guess after all this time I'm going to finally get my gourmet kitchen, hmm? I'll look at the furniture when I get out of here. What I can't get professionally cleaned I'll replace." That idea did brighten her spirits. She'd always hated her living room couch but it had been too expensive to replace.

Clayton's voice turned impatient. "Mom, there's no point. We need to order a dumpster and clear everything out."

Her brain must have still been foggy from her fall, because she was only just now putting everything together. "You're going to try to use this as an excuse to get me out of my house. That's why Bo and Briana are coming here. You all want to gang up on me."

Clayton sat down in the chair by her bed and reached for her left hand, the one without the IV. "Mom, you're taking this the wrong way. We all love you and want you safe."

"I was safe at home."

"I'm sorry, but that's not true," Janie said. When Camille drew in a sharp breath, she continued in a rush. "You left a candle burning and the pot of chicken unattended. I'm sorry if pointing it out hurts your feelings, but I have to tell you the plain truth." Softening her voice, she added, "You already can't drive and now we all have serious concerns about you continuing to live alone. It's time to move someplace with more support."

Camille bit down on her bottom lip to keep it from trembling. "I am very tired. I'd like to take a nap."

Janie's expression crumpled. "Mom, please try to understand. This isn't easy for us, either."

Yet she was the one whose feelings were being disregarded. "Tell Bo to be sure to call or text me before he stops over. *Me*, not *you*."

Clayton tried to reach for her hand again. She pulled it away and said, "I love you both but I need some space."

"Mom."

She reached for the remote to raise the head of the bed. When she was better able to look Clay and Janie in the eye, she said, "Let me have some time alone. Can you at least do that?"

Clayton got to his feet. "I'll come back later."

"Tomorrow will be soon enough. For both of you."

With leaden feet and obvious regret, they got to their feet and headed out.

Only when she was completely alone did Camille allow the tears to fall. She was angry, and she was scared.

What if her children were right and she was the one in the wrong?

Chapter 33

$\mathcal{F}$rank might be guilty of a lot of things, but hesitating to do what's right wasn't one. But now, as he walked down the hospital corridor with a VISITOR badge clipped to his collar and a bouquet of roses in his hands, he slowed his pace to a mere crawl.

Maybe he shouldn't have given in to the impulse to charge over like an old and slightly rusty knight in shining armor. Maybe he should have called Camille first instead of just showing up like he had a right to visit.

After all, he wasn't at Walter Reed visiting soldiers just returned from Iraq. He was just a guy who liked a woman and wanted to show he cared. He'd feel better about it if that woman acted half as interested in him as he was in her.

"Sir, may I help you?" asked a nurse in pale-blue scrubs.

He'd been so lost in thought, he'd been standing in front of the nurses' station like a fool.

Pulling himself together, he smiled sheepishly at the young woman who looked to be about the age of his oldest granddaughter. "Thank you, no. I, uh, was just getting ready to visit a friend."

"Oh, did you need help getting to her room or opening the door? It can be tricky when you have your hands full."

"I'm good, thanks," he said. "I'll head down there now." Did he actually look like he needed help turning a door handle, he who had commanded thousands of soldiers?

He would think about that later. Now, fortunately, when he walked into Camille's room her eyes brightened.

"Frank! What are you doing here?"

"I wanted to see you," he said simply. He took in the bandages, the sizable bruise on her cheek . . . and the dark smudges under her eyes. "I was concerned when I heard about the fire. How are you doing?"

"Not so good, if you want to know the truth."

Now he knew he'd done the right thing. Stepping forward, he set the bouquet of roses on her table and reached for the hand that wasn't attached to an IV. "I'm so sorry, Camille. I'm just grateful you weren't hurt any worse."

Belatedly he realized he really had no idea how injured she was. Maybe she was badly hurt and that's why she was still in the hospital. "I mean to say, I've been worried about you."

"Thank you."

Her voice was as gracious as ever, which gave him hope. On the other hand, she sounded far more fragile than usual. His worry for her grew. "Talk to me," he said as he took the seat next to her bed. "What is going on?"

Her lips twitched. "Now you sound like the general I know."

"Ha, ha. I'm serious."

"Seriously, I've been better." Averting her eyes, she said, "The doctors seem to think I'll be okay, but this darn lump on my head has gotten quite a few of them in a dither."

"How serious is it?"

"Not as serious as they first feared, thank goodness. The swelling has lessened . . . and so has my headache." She smiled weakly. "The burns on my arm are better, too, though I imagine I'll have a good-sized scar."

"We'll be a pair then. I've got a couple of scars, too."

Her smile widened. "You, Frank?"

"I didn't always sit on my rear end, Camille. There was a time I was on the field in the thick of things."

"Maybe one day you can tell me all about it."

Which meant she wanted to see him again. On another day, he would have grinned. Now, though? He could care less about telling war stories. "It's not that interesting. Like you've said, those days are behind me."

"That was rude of me. I'm sorry." She sighed deeply.

That broke his heart. He liked the feisty version of the woman he'd become so fond of—she kept him on his toes. Becoming more worried, he murmured, "I think there's something more going on besides burns and bumps. What is it?"

And just like that, her brave smile faded. "I don't know where I'm going to live."

He took her hand again. "Now that is something I can help you with. I'm a pro at finding temporary housing." And he knew enough people in the area he was sure he could find her someplace nice. "Don't give it another thought."

She shook her head. "No, Frank. It's getting worse. My children are now even more determined that I don't live by myself anymore. They're dead set on my moving to a retirement home." She gave a halfhearted shrug. "I don't know. Maybe they're right. The fire was my fault, Frank."

"How so?" he retorted, becoming angry. "Did you torch your house on purpose?"

"No, of course not. But I had left a candle burning near an open window. The wind knocked it over and it caught the kitchen rug on fire."

Camille looked so guilty you'd think she was confessing to murder. "That's unfortunate, but it was an accident."

"Yes, but I should have been more careful." She fingered the thin blanket, avoiding his eyes. "I was outside weeding. When I heard the smoke alarm, I ran inside. All I saw was smoke—and, you see, I'd left a pot of chicken boiling on the stove and at first, I thought it was the pot that was smoking. I ran in and started looking for my phone to call 911. But I was caught unaware by the smoke and the flames, then I knocked into something and fell."

Hearing the story made him realize just how close he'd been to losing her. "That sounds really scary." Lowering his voice, he added, "But you need to stop acting like everything was your fault. A lot of people would have reacted like you did. Believe me, no one knows how they'll react in a crisis until it happens."

Tears filled her eyes. "You mean that, don't you?"

"Of course I do." Thoroughly confused, he reached over, pulled a couple of tissues from the box, and handed them to her. "Camille, what is troubling you so much?"

"My children say I made one mistake after another. They're really disappointed in me." She turned her face away, but her shoulders were shaking with unshed tears. "I've started to think that they're right."

Not caring about protocol, he moved to sit beside her on the mattress. "Come here," he murmured as he carefully pulled her in close.

She placed a hand on his chest. "I'm going to get you wet."

"I can take it. Cry all you want, soldier." As he'd hoped, she giggled around a sob. Then she leaned closer, pressed her head to his chest, and cried some more.

Rubbing her back, thinking of how upset she was and how unfair her children were being, he began formulating plans to make her feel better. It wasn't entirely selfless. He didn't want her to move across the country. She'd become too important to him.

"Hello, Camille!"

Camille pulled away from his embrace as Chelsea from

the senior center appeared at the door. She wiped her cheeks and said softly, "Hello, Chelsea."

"Oh! I'm sorry. I didn't realize you had company. I can leave—"

"No, no, dear. It's okay. I was just having a little cry. Poor Frank here was stuck dealing with it, so you came at the perfect time."

Chelsea was still standing awkwardly near the door. It was obvious that she wasn't sure whether to stay or go.

"Do you often make hospital visits, Chelsea?" Frank asked as he returned to his chair.

"Hmm? Oh no. Camille and I are neighbors." She smiled at Camille. "She watches my son from time to time."

Camille's expression warmed. "I enjoy my time with Jack. He's a lot of fun."

Seeing the younger woman's obvious fondness for Camille shine through, he made a decision. Camille needed more people on her side. "Have you spoken with Chelsea about what's been going on?"

Camille's eyes widened. "Frank, don't interfere."

"I understand wanting to keep things private, but this is important." With a glance at Chelsea, he added, "I'm sure she knows a lot of people who can help."

Chelsea came inside and stood at the foot of Camille's bed. "Maybe you should tell me what Frank is talking about," she said gently. "I'd like to help."

"I'd rather not."

Frank was about to chide her for her stubbornness, but Chelsea just chuckled. "Oh, Camille. Even sporting bandages and a hospital gown you're pulling an attitude."

"Don't you start on me, too, Chelsea."

"Do you really want me to go over your head to get the whole story? I can pull Frank out into the hall right now."

He made a move to stand up. "I could give you an earful."

As Frank expected, Camille looked fit to be tied. "You wouldn't."

Chelsea nodded. "Just because I love you doesn't mean I won't play hardball."

"Tell her, Camille," he coaxed. "She's going to know eventually."

"What is it?" Chelsea suddenly paled. "Oh my gosh. Camille, are you sick?" She lowered her voice. "Do you have cancer?"

"No, nothing like that. It's . . . well, my children want me to move to Florida."

Chelsea glanced his way. Frank nodded. "They want to put her in a senior living center near her oldest. Obviously, Camille doesn't want to go."

"Just tell them that. I'm sure they're just worried about you. Once they realize you're fine, they'll back off."

"I'm afraid it isn't that easy. See, I don't have a house to live in now."

Chelsea pursed her lips together. "Oh, right."

"Please don't worry, dear. I'll be fine," Camille said, shooting Frank an irritated look. "I'll figure something out."

He cleared his throat. "I wasn't tattling on Camille. I'm going to place some calls. I'm sure someone I know will know of a place Camille could live for a month or two until her place gets fixed up."

"Or, I could probably help you find something, too," Chelsea said. She paused. "You'd like to stay here in town, right?"

Camille hesitated, as if she was afraid to divulge a dark secret. "Yes," she said at last. "It's my home and all my friends are here. I can walk anywhere I need to go and get things delivered for everything I can't. I feel safe here." Her voice grew stronger. "I don't want to get shuttled off somewhere new, especially somewhere on the other side of the country."

"Then don't worry, I'm sure we can figure something out." Chelsea's expression was warm and caring. Full of compassion. "I don't want you to go, either."

Seeing how honestly Camille had shared her feelings—and how sweetly she had responded—was a huge relief. Frank felt the knot that had been settling in the center of his back start to relax.

Time to put a plan into action. "Chelsea, how about this. I'll get on the phone and check into some temporary housing options. After I get some leads I'll report back and you can help me run them down."

Chelsea shook her head. "I just realized that there's no need for that."

"Why?" Camille asked. Her eyes brightened. "Do you already know of someplace I could go until my house is fixed?"

"I do." Chelsea smiled. "Actually, I can't think of a better place for you to finish recuperating, either." She drew a breath. "I want you to live with me and Jack while your house gets repaired."

Camille already looked more optimistic, Frank was delighted to see. "Are you sure you have room for one petite woman with a big attitude?" he asked Chelsea.

"I have a guest bedroom just waiting to be used. What do you say, Camille?"

"I say that is very kind of you, dear, but I couldn't impose."

"Oh, stop. I promise it's not an imposition. I have an extra bedroom. Plus, you'll be able to supervise the remodel if you're right across the street."

"I bet she might even be able to help you with Jack from time to time," he added.

Chelsea smiled. "We would both love that."

"Oh, Chelsea. This is too much. It's too generous."

Frank knew if their roles were reversed and he was the one lying in the hospital bed, he would feel just as hesitant. "How about everyone sleeps on it. I'll give you a call tomorrow and you can tell me your answer then."

"Of course this is totally your decision, Camille. If you

would feel more comfortable somewhere else, you can tell me that. My feelings won't be hurt."

Camille looked a little dazed by the turn of events. "I'll let you know tomorrow, dear."

Chelsea nodded. "Great! It sounds like we have a plan, then." Gathering up her purse, she headed for the door. "I'm so glad I stopped by! Frank, take care of our girl and make sure she rests."

"Always," he replied before realizing that he was making assumptions. But it sounded right.

With a chuckle, Chelsea departed.

When they were alone again, Camille sank back on the pillows. "I can't believe she offered to have me live with her. What a sweetheart."

"You're right. She's a peach."

"I suppose I should tell you that I'm not all that happy with your high-handed behavior."

"You don't have to do that." Sitting back by her side, he reached for her hand once again. "You could just tell me that you understand that I'm trying to help."

"I do." She sighed. "I just don't know what I'm going to tell my kids."

He knew what he would tell them. He'd remind them of the respect that they owed their mother. And that there was more than one way to help Camille live safely and happily.

But he couldn't speak for her. "I reckon you'll know the right thing to say when the time comes," he murmured.

Before his eyes, she sat up a little straighter. "You're right, Frank. I just have to hope and pray that it goes better than I fear it will."

"I used to tell my soldiers that life on earth isn't always fair or easy. There's a reason it's not called heaven."

Chapter 34

Chelsea didn't consider herself to be impulsive by nature. She had carefully weighed the pros and cons before taking her job at the senior center. She wrote out to-do lists and worked hard to get those tasks done in a reasonable amount of time. She'd even cut out pieces of newspaper in the dimensions of the couch she was considering buying and taped them to the floor—much to Jack's annoyance.

She was proud of her thoughtful approach to life.

Of course, she was also aware that she let all that control and careful decision-making fall by the wayside from time to time. Hadn't she let herself have a little too much to drink, slept with a guy she barely knew, and turned her life upside down?

She'd learned a good lesson from that experience, and it wasn't just to not get drunk.

No, it was that being impulsive didn't necessarily lead to regret.

Which she hoped would be true of this latest impulsive decision.

Jack waved when he saw her car in the pickup line. "Hi," he said, hopping into the car.

She smiled. "Hi, back. How was your day?"

He shrugged. "Okay, I guess."

"You guess?" she asked as she pulled out of the parking lot.

"It was just a regular school day," Jack said. "Some days are uneventful, Mom."

Uneventful? Sometimes he sounded far older than his years! Chelsea chuckled. "I can't disagree with that."

"How come you picked me up today? Where are we going?" His expression fell. "Do I have to go to the doctor?"

Jack hated shots. "No. Why would you think that?"

"This is the way to the doctor's office."

She realized then that they actually were very close to the pediatrician. "That's true, but I had something else in mind. I thought maybe we'd go to Granger's Last Stand and have an early dinner. What do you say?"

"That sounds good."

Chelsea smiled to herself. Now that she had alleviated his worry about getting a shot, Jack was in his usual easygoing mood. This was his norm, but every once in a while he showed that he was her son by meeting any change in his routine with suspicion.

Even at four o'clock, Granger's was busy. At least half the tables were filled and the jukebox was playing. "It never ceases to amaze me how many people come here," she said.

"I guess people are always hungry."

"You have a good point. So, do you know what you'd like to eat?"

"Uh-huh. A cheeseburger and fries. What about you?"

"I'm going to get the same."

"Not your chicken salad?" She usually got a fried chicken salad when they were out together. It had just as many calories as a burger, but it was twice as good, she thought.

"Not tonight. I think a cheeseburger will hit the spot."

When Jane, their server, came to take their order, Chelsea nodded to Jack to go first.

"I'd like a cheeseburger deluxe, please."

"And to drink?" the server asked.

"Water, I guess."

"How about a root beer float?" suggested Chelsea. That was his favorite.

"Um, okay."

After the server took Chelsea's order and walked off, Jack scowled at her. "Something's wrong, isn't it?"

"Why would you think that?"

"Because you never let me get a burger, fries, *and* a soda."

"I do, too."

"Oh no, you don't. You always tell me that everything in one meal can't be good for you. That's why you always make me get milk or water."

That was true, actually. "Well, today I changed my mind."

He shook his head. "You don't change your mind, Mom. What happened?"

"Okay, fine. There is something I need to talk to you about that's pretty important." She stopped to smile at Jane, who had returned with their beverages.

"Does it have to do with Will?"

"Will? Ah, no." She realized, to her surprise, that she hadn't thought about him in days. "It has to do with Miss Camille."

His eyes widened. "Is she real sick?"

"She's still in the hospital, but I think she's on the mend."

"She's been there a long time."

"I know, the doctors are being cautious. I saw her today and I promise, she's recovering."

He took a gulp of his drink. "What's wrong then?"

"Well, her house is in bad shape."

"I know that, Mommy. Her house was on *fire*." Looking pleased with himself, he took another gulp of soda and chased it down with a big bite of ice cream.

"Jack, Miss Camille can't live in her house while it gets repaired, so she's going to need a place to stay. It could be a month or two."

"That stinks. Where's she going to go?"

"Well, I was wondering how you felt about her moving in with us. She needs friends around, plus we're right across the street from her house, so she'd be able to oversee the repairs."

"Okay."

Chelsea studied his expression. "Okay to what?"

Their plates arrived and Jack picked up a french fry before answering. "Okay to Miss Camille moving in. What else would I think?" He bit off half the fry.

"Do you have any questions?"

"No. We're her friends, Mom. Obviously we should help her."

Jack was right about that. Maybe she'd been overthinking everything. "Okay, then. I'll tell her tomorrow. Thank you, Jack."

Picking up his cheeseburger with both hands, he grinned. "Mom, sometimes you're so silly. I would've said yes no matter what. You didn't have to get me a cheeseburger *and* a root beer float."

"It wasn't a bribe." Okay, it totally was, but she didn't have to admit that. "I just thought we needed a treat."

He grinned as he dug into their very filling treat.

That night, Chelsea wandered into the guest bedroom. There was an old comforter on the bed, which she'd bought at Target when she was pregnant and living at home. It had been washed so often it definitely looked a bit ratty.

Come to think of it, everything in the room seemed pretty old and worn.

She'd never been in Camille's bedroom, but she'd certainly been in her kitchen and living room numerous times.

Everything there was neat as a pin and well taken care of. Though Camille would never criticize her new, temporary home, Chelsea felt the urge to step things up.

Grabbing a pad of paper, she sat on the bed and started listing things she could do that she hoped would make Camille comfortable and happy.

Her phone buzzed, and she answered distractedly. "Hello?"

"Hey, Chelsea. It's Anderson."

"Hi," she said around a smile.

"Did I catch you in the middle of something?"

"Yes, but I'm glad you called. What are you up to?"

"I went out for a run and now I'm sitting on my back porch. I was just thinking about you, and about our conversation the day before yesterday. It meant a lot to me. Thanks for that."

She thought back to the vulnerability in his eyes—and to the way he'd pulled her into his arms when she hugged him. For a few seconds, she'd felt close to him again, as if all the words and guilt and confusion didn't matter anymore. As if the bond that had always existed between them was still as strong as ever. "You don't need to thank me for that, Andy."

"I also wondered if you'd like to go out this weekend."

Here it was. At last, Anderson was calling her up and asking her out on a proper date. No, not *at last*. Once again.

As if it hadn't been working properly for a decade, her heart started hammering in her chest. The touching tentativeness in his voice made her want to pretend—even just for a couple of seconds—that they were the two people they used to be. That he was the so-hot, so-nearly-unobtainable Andy Kelly, star quarterback, and she was the only girl he had eyes for.

But all of that had been a long time ago.

"Chels? What do you think?"

She wasn't quite ready. That's what she thought. As tempting as it was, it was too sudden. Luckily, she had a perfect excuse: Camille. She was due to be released from the hospital soon and no matter where she decided to live, she was going to need a friend. She sighed. "Thanks, Anderson, but I don't think I can."

"You already have plans?"

"Sort of."

After a pause he said, "Listen, I heard that you've been dating some guy from the air force, but I don't want to give up on us. I still want something more, Chels."

She knew in that moment that if Anderson could allow himself to be vulnerable, then she could, too. "I'm not interested in that air force guy."

"No?"

"No. Um, it has to do with my neighbor whose house burned down."

"What?"

Realizing that he would be the perfect person to talk things through with, she said, "Can you come over? I'd love to tell you about it in person."

"I'll be there in thirty."

After they hung up, Chelsea let herself wonder if it was okay that she was so relieved that he hadn't hesitated.

Chapter 35

Anderson had never thought he'd be the type of guy to phone a friend for relationship advice. At this point, though, he was willing to do whatever it took to not mess things up again with Chelsea. What he needed was a pep talk.

The way he figured it, he could call his parents, who knew Chelsea and their history; his brother Carter, who would have a lot to say but wasn't so good at listening; Mark, who was pretty serious about most things; or Greg, who came off as a player but was probably the most sensitive of them all.

Anderson quickly made his choice. He didn't want to rehash the past with anyone in his family and didn't want to analyze his life choices with Mark.

As Greg's number rang he tried to remember if he was on shift or not.

"Yeah?"

"You home or at the station?"

"I'm at the station but it's dead. What's up?"

"I need advice about Chelsea."

"Yeah? And you called me?"

Greg sounded delighted, which was nice but also a sign that the call would be rubbed in his face for the next decade. "Yeah, but only because your number's easy to remember," Anderson retorted. He had no doubt Greg could see through his flippancy . . . but at least he wasn't sounding quite so desperate.

"So what's going on?"

"Well, you know how I've told you that we had a past. That she'd been my girl."

"Yeah . . . and you've also told me about Jack, buddy. I also saw the three of you together over here. What's up?"

"I called Chelsea and she asked me to come right over."

"Uh-huh, that's good, right?"

"I don't know, she said it had something to do with the house fire across the street from her."

"Like, about the cause? Wait, did the inspector say it looked suspicious?"

"I wouldn't know. I'm just a paramedic. But I don't think it's that, anyway." He was pretty sure it wasn't that. But what if he was wrong and about to make an ass of himself all over again?

"What else could it be?"

Anderson decided to come clean. "I told her that I knew that she'd gone out with that major."

"Ah."

"Ah, what? I shouldn't have mentioned him, should I?"

"No, it's probably good that you did. What did she say?"

"She said she wasn't interested in him."

"Great. What's the problem, then?"

"I don't think it's that easy. That's when she mentioned her neighbor's house and asked me to come over."

Greg's voice filled with amusement. "Buddy, do you think Chelsea just did the same thing you did?"

"You've lost me."

"Do you think she needs a sounding board, or wants to see you?"

"I'm pretty sure she wants to see me."

"There's your answer, then."

Sometimes Greg's mile-a-minute speech left him feeling like he was struggling in remedial English. "I'm still lost, man. Sorry I didn't go to an Ivy League school like some people. What in the heck are you talking about?"

"First, I was asked to leave that Ivy League school after two semesters, so it really doesn't count."

Anderson drummed his fingers. "Still . . ."

"Still, what I'm saying is that Chelsea might *say* she wants to talk to you about the house but you're missing the point."

He was still in the trees. "What's that?"

"You idiot! That she could have told you about the neighbor over the phone but she asked you to come over. Now, here's your pep talk: before you waste any more time, take a shower and head over there."

Greg was right. "Okay, gotta go."

"You're welcome."

"Thanks, Greg, I—" He heard the bells in the background and finished, "Be careful."

"Yeah, you, too."

Striding to the shower, Anderson grinned to himself. Greg had unconsciously responded like he, too, was heading out into potential danger.

Unless Greg had been thinking one step ahead—again—and was cautioning him to be careful with Chelsea.

Turning on the shower full blast, he stepped into the cold spray. Of *course* that's what Greg had meant. He was an easygoing guy, but quick on the uptake.

A whole lot quicker than him.

*H*e knocked on the door forty minutes after Chelsea's call. On his way over, he ran into the grocery store and grabbed two pints of Blue Bell ice cream for Chelsea and a carton of Moose Tracks for Jack. Then he decided to run to the liquor store next door and pick up a six-pack of beer and a bottle of rosé. He'd almost added flowers into the mix but thought that might be coming on too strong. For some reason, flowers seemed a lot more personal than liquor and her favorite ice cream.

When Chelsea opened the door, she was wearing a pair of dark jeans, black flats, and a white fitted turtleneck. Her hair fell in loose waves around her shoulders, just the way she wore it in high school. She looked like an older, sexier version of the girl he'd once walked to every class.

"Sorry I'm late," he said. "But I did bring sustenance."

Her eyes widened as she took in the paper sack from the liquor store and the plastic bag of ice cream. "Is that Blue Bell?"

"It is. I got you Cookies 'n Cream and Rocky Road. And Moose Tracks for Jack."

"He loves that. How did you know?"

"He's a kid. I knew."

"And the paper bag?"

"What else? Beer and wine."

"You are being so good to me."

"And you, Chelsea Davis, are so easy to please." Leaning down, he pressed a kiss to her brow.

"So, what would you like?" he asked as he followed her into the kitchen. "Liquor or ice cream?"

"A glass of wine, I think. But maybe we could have a treat later?"

So she wanted to hang out for a while? He was completely down for that. "Yeah, that sounds good." Opening up the sack, he pulled out the bottle of rosé. "This okay? It's cold."

"That would be amazing." She pulled out a corkscrew and handed it to him, then opened the cupboard. "Do you want a glass or are you having a beer?" She looked over her shoulder. "Or water? Are you on call?"

"I'm not on call. So a beer would be great."

After they were situated, he looked around, saying, "Where's Jack?"

"At a sleepover. He doesn't do that very often, but his friend's family took him to a soccer game in the Springs."

"That sounds awesome."

"It is." She smiled. "His friend's older sister had other plans, so there was an extra ticket. Lucky, huh?"

"Yes," Anderson responded, almost smiling. It was obvious she was avoiding talking about why she'd asked him over, just like in high school when she didn't want to talk about something. It had taken him a while to figure out what she was doing, and even longer how to encourage her to speak her mind without him sounding like a pushy jerk.

Maybe he'd learned a few things over the years, or maybe he was still fumbling around. But he needed to do *something*.

She could talk about anything and everything all night unless he prodded her.

Hoping he'd learned to be more diplomatic in the last ten years, he said, "Chelsea, I know that you're worried about something."

"I know . . ."

"Well then, I think it would be better if you just came out and told me."

She smiled. "I guess some things never change, huh?"

He shrugged. "It does seem like you still worry about choosing the right words."

"And you still prefer to tackle a problem head-on."

"Maybe." He took a sip of his beer. "So . . ."

"So Camille needs a place to live."

So, that was what they were going to talk about. Okay, then. "Camille is your neighbor?"

"Right. See, I know her renovation is going to take some time, what with building inspectors and insurance claims and all the work itself."

"That's true. I've heard it can take as much as a year

after a fire." When she didn't reply, he said, "Is Camille's house what you're worried about?"

"Yes and no. I mean, yes, but that's not what I wanted to talk to you about."

"Chelsea, what is it?"

"I said she could move in with me and Jack."

He raised his eyebrows. "That's really kind of you." Instead of answering she took a sip of wine, and he added, "I didn't realize you were so close."

"We aren't." She frowned. "I mean, she's helped me with Jack over the years, and I've picked up groceries for her on occasion, but we don't spend a lot of time together otherwise. I mean, apart from at the senior center." She paused. "Huh, maybe we are kind of close?"

"Does she have nowhere else to go?"

"Unfortunately, she does. Her kids want her to move to a retirement community in Florida."

"Wow."

"I know, right? She's really upset."

"I'm sorry. I was actually thinking that that sounded pretty cool."

Chelsea threw him a look. "I can't believe you said that."

"Why not? My parents would love to retire someplace warm where they could play golf in the sun every day. But they'd never leave because we have so much family here."

"Well, Camille feels a little differently. She loves living in Woodland Park. She doesn't want to go but they're making her feel like they want to put her out to pasture."

"She should tell them that." Seeing that look again, he backtracked. "Okay, so she *has* told them that."

"Yes. They're using the fire as the perfect excuse to say she's mentally incompetent to make her own decisions."

"Ouch." That put a whole different spin on things.

"I know!" She sipped her wine before leaning forward. "They're being *awful* to her."

Her eyes were so filled with righteous anger he smiled. "So you've made up your mind?"

"Not exactly. See, I went to visit her at the hospital and one of her friends was there. Since I know them both, Frank kind of roped me into their conversation, and on the spur of the moment I invited her to come live with us. But she said I should take time to think about it."

He grinned. "Which is where I come in."

"Yes." She sighed. "What do you think I should do?"

"Have you talked it over with Jack?"

She nodded. "Jack said that it's fine with him. But he's just a little boy. He isn't going to think about the day-to-day implications."

"Which are?"

"Well, obviously, we're used to it being just the two of us in the house. Now the three of us would have dinner together. And maybe she'd want to watch TV or something while I was helping Jack with homework. I worry that he might get tired of sharing his space—or sharing me. And I'm worried about not having time to do enough for her—or trying to do too much and crowding her! And it's pretty uncomfortable to think of coming between Camille and her children."

"That's a lot of worries."

"Thanks for pointing that out."

So much for his attempt at humor.

She bit her lip. "Anderson, I want to help her, but I also don't want to disrupt our lives so much that I regret wanting to help her."

Man, she was still so sweet. It was what had drawn him to her in the first place, had drawn her to him again. Chelsea was yet again trying to do the right thing but second-guessing herself in case she'd overlooked some contingency.

However, if he knew anything about the woman in front of him, it was that she was strong. She could handle anything.

"I'm sorry, I can't tell you what to do. You're going to have to figure this out on your own."

She looked like he'd just kicked a puppy. "That's all you have to say?"

"I trust you're going to make the right decision no matter what. You don't need my two cents."

"I might."

He smiled slightly. "How about this, then? I'd like to tread lightly, since I'm trying to get back into your life, but Chels, I want you to give us a fair shot."

"I can't believe you brought that up again. I told you I'm not interested in Will."

He believed her . . . but he also knew that it was just a matter of time before another man saw how special she was. "I can't help it. Knowing another man got to take you out has been difficult for me."

"Is that what you're so worried about, Andy? Your competition?"

He weighed his words with care, wanting to show how much he valued her feelings, but still make it clear that he thought he was the best man for her and Jack.

"No. I'm worried about losing you before I even get the chance to show you that I'm better with you, and I believe you're better with me. We're better together."

"I told you that I thought we should go slow."

"I'm good with that." He smiled softly. "I just want you to go slow with me."

Her eyes widened before her expression warmed. "I hear what you're saying, 'kay?"

It wasn't what he wanted, but it was better than he'd feared. Reminding himself to not push, he leaned back. "Okay, back to Camille. If it's any consolation, I think you already know what you want to do."

"Really?"

"You extended the invitation, you've talked to Jack, and now you've talked to me about it. There must be something inside of you that feels good about offering Camille a place to stay. I think you should trust yourself."

"You're right."

Her voice was whisper-soft. And so sweet, it made him return to the past, when she was so shy that she blushed the first time he held her hand as they were walking down the school corridor.

In a stronger voice she said, "I'm going to tell Camille that I still want her to come here."

"You sound positive now."

"I was imagining how I would feel if I said no. I'd not only feel guilty but I'd worry about her." Twirling her wine-glass, she said, "Plus—and I know this is selfish—it might be really helpful to my schedule. Camille already watches Jack one afternoon a week, but this way she could do it more frequently." She paused. "Wow, that's really bad, isn't it? I mean, she's lost her home and I'm worried about child-care."

"I think you're being smart to think everything through."

She nodded. "Okay, then. Decision made."

"Good for you." He leaned back on the couch.

"Thanks so much for talking it through with me."

He loved the way she was looking at him—like he'd saved the day. Though he hadn't done anything more than validate her feelings, he couldn't deny he liked being some-one she needed. "No problem. I hope it goes okay."

"Me, too." She smiled at him. "I'll keep you updated."

This was the perfect time to remind her that he wanted to take her out on a date. "I'd like that. Maybe I could stop by to help sometimes. Or, if things go well with Camille and Jack, take you out."

A full second passed. Then she nodded.

"Yeah?"

"Yeah. I like the idea of us moving forward. I think it's time to stop apologizing and move on."

Moving on had a good ring to it. It was past time to stop

pulling out old hurts and concentrate on their future. "I like moving on, too."

Holding up her half-empty wineglass, she said, "Let's make it official. Here's to moving forward."

He gently tapped his beer bottle to her glass. "Cheers."

"Cheers." She set her glass down. Bit her bottom lip like she always did when she wasn't quite sure about what to do.

"Come here, Chels," he murmured, pulling her into his arms. She hesitated for a moment, then pressed her hands on his chest. Rested her face in his neck.

When she relaxed against him, he held her a little closer and pressed his lips to her head. There was that faint scent of honeysuckle again, spurring his memories, giving him hope.

"This is nice," she whispered.

"It is." He swallowed hard, suddenly emotional. He held her for a few seconds longer before reluctantly pulling away.

Confusion clouded her eyes before she smiled slightly. "I guess it's time for you to leave."

"Yeah." One day he was going to hold her in his arms all night long, but today was not that day.

Chapter 36

*I*t felt a little strange but also very right to collect Camille from the hospital with Anderson. She knew his medical knowledge would help in transporting her and answering any questions that arose about her care.

In addition, Chelsea was worried about leaving Camille alone while she went to Camille's house to collect any personal items she wanted—assuming they weren't damaged by the fire—and Anderson could do that for her.

Beyond all those practical reasons, though, was the simple realization that she liked being around him. He calmed her down when she got frazzled. He made things easy instead of harder. He also, just like all those years ago, was able to convey in one touch or look that she wasn't completely on her own. That he cared about her. He hadn't hesitated when she asked for help. She was so grateful for that.

"Are you nervous?" Anderson asked as they walked down the hall to Camille's hospital room. Today he had on tennis shoes, a pair of worn, soft khakis, and an even older green T-shirt with the word ARMY printed across his chest in bold, black letters. He looked like Anderson, casual, comfortable, and kind.

Which was probably why she decided to be so honest. "I'm petrified. At least Jack's at school and I can spend most of the day helping Camille get settled."

He stopped in his tracks. "Wait, petrified? I thought you said you and she got along well."

"We do! I'm worried about everything else. I've never looked after an older person before, or someone who's been in the hospital. Like, I want to encourage her recovery, but not push her to do too much. It seems kind of tricky to walk that line."

"I guess so, but you're going to be able to handle it. Plus, I'm always just a text or phone call away."

"Thanks. That really means a lot."

He shrugged off her words. "It's nothing. I would help anyone in Camille's situation. It's an honor to help her. So you're not putting me out."

His words did make her feel better. "Sorry, I guess I just don't want her to regret taking me up on the offer."

"She won't. Now, stop worrying and come on." He gave her an encouraging smile and she knocked lightly on Camille's door.

Chelsea was surprised to hear multiple voices in the room, some of which sounded agitated. When no one replied to the knock, she knocked louder, then carefully turned the handle.

She expected to find Camille all dressed and ready to go, speaking to a doctor or nurse about her discharge; instead, Camille was still in her hospital gown and a tattered robe, which was so very un-Camille-like.

The others in the room were two men and one woman who all looked so much alike that they could only be Camille's children.

When she and Anderson entered the room, all four people turned to stare at them.

"Yes?" the woman said impatiently.

After exchanging a quick glance with Camille, Chelsea took another step inside. "Hi, I'm Chelsea Davis. I'm one of Camille's neighbors." She walked farther into the room. "This is my friend Anderson Kelly."

"Hey," said Anderson. Though it was obvious that there was something else going on, he added, "We're here to take Camille home."

"Excuse me?" said one of the men, who was tall and balding.

Anderson simply rested his hands behind his back and looked right back at him.

The tension in the room increased.

Feeling foolish for not speaking directly to Camille, Chelsea said, "Are you feeling okay? Does the doctor want you to stay longer?"

"Not at all," Camille said. "Everything is fine, especially now that you're here."

"Mom, really?" the younger guy said.

"Chelsea, Anderson, please allow me to introduce you to three of my four very concerned children." Somehow managing to look haughty, even though her hair wasn't styled, she didn't have on any makeup, and she was wearing hospital clothes, Camille waved a hand. "This is Janie, Clayton, and Bo."

"Would you like us to come back in thirty minutes or so?" Chelsea asked.

"Not at all." Frowning at her kids, she added, "I'm sorry to say that you've just walked into a family disagreement. They're not pleased that I decided to go home with you instead of one of them."

"I see," Chelsea said, though she didn't see at all.

Janie, who was petite like her mother and also shared her pale-blonde hair, raised a placating hand. "Listen, I know this isn't a great first impression, so I'm sorry for that, but Mom isn't—"

"What she's trying to say," Clayton interrupted, "is that

while we're very grateful for your offer to give Mom shelter, we think it would be best if she lived with one of us. We know how to look after her."

Chelsea didn't like their condescending attitude. Camille was only in her midsixties and she was not only mentally competent but physically fit.

Nor did she like how her kids were practically shooing her and Anderson out the door.

That said, she realized that Janie was right about one thing. Camille was her friend, but that didn't mean that she knew everything about her life or her health.

She exchanged a glance with Anderson.

Bless him, he spoke right up. "Camille, ma'am, what would you like to do?"

Relief filled her eyes as she lifted her chin. "I would like to do what I'd planned. I would like to go home with Chelsea so I can supervise the repairs to my house."

That was all Chelsea needed to hear. "Well, all right then. Let's get you ready so we can be on our way. Where are your clothes?"

Camille looked at her children. "You said one of you would stop by my house?"

"I did, Mom," Bo said, speaking for the first time. "Luckily, the fire inspector and a cop were there. They let me go upstairs to get some of your things, but they warned me that no one else was going to be allowed in anytime soon. You're likely gonna have to go shopping."

Some of the light in her eyes dimmed. "I see. Well, where is what you did pick up?"

"It's out in the car. I'll go get it."

"Wait, Bo," Clayton barked. He turned to their mother. "Are you really sure about this?"

"Yes, absolutely."

"Mom's right," Bo said in his low, rough voice. "That's what I've been saying for an hour. It's for *her* to decide where she wants to live."

As soon as Bo was on his way, Chelsea tried to smooth things over. "Anderson is a paramedic, so he can help Camille if she has any medical emergencies. I mean, he's just a phone call away."

Clayton ignored her. "I understand that you don't like change, Mom, but I think you're making a big mistake," he said. "We could sell your house and use the money to set you up well in Sarasota. You'd be happy there if you'd just give it a chance."

"I'll be set up well *here* just as soon as the house is repaired. I've made up my mind."

Janie threw up her hands. "I love you, Mom, but this just isn't right," she said, and as Chelsea watched in shock, she walked out of the room without a word of good-bye.

"Don't worry, Chelsea," said Camille. "Janie doesn't like not getting her way. She'll come around in time."

Looking glum, Clayton handed Chelsea his business card. "My cell phone number is on there. Would you please text me your number later?"

"Of course."

"Thanks." He took his mom's hand and said, "Even if you don't want to move across the country, we'd be really happy to have you with us."

"I know that, but I'll be happy at Chelsea's. Try not to worry so much, Clay. Trust me."

Bo returned with his mother's bag, and a few minutes later both of her sons left.

"Well, there you have it," Camille said. "My loving brood."

Camille's voice was so sarcastic, Chelsea couldn't help but smile. "I'm sure they mean well."

"Indeed. Now, come help me sort through what Bo brought."

"I'll go out to the nurses' station and see what they need in order to discharge you," Anderson said.

Chelsea smiled at him. "Thanks."

When they were alone, Chelsea unzipped the bag and

found quite a few outfits neatly folded inside. "He did a good job, I think."

"It seems so." After picking out a soft, pale-pink sweat-suit, Camille got to her feet and slowly walked into the bathroom to change.

Grateful for a moment to herself, Chelsea sat down on the edge of Camille's bed. She couldn't stop thinking about the way Janie had stormed out of the room, like a teenager flouncing off to sulk.

"The nurse said the discharge papers are all in order," Anderson said on his return. "All they were waiting for was us to come get her." Lowering his voice, he added, "It seems the whole floor knew that Camille's three children were being obnoxious."

"I hated being in the middle, but oh my gosh! They were awful."

"They really were." He rolled his eyes. "I don't get why they're being such jerks. You did good, though."

She smiled up at him. "So did you." Chelsea kept a smile on her face when Camille came out of the bathroom, dressed. She tried to appear calm and positive while a nurse gave Camille her discharge instructions, while they gathered her things, and when they drove back to the house.

Only then did Chelsea start to worry that Camille might break down when she saw the condition of her home. Instead, she only pursed her lips and said, "It's a real mess, isn't it?"

"Yes, ma'am," Anderson replied. "But houses can get fixed."

Camille smiled. "Indeed they can. A whole lot more easily than people. I'm very grateful I wasn't injured any worse."

Feeling a bit more relaxed, Chelsea led Camille inside her house and up to the small guest bedroom at the top of the stairs. "This will be your room, Miss Camille."

Camille stopped in the doorway, and stood, staring.

It must seem pretty depressing, Chelsea guessed. "I know it's not much, but I actually got a new mattress for that bed last year, so I know it's comfortable. And Jack and I cleaned out the closet for you." Increasingly nervous, she started talking even faster. "I promise, tomorrow or the next day, we'll go over and see what else of yours we can bring to make it feel more like home."

"Chelsea dear, I'm not upset. Not in the slightest! Actually, I was just standing here thinking how blessed I am to have a sweet girl like you in my life. Everything is perfect."

"It's far from that, but Jack and I have talked, and we're going to do our best to give you everything you need, including privacy."

"Please don't worry about a thing. Now, I'm going to have a little rest. Why don't you go back downstairs and visit with your guy?" She lowered her voice. "By the way, he is very handsome, scars and all."

Chelsea couldn't help but laugh. "He sure is. To be honest, I never even notice his scars anymore."

"That's how it should be, I think. All of us are more than our flaws, don't you agree?"

Chelsea felt a lump form in her throat. She and Anderson had both made mistakes. They weren't perfect, but those imperfections made them unique. "Yes, ma'am," she said softly. "And, that's true of generals, too."

Camille's cheeks turned pink. "Touché, dear."

Chelsea smiled. "I'll be back in a little bit."

"Take your time."

*How's she doing?" Anderson asked when Chelsea met him in the living room.

"Okay, I think. She didn't seem to mind that the bedroom's nothing fancy."

"It's obvious that she's grateful to be here. Now, come here."

She walked into his open arms and leaned her head against his chest, enjoying again how strong and solid he felt. This is what she'd been missing, she realized. Someone to lean on. "I really am glad you came with me."

"Me, too."

In no hurry to tell him good-bye, she murmured, "Jack will be home soon. Do you want to stay for dinner? It's just pork chops and two veggies, but there's plenty for four people."

"Thanks, but I'll take a rain check. I promised my parents that I'd stop by tonight."

"Oh, of course." She pulled away.

"Hey," said Anderson, "what just happened?" He brushed a loose strand of hair from her face.

"Oh, I just realized that everything between us must have affected how your parents see me."

Resting his palms on her shoulders, he shook his head. "It didn't."

She didn't see how that was possible. As a teenager, she'd spent almost as much time at his house as hers. More than once his mother had said that Chelsea was like another daughter to her. "Are you sure?"

"You have to remember that I had broken things off with you first. My mom didn't blame you for anything. She would've been happy if we got married before I went to basic training, just like those couples in World War Two."

"That's funny. My mother, no, but I think my father would've been okay with us marrying so young, too. I remember him saying he was in no hurry to get to know another guy all over again."

Looking into her eyes, he said, "Here's the thing. I'm glad we weren't 1940s sweethearts. I'm glad we didn't get married right out of high school. We would've probably been miserable. I was cocky and full of myself. I needed to grow up."

The truth of his words struck her deeply. His honest insight helped all the regrets she'd held so deep in her heart heal a little more. "I did, too. Besides, if we'd gotten married, I would have never had Jack."

"Which would be a shame, because he's a cool guy."

"I think so, too."

"So, don't go worrying about my parents!"

"Well, tell them hello."

"I will. Don't forget, they still want to have you and Jack over one day."

"I won't forget."

He stepped forward. "There's something I can't forget," he murmured as he curved a hand around her jaw. "And that's what it felt like to do this." He gently lifted her chin. And claimed her lips.

She hadn't forgotten those kisses, either. From his hand cupping her jaw, as though he was afraid she'd pull away, to the way her body melted against his, Chelsea hadn't forgotten a single detail about kissing Anderson.

Just like in years past, she raised her arms and curved her hands around his neck. Opened her lips when he deepened the kiss.

And sighed with regret when he finally pulled away.

"Man," he murmured, "are you okay?"

"Oh yes. What about you?" she teased.

His cheeks flushed as he chuckled softly. "I'm not sure. I've been dying to kiss you again, but I wasn't expecting that today."

"Me, neither." Her limbs felt languid, her head a little buzzed, like she'd just sipped too much champagne too fast.

She had enjoyed other kisses, she wasn't going to lie about that.

But there was something just plain different about a kiss from Anderson Kelly. It was more familiar, more emotional, more everything. No, it felt like coming home.

Chapter 37

J'm here!" Anderson called out as he stepped inside his parents' sprawling house. When no one answered, he shook his head. This was typical. His mom and dad had bought the huge house out of foreclosure. Though he and his brother and sister had tried to talk them out of it, their parents had insisted it was their dream house.

Now they said it was also their money pit, fitness center, and the reason they no longer went on vacations. There was simply too much to do.

Every year they picked a room to remodel, if only to update the faded oak woodwork and scratched ceramic tile, but they couldn't help redecorating, too. The problem was that neither of his parents had very good instincts. The result was a mishmash of styles and decor, some more successful than others.

They were currently working on the bathroom in the basement. Which was probably why no one had answered the door.

After pulling off his muddy Sorels, he padded down the hall toward the kitchen, where two Crock-Pots were going full blast and something that smelled like barbecue chicken was warming in the oven.

His mouth watered in response. His mom might not be able to decorate very well, but she was an excellent cook!

"Hello?" he called out again. When there was still no answer, he shouted, "It's me! Anderson!"

"In the basement, honey!" his mother called. "Come on down."

"'Kay." After spearing a pair of green beans out of the Crock-Pot with a fork, he headed downstairs.

Halfway down the steep wooden staircase he heard the distinct sound of Rascal Flatts crooning. That told him two things: his father wasn't home (he wasn't a country fan) and his mother was doing something she didn't like (Rascal Flatts seemed to calm her nerves).

Just as the group belted out the final chorus of "Bless the Broken Road" he found her on a step stool stripping the god-awful paisley wallpaper. When he saw her wobble as she stretched for a piece of wallpaper just beyond her reach, he hurried to stand beside her. "Mom, hop on down off that. You're going to get hurt."

She met his eyes in the mirror. "I've got my tennis shoes on. I'm fine."

"Tennis shoes won't help you if you fall off the stool. Now come down. I'll get the last of that paper."

"Fine." Taking his hand, she stepped down like she was descending a marble staircase. "You don't have to do this, you know."

"I know." He also knew that there was no way on earth he was going to stand there and watch his mother balance on a step stool. Which reminded him: "Where's Dad?"

"He had to run to the store. I didn't have any vanilla ice cream."

He looked down from his new perch on the step. "You could have texted me. I would've picked it up on my way over."

"I know, but your father was eager to get out of the house." She smiled. "I don't know why."

Pulling off a long strip coated with Downy, he grinned. "Me, neither."

"He'll be back soon. Besides, even I'm getting tired of singing along with Gary LeVox."

"Don't tell Dad that," he joked.

"Don't worry. If I say it once he'll never let me forget it."

She picked up a trash bag and started filling it with pieces of wet wallpaper. "So, where've you been today?" Her voice was studiously nonchalant, but he knew that tone as well as he knew that their constant decorating was never going to end.

"It's kind of a long story."

"I'm listening . . ."

"All right, then." He took a deep breath. "I was with Chelsea Davis all afternoon."

"I knew it!" She grinned like she'd just won the lottery.

"What did you know?" he asked suspiciously.

"Only that it was just a matter of time before you two got back together."

"She asked if I'd go to the hospital to help bring home an elderly neighbor."

She beckoned with the universal signal for *tell me more*. "And why did she need your help with that?"

Briefly, he told her about Camille's friendship with Chelsea and Jack and her house almost burning down.

"That poor woman. It's so good of Chelsea to have her over. I guess she doesn't have any family nearby?"

"Well, she does, but they're not exactly getting along right now."

"Oh? What's the problem?" His mom was all attention, delighted to hear more even though she'd never met Camille and maybe never would. His mother was always interested in human nature.

"Apparently they want her to move to a retirement community in Florida."

She frowned. "It's so hot and humid there."

He pulled off another strip of paper. "Yes, ma'am, it is."

"Okay, I guess that was obvious. But if she's happy here in Woodland Park, what's the conflict? I mean, that's the important thing, to find a place to be happy."

His mother was a smart woman. "I don't know the whole story, but Camille wants to stay in town and Chelsea will be putting her up for a while, while her house gets repaired."

"I wish I would've known. They could all have come over for supper."

His parents really were the best, but that might have sent Chelsea over the edge. She was still worried about seeing his parents, still fretting that they blamed her for breaking his heart. Of course they didn't, but he wasn't going to push Chelsea to see them until she was ready. They already had enough to worry about. "Camille was ready for a rest and Chelsea was pretty busy making sure she had everything she needed," he explained. "Maybe another night."

"I hope so. Do you think she'd be upset if I asked her myself?"

"No, ma'am." An invitation straight from his mother would go a long way toward easing her nerves.

"So, I guess things are going well with Chelsea? And Jack likes you, too?"

"Hey, Dad's home." Anderson pointed up toward the sound of footsteps above them.

"He'll come down when he's ready. Now, don't change the subject."

"We need to change the subject."

She rolled her eyes. "Come on now, it's not like I don't know her."

"Things are different now and you know that." Hearing his father on the stairs, he called, "Dad, come give me a hand!"

His mother propped a hand on her hip. "I'm well aware you and Chelsea are a few years older, but I promise, neither of you has changed that much."

"Mom, I don't want to discuss this."

"It's time, though. Past time, I think." Looking as if she was about to offer a revelation, she continued, "Look at you. You have a few scars, but—"

"Leave the boy alone," his father groaned as he joined them.

She opened her mouth, then seemed to think the better of it. "Fine," she said with a sigh.

Anderson grinned. "Saved by my father."

"Your meddling father," she whispered.

"Andy, is your mother making you pull wallpaper?"

It wasn't like he could lie about that. "Yes, sir."

His mother put a hand on her hip. "Porter, things were going just fine before you joined us. You're being a little rude."

"I'm not being rude at all. You two should come on up and relax. And Missy, let me remind you that Anderson came over for supper, not honey-dos. I'm turning off Rascal Flatts, too. I can't take it anymore."

With a grin, Anderson climbed down off the step stool. "Looks like it's time for a break, Mom."

"I suppose." Gazing at the bare wall, she smiled. "We did make a lot of progress though, didn't we?"

"We sure did. It's gonna look great. I can't wait to tell Carter you're finally taking the paper off."

"I'm sure he'll have something to say about that," she murmured. After clicking off the speaker and turning off the bathroom light, she led Anderson up the stairs.

They found Porter Kelly in the kitchen eating a plate of beans.

"Porter!"

"Sorry. I'm starving." He set the plate down and gave Anderson a hug. "You should come over more often. It's obvious that you're needed."

Anderson hugged his father back, thinking that with each year his dad felt a little smaller than when he was growing up, certain that his father was the biggest man around. "Get the ice cream?"

"I did. Your mother made strawberry shortcake. You want a beer?"

"Coors, if you got one."

"I always have one of those." He looked back at his mom. "Missy, can we eat, honey?"

"Of course. The table's all set. I've just been waiting on you."

And so it continued. His parents lightly fussed, served too much food, and treated him like he was something special.

They'd done that ever since he joined the army, and it was the same way they treated Carter whenever he was stationed back home. Their doting didn't stop with the boys, either. They pulled out the same red carpet for his sister, Kim, who was a financial advisor.

He'd grown up secure in his parents' love and acceptance. He'd taken so much for granted!

"You're awfully quiet tonight, Andy," his mother said. "Are you worried about Camille and Chelsea?"

"Who's Camille?" Dad asked.

"I'll fill you in later," Mom said. "Is that the problem?"

"No. Actually, I was just sitting here thinking about how spoiled I've been."

His dad frowned in puzzlement. "What's that supposed to mean?"

"Not spoiled in a bad way. Maybe it's more like blessed. You are just really great parents."

His mother blushed. "We tried our best. That's all."

Anderson debated whether to share what was on his mind with the two people who had never wavered in their support of him. But since he'd already started down this path, he figured he might as well continue. "I really like Chelsea's son, Jack."

"I'm sure he's very likable," Dad said. "Chelsea is a wonderful woman."

"His birth father isn't in the picture. I don't think Chelsea's even gotten financial support from him. She says she's not upset about it, but . . ."

Mom nodded. "Well, she has had her parents around. I'm sure they've stepped up."

"I think so." He turned his fork over a few times before saying what he was really thinking. "It's good they did, since she was all alone. Lately, I've been feeling really guilty about how I acted. I should've been there for her when she told me she was pregnant."

His parents exchanged looks. "You might not like hearing this," his mother said, "but I disagree. And it does no good to rewrite the past."

"I'm not rewriting the past," Anderson said defensively. "I'm trying to tell you something." No, he was trying to do more than that. He was taking responsibility for his mistake.

His father coughed. "Andy, going into the military was a really good thing for you. You served with honor, learned important skills, and even made some lifelong friends. What do you think you'd be doing now if you hadn't signed up?"

"Or worse," Mom chimed in, "quit because of some misplaced guilt?"

"I'm not saying I should have quit. But I let Chelsea down, and I have been feeling guilty about that."

"What happened was meant to happen. You went into the army as Andy Kelly, the star quarterback with a chip on his shoulder. Six months later, Anderson Kelly greeted us at the airport."

"I wasn't all *that* different."

"You were, honey," his mother said. "It's not just that you were two inches taller and twenty pounds heavier, but you held yourself so straight and proud, it was a sight to see. The army turned you into the man that you became."

"That's not my point—"

"That's exactly the point." Dad sighed. "Son, you were meant to be a soldier, just as you were meant to be a firefighter-paramedic. The Lord gave you this path and you've done Him proud. Just as Chelsea took the path she was meant to take."

"I feel like I did Chelsea wrong. I never should've broken up with her in the first place." Before either one of them could interrupt, he added, "I never should've been so mean and judgmental when she wrote to me, either. I mean, who was I to judge? I knew plenty of guys who had one-night stands and never lost sleep worrying whether the woman got pregnant."

"Do you remember what I told you then?" Mom asked.

"You said that you were disappointed with me but you understood."

"I also said that when kids start making adult choices, they have to accept that there are adult consequences. As much as I wished you would've handled things differently, I wasn't going to try to push you two back together. Even mothers shouldn't get in the middle of other people's relationships."

"I appreciate what you're saying, but, Chelsea—"

"Anderson, do you really think you could have swooped in and saved the day?" she asked. "You were practically a kid, just like she was. Plus, Chelsea was strong and capable even then. She probably didn't want you to 'fix' things for her."

"No, she didn't," he murmured. Thinking of back then—and of all that had happened since—he looked from her to his father and back. "Do you think it's too late for us?"

"Not at all," his mom replied. "I think the right time might be now . . . if you're brave enough to stop worrying about things you can't change."

His mom was right. He'd long ago accepted the scars on his body. If he could accept those visible imperfections, surely he should be able to accept his past actions, too. "It isn't too late at all," he murmured.

"You're twenty-eight," his father said drily. "I think you might have a couple of good years left."

"You're right. You're both right."

"All we're trying to do is help you finally leave the past behind. You're home now, right?"

He knew what his dad meant. He'd left home, fought, been injured, and gotten out safely despite his scars, internal as well as external. "I'm starting to realize that the scars I've been wearing on my skin aren't the only ones I've collected."

"And the scars you've received from fighting overseas aren't the only ones you've earned," his mother said quietly. "But don't forget: you're healed now."

"Thanks," he said, though it really didn't convey everything he was feeling.

"You're welcome," Mom said as she got to her feet. "Now, may we please eat the lovely, calorie-laden strawberry shortcake with ice cream?"

"Yes, ma'am." He grinned. Sometimes there was only one thing to say.

Later that night, he gave Chelsea a call. When she answered on the first ring, her voice sleepy and soft, he winced. "Shoot, did I wake you?"

"No, I was just watching TV."

"Another Hallmark movie?"

She laughed softly. "Maybe."

"I think it's cute that you like those sappy movies so much."

"Don't knock my movies until you've tried them. It's nice to have something easy to watch."

"I just called to see how things are going with Camille. Do you need anything?"

"I don't think so."

"How about with Jack? Do you need help getting him to baseball practice? I have the next two days off."

"You know . . . what if I said yes?"

He smiled. "If you said yes, that would mean you're going to let me help you. And that would make me very happy."

"If you take Jack tomorrow, you could come over after. I mean, if you want to."

If? He wanted nothing more than to spend time with her. Time with her *and* Jack. "That sounds good."

"Pick him up at eleven, if that's okay?"

"That's fine. I'll see you then. Enjoy your movie."

"Thanks." Her voice warmed, sounding almost silky. "I mean, thanks for everything, Anderson. I'm starting to wonder how I'd be doing if we hadn't reconnected."

"You're a strong woman. I'm sure you'd be good."

"You know what I mean."

"Yeah. I do. I absolutely do." If they hadn't reconnected he'd still be feeling half-empty. And would still be thinking about the girl he used to love—and how he'd let everything they'd had slip away.

Chapter 38

Now that she was settled in her new temporary home, Camille felt a little bit at loose ends. Chelsea had made sure to tell her to make herself at home, but she wasn't sure how to do that without getting in their way.

That's why she found herself sitting on her neatly made bed with the door closed, wondering when she should come out. She could hear the TV on low and Chelsea and Jack talking over it, so she knew they were awake, but she remembered such precious little moments with her own children, and she didn't want to intrude.

Suddenly she heard Jack calling, "Miss Camille? Are you okay?"

She opened the door. "Of course. Why do you ask?"

"'Cause we've been waiting for you to come out of your room. Mom thought you'd be an early riser."

Now she just felt foolish. Why was she being so tentative? "I was just waiting for you to come get me," she teased.

Jack grinned. "You're funny, Miss Camille."

"So are you." She lightly ruffled his hair. "Now how about you show me where the coffee cups are?"

"Over here," he said as he led her to the kitchen. Chelsea was standing near the coffee machine, holding a large cup between her hands. "Good morning," she said.

"Good morning to you, dear."

"Miss Camille wants some coffee, Mom," Jack said.

"Of course." Extending a bright-red mug, she fired off a series of questions. "Did you sleep well? How are you feeling? Are you dizzy? Oh wait, I'll get it for you." And she pulled back the mug.

"I'm feeling much better this morning, no dizziness at all. And I don't want you to serve me—I can pour myself a cup of coffee."

"All right, then." Chelsea pointed to a pair of white ceramic containers in the shape of milk cartons. "The sugar and cream are in here."

"Thank you." After taking the mug, Camille carefully lifted the handle of the carafe and poured. Pleased when she didn't spill a drop, she added a splash of cream.

She sat down at the table next to Jack. "What kind is that?" she asked, gesturing to his cereal bowl.

"Cinnamon Toast Crunch."

She raised her eyebrows in mock surprise. "You have that at home? What a surprise."

Chelsea chuckled. "I decided to pick my battles."

"Mom said she's not gonna buy it *all* the time, because it's not good for me."

"Maybe tomorrow I'll make us some pancakes."

"Really?"

Chelsea joined them at the table. "Camille, you don't need to do any cooking. Don't forget that the nurse said you've got to take it easy for the next few days."

"I haven't forgotten." She picked up her cup and sipped. "This is delicious—strong, like I like it." She took another sip and sighed happily. Nothing tasted better than morning coffee. "Chelsea, are you off to work?"

"No, I took the day off."

Camille shook her head. "There's no need for that," she protested. She didn't want to be any more of a burden than she already was! "You heard the nurses. All I need to do is take it easy. I can do that without supervision."

"I don't want to supervise you," Chelsea said. "Actually, I thought I could help you make a list of things you need, then do a little bit of shopping."

Oh dear, there was no way she was going to let this young woman do one more thing for her. "Certainly not. I am just fine."

Chelsea's eyebrows lifted. "Camille, no offense, but I heard what Bo said. You aren't going to be allowed inside for at least a couple of days."

"I'll make do with what I have."

"There's no reason for that. I'm happy to pick up a few things. It will be fun. I can get you another outfit or two, and maybe even some moisturizer, makeup, a new nightgown . . . whatever you want."

"This is so kind of you." The reality of what had happened was hitting her yet again.

"It's not a problem at all. There must be a few things you wish you had on hand. Write it all down for me."

When Camille continued to hesitate, Chelsea said, "Listen, either you give me a list of what you need or I'm going to guess. I think we both know you don't want that."

"I'd listen to my mom," Jack piped up. "She'll buy you the worst stuff just to make you wish you would've been honest."

Meeting Chelsea's gaze, Camille chuckled and said, "Well, I can't have that now, can I?"

"No, ma'am."

"All right then, but you must promise that you'll let me pay for them. I can give you my debit card."

"That's perfectly fine. Now, don't be afraid to write a good list, okay? I'm going to go to Walmart and down to the mall in Colorado Springs."

"Are you going, too, Jack?" She certainly hoped he wasn't going to have to sit home with her.

"Nope, I have baseball practice today."

"That sounds like fun."

"Uh-huh."

"How are you going to get to practice? Is one of your friends going to take you?"

"Actually, Anderson volunteered to take him. He'll be here around eleven."

Chelsea's voice was so smooth, Camille glanced at Jack— who, as she'd expected, looked kind of amused.

Well, that made two of them. All Camille had needed to see was the way that man gazed at Chelsea at the hospital to know that there was something special between them. She wondered when Chelsea was going to realize that Anderson Kelly was completely smitten with her . . . and that she might be the only person who didn't know it.

"Since Jack's birthday is just around the corner, I'm going to do a little bit of birthday shopping, too," Chelsea added.

"It's in less than a month, you know," Jack added.

Camille grinned. "Believe me, I know." They'd discussed his birthday many times while she'd sat with him after school. "Have you decided what you want yet, Jack?"

"Uh-huh. New cleats."

"He wants *Nikes*," Chelsea said. She was trying to sound put out, but it was obvious that she was planning to get them.

"Goodness," Camille said. "I suppose I'll have to come see them in action."

The boy's eyes lit up. "You want to come to one of my games?"

"Of course I do. I love to watch baseball."

Furrowing his brow, he said, "Have you ever gone to a ball game *in person*, Miss Camille?"

"Believe it or not, I have. Don't forget, I used to have

four children at home. I attended my fair share of ballet recitals, band concerts, and sports."

"Which ones?"

"Clayton played soccer and lacrosse. But Bo was baseball crazy. What position do you play?"

"Catcher."

"You must have good knees."

"Uh-huh. I'm good at catching balls, too."

"Yes, that's important."

Chelsea opened the refrigerator and pulled out a bowl of cut-up fruit. "I made this earlier. There's also milk, cereal, and bread for toast. Oh, and eggs." She worried her bottom lip. "You should also make a grocery list, so we have stuff you like."

"I'll be fine, dear. And don't forget, I'm used to ordering groceries and fending for myself. I can do that for all of us."

Jack grinned. "It's going to be great having you here, Miss Camille."

"You know, Jack, I was just thinking the same thing."

Chapter 39

*I*t had taken a good fifteen minutes for Chelsea to say good-bye to him and Jack. Only when Anderson pointed to the clock and Jack said she was going to make him have to run laps for being late did Chelsea let them out the door.

Anderson had managed to keep his mouth shut but he'd been pretty amused. Was Chelsea always so reluctant to let her son leave, he wondered, or was it because Anderson was taking him?

After he'd loaded Jack in the car and pulled down the road, Anderson glanced sideways at him. Jack was wearing a dark-blue ball cap facing backward, baseball pants, cleats, and a green T-shirt. "You good, buddy?"

"Yeah."

"I don't think we'll be late. If the coach gets upset you can blame me."

The boy slowly smiled. "I'll be fine. I only said that so my mom would let us leave. The coach doesn't get mad if you're late every once in a while. Only if you're always late."

"That sounds like the coaches I had when I was your age."

"Later on you get in trouble if you're late, right? A couple of my friends said that happens to their older brothers."

Thinking about some of the football coaches he'd had back in the day, Anderson nodded. "Yep. By the time I got to high school, being on time meant being five minutes early."

"I'm gonna do that, too."

"That's actually a good habit to have. When I was in the army, knowing how to be on time helped a lot. A soldier doesn't get too far if he can't be somewhere when he's supposed to." When he stopped at the light, he winked at Jack. "Turns out that's important when you're a firefighter, too."

Jack's tentative smile widened. "I bet."

Seeing the ballpark up ahead, he said, "How long is your practice?"

"An hour. My mom usually sits in the car and reads or does emails and stuff."

"Okay. Hey, I'll probably stick around, if that's allowed."

"Sure," Jack said, but he didn't sound sure at all.

"Is that all right with you?"

Jack's smile had faded. "Yeah, just . . . Why would you want to do that?"

Anderson kept his gaze firmly on the road. "Oh, I don't know. I like baseball. And I think it would be fun to watch you catch." As he pulled into the parking lot he added, "Unless you don't want me to. If you'd rather I didn't stay, I won't. It's up to you, bud."

Jack seemed to be thinking hard. "I guess it's okay," he said, fiddling with his shirt cuff. "I'm not real good, though."

"I understand. Don't worry, I won't yell or anything. I promise."

"Okay." At least he was smiling again.

Anderson pulled into a parking space. "I'll help you get your gear and then you can go, yeah?"

"Yeah." Jack scrambled out of the passenger seat and met Anderson at the back of his SUV. Anderson easily lifted out the black bag with all his catcher's equipment and bats and

Jack put the handles over his shoulders, carrying it kind of like a backpack.

"You good?"

"Yeah." He started to walk away, then stopped abruptly. "Thanks for taking me."

Looked like Chelsea had done a little bit of coaching herself. Anderson fought back a smile. "You're welcome. It's my pleasure."

Anderson saw quite a few other boys just getting out of their cars, so he guessed they weren't running late at all. Maybe they were right on time.

"Hey, Anderson?"

"Yep?"

"I guess you really like my mom, huh?"

Whoa. Well, there it was. He'd been half expecting an interrogation, but when Jack didn't ask him anything on the way over, he figured he was in the clear until the ride home. Maybe it was better this way because there wasn't any time to hem and haw and wonder about finding the right words.

"I really do." Meeting Jack's blue eyes, he spoke slowly, just to make sure the boy didn't mistake what he was about to say. "As you know, she and I go back a long way."

"Mom told me that she used to love you."

And there went his pulse rate, spiking as intensely as if he were in enemy territory without a weapon to defend himself. "I used to love her, too." He paused, then decided to go all in. "Fact is, I'm pretty sure I love her now. She's really great. You should be proud to have a mother like her."

"She's pretty."

"She is. She's always been pretty . . . but that's not why I love her."

Jack looked up at him, his lips slightly parted. Though he stayed silent, it was evident that he was hanging on every word.

Kelly, do not *mess this up.* "I love her because she's smart and tough and doesn't give up. Because she's kind to people like Camille, and she's funny and, well, because she's the type of woman to raise a boy like you."

"Like me?"

"Yep, you're pretty great, Jackson Henry Davis. One day, I hope you'll consider me a friend." He cleared his throat. "Now, you'd best get a move on, huh?"

Jack took a couple of steps, then turned back around. "Are you still going to stay?"

Feeling like everything had just slid into place, Anderson nodded. "Oh yeah. I'm not going anywhere." When Jack grinned before hurrying off to his teammates, Anderson finally allowed himself to smile. He might not know anything about this fatherhood thing, but so far he didn't think he'd messed up too bad.

He climbed the metal bleachers and took a seat near the end of the top row, where he settled in to watch the kids practice.

"Hi," another man said as he sat down a few rows below Anderson. "Which one is yours?"

"I'm here for Jack. He's the catcher," Anderson said simply. "You?"

"My boy is that sandy-haired kid on second." The man pointed to the boy who was tossing his leather mitt in the air. "He loves the game."

"Jack does, too."

Just then the coach started calling out directions. Jack looked up into the bleachers and gave Anderson a small wave.

Anderson gave him a small salute back.

*A*n hour and a half later, Anderson pulled onto Chelsea's driveway and turned off the ignition. Before they got out, he decided to touch base with Jack again. "Your mom said I could come over for a while. Is that all right with you?"

"Yep, she told me you might stay awhile if you had time."

"You're gonna have a lot to tell your mom and Camille," Anderson said as they got out of the car. "You hit a double and it was awesome."

Jack grinned. "I got an out, too. The coach said I'm getting to be a better catcher."

He headed for the front door, and Anderson whistled low. "You forgot your stuff, buddy."

"Oh. Yeah." He returned to the rear of the SUV, where Anderson had opened the door. "My mom usually carries this in for me."

"Maybe you can start doing that yourself, yeah? You're old enough to carry your own stuff."

Jack looked a little put out, but he silently hefted the bag.

Anderson lagged a step behind, letting the boy be the one to open the door and lug his equipment bag into the house.

"Mom!"

"Don't yell, Jack. And don't toss your bag down in the middle of the hall," Chelsea called out.

"I'll get it later," Jack said.

Before Chelsea could answer, Anderson shook his head and said quietly, "Pick it up and put it where your mother wants it." To his relief, Jack picked up the bag again and, to his greater relief, Chelsea didn't look mad that he'd stepped in.

After the boy headed to his room, she smiled at him. "Thanks for backing me up. I don't know how many times I've gotten on his case for dropping his things in the middle of the floor."

This feels so right, thought Anderson, *coming home to Chelsea and working as a team.* "I figured," he said. "Lord knows my mother told me the same sort of thing many times. But if I overstep, never be afraid to let me know."

"I won't." She looked up at him and smiled.

Which gave him the perfect opportunity to lean down

and kiss her lightly on the lips. "How was your shopping trip?"

She blinked. "It was good. Want to come into the kitchen and get a drink while I tell you all about it?"

"Yep." He followed her, liking how she looked in a pair of white jean shorts, a navy long-sleeved T-shirt, and bare feet.

Chelsea talked about Walmart and Camille and some sale over at Kohl's while he got himself a glass of water and leaned against the counter, listening.

After ten minutes, she grimaced. "Oh my gosh. I've been going on and on about stuff you probably couldn't care less about. I'm sorry."

"Nothing to apologize for. I want to hear about everything."

"You're serious, aren't you?"

When he nodded, she blushed, just like she used to do back when they were kids.

And just like all those years ago, he thought there was no better sight to see.

Tenderness filled him. He loved being the man who could still make her blush. No, the man who could still make her happy. Reaching for her hand, he linked his fingers through hers. "Now, what else did you all do?"

When she started talking again, he rubbed his thumb along her knuckles and imagined coming home to moments like this all the time. He prayed it wasn't too much to hope for.

Chapter 40

*T*wo weeks later, when Camille knocked on the door of her office, Chelsea knew the woman was up to something. After all, they now ate breakfast together every morning and sometimes even exchanged little notes, reminding each other about their late-afternoon schedules.

Actually, they'd become good friends. Camille was not only helpful with Jack, she also was an excellent sounding board. Now, several times a week, they'd sit in the living room together after Jack had gone to bed and simply talk about life. Chelsea had counseled Camille to give her children time to come around while Camille had encouraged Chelsea to be kinder to herself and not feel so guilty if she had to leave work early to take care of Jack . . . or if she was ten minutes late to pick up Jack from baseball practice.

They really were helping each other out.

All in all there was no reason for Camille to need to speak to her privately at the senior center . . . unless she wanted to make sure they were having a private conversation away from little ears.

"Chelsea, do you have a minute?" Camille asked that morning.

"Of course, but you know you don't have to knock. Just come on in." Chelsea paused, feeling puzzled. "Or you could have just told me whatever was on your mind over breakfast this morning."

Camille stepped inside, but didn't sit down in one of the two comfortable chairs in the corner of Chelsea's space. "I probably could've done that, but I wanted to think about how to phrase this."

Uh-oh. That sounded ominous. Was Camille upset about cooking so much? Had Jack been disrespectful? Or, perhaps, something new had happened with her children? "Camille, what is it?"

Camille folded her hands demurely in front of her loose-fitting sweater and leggings. "It's this . . . I think you need to start doing some of that dating we talked about."

Chelsea stared at Camille, surprised. "Anderson and I have been seeing quite a bit of each other."

"You have, but always with Jack in tow—and sometimes even with me, too."

"We like being with you and Jack."

"I'm glad, dear . . . but it's time you went out on a proper date." She smiled slightly. "Like, in the evening."

Anderson had said the same thing, Chelsea thought with a twinge, but he hadn't mentioned it in weeks. "I'm just following his lead."

"Dear, you need some straight talk."

Chelsea was beginning to be very glad she was sitting down. "About what?"

"Anderson is falling in love with you, if he hasn't already."

"Camille!"

"Listen, I'm making a point, which is that he's not going to do anything to mess things up with you. That means he's going to spend his time with you and Jack together until *you* tell him otherwise."

"You're serious."

"I'm very serious. And, just as importantly, Jack feels the same way."

Chelsea was so stunned, she didn't even try to argue. "You and Jack have been talking about us?"

"Oh yes. We've discussed it at some length. You need to give Anderson a call and ask him out." She smiled. "And when you're doing that, make sure he knows that you're talking about just the two of you. You need some alone time."

This was becoming really awkward, really fast. Chelsea felt her cheeks heating up. "I don't know. I mean, wouldn't Anderson have said something?"

"He wouldn't. Now, pick up that phone of yours that's always chirping and give that man a call." She shook her finger. "And I'm going to babysit, so don't act like that's a hurdle."

"Yes, ma'am." There was no way to pretend Camille hadn't made a number of good points. "I'll call him right now."

"Good girl." She smiled. "I'll tell all the gals that we can start our card game without you."

Which meant, Chelsea knew, that they'd all have a grand time congratulating Camille on her idea. "Thank you. I'll join you soon."

"Take your time. You know we spend most of the time sipping coffee and chatting anyway."

When her office was empty again, Chelsea picked up her cell phone and practiced asking Anderson for a date. "I was just wondering if you were free tonight."

Did that sound like the right tone? Or too wimpy?

She tried again. "Anderson, I think it's time we went out on a proper date." She frowned. That was probably a little too stiff.

After growing tired of trying to come up with some-thing cute and encouraging—a grown-up version of her sixteen-year-old self—Chelsea stopped debating, picked up her cell phone, and called Anderson.

He picked up on the first ring. "Chelsea, hey."

Oh Lord. Now what? Suddenly feeling flustered, she said, "Hey, uh, what's up?"

"You called me. What's going on?"

"Oh, nothing," she chirped. "I mean, I'm at work. What about you?"

"I just started my shift."

"Oh."

"What's wrong? Did you need something?"

"No . . . well, I mean, I was hoping that we could go out soon." When he didn't say anything, she added, "You know, like a date."

"Is that right?"

She could practically *see* his grin. "You're teasing me." She closed her eyes. "I guess I sounded pretty stupid."

"No, I was thinking that you beat me to it. I was going to call about setting up our proper date, the one we talked about a few weeks ago, remember?"

Proper date? "Did Camille contact you?"

"Why are you asking?"

So, no. Should she admit that she'd asked him out only because of Camille's encouragement, or let it drop? "No reason."

"Anyway, how does Friday night sound to you? I'll be done with my shift and will have even had a good night's sleep."

Friday would give her time to get something cute to wear and maybe even have her nails done, too. "Friday sounds great."

"Awesome," he said, then started laughing. "Chels, our younger selves would be getting a kick out of this. I think we used to be a lot smoother back in the day."

"You're not wrong, but that's okay. I don't mind being awkward with you."

"I feel the same way," he murmured. "Listen, I've gotta go, sorry."

"Of course. Be safe and I'll see you on Friday night."

"I'll text you before then. Bye."

He clicked off before she could reply.

Chelsea disconnected more slowly, feeling bemused by the whole situation. But, she realized, she was bemused in the best way. In the best possible way.

On Thursday she finally had time to go to the mall in Colorado Springs. After working in the morning, she headed east and went to the Shops at Briargate. She treated herself to a fancy coffee and got two outfits, a new pair of shoes, and even a new purse. Probably none of it was necessary, but she was excited at the prospect of wearing something other than sweats or boring work clothes the next time she and Anderson saw each other.

She'd had so much fun that she lost track of the time. As the hours passed, the pretty sky turned cloudy and snow started to fall.

Now she was driving back to Woodland Park in weather that seemed to get worse with every mile marker.

Honestly, why did it always have to snow at the end of April? Even worse, why did the snow always catch her by surprise? She was from Colorado! Even though she always had an extra coat in the car along with an emergency kit, she wished she wasn't almost an hour from home.

Inching along the Ute Pass, she did her best to ignore the ice that was forming on the guardrails and the dark clouds that seemed to have appeared out of nowhere. Instead, she kept a close eye on the road and the Chevy Equinox in front of her and thought about taking a long, hot bath as soon as she got home.

And about counting her blessings. She had so many. Especially Camille, who had become such a wonderful part of their lives, so much so that Chelsea often wondered why she'd worried about having her live with them in the first place. She was turning into the warm-and-fuzzy grandma that Jack had never had and the kind of friend that Chelsea hadn't even realized she needed.

She'd just glanced at the clock when the Chevy in front of her skidded to the right, hastily tried to correct itself, and then suddenly fishtailed.

Though Chelsea knew better than to slam on her brakes, she had to apply some quick pressure to avoid hitting the car, which she did . . . but her wheels also hit a patch of black ice and slid.

Heart pounding, she attempted to steer into the skid, but it was no use. In seconds, she spun out, hit the vehicle to her left, and did a one-eighty.

Unfortunately, her Subaru wasn't the only vehicle to lose control. It seemed like she was surrounded by blaring horns, screeching tires, and careening vehicles. Before she could stop it, she'd run into the guardrail, bounced off, and slammed into the truck to her right. She heard a crunch of metal followed by a blare of horns, and then only blessed silence.

Chapter 41

$\mathcal{A}$nderson had just taken his second bite of the Chipotle burrito Chip's wife had brought for the crew when the bells rang out.

Hastily eating a third bite, he surged to his feet and strode to his locker. Two minutes later, he was putting on his turnout gear.

Beside him, Dave pulled on his boots. "You get anything to eat, Doc?"

"Almost half a burrito."

Dave sighed. "Me, too. At least we got that, huh?"

Anderson grinned. "Yep. Anything is better than nothing." He'd certainly learned that when he was deployed.

He was in the process of checking his radio when he heard the captain's scratchy voice. "Code 3. MVA. Westbound Ute Pass."

The whole team's demeanor changed, became less relaxed and more focused. Code 3. Injuries reported. They needed to approach with sirens and lights. MVA. Multiple Vehicle Accident. That meant Jaws of Life, multiple trucks and ambulances.

Personnel piled into the trucks. The lieutenant was alternately barking orders at them and speaking into his radio.

"We good?" Anderson asked Chip.

"Affirmative." Chip had already started the SUV. Though two or three ambulances would meet them at the scene, the snow might delay them. The SUV, on the other hand, would get them through everything.

"Dave?" he shouted.

"Here, Doc," Dave responded as he hurried to join them. "Sorry, the lieutenant suggested we bring additional boards."

So it was even worse than he thought. As they pulled out behind the ladder truck and main engine, he mentally prepared himself for the scene ahead of them.

"Sheriff is already on the scene. More support coming from Manitou and Divide."

"It's bad," Dave murmured.

Usually Anderson would roll his eyes or say something about Captain Obvious. But he knew Dave was nervous. The reports coming over the radio told him they were heading into a scene that could overwhelm a rookie tech.

"You're gonna do fine, Dave," he murmured. "You're well trained and you've handled yourself time and again. Just remember, one person at a time."

Dave nodded but didn't look reassured. After a second's pause, he blurted, "But what if there are too many . . ." His voice drifted off. "Never mind."

Guessing what they were going to find never helped. In a firmer tone, Anderson said, "Don't do that. Don't get ahead of yourself. One step at a time, yeah?"

"Yeah."

"Good." As they approached the crash site, Anderson saw a maze of flashing lights and heard the low hum of sirens. The snow was miserable for everyone and dangerous for inexperienced drivers.

As Chip pulled to a stop, Anderson fastened his coat and opened the door. "Stay alert, Dave, and stay by my side."

"Yes, sir."

He'd expected to see a parking lot and he wasn't wrong. First glance told him that at least five vehicles were involved.

"Doc!" Mark called out. "Over here."

Bracing himself against the wind and the snow that felt like ice pellets against his skin, Anderson strode forward. Dave followed behind, carrying a backpack of emergency supplies. The vehicle was an ancient Honda that had flipped on its side. Mark and Sam were already on the scene, operating the Jaws of Life.

"What do we got?" he asked.

"Young male, head wound but conscious."

He went to the small opening. Taking care to work around the two firefighters who were actively pulling the metal apart, he said, "Hey. Hanging in there?"

"I don't know."

Anderson continued talking, anything for the kid to focus on besides his pain. "My name's Anderson, but everybody calls me Doc. We're going to get you out and get you to the hospital, okay?" Seeing that the kid was responding to a voice of authority, he added, "Your job is to hang in there, understand?"

The boy nodded and seemed to relax slightly.

"Good. Now, tell me your name."

"Cooper."

"Cooper, good to meet you," he said as he checked his pupils.

"Am I going to be okay?"

"It sure looks that way. Now, tell me, how old are you, Cooper?"

And so it continued. He kept up a steady conversation while the men around him worked to create an opening through which they could extract the victim.

Thirty minutes later, he and Dave had the seventeen-year-old on a board and were moving him to the ambulance.

"You did good, Cooper," he said. "As soon as we get to the hospital, I'll call your parents."

"'Kay."

"Hey, Doc," Chip called out, "we need you!"

Anderson looked over at him in confusion. Speaking into his radio, he said, "I'm transporting this kid to the hospital."

"Change of plans. I'm going to help Dave load and transport to General."

Now that they'd gotten Cooper into the ambulance, Anderson turned—and was surprised to find himself face-to-face with Chip. "What's going on?"

Chip took a deep breath. "I'm sorry, Doc. It's Chelsea."

"Chelsea? What about her?"

"She's here." Anderson stared at him in confusion, trying to process what he was hearing. "Chelsea's in good hands," Chip went on, "so don't worry. She's being seen to by Divide. You know how great that team is."

It felt like the words were sinking into his brain only in fits and starts. He blinked. "Wait. You're saying she was in the accident?" He looked around, even though it was impossible to see—not just because of the snow but because there were cars piled up everywhere, and about a dozen emergency vehicles scattered around. "How bad is she? Is she okay?"

He expected reassurance, but Chip just pointed to two vehicles about ten yards away. "She's over there, Doc. Gray Subaru Outback. Greg's with her, too."

"Thanks." But he hesitated, duty warring with emotion.

"Cap told me to get you. Dave and I'll take care of the kid. I promise, we've got this. Now go."

Finally Anderson found Chelsea's vehicle; it had been rear-ended and looked to have crashed into the guardrail. Through his cloud of confusion, he realized that he hadn't even thought about getting his kit.

When he got to the scene, he was relieved to see that the crew had Chelsea out of the car and on a stretcher. Someone had put a blanket over her, but one of her arms was exposed. She looked so young and vulnerable. Even from a distance, Anderson could see that she had multiple injuries to her face, arms, and hands.

At least she was awake.

"Oh my God. Chelsea," he breathed as soon as he reached her side.

"Anderson?" Her brave expression seemed to dissolve before his eyes. "I can't believe you're here. I'm so glad."

He crouched down by her side. "Me, too, baby." Looking over at the tech, he said, "How is she?"

"Possible fracture of left tibia and collarbone. Multiple contusions but otherwise I'd say she's lucky."

He would say so, too. There was at least one fatality and two other victims had sustained serious injuries. "Don't worry, Chels. They're going to get you on the ambulance and get you taken care of."

"What about you?"

"I've got to stay here, but I'll be there as soon as I can, babe."

Disappointment filled her gaze but she nodded. "Could you call Jack and Camille and my parents?"

"Yep. I'll call everyone as soon as I possibly can. Don't worry. I'm not going to let you down."

"I won't. I just don't want Jack—"

"I'll take care of him. I *promise*." He tried to imbue every word with his sincerity so she'd know she could trust him.

Her expression showed relief as everything he was saying finally sank in. "Okay." With a sigh, she closed her eyes.

He hovered over her, aching to hold her and whisper a thousand promises, a thousand vows that he would never disappoint her again.

"Anderson. Bud! Step aside. We've got to load her," Greg said.

"Sure." Leaning down, he kissed her brow. "See you soon, baby."

Without opening her eyes, she murmured, "See you."

Reluctantly, he straightened. "Greg, please t-take"—his voice cracked and he cleared his throat—"good care of her." Then he took a deep breath and forcefully pushed all thoughts of Chelsea to one side. "Captain, Kelly here," he said into his microphone. "Where do you want me?"

"Black Ford Explorer. Multiple injuries."

"On it." He jogged toward the vehicle and reported in.

And then did what he was trained to do. His job.

Chapter 42

Camille had been through a great many things, but few as gut-wrenching as the past four hours. After Anderson had called her with the news about Chelsea, she'd taken an Uber to Jack's school. School was going to be out soon and she didn't want him riding the bus home.

Luckily her name had been on the list of emergency contacts, so the secretary hadn't argued about Camille picking him up. After they got back to the house, she told Jack about his mom's accident.

After one hour passed and then two, Jack looked near tears. "Can't we go sit at the hospital instead of here?"

"Are you sure about that?"

"I'm sure."

"All right then. I'll see what I can do." After debating back and forth, Camille called Frank for a favor. After explaining about Chelsea's accident, she said, "I need to take Jack up to see his mom. Would you please take us? It's getting dark. I don't want to do another Uber."

He didn't hesitate for even a second. "I don't want you taking one, either. I'll be there soon."

Relieved, she sat down on the couch next to Jack. The boy had been quiet ever since she'd told him about his mom. She was worried that he wasn't letting out his feelings.

"Frank is coming to pick us up and bring us to the hospital," she said gently.

"I hope Mom's okay," Jack muttered.

"Anderson said she had a broken collarbone and a broken leg, but they already set her leg. She won't even need surgery."

Jack nodded but he didn't look too optimistic. "He said she needed stitches, too."

"That's true."

His bottom lip quivered. "What if she's hurt really bad and Anderson didn't want to say?"

Camille knew Jack well enough to know he didn't need sugarcoating. "Honey, your mother *is* hurt pretty badly, but here's what you have to remember: *she's going to be okay.*" She leaned down so she could look into his eyes. "Of course you're worried, I understand that. But try to be positive, child. No need to assume the worst."

His throat worked before he spoke again. "I don't have a dad, you know. I mean, I have one but he never wanted me."

"He missed out, then."

"And my grands . . . they're nice and all, but they spend most of their time on cruises or golfing or something."

She wasn't exactly sure where he was going with this, but he seemed to be feeling alone in the world. "When I called your grandparents, they were very concerned. They love you and your mom very much. They offered to come back home from their trip right away."

"What did you tell them?"

"Just what you heard me say, Jack. That they could do that, but it wasn't necessary."

"Oh."

Camille didn't want to overstep, but she thought even an eight-year-old could appreciate what she wanted to say. "Jack, dear, I think we need to talk for a moment before Frank arrives and we get on our way."

"What about?" His voice was that special eight-year-old combination of belligerence and vulnerability.

"About life." She held out a hand. "No, don't tune me out. Listen. I promise, this won't take long."

When she saw she finally had his complete attention, she said, "Families are funny. You're related by blood and there's love there. But that doesn't mean each and every family member is someone you can depend on come hell or high water. And that's okay. See, you can find other people in your life to depend on, too. People like best friends, or your mother's friends, or even your old lady neighbor across the street."

He giggled. "You're not *that* old."

"Well, I'm okay with how old I am." She winked. "I even have a new boyfriend, so I'm doing fine, right?"

She chuckled at the sight of Jack trying not to wrinkle his nose.

"What I'm trying to say is that you've been blessed with a terrific mom and grandparents who live nearby even though they aren't perfect. You're also blessed with a whole lot of people who care about you and your mom even if we aren't family."

"All right."

She lowered her voice. "I'm not going to let you down, Jack. I'm going to help take care of you. I promise."

"I'm not gonna let *you* down, either."

Oh, this boy. Had she ever gotten a promise so sweet? Gathering herself, she lightly slapped her thighs. "Okay, then. Let's get ready for Frank to pick us up."

But instead of jumping to his feet, Jack hesitated. "Miss Camille, can I ask you something?"

"Of course, dear. You can ask me whatever you want."

"Well . . . did you say that stuff about not depending on your family because of what your kids want to do?"

Boy, that stung, but she couldn't deny it. Jack knew her story and she wanted to be honest. Weighing her words carefully, she said, "That's part of the reason. I mean, it's no secret that my children and I are currently having some differences of opinion about where I should live."

Looking him directly in the eye, she added, "But I'll tell you this—just because we don't agree on everything right now, it doesn't mean I don't love my children or that they don't love me. I'm sure things will get patched up soon."

"I don't like that they're trying to make you move."

Her pint-sized protector! "I don't like it, either. I want to stay in Woodland Park, near all of my friends."

"Like Frank."

Hiding her smile, she nodded. "Yes. Like Frank. And your mom. And Anderson. And you, Jack." She got to her feet. "Now can we get ready already?"

"Yes, ma'am."

*A*n hour later, Frank was dropping them off at the hospital's main entrance.

"Are you sure you don't mind waiting on us? I'm not sure how long we'll be."

"I don't mind."

"It might be a while," she warned. "I don't want to inconvenience you any more than I already have."

"This was nothing, Camille." Smiling at Jack, he added, "Plus, I enjoyed getting to know Jack a little better."

"Thanks."

"You two go on ahead. I'll park the car and go sit in the waiting area," he said as they got out.

Fifteen minutes later, after waiting to check in, get approval for a child of Jack's age to visit, then navigating the maze of corridors, they finally entered Chelsea's room.

She was in a pink hospital gown, her leg in a giant cast, and sported a variety of bandages, bruises, and more than a few cuts decorated with black stitches.

Jack hovered in the doorway, looking a little afraid to approach his mother. But when she opened her eyes and saw them, her face lit up.

"Jack! And Camille, too. Hi!"

Camille smiled at her. "Hi, dear. We are so glad to see you." Remaining by the door, she urged Jack forward. "I'll wait here for a spell," she whispered.

Nervously, Jack took a step into the room but didn't approach the bed. "Mommy," he said hoarsely, "are you okay?"

"I am. Really. I've got a hurt collarbone and a broken leg, but otherwise I'm not too bad."

Jack frowned. "That still isn't too good."

Still putting on a brave face, Chelsea said, "I know, but I'm going to be fine. If the doctors and nurses weren't so concerned about some of the bruises, I'd even be able to go home."

"When will you get out?"

"Tomorrow morning. They're keeping me here just to be on the safe side. That's all." She motioned him forward. "Now, come closer and let me see you. I need a special Jack hug."

Camille was touched by their sweet conversation. Jack approached his mother's bedside and tentatively gave her a hug. Though it was obvious that it wasn't easy for her, Chelsea hugged him back. "Mmm," she said, "that's the best part of my day. I feel better already." Then she whispered, "I love you so much, baby," before raising her voice again. "Now, have a seat and let me say hello to Camille."

Looking a lot more like his normal little-boy self, Jack sat on the chair and smiled at Camille. "Your turn," he sing-songed.

Stepping forward at last, she grinned. "So it is."

"This is a switch, isn't it?" Chelsea asked when Camille was close enough to gently give her a hug as well. "Just a few weeks ago I was the one visiting you."

"Let's hope that we stop this foolishness soon. I'd be very happy if we both stayed out of this place."

"You and me both." Chelsea smiled, but Camille could see lines of weariness around her eyes. It was obvious that the young woman was both exhausted and in pain. Chelsea clearly needed to rest.

"Is there anything I can do for you, dear?"

"You're watching Jack. That's enough."

She looked over her shoulder at Jack, who had gotten to his feet again. "He's no trouble. Actually, I think he watches out for me more than I watch out for him."

"This afternoon I helped Miss Camille when she didn't have her reading glasses on."

"You two are a good team." Chelsea tried to smile again, but it turned into a yawn.

"I think we are, too." Camille put her arm around Jack's shoulders and said, "I think we should let you get your rest."

"Already?"

Chelsea yawned again, and Camille exchanged a knowing look with Jack. It was obvious he was on the same page. "Frank's waiting for us in the lobby. He's probably ready to get out of there. Dear, how are you going to get home tomorrow?"

"Kaylee or Mallory will pick me up. I should be there by the time you get home from school, Jack."

"Oh good," he said.

Camille was pretty sure that Anderson wasn't going to sit back and let someone else bring Chelsea home, but she kept that thought to herself. "Jack, let's go find Frank and sweet-talk him into taking us through the drive-thru."

"I hope he likes McDonald's."

"I have a feeling he's going to like anything you do."

Looking back at Chelsea, she smiled. "We'll see you to-morrow, dear. Get some rest."

"Thanks. Jack, come give me a kiss."

Jack kissed his mother's cheek. "I'm sorry you got hurt, Mom."

"I am, too, but I'll get better."

"Okay." He glanced back at Camille. She could see that he was ready to go. She didn't blame him. It was hard for anyone to see a loved one lying in a hospital bed, but especially a child.

After gently squeezing Chelsea's hand and extracting a promise that she would call if she needed anything, Camille escorted the boy out of the room.

*A*nderson had been to General about a hundred times but never beyond the emergency room. And never without a uniform on, in an official capacity. He was learning that visiting a patient was a whole other story. It had taken a full fifteen minutes to get to the front of the line and show his identification, then make his way around the maze of the third floor. So far, two nurses and an orderly had had to redirect him.

And now he was, unbelievably, lost again.

Just as he was about to swallow the last amount of his pride, he spied Camille and Jack walking down the hall. He strode toward them. "I'm so glad to see you."

"How come?" asked Jack.

"First, because it's you two . . . and secondly, because I've been looking for your mother's room for the last ten minutes."

"That's easy." Jack turned and pointed to a door straight down the hall. "Mom is in Room 387."

"It took us a bit, too, Anderson."

"So, you saw her. Is she okay? Can she still have visitors?"

"She's good," Camille said. It was obvious that was for Jack's benefit. It was also obvious that there was quite a bit that she wasn't saying.

"She's coming home tomorrow," Jack announced.

Squeezing his shoulder, Anderson smiled. "I'm glad. Well, I better go see her before I get lost again." Suddenly remembering that Camille didn't drive, he said, "Hey, I'd be glad to take you both home after I visit with Chelsea."

"Thank you, but we have other plans," Camille said mysteriously.

Jack bounced up and down on the balls of his feet. "We're going to the burger drive-thru with Frank."

"That's very cool! I won't keep you then." Sharing a smile with Camille, he turned and headed toward Chelsea's room, thinking that both Jack and Chelsea were lucky to have Camille in their lives.

Chapter 43

*H*e was still smiling when he walked into Chelsea's room. Then his smile faded.

She was asleep, but she didn't look peaceful. She looked like she'd been in a car accident. Bruises had formed on her face, stitches crept up past her hairline, and the contusions that weren't bandaged looked angry and irritated.

What concerned him the most was the beginning of another fierce bruise on her collarbone. He'd helped enough accident victims to know that she probably had some good-sized bruises on her chest and abdomen in addition to the broken bone.

As he sank down into the chair next to her, he was hit by the full effect of her injuries—and what might have happened if her accident had gone south just a few more yards. She could have been far more seriously hurt, maybe even fighting for her life like at least one other victim was.

Or she might not have made it.

He could've lost her.

Tears pricked his eyes as he forced himself to imagine

what could have happened. What would he be doing at this minute if Chelsea had—died? His world would've gone dark.

The tears fell faster, and he cursed himself for indulging in what-ifs. Pulling out a tissue from the box beside her bed, he swiped his eyes. Somehow he managed to knock over the box in the process. It clattered against the table as it fell to the floor.

And startled Chelsea enough to open her eyes with a jerk.

"Crap," he muttered.

She looked around in alarm, then her eyes fastened on him. "Andy?"

Boy, he loved hearing his old nickname on her lips. "Yeah, sweetheart. Hey."

"Hey." Looking confused, she whispered, "Have you been here long?"

"No. I only just saw Jack and Camille in the hall."

"I must have drifted off. I'm sorry."

Seeing that her lips looked parched, he picked up the large plastic cup filled with ice water and brought it to her lips. "Sip."

She did as he asked. "Thank you. That feels so good."

"Is your throat sore?"

She nodded. After she swallowed another bit, she appeared a little more alert. "How did you know?"

"Comes with the territory."

"Oh, of course." She looked away, almost like she was embarrassed to have forgotten something so obvious.

Leaning forward, he rested his elbows on his thighs. "Are you in pain, Chels? Do you need something? I can call the nurse for you."

"I think I'm okay for now."

But seconds later, tears formed in her eyes. "What's wrong?" When she didn't say anything, he pushed a little harder. "You might as well tell me. I'm not going to leave when you're so upset."

She took a deep breath. "I keep reliving the crash. Anderson, I felt so out of control, it was terrifying. For a few minutes, I even thought I was going to die."

He'd had moments like that back in Afghanistan. Shoot, he'd even had moments like that on the job. "Honey, that's normal. What you've just been through was scary as all get-out."

She shook her head. "No, what I'm trying to say is that all I could think about was how scared I was . . . and how I had held so many worries and problems close to my chest. I don't know why I thought something that happened almost ten years ago was so important. I'm sorry, Anderson."

He was floored. That's what she'd been dwelling on? "Chelsea, I've said this before and I'm going to keep saying it until you believe that I'm being sincere. Everything was my fault."

"I'm not a child. We both know that isn't true."

"I think it is. I'm the one who wanted us to see other people. I'm the one who freaked out when you were pregnant. Even after I cooled off and felt bad about the things I said, I didn't reach out to you. I acted as if my pain was so important that what you were going through paled in comparison." He took a deep breath. "No, that's not entirely true. I was hurt, so I wanted you to be hurt, too."

When he finally stopped talking, he met her gaze. "Does any of that make sense?"

She smiled slightly. "It does, but does rehashing everything that we felt ten years ago even matter anymore?"

Chelsea was right. They could continue to apologize and continue to wish they'd done things differently. But the truth of the matter was that they were different people now. He knew without a doubt that if he were standing next to his nineteen-year-old self, he would have told him to get a clue and concentrate on what really mattered.

Was he willing to do that now?

"Chelsea, I still love you."

She blinked. "What did you say?"

"I still love you." He took a deep breath. "Honestly, I never stopped, I just pushed it away." He lifted a shoulder. "I've always loved you, Chelsea Davis. I love you today and I'll love you tomorrow and the next day and the day after that."

He winced as he spied more tears leaking from her eyes. "Listen, no pressure, okay?"

"No pressure?"

"What I'm trying to say is that it's okay if you don't feel the same way or . . . whatever . . . I just wanted you to know."

He could practically see her mind spinning. Then, she seemed to make up her mind. "I guess if you can be brave, then I can, too. I still love you, too."

He smiled. "Look at us."

She smiled back at him. "We have absolutely the worst timing on God's green earth."

"Maybe, or maybe not." Looking at her hospital bed, he quickly sized it up, then made a decision. Carefully, he lay down on her uninjured side and adjusted her so that her head was resting on his chest. "You okay?"

"You can't get in here with me! You're going to get in trouble!"

"Probably, but I'll handle it. There's no way we're finally going to admit that we love each other and stay two feet apart. There's no way I'm not going to hold you after seeing you in that accident. Now, are you okay? I'm not hurting you, am I?"

"Not at all. I'm good, Anderson."

He gently rubbed her back. "Me, too."

Seconds later, he felt her body relax and knew that she'd drifted off to sleep. When the nurse came in, she scowled, until she recognized him.

"You might be a paramedic, but you can't go around hopping into bed with patients, Anderson Kelly."

"I know. But give me five more minutes, 'kay, Brenda?"

She folded her arms over her chest. "What about the fact that visiting hours are over? There are no exceptions, Doc. Not even for pretty cute firefighters."

"Five minutes, then I'll leave. Please? This is my girl."

She rolled her eyes but nodded. "When I come back in six minutes you had better be gone."

"Fine."

When they were alone again, he kissed the top of Chelsea's head and stroked her hair. She shifted and snuggled even closer, making him wish he could stay there all night, holding her in his arms. He wanted to be the one who soothed her worries and calmed her fears—and not just for one night, but every night. He didn't want her to ever wake up alone again.

Chapter 44

Chelsea didn't know whether to give thanks for all the help she was receiving or try to find a creative new way to ask for everyone to leave her alone.

She'd been home four days and her cozy house was beginning to feel like Grand Central Terminal.

Not only was Jack constantly checking on her, but Camille had commandeered the kitchen, Anderson had asked for the week off to spend with her, and even Kaylee and Mallory were stopping by on a regular basis.

Today she'd received a huge basket of goodies from everyone at the senior center. Jill had taken up a collection from the staff and all the senior citizens they served. It was filled with homemade and store-bought goodies, from two lasagnas to an apple pie to piles of brownies, plus gift cards for restaurants that delivered.

It was all wonderful but it was also a bit overwhelming.

Okay, a lot overwhelming.

Thank goodness she'd begged her parents not to return from Phoenix just yet. She just didn't know if she could take her mother diving into the mix.

"You know, you're acting awfully grumpy for a woman being spoiled," Kaylee said.

"I know. I'm sorry about it, too. It's just a lot of attention, you know? Two months ago, Jack and I were usually alone."

"There's also the fact that you have a giant cast on your leg and a broken collarbone," Kaylee added. "I'm sure that's hard."

"I am sore, but it's honestly not too bad. It's everything else that I'm finding hard."

"For the record, I don't think Jack minds all of the fun and food," Mallory added. "He asked me if you needed to know how many brownies he was eating."

"What did you tell him?"

"Of course not." When Chelsea shot her a wounded look, Mallory added, "Come on, Chels. It's just brownies."

"You're right. Sorry."

"What's going on with you? Is your leg bothering you?"

"No. I mean, it's sore, and this heavy cast is hard to manage. It's almost impossible to get around without knocking into something."

Mallory grinned. "I'm going to take that as a sign that you're feeling better. You wouldn't be complaining about knocking into things if you didn't want to move around."

"She does have a point," Kaylee said.

Thank goodness she had two good friends who could put her in her place. "I'm sorry, guys. You're right. I should stop complaining."

"I didn't say you couldn't complain. What are friends for if not to validate your every gripe!" Looking suddenly gleeful, Mallory leaned forward. "But if you want to change the subject, how about you tell us all about the latest developments with you and Anderson?"

Chelsea tried to look nonchalant. "What makes you assume that there have been developments?"

"No reason . . . except that I saw you two kissing yesterday."

"Oh, for heaven's sake."

"Act outraged if you like, but it was noteworthy," Mallory retorted. "A very noteworthy kiss."

Kaylee sat down on the side of Chelsea's bed. "What happened?"

Chelsea hesitated. To talk about it felt like giving up a small portion of the romance that was blooming between them. On the other hand, if she kept it to herself and Anderson found out, he would be upset. She wouldn't blame him, either. If she thought he was keeping their relationship a secret, she would feel hurt or maybe even worry that he was having second thoughts.

So, there really was no choice.

"We're in love," she blurted out.

Mallory raised her eyebrows. "Is this official?"

"Yep." She smiled. "Anderson told me that he still loved me when I was in the hospital."

Mallory gasped. "And what did you do?"

"I knew I had to be brave and tell him right back."

Kaylee smiled suggestively. "And I guess things just got better from there?"

Chelsea nodded. "They sure did," she said, adding silently to herself, *It's been absolutely perfect.*

Chapter 45

"How's it going at Chelsea's house?" Frank asked as they walked over to Camille's house for the daily inspection.

Camille had to smile as she thought of the best word to describe it all. "Chaotic."

"Whew. I bet you're ready to get home."

She laughed. "Sometimes, yes. I didn't realize it, but I really am used to the quiet. To a lot of quiet." She paused, considering. "But other days, I sort of dread going back home. I like always having something to do. And there really is a lot to do, since Chelsea can't get around on her broken leg too well."

He unlocked her kitchen door and then followed her inside.

"Well, it looks like they've finished the wiring. I have half a ceiling."

"You do, indeed." He pointed to a new portion of dry-wall. "Half a wall, too."

When she'd met with the remodeling company, they'd suggested some updates and changes to her kitchen. More cabinets, some easier storage solutions, a nifty dishwasher that was raised so she didn't have to bend over so much. Actually, she'd learned a lot from the husband-and-wife team about remodeling for the long term, like repositioning some outlets so they'd be easier to reach, widening some doorways in case one day she needed a walker or a wheelchair—she'd even switched out her bathtub for a wide shower with safety bars in it.

They'd also suggested getting rid of her dining area and replacing it with a cozy banquette set and updating the formal living room with a wood floor, a gas fireplace, and some comfortable sitting areas. They'd convinced her that the whole arrangement would be less formal and more inviting—something that she thought was overdue.

"I'm excited about this house, Frank. My contractor's mother is my age and he's suggesting lots of great things that I would've never thought about. Even something as simple as making the lights brighter, or using smart technology to monitor the heat, the AC, even the speakers and security."

Frank raised his eyebrows. "You're going to have a pretty fancy house, Camille."

She chuckled. "I am, but it's going to be practical, too. What's important is that I'm going to be able to age gracefully in my own home."

"Sounds like a silver lining."

"It is, indeed."

"You're going to be happy here. I can feel it in my bones."

"I hope your bones are right," she joked. They walked around the gutted space some more, mainly just to wander. Since they visited every day there wasn't much new to see. "Would you like to walk down to the senior center?"

"I thought maybe I could buy you an ice cream instead."

"Really?"

"What do you think? Fancy a cone? Or we could go big and get sundaes. It's ladies' choice."

"Boy, you're feeling bold today."

He chuckled. "What do you say?"

"I say that I'd love one. Thank you."

"Do you need anything from your room?" He eyed her light cotton sweater. "Will you be warm enough?"

"I'll be fine."

As they made their way down the sidewalk, they passed several people they knew. More than one person gave them a second glance, which was no surprise, she thought. Frank Robards was an imposing presence, and she'd been alone for a very long time.

"You've got a Cheshire cat smile, Camille."

She chuckled. "I probably do. I was just thinking that our stroll has caught the attention of a couple of folks."

"People like to look and talk. It's the same everywhere." He cleared his throat. "Does it bother you?"

"Not in the slightest. I've decided if I can get through these past few weeks with the fire and the showdown with my children, I can get through anything."

He frowned. "I hate that your children's attitudes have brought you as much hardship as that fire."

"They're not perfect and I'm not, either. But that's okay. We'll all be good again." One day, she hoped.

"I hope so. Ah, and here we are." He opened the door to Bell's Ice Cream. "Looks like we're not the only people who decided that ice cream was a good idea."

"I don't mind the crowd if you don't."

"Not at all."

When they got to the counter, Frank said, "Want to split a Gold Rush Sundae?"

She glanced at the description. Three scoops of ice cream, caramel and hot fudge sauce, with crushed Heath bars on top. It sounded decadent and delicious, and she couldn't recall the last time she'd indulged. "Of course."

After he paid, they took their number and went to find a table. One of the high school kids would bring it to them.

"Here you go," Frank said. "Over near the window."

She started to follow him over, then stopped to chat with a couple of ladies she knew from the last painting class she took.

When she was done, she turned—and drew up short. Frank was speaking to none other than Bo.

He turned and gave a tentative wave. "Hi, Mom."

"Bo. This is a nice surprise."

"Allyssa's in the bathroom. She had a sleepover up here and I came to pick her up. We decided to get an ice cream before heading home."

That pinched. It had been a month since she'd seen her seventeen-year-old granddaughter. "I look forward to seeing her."

"She'll be happy to see you, too, Mom."

She glanced at Frank, who was looking every inch the general, with a forbidding posture and hard stare. Yes, she'd certainly acquired a defender in him.

"Mom, I'm sorry about everything."

Years ago, she would have hugged Bo and told him to forget about it. But not any longer. She'd learned to stand up for herself . . . and the fallout from the past month wasn't going to go away with a hug and a pat on the back. Bo and his siblings had caused her a great deal of pain.

"I'm glad to hear that you're sorry," she said. "I'm also sorry that you all tried to boss me around like you did."

He visibly winced. "I don't blame you for being mad."

"I have every right to be." She hesitated, wondering if she should say what was in her heart instead of keeping it to herself. "I must admit that your part in this plot surprised me, Bo. I thought you understood how happy I am here."

Looking frustrated, he nodded. "I did. I mean, I do. The problem is that the others sounded so right. Even when I disagreed, it was hard for me to say they were completely wrong. I've felt stuck in the middle and it's sucked," he mumbled. After a pause, he cleared his throat. "However, that's not the point. I should've done more to help you. At the very least I should've made sure you knew that you weren't alone."

"Yes, you should have," Frank said.

Bo's eyes twitched but he didn't reply. Camille appreciated that. She also knew that Bo wasn't the instigator. He'd never been that type of person. "I love each of you, and I appreciate your concern. But I'm not ready to be told what to do yet."

"I understand."

"You should come by the house one afternoon. I'll walk you through it. We're making some adjustments for my age. It's going to be better."

"I'm glad. Ah, here's our girl. Hey, Lyss! Look who I found."

"Gram!" Allyssa trotted over and gave her a big hug. "What are you doing here?"

"I just happen to be on a date. This is Mr. Robards."

"Call me Frank," he said.

"Hi." Her granddaughter's eyes twinkled. "Are you really Gram's boyfriend?"

Frank grinned. "You should be asking your grandmother that."

Her pretty granddaughter looked at her mischievously. "Is he, Gram?"

Camille decided she wouldn't mind being coy. "Maybe."

"We're in the going-out-for-ice-cream stage of dating, young lady," Frank said. "But if things progress to dinner out, I'll let you know."

Allyssa grabbed her hand. "Gram, you have to text me about your dates."

Bo was actually blushing. "Lyss, don't pester Gram about her personal life."

Camille was just about to reference the pot calling the kettle black when Allyssa spoke up.

"Dad, that's all you and Aunt Janie have been doing."

"What are you talking about?"

"Oh, come on. Rowan and I have talked about how you've all been bullying Gram. We don't like it."

Another time, Camille would've probably told Allyssa to be more respectful. Today, though, she couldn't help but feel a little vindicated. Bo looked embarrassed and a bit like a bug stuck on a corkboard with a straight pin.

"Frank, I think we better get to our sundae before it melts all over us."

"I was thinking the same thing." After a beat, he held out his hand to Bo. "I'm glad we met. I'm sure we'll see each other again soon."

Bo shook Frank's hand. "Yes, I bet we will."

"Allyssa, you are a delight." Frank shook her hand in a far warmer way.

"It was nice to meet you, too, Mr. Robards. I mean, Frank."

"You can just call him General," Camille said. "That's what half the people in Woodland Park call him anyway. It's kind of stuck."

The teen's eyes widened. "Are you a real general?"

"I'm afraid so," he said with a wink. "Camille, are you ready to sit?"

"Yes, of course. Good-bye, you two."

"Bye, Mom," said Bo as he escorted Allyssa into the line.

When they sat down Camille leaned back in her seat and released a big sigh. "I can hardly believe that happened."

"I'm proud of you. You put that son of yours in his place."

"I had some help. Thank you for that."

"You're welcome, but I think your granddaughter did a better job than either of us."

She chuckled. "You aren't wrong. Oh boy. Do you have any grandchildren like Allyssa? She was born knowing what she wanted."

"I can't say that any of my grands are quite the pistol she is, but I think she's delightful."

"I do, too." Lowering her voice, she added, "I have to admit that while I'm not supposed to have favorites, Allyssa's up there at the top. Her father was a lot like her, too."

"Take a bite of this sundae, Camille. It's awfully good."

She dipped her spoon into the soft ice cream with hot fudge sauce and took a bite. She couldn't resist smiling. "It sure is. It's a shame we talked so much. I have a feeling it might have been even a little bit better five minutes ago."

Frank took her hand. "We'll have to compare the next sundae we share."

Chapter 46

$\mathcal{A}$nderson had ended up taking ten days off. Every day, he'd done his best to bond with Jack, ferry him to his activities, support Camille, take care of Chelsea . . . and court her, too.

He had soon learned that there weren't enough hours in the day to do it all well—especially with Tab in the mix! That cat was always either cuddling with Chelsea or getting in the way of his other jobs.

Tonight, though, he'd gotten lucky: Frank and Camille offered to take Jack and one of his buddies to the drive-in in Colorado Springs. The boys were excited to eat a bunch of junk food and Camille and Frank seemed so smitten with each other that Anderson suspected they were looking forward to making out in the dark whenever the boys weren't in sight.

When they realized they'd be at her house alone for the first time, Chelsea joked, "We're finally having our date and I'm stuck in the house with a broken leg!"—and right then Anderson had decided to take things up a notch.

Sure, it might not be the romantic date of Chelsea's

dreams, but he felt sure that he could make it memorable.
He'd served in the military for eight years; if there was anything he knew how to do, it was to execute a plan of action.

The first thing he did was call Kaylee and ask if she had
a minute to help Chelsea get ready. When she arrived, Anderson went shopping and returned with steaks, potatoes,
salad, a carton of éclairs from the bakery, a bottle of red
wine, and a bunch of flowers.

Then he'd gotten busy setting the table, seasoning the
simple meal, and putting on a clean shirt.

Soon after Kaylee left, Chelsea appeared on her crutches,
and she looked so pretty, she honestly took his breath away.

She was wearing a flowy red dress with a scooped neck-
line. Her golden hair was curled softly around her shoulders, and she had on some kind of eye makeup that made
her blue eyes look even bluer than usual.

"Hey," she said when he'd caught sight of her.

She sounded unsure and sweet. So different from the
confident woman he'd come to know. He embraced her and
kissed her softly. "You look amazing."

"I don't know about that." She frowned down at her leg,
then lifted a crutch to illustrate. "All I can do is hobble
around and knock into things."

"Even with the cast and the crutches, you're gorgeous."

"I was going to wear this dress on our big date."

He pulled her in closer. "I'd say it was worth the wait."

She leaned into him for a minute, then straightened, and
caught sight of the table for the first time. "You've been busy."

He smiled. "I have been. I decided if we couldn't go out
for a nice evening, then our nice evening was going to come
to us."

"This wasn't necessary."

It was. For too long, he hadn't done enough. But now he
was determined to do everything she deserved.

He pointed to the open bottle of cabernet. "The guy at
the store said it was pretty good. Would you like a glass?"

"If you don't mind, could we talk for a few minutes first?"

"Yeah. Of course." He helped her to the couch and to prop her leg on the coffee table even though she protested.

Then he sat down beside her and tried to think of a way to say everything that was in his heart without overwhelming her.

But she reached for his hand first. "Anderson, all of this is really amazing. You've been here every day doing a hundred things for me and for Jack, and I think things between us have been pretty great. But this is making me nervous. What, exactly, is going on?"

It was time to go all in and stop thinking about the consequences. Just like when he was fighting fires, Anderson knew it was time to press ahead—even if there was a possibility of getting burned. "I need you back, Chels."

Pure confusion filled her gaze. "I don't understand," she said. "You have me back. We're together now."

He ignored her confusion. Ignored how hard his heart was beating. He knew if he didn't get the words out—if he didn't get all his feelings out—he would probably turn chicken and keep everything bottled up inside for another month or six.

So, he continued, even if it didn't make sense to her.

"What I'm trying to say is that I don't just love you or want you in my life. I . . . I need you, Chelsea."

She inhaled sharply.

Before she had time to say anything, he continued. "I know I'm really bad with speeches, but listen for a sec, okay?" As soon as he saw her nod, he plunged ahead. "Chelsea, I don't want you to go another day without knowing how important you are to me."

He took a deep breath. "I know there are a dozen reasons to go slowly, and I promise that I'll wait as long as you want . . . if you just say yes."

Her eyes widened. "Say yes to what?"

"To me." Realizing that he still hadn't actually said the

words that she needed to hear, he chuckled softly and, carefully moving from her side to the floor in front of her, he knelt on one knee. "Chelsea Eleanor Davis, will you marry me?"

Chelsea studied his face, then looked down at her hand encased in both of his own. She bit her bottom lip.

And then spoke at last.

"When I was sixteen, and everyone said I should only care about getting into college, all I really cared about was you.

"Even after our letters and my tears and Jack, and all that bitterness . . . way after I didn't want to care about you anymore, I still did."

She was speaking in the past tense. "Are you saying that I waited too long?"

She shook her head. "No, I'm saying that some things are simply inevitable. Like sleepy Monday mornings and cereal going soggy before I've finished it. Like sipping really awful coffee at your firehouse. Like snow falling in April in Woodland Park."

She smiled. "But, in spite of being sleepy, I'm always grateful for my job on Mondays. In spite of that last soggy bite of Special K, I'm thankful to have cereal in the pantry. In spite of that really bad coffee, I'm glad to share it with you. And as much as I dislike April snow, I know that snow will help prevent fires . . . and maybe even keep you safe."

She chuckled. "I guess I'm bad at this, too. What I'm trying to say is that even though we're older, we're harder, and maybe not even the same people we used to be, I still love you, Anderson Kelly. That just like you, I need you in my life. Of course I'm saying yes. Of course I'll marry you. I would love to be your wife."

He moved back to her side and gently pulled her into his arms. And then kissed her like she was the most important person in the world.

Kissed her like he would never let her go again.

And later—much later—when they were sipping wine and taking their first bites of dinner, Chelsea smiled at him.

"This first 'real' date has been pretty amazing, Anderson. I can't wait to find out what you do on the next one."

He gaped at her, and she laughed and laughed. It was the sound he didn't know he'd been waiting to hear. The sound that told him he'd finally come home, at long last.

Chapter 47

SIX MONTHS LATER

I don't know if this old church has ever held so many people," said Chelsea's dad as he walked into the bride's room, which was really the junior high Sunday school room. "Practically the whole town is here." He sounded peeved.

Their guest list *was* huge, and hardly anyone had sent their regrets, Chelsea thought. But surely there weren't that many people waiting to watch her walk down the aisle!

Her father looked a little pale, though. "Dad, are you nervous? It isn't like you to exaggerate."

"I'm not nervous. Well, not much. But there is a heck of a crowd out there, Chels. The sanctuary is filled to capacity and then some—Good thing we have so many members of the fire department here."

"That is a good thing," she agreed with a laugh.

"I just came to tell you that Pastor Wallace said five more minutes. They're bringing out more chairs and they're still seating people."

More chairs. Still seating people. She took a deep breath. "I can wait five more minutes."

"Don't worry. Anderson is looking good. I don't reckon he's going to bolt or anything."

She giggled. "Thanks, Dad, but I'm not worried about anything."

"You shouldn't be. They can't start without you, you know." He cleared his throat. "I'll go back outside and see if anyone needs anything. Hang tight."

"Yes, Dad."

When he left, all the women in the room burst into laughter.

"I don't know if I've ever used this word before, but your father is in a *dither*," said Kaylee.

"He's a nervous wreck," Chelsea agreed. "He hates big crowds and he really hates being the center of attention. Mom said he's been having dreams about tripping while we walked down the aisle."

Kaylee giggled. "You're supposed to be the one worrying about that."

"I told Dad that everything is going to be fine. Even if we *both* trip I'm still going to get married."

"You better. You're going to Mexico tomorrow morning."

They were! While Jack was going to be spoiled by two sets of grandparents—three, counting Camille and Frank!—she and Anderson had booked the most amazing casita in Acapulco: their own bungalow with a private pool. The travel agent said the resort even delivered fresh flowers and coffee and pastries every morning. All she and Anderson had to do was live in their own little honeymoon hideaway for a full seven days.

"I can't wait until we get on that plane. That's when I'll know that everything is really happening."

Samantha chuckled. "Oh, it's happening. I've never seen Doc look so determined."

"He looks handsome, too," said Kaylee. "I thought he

was going to wear a tuxedo, but he's wearing his army uniform."

"He *was* just going to wear a tuxedo," Chelsea replied, "but the moment I saw his dress uniform, I asked him to consider wearing that."

Mallory pretended to fan herself. "He's got a chest full of medals, Chelsea."

Those medals were impressive, but as far as she was concerned, the scars on his body served the same purpose. He'd done things that few people were willing to do. She was proud of every bit of him. "He's a true hero, he just doesn't like to talk about it much." Thinking of the other man in her life, she said, "How's Jack?"

"Standing proudly next to Anderson," Kaylee said. "I've never seen a more adorable best man."

Mallory chuckled. "Whatever you do, don't call him 'best boy.' I made that mistake last night and he informed me he wasn't a kid."

Chelsea grinned. "Well, he is almost ten now."

The door opened and Bridget, their wedding planner, poked her head in. "Time to take your places, ladies. Chelsea, your father will be here in a minute. He's, ah, just calming down."

"I bet someone gave him a shot of courage," Mallory said.

Chelsea chuckled. She couldn't see her father taking a snort, but he was so nervous he just might.

Getting to her feet, she said, "I guess it's time."

"Hold on," Kaylee said. "We've got to fluff this thing."

Kaylee wasn't kidding. She had made Chelsea a bright-white strapless gown in thick satin. Layers of tulle poufed out the skirt, making her feel like a princess. Even though it wasn't especially comfortable, she loved it to bits. It was the dress she'd dreamed of ever since she was a kid.

Her hair was down, just the top of it pinned up in a silver

comb, and now Kaylee was arranging her full, lace-edged veil. The door opened and Bridget started waving them forward. One by one her bridesmaids departed, each holding a bouquet of red roses.

Her father was waiting by the doorway. "You look beautiful, child. Just perfect."

"Thank you, Dad."

He held out his arm. "Are you ready for this?"

"Of course."

He took a deep breath. "I've never seen you happier. I—I'm so glad."

The processional began, and Bridget beckoned to them. "Now," she said.

"That's our cue, Daddy," Chelsea whispered.

"I know. I've got this."

Slowly they set off. Her hand was resting lightly on her father's arm, but the rest of her was vibrating at the sight of the crowded church. Her father hadn't exaggerated. It seemed as if practically the whole town was there.

And then there, standing next to Jack, was her guy, Anderson Kelly, standing straight and tall, his dark-blue uniform adorned with ribbons and medals. The scar on his cheek was there for all to see. Chelsea didn't think there was a handsomer man in all of Woodland Park, Colorado.

Anderson's gaze didn't waver as he watched her come down the aisle. When her father lifted her veil and their eyes met, Anderson smiled. It was the same smile he'd flashed when he'd first helped her pick up her books all those years ago. When he used to hug her after his football games or saw her across the room at a party. When he'd sat by her hospital bed and heard that she loved him, too.

"Chels, come here," he whispered. Holding out his hand.

It was her invitation to come home at last. To come home to him.

Smiling brightly, she left her father's side and stepped forward. There was nowhere on earth she'd rather be.

Acknowledgments

I'm so grateful for the many people who helped to make this novel a reality. First and foremost is my husband, Tom. He's always offering encouragement and support. From the moment I told him that I was thinking about writing a firefighter romance featuring Army veterans, he was all in. He drove me up to Woodland Park multiple times, hung out with firefighters with me, helped with research, and even gave me the push I needed to chat with several veterans returning home from a deployment.

A huge thanks also goes out to my agent, Nicole Resciniti of the Seymour Agency. She not only suggested I try to write outside my usual genre, but has been with me every step of the way through the writing and publication of this novel. Every author should be so blessed with such support.

Many of the scenes wouldn't have been possible without all the help from Tiffany Adams. Her experiences as a nurse in a military hospital helped tremendously. A big thanks goes out to Maddy Moviel, as well! Maddy very patiently answered my many questions regarding emergency rooms and Woodland Park.

I'm also very indebted to the team of firefighters I met from the Northeast Teller County Fire Department. They very patiently showed me around the station and allowed me to climb up in firetrucks and take tons of pictures. They also answered all kinds of questions about their jobs. I changed a few details for the sake of fiction, but I hope and pray that I conveyed my sense of awe and gratitude for the danger these men and women place themselves in every day.

Finally, I can truly say I've been honored and blessed to work with Tracy Bernstein on this book. Tracy's editing, encouragement, and belief in what this story could be was incredible. It's because of her that *Coming Home* is a novel to be proud of. Tracy, thank you for not giving up on me.

Turn the page for an exclusive
preview of Shelley Shepard Gray's next
Woodland Park Firefighters romance

Moving Forward

Coming from Berkley in 2023

$\mathcal{G}$reg pressed a hand against the cool metal wall of the fire engine as Chip veered right. Through the window, he saw two pickup trucks hastily pull over to the side of the road as Chip, the fire truck's engineer and driver, picked up speed. "Whoa, cowboy," he teased. "The goal is to make it to the fire in one piece, right?"

"Stop worrying, Tebo. I got this." Chip blared the horn at a stubborn driver, then gunned the gas. After a second's pause, the engine lurched forward like it was entered in a Formula 1 race.

When Chip blared the horn as he sped through another intersection, Greg took care not to look out for oncoming traffic. Every once in a while, all the lights and horns played with his head—a gift that kept giving from Iraq. This was one of those days.

He breathed deep and attempted to center himself by silently counting backward from twenty—no small feat while traveling inside a speeding fire truck.

"Idiot," Chip muttered as he blared the horn again.

Feeling his vision swim, Greg started over again. *Twenty. Nineteen. Eighteen. Seven—*

"Greg, what's up with you?"

"Huh?" With effort, he pushed aside his numbered life-line and turned to the person in the jump seat next to him.

Samantha Carter grinned at him. "You okay, T? You're looking a little uptight. What's up?"

He wished he'd been able to hide his discomfort better. "Nothing."

She arched a brow. "Want to try that again?"

Irritation surged forward. Just in time, he bit back an impatient reply. The truth was that it wasn't just the sirens that had been giving him fits today. Almost everything, from the alarm on his phone to the Xbox game the guys were playing last night to the flickering lightbulb in the kitchen had rubbed him wrong. Greg couldn't deny it; he'd been short-tempered during the entire forty-eight-hour shift. He hoped it was because it had been slower than usual.

Too much time on his hands was dangerous for him. Too much time meant hours staring into space instead of actually sleeping. Too much time to think about his father's upcoming visit from his hometown in West Virginia. Too much time to wonder if he'd chosen the right profession after the army.

Of course, none of that could be shared—especially not while Chip was driving hell-for-leather.

"Aw, don't worry about me, Cat," he said softly, using his pet name for her. "I'm good. Just glad this shift is almost over."

Sympathy filled her gaze. "I'm with you. I hate boring shifts."

"Four minutes," the captain said through their radios. "Fire looks to be contained, but be ready for anything. This is a garden center. Lots of substances that can ignite."

"Roger that, Cap," Greg said as he fastened the buckles on his turnout coat.

Chip screeched to a stop. Greg stepped out of the truck, Samantha on his heels. In front of them, a pretty good fire was burning, but as the captain had reported, it didn't look to be out of control. Lightning had struck an old scrub oak that should've been cut down years ago. Though the fire had engulfed the surrounding pasture, the spread was slow, mainly due to the storm that had just passed through—and the fact that next to the pasture was the field of plants and shrubs that the nursery owner was growing.

As he began pulling out the hoses to hook up to the hydrant, he spared a glance toward Anderson and Dave. They were also in full gear but holding a stretcher. Belatedly, he remembered that the dispatcher had said the owner had a heart condition and might need help.

When he heard a curse and the intense string of orders from the captain, Greg was brought back to his job and focused on the fire that had found more fuel.

"Here we go," Sam muttered as she headed toward the flames.

He took position about four feet from her and braced himself as the water surged forward. Within five minutes, another truck arrived, along with the big Mack tanker truck. Sirens filled in the air as more orders rang out and other firefighters joined in.

When a new burst of flames erupted, he moved farther to his left, braced his feet, and attacked the fire. As the pressure from the hose increased, his biceps contracted.

Another firefighter stepped beside him. When their eyes met, he gave a thumbs-up sign. Greg did the same thing back, assuring the guy that he was okay.

The noise from the flames was deafening. Greg zoned out everything except for the job—and his brain practically sighed in relief.

Thirty minutes later, the last of the flames were extinguished. Only smoke remained.

Greg breathed a sigh of relief—and couldn't help but reflect on how intense the moment had been and how quickly it had been replaced by a feeling of satisfaction.

He stayed in position, waiting for directions.

"Sam, you stay on-site. Tebo, go assist Doc with the victim," Captain ordered.

"On it." He dragged the hose to the truck, where Chip would unfasten it from the valve and secure it back into place. Less than a minute later, he strode through the open door of the garden center to assist their paramedic Anderson Kelly, known to most of them as Doc.

But instead of the older woman he expected to see, he discovered Doc crouched next to a young woman with bright-blue eyes and a mass of auburn hair. She was holding an oxygen tube under her nose while Anderson was checking her pulse.

The woman seemed to tense the moment she saw him approach, so Greg lifted his breathing apparatus from his face. Some victims were so shook up that being surrounded by firefighters with their faces covered was difficult.

"How can I help, Doc?" he asked.

Their usually calm and collected paramedic looked annoyed. "Glad you're here, T. I'm on the phone with the hospital and the new guy in receiving is acting like I've got nothing better to do than hang on hold. Keep an eye on her vitals."

"Roger that." He smiled slightly at the woman. Lowering to a crouch as well, he said, "Hey. My name's Greg. I'm going to sit with you for a bit. All right?"

When she nodded, he smiled again, just like they were at a bar or in line at the grocery store or something. "What's your name?"

"Kristen."

"It's real nice to meet you. Sorry it's under these circumstances, though."

"Me, too." When she attempted a small smile, he relaxed slightly. She seemed to be coherent.

"How are you doing?" Some victims needed a gentler hand than others. To a lot of his coworkers' surprise, he always seemed to have patience to spare for their victims, even when they behaved erratically. It was only with his coworkers that he sometimes became short-tempered.

"I've been better," she said weakly. "Were you out fighting the fire?" She closed her eyes. "That was a dumb question."

He was starting to think she was more affected by the fire than she was letting on. "I did help out with the fire." Leaning forward a bit, he looked directly in her eyes. "It's completely out, Kristen. You're not in any danger now."

She breathed deeply. "I'm so grateful. If y'all hadn't arrived, I would've lost everything."

Noticing on the monitor that her pulse was starting to accelerate again, he reached for her wrist. "This plant shop is great. Is it your family's place?"

Some of the warmth in her eyes cooled. "No, it's my garden center. I started it."

"Sorry if calling it a plant shop was rude." He smiled at her. "Blame it on me being a small-town hick from West Virginia."

"You're far from home, too. I'm from Houston."

"I heard that *y'all*. Good to meet a fellow Southerner." As he checked her pupils, he said, "When you're better, I'll have to stop by and get some tips. I can't keep a thing growing out here in Colorado."

"Well, there's a whole lot more rain back there."

"That's a fact."

He was about to ask her how a city-girl Texan came to be living in the foothills of Pikes Peak when Anderson joined them again.

Her eyes darted to Anderson, but instead of looking pleased, she looked stressed again. "Any luck?"

Anderson looked just as serious. "Yes, ma'am. I talked to your cardiologist. You need to head to the hospital with us. So, I need you to stop fighting me and get on the stretcher."

Kristen looked at Anderson like he'd just asked her to pick up a toad with her bare hands. "Can't I at least walk out of here?"

Anderson didn't even pause. "No, ma'am. It's protocol. There's still danger of fire, too." His tone turned even firmer. "It's better to be safe, right?"

But instead of agreeing, she looked mutinous. "Listen, I know my heart and I know when I'm in trouble. I'm okay."

Looking over at his buddy, Greg realized that Anderson was just about at the end of his rope with her. That was a surprise. Anderson rarely got flustered.

It was time to do an intervention before either Doc or Kristen *had words*. "How about you give Anderson a break, Kristen?" Greg interjected smoothly. "We're all just trying to do our jobs here, right?"

She turned to him, looking contrite. "I'm not trying to be difficult. It's just that I need to stay here. Like I said, this is my business. Everything I have is in this building."

"In that case, let's get a move on," Greg said. "The sooner we get out of here, the sooner you can come back."

When still she hesitated, he added, "Please, Kristen. There really is no other option."

"All right." Before either of them could help her, she surged to her feet, then immediately paled.

When her eyes started to roll, Greg reached for her, catching her as she fainted. Picking her up in his arms, he carefully arranged her on the stretcher. "She's a pistol, right?"

"She's stubborn, that's what she is," Anderson muttered.

Greg couldn't deny his buddy's assessment, though there

was a part of him that admired her. She was a go-getter who was concerned about the business she'd built, and who could blame her?

Seeing that she was already coming around, he smiled at her when her eyes fluttered open. "You okay?"

She blinked. "Did I just faint?"

"Yep."

All of the spit and fire she'd been displaying slowly edged out of her countenance. "I'm so sorry for the trouble." She hardly moved a muscle as they carted her out and helped her get situated in the ambulance.

Crawling in after her, Anderson waved Greg off. "Thanks, buddy. I owe you," he added as the door closed and they sped away.

Greg stayed where he was for a moment, thinking about Kristen and the fact that she was too young to have a cardiologist on speed dial.

*T*he Pikes Peak Regional Hospital, located in the heart of Woodland Park, was state-of-the-art, attractively designed, and relatively comfortable. The staff were mostly a kind bunch. As hospitals went, it wasn't a bad place to be.

But still Kristen hated every bit of it.

"I need to get out of here," she said. "Please sign the release forms."

Dr. Gonzales was her favorite physician and one of the best cardiologists in the state of Colorado. It was Kristen's good luck that he'd bought a house in the woods just outside of Woodland Park and saw patients once or twice a month at Pikes Peak.

He had such a good reputation, he was the reason she'd moved to Woodland Park; his opinion was one of the few her parents would accept without question.

Unfortunately, Dr. Gonzales was extremely difficult to boss around. Which was why she was still dressed in a hospital gown and tethered to three cords and monitors instead of wearing tennis shoes and jeans.

"You had a pretty close call, young lady," he said without a moment's hesitation. "Don't pretend you're not aware of that."

"But I can rest just as easily at home."

"My dear," he began as he sat down in the chair beside the bed, "do you really think I believe you'd lie in bed bingeing on Netflix instead of going at your usual speed? Especially when a portion of your garden center recently went up in flames?"

She couldn't stop the blush that was fanning her cheeks. "I could promise not to work."

"You promising not to work is like me promising to finally take a monthlong vacation. It's practically a lie."

"That's not very nice."

"Neither is ignoring my advice, but we know you've done that more than once."

She averted her eyes. She hated seeing that combination of disappointment and exasperation on his face. It was also pretty embarrassing that they'd played this game before. "I *am* sorry."

"You should be."

"I'm afraid I'm not much of a bingeing type of gal, Doctor." She could say that she'd had to sit quietly in bed for far too many days to ever do it again willingly. But really, she felt that being busy was simply in her makeup.

"That's not a bad thing, but I suggest you think about watching more television for the next twenty-four hours." Dr. Gonzales waved a finger at her like she was a naughty four-year-old. "And you know what I'm talking about, Kristen. Play games on your computer, talk on the phone, read a book. Maybe even read two. Whatever you do, make sure your body does nothing but concentrate on getting better." He lowered his voice. "*Do you understand?*"

"Yes, Dr. Gonzales."

He raised his eyebrows. "And?"

"And I promise I'll be good and do what I'm supposed to do."

After checking his watch, he got to his feet. "Your test results should be in later this afternoon."

"And then?"

"And then, if your numbers have improved, I'll sign your discharge papers for tomorrow afternoon." He stared intently at her over the rims of his glasses.

"Thank you for taking the time to see me, Dr. Gonzales."

"I always have time for you, my dear. Now, be good."

When the door closed behind Dr. Gonzales, Kristen at last let down her guard. She leaned back against her pillows, pressed her palms to her eyes, and tried not to cry. She really hated crying in front of other people. She didn't like anyone to see her being weak—plus, she wasn't a pretty crier. Within seconds, the skin around her eyes got blotchy. Her friend Danielle said that after a crying jag Kristen always looked like she'd gotten stung by a swarm of bees.

It was a silly concern, but there was something about being in a hospital gown and looking her worst that really got to her. She hated feeling vulnerable.

Which summed up everything she hated about her condition, pulmonary arterial hypertension, or PAH for short. She'd been born with a heart defect, a small hole in her left ventricle. She'd had surgery but there were still a number of lasting effects that would be with her the rest of her life.

Living with her condition meant that she had frequent checkups. It also meant that she'd been poked, prodded, scanned, and examined more times than she could remember.

Oh, well. Just one more day of sitting in this darn bed. Just one more day of hoping and praying that her latest test results were good. Then she could go home and attempt to repair all the damage the fire had done to the garden center.

"Knock knock, are you up for visitors?"

Glad that she was wearing a zip-up hoodie over her hospital gown, Kristen pressed the remote on her bed to sit up a bit.

Sure it was someone from work, she smiled.

But instead she saw a stranger. He had dark hair, light brown eyes, and seemed to be at least six foot five. He also had impressive biceps and a scruffy beard. He wasn't classically handsome, but he was the type of guy who deserved a second look. That meant she didn't feel bad for taking a moment to check him out before sending him on his way. "I'm sorry, I think you're in the wrong room."

He paused in midstep. "Oh. Sorry." Seeming flustered, he looked down at his feet for a second. Ran a hand over his scruff. "I'm not in the wrong room, but I don't know what I was thinking. I should've realized you wouldn't remember me."

Once more giving thanks that she was more or less covered up, Kristen said, "Have we met?"

"We have. About twenty-four hours ago, give or take. My name is Greg Tebo. I was one of the firemen who was at your nursery."

She had a spark of memory. Of this guy in a full fireman's uniform crouching next to her . . . right before she fainted.

She smiled. "I do remember you. I'm so sorry. I should've recognized you."

"No, I know better. Being in full uniform does cover up most of my best features."

She laughed. "Not your smile. I think that's the same."

His smile widened. "I was just here checking on the mom of one of my coworkers when I heard you were still here. I thought I'd stop by to say hello."

"I'm glad you did. Now I can say thank you for saving my business. And for helping me when I was being stubborn with the paramedic."

He laughed. "You're welcome, Kristen. I could say it's my job, but I'm also glad it gave us a chance to meet."

"I feel the same way."

Pointing to the chair, he said, "Mind if I stay a couple of minutes?"

She couldn't figure out why he'd want to, but she wasn't about to turn him away. "Of course not."

He sat down in the small chair like it was the most comfortable thing in the world. "So, how are you feeling?"

"Okay."

His expression was sympathetic. "Sorry, that's kind of a stupid question to ask someone who's sitting in a hospital bed."

"No, I think it's kind of you to ask. All things considered, I really am feeling okay. I hate being in the hospital, but I'm grateful to have people looking out for me."

"Where's your family?"

"Texas."

"They coming out?"

"No."

"That's too bad."

"This probably won't come out the right way," she said, "but I'm glad they aren't. They have a habit of overreacting a little bit." Actually a lot.

"When are you getting sprung?"

"Hopefully tomorrow." Unable to help herself, she added, "As long as I'm a good girl and my tests come back all right."

Amusement lit his eyes. "Is that a line on the discharge form now? Was the patient a good boy or girl?"

"No. I'm afraid it's a joke between me and my cardiologist. I have a pretty bad reputation when it comes to following doctor's orders."

"Sounds like you've been in the hospital before."

"I have. I was born with a minor little heart defect. It's all healed, but every once in a while it acts up."

"You're the first person I've ever heard mention having a *minor little* heart defect."

"And . . . that is probably why I have to be given warnings to be on good behavior." Tired of talking about her flaws, she said, "How are you, Greg?"

"I'm good. I have another forty-eight hours off before I go back on shift." He stretched his arms. "I plan on spending most of the day tomorrow sitting on my deck and being lazy."

"That sounds like heaven. I really meant what I said. Thank you for saving my business. One day you'll have to come by the shop. I'll set you up with a couple of pepper plants. Next thing you know, you'll be eating your own jalapeños."

"I might take you up on that."

"I hope you will. Anytime." She couldn't stifle a yawn.

Greg stuffed his hands in his pockets. "I think that's my cue to get out of here."

"I guess so." Kristen was sorry to see him go, but she really shouldn't expect more. He probably did these quick hospital visits all the time.

"Hey, Kristen?"

"Yes?"

"Any chance I could have your number?"

"Why?" That must have sounded rude, but she was totally shocked.

He looked taken aback but he quickly recovered. "Uh, so I can give you a call. Is that okay? Or, are you seeing someone?"

"I'm not seeing anyone," she hurried to say. "I mean, yes, you can have my number."

He pulled out his cell phone. "Ready when you are."

After she recited it, he texted her so she'd have his, too. "Save it, all right?"

"I will. Thanks again for coming by."

"I'm glad I did. And, uh, do me a favor and try not to

give the staff here too much trouble. I'm glad they're looking out for you."

"I promise. I might be acting like a pill, but I'm grateful for them. Enjoy the rest of your time off."

"Always."

When the door closed again, she couldn't help but smile to herself. Greg Tebo was a hunk—and he'd asked if she was seeing anyone! Even though she was sitting in a hospital bed in an ugly gown. Even after she'd been honest and told him about her heart condition! If ever there was a silver lining to a bad situation, this was it.

Then she thought of all the things John had said before breaking up with her. No one wanted a woman who was so much trouble. It was probably just a matter of time before Greg came to the same conclusion. *You better watch it, girl,* she thought to herself. *Your heart has enough problems without letting your guard down again.*

Ready to find
your next great read?

Let us help.

Visit prh.com/nextread

Penguin
Random
House